# BLOOD EMERALD

By

# Amber Anthony

**ISBN: 978-0-578-44499-4**

**Credits**
Cover Artist: Kelly A. Martin, kam.design
Editor: Professional Editor Services
August 2020

# Praise for Blood Emerald

*"Rick Hiatt is a hero to die for in this stunning standalone. Literally. We were first introduced to this devilishly handsome vampire in the first book of the Blood series. Now, Rick is the leading man in this second installment and readers are going to melt as his story unfolds. The context is immaculate, and the characters are wonderfully flawed. Although the heroine is fascinating and complex, Rick and his dominating ways are the tugboat dragging readers through a flood of emotion. Amber Anthony does no wrong when it comes to sculpting a man who is brought to his knees by a savvy woman."* I.C., USA

*"I did not read the first book and I did understand what was going on, so you don't have to the read the first book. But I am going to. I loved this book. The writing was sharp and interesting. The story was amazing. The characters were very well developed. I absolutely recommend this book. I am definitely a brand-new fan!"* P.G.G., USA

*"I was captivated from the very beginning of this magical tale, unable to tear myself away from the lovable cast. Rick Hiatt won my heart with his charming wit and tender devotion for his beloved Anna. This sensual romance is positively a five-star read. What a divine adventure awaits the reader inside the five-hundred-year-old realm of the Hiatt empire. Looking forward reading the sequel, Blood Dragon!"* – A.M.D.

## Brenner's Edicts for the Undead

1. Vampires are the ultimate Doms.
2. Stay out of mortal's relationships, *no good comes from intervening.*
3. Never get involved with mortal females, *they break too easily.*
4. Emotional relationships with mortals are difficult, *they can't detach.*
5. Immortality is an illusion, *vampires can be killed.*
6. The number one mannerism for appearing human*: inhale/exhale, repeat.*
7. To be irresistible to donors, *hang out with your fangs out.*
8. The first bite is the sweetest.
9. Pale is the new tan.

## The Vampire's Golden Rule

*It's not the bite you get,* it's the bite you give.

## Dedication

To chance meetings and those who said 'Yes'.

# 1

Rick Hiatt got no rest on the jet. No donor on the flight, so he fed on that low fat, vegan, homogenized, bagged blood he hated. That wasn't the only reason he was edgy. He recounted the ballroom disaster in Barranquilla, Colombia at The Lust for Life vampire-exclusive resort. Initially, the event had been staged like any of the Saturday night grand buffets. The dining Vamps bid fiercely for the thirty seats; it was the crème de la crème of the sanguine new age. These jaded high rollers found even Rick's exotic BDSM clubs *so* last week.

The chandeliers were dimmed before the undead entered the room. For the right price, they would find a god or goddess in every corner, tanned and plumped by a month of the sun and richest foods. The sixty donors, willing to trade their life's blood for the ecstasy of the vampire's bite, lounged languidly on leather fainting couches awaiting that orgasmic thrill. Each of them spent their days on the beach between eating, drinking and receiving the ultimate spa services. Their blood was primed perfectly to sing of oysters and marbled beef, the finest wines, and liquors. Their young, tremendously toned bodies were waxed to silky smoothness leaving only the fragrant hair on their heads. These pampered few were the stable for the resort. They rotated their bodies and blood every fifty-four days to feed the rarified echelon of billionaire vampires. Tonight after 'work' they'd return to their suites and begin the cycle again.

The feedings began with playful tumbles, vampires slipping out of their robes to press living flesh against their tomb-cold bodies. Rick and Adam were invited to be monitors months ago, before the current party drug fracture within the vampire world. They were known for their abilities to handle entitled vamps and jaded donors with firm diplomacy.

Master Adam Lachlan, Rick's Senior Dom, slipped silently between the fainting couches and the draped walls exchanging nods with Rick. Their gazes met across the room at the first pained murmur. Rick's reflexes tensed at the male donor's cry. This was not the expected orgasmic moan, but a visceral shriek. The feasting heads down over their meals lurched at the irregular sound, and then rose in peculiar unison.

Rick saw unbridled bloodlust in newly turned vamps, but never, *never* with experienced vamps, and never in such great numbers. Rick and Adam were trapped in the center of the melee, unable to aid the wounded humans. Back to back, he and Adam were barely able to protect each other. The transformed monstrosities acted out their carnage with killings that began as sexual eroticism and ended in extreme mutilation. When the last mortal heart silenced, they turned on each other, and the weaker undead fell prey to their stronger brethren.

Rick and Adam deflected and outmaneuvered countless attacks. When balancing on blood-slicked marble became overwhelming, they fell to their knees and continued to fight. Adam's lamentation rose to Valhalla. Thrown back onto his elbows, Rick marveled when Adam's spine undulated and lengthened. He extended each leg and turned it outward as it muscled and formed claws. His hands clenched and rested at his hips as wings extended from his back. His arms lengthened into front legs, muscular and long, each ending in three vicious claws. He dropped his head as great curved horns grew from his skull. As his neck lengthened and his gaze swept the ballroom, a mace-like tail unfurled. Within seconds, he transformed into a Fire Dragon. Adam's cool Nordic looks warmed to ombre shades of carmine and gold. To Rick's amazement, the beast rolled his shoulders, releasing his leathery wings, testing their flexibility.

The Dragon's head swayed. His gaze swept the ballroom, seeking and finding Veronique Moreau. She was the Queen of Hearts who masterminded this carnage. She stood at a railing watching coolly from the mezzanine, totally unmoved by the plight of the mutilated dead. For a moment, Rick expected the creature to flame her, frankly, hoping he would.

With a definitive stomp of one great foot, the beast arched his long neck. Before Rick could regain his senses, the Dragon crouched low and with his snout, rolled Rick onto his broad, armored back. His great wings spread, fanning the scent of brimstone in the ballroom. Massive feet plodded over the dead toward the balcony. His claws balanced on the precipice. Then, with a bunching of his powerful haunches, the beast leapt to the sky. His wings caught the air, beat against the downdraft and soared above the treetops. Rick tucked his head down and held fast to the scaled neck of the ancient creature as they rose above the coastline and headed for the Andes mountain peaks.

* * * *

Now, in the safety of his elegantly appointed corporate jet, Rick's hand still shook imperceptibly as he held the Baccarat tumbler filled with blood. He survived a lot in his five hundred years. The perennially handsome former Peer of the Realm fought in many battles and prevailed in them all. Nothing prepared him for what he witnessed this weekend.

Veronique Moreau was a darkly, evil Princess since the day she was turned, centuries ago. Combine that nature with the kind of money she raked in when she developed the vamp party drug Humanité, and it produced the lethal combination they witnessed in Barranquilla.

Rick couldn't see the appeal himself. Why would anyone become a vamp and then take a drug to pass as human a few hours at a time? It wasn't like he missed the ability to cavort in sunlight. He found night time pursuits much more pleasurable. Still, the vamps who used it loved it. Now that Veronique increased its addictive properties, it became a threat rather than an annoyance.

He and Matt Brenner, Rick's business partner and best friend, banned the stuff from their clubs once its addictive qualities became known. They created a BDSM empire catering to Vampire/Doms and willing donor/subs who traded sexual ecstasy for blood. They hadn't built their entertainment mega-conglomerate on vamp or human misery, and they didn't intend to start now.

Their nightclubs—both legit and clandestine—began as speakeasies and morphed into S&M playgrounds in the 1920s. Now they enjoyed an incarnation as BDSM clubs. He and Matt blended talents that proved phenomenally successful. Matt managed security, personnel, and the physical plants, and Rick managed guest relations, business, and finances.

One set of clubs grew to more than eighty in cities all over the world. If one vamp required several donors, a million vamps required legions, and they all needed a home. Little by little, Consort Group became Consort Group International or C.G.I. They expanded their reach into other areas until now Matt and Rick owned a diverse number of businesses.

The two were as close as brothers, and Rick knew Veronique had a score to settle with his best friend and business partner. In her current egomaniacal state, God knew what she might do, either to Matt or to his new bride. Rick decided Matt needed to be warned.

He grabbed up the ringing phone, "Hiatt."

Matt's buoyant voice sang back to him. "Hey, old man, the Captain said you called. What up?"

"Where are you?"

"Juneau, you know?"

"Well, that's delightful; I'm sure," Rick replied tersely then dialed it back. "You and Cat must be making the most of that yacht. You sound relaxed."

Matt hesitated, "You don't." Rick could hear Matt's concern over a few thousand miles, "What's going on?"

"I just left a bloodbath orchestrated by Veronique." Rick heard a swell of loud music and a navigation horn. A door slammed, followed by quiet.

"What the git has she done now?"

"Have you ever scented a donor's fear as some hopped-up vamp tore open his chest?"

There was a moment of dead silence. "Ronnie orchestrated that? How?"

"Humanité. She altered the formula to make it more addictive."

"She did what?"

"This new formula, when it wears off, removes all restraint." Despair sat heavy in Rick's voice.

"Rick, slow down."

"You know, Matt, I've been proctoring these events for a while. At their wildest, I've never seen anything like this. We were at Lust for Life, Ronnie was the hostess. It started like any Saturday night. Then, at first bite, they went savage." Rick's voice choked, "Ronnie stood there like some Ring Master at the Devil's Circus."

Another long pause. "Did Adam make it out okay?"

"Physically he's okay. Mentally, he's up in the mountains trying to regroup."

"Is that the safest place for a man who's just gone through this?"

Rick hesitated, "It's probably the best place for a Dragon Shifter who hasn't shifted in over two hundred years."

"Whoa, he what?"

"If he hadn't shifted, I wouldn't be talking to you."

"Do you want us to come home, Rick? Because we will…"

"No. Ronnie's lost her senses. Gas up that yacht and head for open waters. Do it quickly and quietly and keep an eye out."

"You think she's coming after me?"

"I'm afraid she might go after Cat."

"Should we hunker down and prepare for it?"

Rick heard the tremor in Matt's voice. "I have no idea. You know how spiteful she is, but she may have other things to worry about right now. As soon as I get Council clearance, I'll do what I can to terminate her."

"Rick, if you need me, I'll come back. Whatever you need."

"I know you will, dear boy. Give my love to your beautiful bride."

Rick cradled the receiver and fell back in his seat. He let out a long sigh and shrank into the upholstery. *If word of this gets out, Vampires will be hunted to extinction.*

* * * *

The Tesla P100D was parked in his private hangar at the airport. Occasionally the nights were his alone, and he savored time to drive and think. With this car, he didn't even have to drive. His carry-on bag hit the trunk with a thud, and it wasn't long before he was out on the 101. At two in the morning, traffic was relatively light, so he let the car drive itself and turned his thoughts to what should have been an ecstatic feeding in a dream setting.

Rick was an acknowledged expert Dom. He knew donor-subs experienced sexual euphoria as a result of a well-given bite. It drove mortal subs back time and again. Male or female, they craved Rick's discipline and longed for his famous fang-on-flesh feeding. The fact that Veronique had managed to corrupt a beautiful symbiosis was disturbing. Well, that and the fact it put all vampires in imminent danger.

When Veronique and her psycho vamp sire, Papa Moreau, threatened the life of Matt's lady-love, Rick took care of Papa personally. He thought Papa's termination would inhibit Ronnie's criminal inclinations. Obviously, he was wrong. With Papa out of the way, Veronique was completely off the chain, and Rick laid the blame for the new menace right at his own door. He should have taken her out along with her sire.

Now, Matt was off honeymooning, and even as he and Cat were bonding, Rick seriously needed his best friend's help. Tonight, Rick was also without Adam to manage The Gaoler. So there went Rick's right hand and his left. *Have I ever felt lower?* This was no pleasant slip into chaos, he felt every blow.

Thankfully, Matt's deputies for his responsibilities at C.G.I. were taking care of business. Rick couldn't begrudge them a learning curve; he and Matt ran things together for almost a hundred years. A replacement for Adam was more problematic. He not only managed their flagship BDSM club, their member donors and vamps had specific and particular relationships with him. For the past twenty-five years or so, Rick and Matt were happy to let Adam handle it. Neither donors nor vamps were willing to trust their kink to just anyone, you don't change dicks in the middle of a screw unless you specify first.

Rick worked himself into a fit of frustration by the time he pressed the remote on the garage barrier and turned into C.G.I.'s indoor parking. Agitated, he took the ramp's corner too quickly, his tires squealing in response. *Bollocks, What am I going to do about Veronique and her drug-crazed, vampire freaks? She is making the vamp community far too conspicuous and it...*

Rick swerved into his reserved parking space inattentively, just as a waif-faced specter emerged from the shadows. He braked in panic when the headlights illuminated her swirl of flaming hair. The car jarred to a halt and Rick was out the door before it stopped rocking.

"God's bones! Are you trying to fecking kill yourself? Have you fallen into madness?" As a vampire, he had no adrenalin to surge, but he shook anyway. Exasperated, he ran a hand through his thick caramel brown hair and drew in several unnecessary calming breaths.

She shook too. She had retreated into the darkness, back against the rough concrete wall to get out of his way. "I'm sorry. I didn't mean to..."

Rick searched her face. She seemed an apparition with her pale, porcelain skin, jade eyes that dominated her entire face, and that mass of titian hair. Recognition dawned on him. "Wait a minute, I know you." He pointed to her. He always thought she looked far too young and delicate to be a donor. "You're Matt's donor. The hanger-on always dawdling in the lounge. You're..." He snapped his fingers trying to drudge up the name.

"Anna." Her voice was melodious and filled with embarrassment.

"Yeah, Anna." He agreed with a scowl. "We banned you. What are you doing here?"

"Matt banned me. That's why I'm in the garage. I knew where your parking space was and I..."

"So, you thought you'd stand in it till I ran you over?" He bellowed melodramatically.

"No. I couldn't get into the club, and I couldn't get up to the Consort offices. I have to see Matt, so I..."

"You're banned. We have nothing more to say to you."

"If it meant vampire lives, would you speak with me?"

"That's pretty desperate." Rick's whiskey brown eyes searched her face closely.

Her voice grew more strident, "I need to talk to Matt."

Rick shook his head, close to pity for this mortal girl. "Look, Matt just got married."

"Married! Matt?" Her tea-rose complexion paled to near vampire transparency.

"Hitched. Jumped the broom. On his honeymoon as we speak. So, if you're really concerned about our safety, tell *me*. If this is a ploy to get Matt back, it's been done before. Which is it?"

Hot tears filled her vividly celadon eyes. She swallowed hard. "It is about your safety. Though why I should care at this point, I don't know."

Rick took a long beat, assessing her. He opened the door and slid into the car with a gruff, "Get in. You have two minutes."

Seemingly defeated, Anna slid into the passenger seat. "I've been out of the life for like, what, a year?"

Rick's eyes narrowed, "While you're young, dear, get to the point." He inhaled deeply. "You been smoking a little weed tonight?"

"No. I don't do drugs." She sniffed at her coat defensively. "I was at a party…"

"And the 'party' so filled you with paranoia, you came running over here? Are you sure you didn't inhale? Get a little contact high?"

"I don't like you." Anna's words stunned him. Rick blinked hard. No, this slip of a girl really said she didn't like him. That she had the moxie to declare it so emphatically in such close quarters to a vampire was unprecedented. In his gob-smacked silence, she barreled on.

"I think you're pretty much an ass, and I'm not sure you deserve to know what I know." She said it evenly, acerbically, but without a huge amount of heat. Rick inhaled deeply, scented her honesty and believed her. That pissed him off.

"Unlike Saint Matt?" In a split second, his fangs dropped, and he was on her with the stench of the undead. "You do not sit in judgment of me, Cupcake. You aren't even in the food chain anymore."

"Stop it, stop it, stop it!" She spit back. "Listen to me! I know Matt worked very hard to keep vampires invisible and I know that's what this place…" she made a sweeping gesture, "is all about. I think something horrible is about to happen."

Rick growled a forewarning. "I think you're right." He used his preternatural strength to subdue her, clenching her against him. He was immediately stunned by his body's response to her lithe, flushed form pressed against his cool, hard length. It pissed him off even more that his anatomy over-rode his gut instinct. In a split second, he regained his vampire senses, baring ivory fangs, grazing the elegant column of her neck, savoring the flavor of fear her few crimson drops deposited on his tongue. He enjoyed the spirit of her resistance, the way it pumped her blood frantically around her beautiful body and dilated the pupils of those huge green eyes. He fancied she'd look much the same in passion, and his cock swelled further at the thought.

Anna cringed, fighting fiercely against him. Rick traded the taste of blood for hot tears and in their resulting tussle; two words caught his attention. "Vampire Slayer."

Grating laughter erupted from his chest at the words. He released her and retreated back across the console, now the concerned thirty-year-old club owner with a fading stiffy. "Seriously? You think you met a vampire slayer?" He chuckled, shaking his head in disbelief. "That's your big emergency? You're adorable."

*So adorable I could just eat you up!* Rick ran his tongue over his canines. *But I need to dial back my stiffy, thrall you and move you out.*

Anna's intense jade eyes grew frigid. "You're wasting my time, Mr. Hiatt. I gave you the warning, the consequences are on your head."

Rick didn't try to stop her as Anna fumbled with the unfamiliar door handle and stumbled from the car with as much dignity as possible. He watched her back, ramrod straight, as she made her way down the winding vehicle ramp. Sitting amidst the scents she'd left behind, still oddly stirred by her, Rick pulled the rear-view mirror toward him and corrected his ruffled appearance. *This day just gets better and better.*

* * * *

Anna's tiny sub-compact didn't take up much room in the on-street parking space she found not far from the Consort Building. It was late, she was shattered, and Matt was married. Married! *That asshat Hiatt just couldn't wait to tell me, could he?* She leaned against the car door as she fished in her pocket for the keys, her eyes filling with tears she'd desperately fought in his presence. A slow, low wail escaped her before she clamped her teeth together to shut it off and dropped into her seat. She brushed furiously at her waterworks and gunned the engine to get herself the hell out of here.

Rick Hiatt and everyone associated with him could be obliterated by Carl Sterling for all she cared. Knowing Rick and the other Vampire-Doms at the club, they'd cut through Carl's bravado like a knife through, well, blood. Unless Carl was lucky enough to get the drop on one of them, he was more likely to be the dead one. Anna intended to wash her hands of the whole lot of them. *I have one more week at the playhouse, and then I'm out of anything to do with vampires forever*, she resolved, hoping she followed through on that pledge. *Vampires are undeniably seductive.*

* * * *

Rick dropped into oblivion as soon as he hit the slab. His last conscious thought was of the lovely Anna, her wide emerald eyes blinking back tears. He felt a little guilty about that. Then, blessed nothingness until the insistent Responder Sergeant McGrath flipped on every light in Rick's peaceful mausoleum and shook him.

"I'm sorry, Mr. Hiatt, I told him you'd be exhausted from traveling, but..." his assistant began, until the burly vampire cop fixed her with a disapproving glare that sent her right back out the door.

"Always happy to help the responders." Rick arched a brow and gave the man a lethargic smile. "What's up?"

"I have an urgent matter for you, sir. It involves one of your security staff, Brett Olson."

"The nervous kid in the lobby?" Rick stood, grabbed the silk robe off the hook on the wall and drew it on.

"Some night clubbers found him staked and left for dead in the alley. We were monitoring the police scanner when they called it in. Luckily, we got there first."

"Is the kid okay?"

"It could have been worse if that couple hadn't stumbled in around four in the morning to hump in the alley. But drunks being drunks, what can I say? They called it in before the sun came up, so we were able to get him out of there. He's downstairs in one of your suites. I thought you might want to sit in on the interview. We haven't had a staking in thirty years."

* * * *

Brett Olson was not the quintessential picture of a vampire. A little doughy with a baby face and pretty high strung. Rick liked the kid all right, but right now he felt like he was talking him off a ledge.

"Brett, sport, wild man, what happened?"

Brett winced and sucked deeply on a blood bag, huddled in the depths of a leather easy chair.

"No, Brett, really, I'm not kidding you, this is mid-century drek. We need to know whatever you can tell us."

"I don't know, Mr. Hiatt. He just took me down." Brett mumbled.

McGrath was on it immediately. "He took you down, or he staked you? Did he get you down before he staked you? What did he look like?"

"He hit me from behind. I didn't see his face."

"Tall? Short? Muscular? Old? Young?" The vampire cop persisted.

Bret shrugged and gestured at his girth. "Big enough to take me down."

"Did he say anything?"

Brett was silent for a moment, teasing the memory back to life. "He said, 'This is for ramseyblack.' What's a ramseyblack?"

Rick and the responder exchanged meaningful glances over his head.

"Ramsey Black? You're sure about that?" Rick enunciated the two words.

"Ramseyblack. Is that a name?"

"Okay," Rick stood to leave. "Good information, kid. Finish that blood and catch some slab time. Anything I can do for you?"

"No, sir. I guess I'm okay."

"That's good. Take some time off." He swung out the door, McGrath close behind. They paused in the dimly lit hallway.

"Ramsey Black?" The responder repeated. "I thought that S.O.B. died years ago. Hell, he'd be a hundred years old now."

"No, the guy said, 'this is *for* Ramsey Black, not this is Ramsey Black. Who the fu… is this vamp slayer wannabe? How does he know about Black? Hell, how does he know about vampires?"

* * * *

In his penthouse, looking out over the breaking dawn of the city, the day's discoveries sent five-hundred-year-old memories crashing through Rick's mind. Vampire slayers were ancient, and he was more ancient still, sired in a time when vampires were thought of as witches or demons, not as the undead. It had been centuries since he had to worry about being hunted by a vampire slayer. Logic would suggest a few remained. If Veronique's activities brought vampires increasingly out of the realm of fantasy and into actuality in mortal minds, there would be many more slayers joining the ranks. He would be thrust back into the perils of the sixteenth century.

Present day Los Angeles faded as Rick recalled his ancestral home in Ireland. He'd heard the story of his birth repeated so often he felt as if he was an unseen observer instead of the struggling bairn in his mother's womb.

* * * *

*Ireland, 1513*

Mary's Ladies in Waiting had often told him of their fervent prayers for his mother's deliverance. She had suffered enough, hearing her husband, Sean Fitzjarrald was mortally wounded. Conveyed back to Erne Castle over the saddle of his horse, he died in the wee hours of 3 September 1513. The sight of her fine-looking husband lifeless and cold threw Mary into a damning delirium.

Whereas the household was celebrating their recent move into Erne Castle, the unforeseen events left the family feeling robbed. The funeral thrust them into black crepe and covered mirrors, and within hours of Sean's internment in his crypt, Mary's belly clutched in pain.

Mary's lamenting howls escaped her lips and rolled down the hallways. It broke the midwife's heart, and she was sure it filled the anxious family with dread. The Ladies in Waiting would surely speculate about whether Mary's dead husband could hear his poor wife.

Sadly, by dawn Sean's sweet Mary joined him in the afterlife, surrendering to the angels within minutes of delivering their son. The handmaiden's mournful wails heralded her fate and drew the family into the bedchamber. Mary was at peace. There was nothing to do now but welcome the newborn into the family.

With acquiescence and a dampened joy, the infant's eldest brother, Ian, held the child up for those gathered to see. "He's quite a scrapper is he not?"

His wife, who would become the baby's adopted mother, lifted the blanket and beheld her new son.

"He will be known as Richard Fitzjarrald," his brother whispered.

* * * *

*Los Angeles, Present Day*

Rick dressed for the night, giving up on any rest. A quick pint from whatever donor lingered at the club would sustain him. He had safety decisions to make about this damn vamp hunter that could impact the entire Los Angeles, vampire Family. He only hoped he hadn't burned bridges that might be crucial to them now.

There were times when he could be too much of a smartass prick for his own good, Rick mused. It was born of being several hundred years old and perched at the top of the food chain. It didn't hurt that he was also handsome, physically fit and with vamp appeal, able to bed anyone who struck his fancy. Being called out on it? That pretty much went down like acid. Hadn't little Anna Cupcake tried to warn him less than six hours ago? And he had not listened.

Still, he wasn't entirely ready to give her a pass. Oh, yeah, she seemed all soft sweetness and light, but was that the truth? Where was his highly tuned vamp sense when he needed it? Probably floundering somewhere between his legs. What did she really want? Was she truly trying to warn him—or at least warn Matt—or was she in on it? That question burned the brightest. Was this some kind of payback? If so, Karma could be a bitch.

He walked purposefully into the membership office of the Gaoler. "Get me the personal info on that Anna girl who was Matt's groupie."

Helen, the matronly woman in charge of mortal donors, tapped a few strokes then looked up from her computer. "Anna Curley? That cute little thing that looks like a bonbon? I swear if I were her mother, she'd never have come through our door."

Rick raised a slightly aggrieved brow. In his experience, no one was that pure, and she was more cupcake than bonbon.

"She lives in Pasadena, or at least, she did last year." Helen withdrew her readers and leaned in conspiratorially. "Gossip is, she works at the Los Angeles County Museum of Art. The one across the street—an art historian or something. Probably a tour guide." She peered at Rick. "What brings her up? I was really glad when Matt canceled her card."

"Get her on the phone. I wanna talk to her."

"You're not gonna let her back in, are you?"

"I didn't know you were in charge now, Helen." He snapped in a way he was sure betrayed his interest in the girl. "Just get me in touch with her."

Helen drew back, clearly affronted. "Yes, sir. I'll call you when I know something."

Rick sighed. Lately, he was batting three hundred in the asshole competition.

# 2

Rick's call-back waited on voicemail a few hours later. "Anna will be at the Hawking Theatre tonight, boss," Helen informed him. "It's in Burbank. They're doing a live-action vampire role-play."

Rick clicked off the message. "People do that?" he wondered aloud.

* * * *

Brett pulled himself together to accompany Rick when they drove into the parking lot behind the theatre. It was a 1950s retro place, with a loud print carpet in the lobby and faded seats with leaning springs in the audience. The role-play started before they arrived. Rick wasn't concerned about the action, he was much more interested in what Brett could discern from the actor's voices and scents.

"Anyone smell familiar here?" Rick pressed in subtones too low for humans to pick up.

"No." Brett paused. "There is this one scent, but I think it's a female…"

"Yeah, I know who that is. She's not who we're looking for. Listen to the voices. Anyone sound like the guy who staked you?"

Brett looked profoundly uncomfortable. "I don't know." He sighed deeply. "I can't tell."

Rick fixed him with a serious gaze. "Okay, buddy, you wait here. I'm gonna go down and see someone at intermission. But let me tell you, we're starting a vamp self-defense class at the Gaoler next week. You and every other vamp on staff are gonna be there, and next time something happens, you'll be able to pick a scent and voice out of a crowd at the Staples Center."

Brett gave him a wan smile before Rick strode down the stage-left theatre aisle, his scent-sense guiding him directly to Anna. He wound his way between set dressings, curtains, and role-players, eyeing with interest the guy in the tux and red-satin-lined cape. He zeroed in on Anna at the props table.

Rick pressed up behind her and hissed, "Well, this is interesting. Does art imitate life?"

Anna whirled around, checking over both shoulders to see if anyone noticed him. Of course, they had, several female cast members all but drooled over the tall, good-looking guy in front of her. "I didn't know there was an art to what you did."

"Mind telling me what you're doing at vampire role-play?" Rick's gaze darted up to the rafters and back down. He flinched as the caped man skirted behind the scrim, leaving behind an odor of bravado and surging testosterone. Rick had much too much of that already.

Anna lowered her voice, "That would be your business because…?"

"Because I asked you. What are you doing here?" He insisted, his lips a grim line on his handsome face.

"The better question is, what are you doing here? You made it clear last night you had no interest in what I had to say." Anna was cool or at least attempting to be.

Rick rolled back and forth on the balls of his John Lobb loafers and slid his hands into his pockets, "You were drummed out of the life and look where you ended up." He glanced around the backstage with disdain, and his gaze landed back on her.

Anna bit back her anger, "No matter what you may think, my life doesn't revolve around vampires."

"All evidence to the contrary." Rick gestured smugly at the rack of costumes, the eight-foot table of props, and the prosthetic fangs. He felt all eyes were on them, privy to a lover's quarrel.

"Whatever." Anna turned back to her props and gritted out louder than before, "To retain dramatic authenticity, the audience is not allowed backstage." She looked at him coldly. "You need to leave."

"I can beat you home tonight," he snarled.

"Oh, I'm *so* scared."

Rick inhaled deeply, scenting her. "I know you are. I can smell it on you."

Anna's eyes narrowed darkly, "You still need to leave."

He grabbed her elbow, forcing a smile when he knew they were being observed. "We need to revisit last night's conversation. And Cupcake, you don't need to like me, to obey me."

"Fine. Clear my name at the door. I'll come to you."

* * * *

Sir Richard Hiatt felt every bit the masterful Dom tonight. Even under threats to his Family, he returned to the Gaoler and to his work. In the public demonstration room, his gaze swept the audience of totally uninspired Vamps and donors watching a not-so-stirring demonstration. As Derrick, the Dom on stage began to lose their attention, Rick swept into the dimly lit chamber. He pressed his palm on Derrick's shoulder in a silent command to step aside.

Rick's reading of the couples waiting to be titillated and motivated to commence feeding, told him they needed to be shaken. They came to be surprised, so he'd give the people what they wanted. He removed his suit jacket and rolled back his crisp white shirt cuffs. Rick hefted the weight of an exquisitely crafted red and black suede flogger before he began to speak. He had the room's full attention now. Running the individual leather thongs lovingly through his fingers, he savored the suede's suppleness.

"Somewhere between the lesser barriers of damsels in distress and group sex, through the land of body modification and fetishes, is that seemingly forbidden land of impact play."

The crowd murmured.

Rick turned to the disconcerted Dom. "What I see tonight, Derrick is not the slow building rhythm and the deft impact that gives a sweet warm-up effect." Rick walked to the donor, trussed to the St. Andrew's cross, her fine naked ass patiently waiting for the kiss of the flogger. Rick's palm cupped her ass as Derrick clenched and unclenched his fists.

"Ladies and gentlemen, correctly flogged buttocks become very warm to the touch when a Dom has suitably brought the flesh to a blooming flush." Rick strolled to stand close to the titian-haired donor. "My sweet, hold this for me." Rick pressed the handle of the flogger into the donor's handcuffed hand.

"Yes, Sir."

Rick led the ousted Dom to the larger St. Andrew's cross and pushed him into the wood, hiding his own grin of satisfaction. "Drop your trousers. Assume the position." Rick's voice was steely.

"Yes, Sir." The vampire surrendered his trousers and raised his arms to be cuffed.

Rick swaggered behind the vamp and grabbed Derrick's dress shirt in his fist, shredding it in one move. The crowd gasped. Rick strode back to the edge of the stage, meeting each of their gazes.

"What do you know about 'switches'?" His fans sat silent and stunned as Rick continued, "No, switches aren't usually Bi, they aren't confused, and they can be real subs or Doms."

Rick returned within whispering distance of the redhead and removed her shackles. Whatever he said to her was inaudible to the rest of the mortals in the dungeon. He stepped back from the lovely woman. "Switches get a negative reaction from purists. But switches can choose; it just depends on the day and their own internal stimulus."

The tied-up vamp jerked at the sharp crack of the flogger and Rick guessed he was ready to piss himself. The redhead's boots breached his space with loudly ringing steps.

"Are your safe words in place?" When his participants confirmed, Rick stepped back, allowing the audience an unobstructed view.

All the commotion in his world had caused Rick to flip his own switch tonight. He expected Anna to be delayed and he couldn't be left alone with his thoughts.

Samantha, the redheaded donor, stepped back an arm and nearly a flogger's length from the trussed-up Vampire. Artfully, she began flipping cool leather straps down Derrick's back in a figure eight pattern. Starting at his neck, she ran the whip down his back, over his first-rate ass and flowed down his muscled flanks to his thighs and calves. Different reactions arose from the crowd as Samantha moved in front of Derrick and dragged the flogger over his face.

Those who knew the exhilaration of well-seasoned leather sighed in expectant satisfaction. Samantha walked into the audiences' view and unleashed the flogger lightly and rapidly. Slap, slap, slap, up Derrick's calves.

"More, Slave?"

"Yes, Mistress."

Moving rhythmically, Samantha swayed as her flogger caressed Derrick's thighs from back to side. Rick could almost feel the sting of the tails wrapping around his thighs as Samantha's flogger popped against the side and front of Derrick's.

The audience on various chairs and lounges began to feed as their libidos revved. There was a universal groan as the leather popped right up between the crack of Derrick's ass.

Rick recalled tongues of leather reaching around hungrily, giving him that erotic bite eons ago. He drew in a sharp, unnecessary breath when Samantha grabbed Derrick's shoulder length dark hair at the nape of his neck.

Samantha blew a kiss into his ear, then hissed an inhalation through her teeth. Derrick's body visibly tightened.

Rick's desire for domination at the Gaoler vacillated. He would say in the centuries he had practiced BDSM, he was seventy percent Dominant versus thirty percent submissive. As a newcomer, he'd learned submission, and he'd studied at the knees of the greatest Doms. For decades he commanded complete dominance, followed by years of obedient submission. Had he been entirely dominant or entirely submissive, Rick admitted, he would have missed some of the finest times of his life.

Rick drew his wandering attention back to tonight's performance. Before he had arrived at any solid conclusion, he was shaken by silence on the stage. The 'show' ended with Samantha uncoupling Derrick's wrists and ankles and leading him to the blood-red leather fainting couch to recline and feed from her neck. There was a new Dom at the Gaoler, Rick thought with amusement, and he knew it was time to be as flexible as Samantha.

The power exchange and all that was great. It was thrilling to be a Dom, the one in charge, to have a sub's willing body at his command. It was equally fulfilling to be a sub, able to cede blind trust to his Dom. But something was missing. The rigidity of the roles hindered true fluid symbiosis between partners. Neither could expose their genuine selves at the moment. Isn't there something more? Something different? Some way for lovers to drop the roles and connect?

*Oh, bollocks!* He thought with surprise. *That's vanilla sex! Preposterous! This is a subject for another day.* After all, he didn't currently have someone he would call a lover.

* * * *

Anna worried her bottom lip as she drove from Burbank to the club on the Miracle Mile. She hated the gut-churning anxiety swamping her whenever she encountered Rick Hiatt. He'd always had that effect on her. Frankly, he scared the hell out of her in a forbidden, delicious kind of way. If Matt was a reluctant Dom, Rick was the real thing, and someone she wanted no part of— did she? *If you're honest*, the devil on her shoulder taunted, *he kinda turns you on with all that force and lust.* "Not in the real world," she countered firmly. *He's drop-dead gorgeous, and the rumor is, he gives great bite.* She wanted to clap her hand over that ear and silence that damn honest devil. "That is something I will never find out," she assured herself primly. *We'll see.*

This time, when she got to the parking garage, the gate rose before she even braked. Well, at least she wouldn't have to park on the street. She expected to see Brett, the sweet security guard who usually protected the elevators. Instead, it was the vampress she'd always thought of as 'Venus.'

"I'm here to see Rick Hiatt." Anna forced herself to stand straight and speak clearly and directly to her nemesis.

"Hmmm. Yes. I see that." Venus looked at the memo before her as if it had spoken and Anna had not. "He wants you upstairs in his office." Venus finally deigned to glance at her and gestured with an outstretched flat palm. "You may take elevator two."

"Oh, thank you." Anna surprised herself with the dripping sarcasm in her tone. That little rebellion felt surprisingly good. *That little rebellion could get you killed.* Anna sighed. *I guess I can only be pushed so far.*

* * * *

Rick was seated at the nondescript receptionist's desk when Anna's elevator doors opened. She stopped in surprise. She would have preferred the long walk down the hall to compose herself. *He* was there, accomplishing everyday office tasks. *Yes, he can terrify me and make photocopies, just to show me he can do it all.*

Rick sat watching her, a bemused look in his whiskey brown eyes. He lifted his arm and beckoned her in with two fingers. "I have to finish up this paperwork, and then we'll go downstairs to my place. It's more private." Rick drew together the stapled papers and slid them into a portfolio, "I crave privacy."

Anna shifted her feet uncomfortably. Whatever made her think he was interesting? *Look at those shoulders. He looks like solid muscle under that expensive jacket.*

"To your playroom?" she ventured with a crack in her voice.

A wry grin curved his mouth. "No, Cupcake. Matt has a playroom. I have a dungeon."

"Oh." With a sinking heart, she stood and awaited her fate.

* * * *

Rick marshaled her into the Gaoler elevator that descended rapidly to the lobby level and pressed his hand onto the glass security pad. They descended slowly to the subbasement. On the way, the temperature dropped to a slightly uncomfortable sixty degrees, the light inside the car changed from a fluorescent glow to red L.E.D., and the thrum of a human heartbeat seemed to vibrate right through her. A chill ran up her spine. The dang elevator got to her every time.

Rick caught the tiny movement and inhaled a long, assessing breath, his gaze checking out her every curve.

What did he sense when he watched her like that? Was there a part of him that knew of her secret admiration? She couldn't forget their tussle in the car, the way his strong body felt against hers. She heard once that passion of any kind could be turned to a passion of the sexual kind. Did that include anger? Is that what was happening to her? She shivered again, and Rick's penetrating look told her he knew it was not from cold.

They were discharged into the hallway of dungeons, adorned with crimson leather wallpaper and thick ebony carpet. Here again, the lights were muted, meant to mimic flickering carriage lanterns. Matt's playroom was a few paces to the right, how she longed for its safe familiarity. Instead, Rick led her a few silent paces to the left—his personal space. When he pressed his hand to the security panel, the door swung slowly open and left Anna with no illusions. This was no playroom. 'Dungeon' described it perfectly. Flippancy drained right out of her as if an artery was opened.

Rick gestured her toward a highly carved and polished wooden chair. "Be seated," he instructed briskly and sat in a similar piece.

Anna's body recoiled at the hard, flat surface of the square chair. Awkwardly, she settled back against the carving of a raven posed rampant over a battlefield. She settled along the throne's arms only to realize her hands rested atop ominous claws holding masked faces of agony and ecstasy. Her hands flew back to her lap with a hitch in her breath. It was all positively medieval.

Her gaze swept the room noting a St. Andrew's cross, several different sized spanking benches, polished cases of assorted sex toys, whips, and belts. Across the room sat an outrageously oversized canopied bed. None of these fixtures consoled Anna. Nervous, knowing Rick could hear her run-away heartbeat and scent her tension, she chose to say nothing and kept her eyes cast firmly on the floor.

He let her squirm for what felt like an hour before he spoke. "Let's return to last night's subject."

Anna jumped. "About why I wanted to talk to Matt?"

"Yes."

"About vampire slayers."

He nodded regally.

"I know they're real," she insisted, a little defensively.

"I know they're real," he agreed.

"No, I mean, now, today, there are vampire slayers. Or, at least, vamp hunters." Worry now overrode her nerves.

"Where are they?" His tone was so intense she retreated into the back of the uncomfortable chair.

"He was at the theatre tonight."

"Van Helsing?"

"Yes."

"Address me properly," he snapped.

Anna stuttered. "I…I mean, yes, Sir." *Damn it! I know better than that!* "His name is Carl Sterling, Sir."

He nodded an acknowledgment. "How do you know he's a vampire hunter?"

Anna babbled out the information. "The party I went to, Sir, I went to the bathroom, I wasn't feeling well, the place put me on edge. So, I went into the bathroom, and I overheard him. He was discussing his family, bragging about coming from a long line of vampire hunters."

"Could he have been just poppin' off? Drunk talk?"

"Well, maybe, but he talked about his grandfather's murder. His throat was bitten out." She slid her hand to her own throat. "And…and I thought…"

"You thought it was a vampire?"

"Yes, Sir."

The room took on a definite chill. Anna half-suppressed a shiver.

Rick weighed her words judiciously "Just because his grandfather was killed by a vamp doesn't mean Sterling is a vampire slayer."

"I…I don't know. It was everything he said, and it was nothing in particular."

"Explain."

"Yes, Sir. The party was at his house. The décor is crazy, eclectic, with all sorts of antiquities." She moaned in frustration as she tried to describe her impressions.

"Antiquities? Explain."

"Sir, he has a lot of silver."

"What do you mean by a lot?"

"He has a wall of silver weaponry…"

"Why do you think they're silver?"

Anna squirmed on the torturous chair. Rick, on the other hand, seemed born to it, perfectly relaxed. "The party kinda migrated into the 'vampire' room, and he took a knife off the wall, and he was playing with it." Anna's eyes closed as if to see the scene again, "and he was roleplaying back and forth. The minute he put the knife on this girl's breast, you know, acting like he was torturing her, she started screaming…"

"Could it have been any other white metal?"

Anna shook her head. "Sterling said, 'If she were a real vamp, she'd be screaming because this is .925 silver.' And he held the knife up for everyone to see."

"You don't think he's a bit of a braggart?"

"Well, yeah, I do, but I'm not sure he's bragging about this." She shrugged and thought for a moment. "I know how I can be sure."

"Go on."

"He'll be out of town for three weeks. He asked me to take care of his dog, I moved into a place not far from him. He gave me the alarm codes; I can disarm the security system. You can see it for yourself."

"I believe I will. When does he leave?"

"Day after tomorrow." She raised her gaze to look into his eyes and was surprised to find warm concern. She stared, mesmerized for half a second, and then finished lamely, "What do you think?"

"I think you could use a beverage." Rick stood abruptly. "Why don't we go to the bar?"

*Drink with you? I'm not sure I can swallow.* "Thank you, sir. Do you think this will help?"

"We'll see, thank you for bringing it to me." And then he smiled. *I'll bet he thinks that's the panty-dropper smile.* She'd never seen him smile before. *It kind of is.*

* * * *

Anna tugged on his hand in hesitation when they reached the door of the bar. Nothing about it had changed. It still bore the substantial dark wood, padded bar stools and frosted glass that screamed Irish Pub. She was sure all the personalities were the same. "Do you think this is a good idea, Sir?"

Rick chuckled. "You worried about my rep, Cupcake?"

"Um…" Anna blinked and shook her head, but she couldn't help remembering the cruel comments that circulated about Matt when they'd been feeder/donor.

"Let's risk it." He winked charmingly.

Anna couldn't miss the stares of the occupants. Rick preceded her at the door and held out his hand to draw her inside. She was gratified by his gentlemanly gesture and knew it signaled to the whole club she had a new status in his eyes. Apparently, she was no longer persona non-grata.

"Let's get the booth in the back," Rick suggested.

What could she say? *No, I prefer it out here so I can watch everyone gawk at us, especially that bitch, Tina?* Revenge was sweet, watching the bar patrons trying to pick their chins off the floor was sweeter, but she'd rather spend some time alone with Rick. That admission shocked her. She never thought of Hiatt as someone she enjoyed hanging with.

"Jameson Black Barrel and B negative, Bobby." He instructed the bartender on the way to their table. "How about you, Anna?"

"Uh, I'm driving, Sir, and with everything that's going on, I think maybe a Coke."

Rick nodded appreciatively. "Very wise. A Coke for the lady, please. We'll be in the back."

Rick caught her hand and zigzagged between small round tables in the bar's dim light. While the patrons got their drink-on post-bite, they spied on Rick's fluid movements. Every patron in the bar hushed and turned to watch them go and then immediately broke out in a hub-bub of comment. Behind him, taking tiny steps, Anna's curves caught someone's shoulder—it was Tina. The bleached blond took an exaggerated look at her, casting silent shade behind Rick's back. She dropped her sneer and returned her attention to the male donor beside her.

Anna giggled. Rick raised an inquiring brow and turned to survey the room. The other guests instantaneously turned their attention to their own drinks.

"The pastime around here isn't sex—it's gossip." Rick shook his head. He gestured toward the padded round booth and didn't seat himself until she seemed comfortably settled.

* * * *

Rick pressed against the padded seat back and appreciated the lass before him. The crimson leather of the booth cast an uncommon glow on Anna. She was a pearl within a tufted jewel box. Rick's voice nearly caught. "So, tell me about yourself, Anna." He tilted his head toward her. "You say you live in Laural Canyon?"

"Uhum. I mean, yes, Sir." She stuttered self-consciously. Bobby set the drinks before them. "It's a little far from work, but I have a couple of different routes to get there, depending on the traffic, and since I can't afford to live in Beverly Hills…"

Rick laughed easily. "Few people can. I guess it's closer than Pasadena. You work at the museum across the street?"

"How do you know that?"

"Helen."

"The coordinator of mortal donors, of course," she said, hiding a blush behind her hair. "For a second there, I wondered if vampires could read minds."

He chuckled again, perversely enjoying her awkwardness. To tell the truth, he was tired of smooth, polished subs who glided through their interactions. They were boring. This girl was off-the-cuff, honest, refreshing, but so nervous in his presence she could barely maintain eye contact. He disciplined himself back to follow the conversation.

"I was very fortunate, Sir. I'm a Junior Exhibition Coordinator. I guess I was just in the right place at the right time, and I agreed to take the historically small salary…"

*Enough,* Rick thought, *I want to see her eyes.* He extended his arm across the table and with two fingers, gently raised her chin to emphasize his interest. "I've known you for ten minutes, and I already know it was more than luck." He countered warmly and then turned up his intensity. "What made you get involved in this vampire role-play thing?"

"Oh," Anna studied the moisture dripping down her chilled glass and squirmed. "I guess I missed, you know…"

*There goes our eye contact,* Rick thought irritably. *Lost to embarrassment.* "You missed *us*, not the bite?" Rick sat back flabbergasted and crossed his arms over his chest, preparing himself to read her more accurately.

"Well, yes, Sir. I mean, I never really understood why Matt banned me…"

There was a beat of silence between them. The raucous squeal of two donors entering the bar broke their stares.

"Anna." *Please, just look at me!* Rick's tone became serious. "I know exactly why Matt banned you." *That got her head up!*

"Well, it was decent of him to tell *me*! I've never been fired before!"

Rick ran his finger down the bridge of his nose, and stopped to stroke his bottom lip, rolling his mental dice. If he told her the truth, would she take her fine innocent ass back to her mortal reality? *Go for broke,* Rick decided, sitting a bit straighter.

"He thought you were too young." He watched for her reaction, but his words didn't seem to offend her as he expected. "Matt felt you were too special to get involved with us."

Anna's brows knit. She pouted, earning her Rick's closing statement.

"Anna, it was a compliment." He forestalled her further protest with a raised hand. "I know it didn't feel that way to you at the time."

"Yeah, well…May I ask you something, Sir?"

Rick nodded, primed to be blindsided.

"This woman Matt married…is she a vampire?"

*And…we're back to Matt.* "Why does that matter?" Rick's lips curled in a juvenile smile as he held his glass and slowly rotated the cocktail straw around the rim. "Matt, Matt, Matt."

Anna slid her glass forward as she leaned toward Rick. Her lips tightened around the red cocktail straw as she drew cola into her mouth. His eyes riveted to her unconscious show. As much as he wanted to banish the thought, he could feel her lips drawing on a particular part of his body. She swallowed hard, and he swallowed harder.

"Won't you tell me?" Anna prodded as she stared up at him.

*Now I get unlimited eye contact.* Rick tapped a nervous finger on the table before he shifted sideways in the booth, in hidden effort to adjust himself. He inhaled, measuring the room's pheromones. A glance around confirmed he was the only vampire in the room and yet, he was the one feeling cornered.

Ego protesting, he aimed for a brotherly tilt of his head and tone of voice when he spoke, "You knew Matt, he'd never get involved with a mortal. Yes. She's a vampire."

"Okay." Her reply was barely audible. "So, if he's married now, may I come back?"

*Not in a million years.* Rick was silent for a long beat, studying her. "I would have to get Matt's signature on that."

Anna's smile fell like hope evaporating.

"Matt and I don't share the same opinion about vamp/mortal interactions. You know what stumps me? From what I hear, you're really not into BDSM. If Matt's off the table, why would you want to come back?"

She opened her mouth to answer but seemed at a loss for a reply.

"Don't answer tonight. You think about that for a while and get back to me."

"Yes, Sir." Anna breathed.

"You've graduated from college. You have a career. Do you have family nearby? You date—and I don't mean that vampire-role-play guy?"

"Oh, I'm not dating Carl Sterling, Sir. He's a silver-plated jerk. I'm not dating anyone right now. And my family, well," her mouth turned down. "They're on the other side of the States."

Rick scowled. "You started to think of us as your family?"

"I...sort of...I guess." She added quickly. "Sir."

"It's time we found you some mortals to bond with."

Anna gave him a dazed nod.

"If you're through with your drink I'll see you to your car."

She hurriedly drained her glass. "Yes, Sir."

* * * *

"Tomorrow is Sunday," Rick started as they emerged from the parking garage elevator. He found his hand gravitating to the small of her back. He wanted to ask what her plans were for the day. *Not a good idea.* "So, Sterling leaves for his cruise on Monday?"

"Yes, Sir."

"I'm sure you're working all day. What time do you plan to go by and feed the hound?"

"Around six."

"Excellent. Text me the address, and I'll meet you there." He frowned. "Wait, you don't have my number, do you? Give me your phone."

She dropped it in his outstretched palm, and he added info to the address book.

"There now, that's my private number. Emphasis on private, if this number goes anywhere, I'll know where they got it."

Anna blushed, and Rick could not resist inhaling a whiff of her tempting scent, so infused with that odd mixture of obedience and obstinance. He guessed the seclusion from her family had taught her to be indomitable as well as sensitive. That was good, she'd need that combination to be successful in life.

He handed her into her car, a tiny skateboard of a thing no one should drive in L.A. "Thank you for looking out for us, Cupcake," he said in dismissal and bent to kiss her cheek. "Until Monday."

"Yes, Sir. Until Monday."

Rick watched her touch her cheek in wonderment as she backed out of the parking space. His other brain stirred for the second time this evening.

A lumbering hulk of an SUV nearly ran her into the wall as he watched. Anna waited patiently for the larger car to pass, but Rick was irked. Damn that wretched little car, of hers, he thought. He would have to do something about it. He wondered if it had been a family graduation present since it was a new model. If it was, they certainly didn't know anything about driving California freeways. He knew winning the prized position of Junior Exhibition Coordinator was more than luck. Matt's fine hand was in it, Rick was sure. C.G.I. was a generous supporter of the LAC Museum of Art, but dammit, they needed to come up with a better salary. A girl couldn't live on a subsistence salary in Los Angeles… He walked back to the lobby whistling. He couldn't remember the last time he whistled.

* * * *

Despite his current diversion with the delectable Anna, Rick was beginning to sense a brooding malevolence toward his undead Family. Methodically he undressed and showered the outside away. Before the World Wide Web, it had been easy to 'be' someone for ten to fifteen years, and then, with a competent attorney, he'd bequeath every worldly possession to his 'son' and relocate to another thriving city. He suspected C.G.I. had overstayed their market visibility in L.A. Despite the financial hit they would take for relocating, they should trade familiarity for survival. One vampire hunter was enough to incite a torch-bearing mob.

With tonight's discovery, Rick was entirely rethinking North and South America as a preferred location. Switzerland was looking better with each pulse of the shower. He hoped fatigue would overtake him as he went horizontal and closed his dry eyes. Within his tomb, silence ticked, and Rick began to fidget. Generally, he took the same corpse-like position each morning. This morn he twisted left to right until he rose fitfully and found sanctuary in his soaking tub. Ice cold water and a few drops of essential oils brought him down from an unaccustomed mental ledge. Rick's eyelids grew heavy, while he floated to tumultuous memories.

# 3

*Ireland, 1534*

It had been a time of torment in Ireland, a time of total rebellion against English rule, to which his family had sworn allegiance. Rick had been Richard Fitzjarrald in those days, Duke of Erne, Earl of Mayo. His half-brother, Ian, led a rebellion earlier that year and marched on Dublin intending to overthrow the English. Rick counseled against the rebellion and fought against the siege, but with Henry the Eighth paranoid and watchful of the Irish, he was in a perilous spot.

Rick was home for a respite between battles when an itinerant craftsmen's wagon broke down within sight of the castle. The most divine of women, Tsura, somehow managed to surmount the mote, scale the walls, evade his sentinels, and knock at the castle door. His presence in the great hall was all that kept her from death. His brothers wanted her beheaded or at least jailed as a spy. Rick overrode them all and listened to her plight.

He was fascinated not only by her beauty but by the fact, her arrival at the castle door was virtually impossible. He was convinced she employed witchcraft, and with the difficulties he and his family faced, Rick was willing to engage any benign practice that gave them an edge. He personally led the rag-tag band to dry quarters in the farthest corner of his massive stables. Though he offered food, they declined it, only accepting jugs of the strongest red wine. That gave him pause, wondering if he admitted a band of drunkards.

Rick was an upright man, loyal to the King, despite Henry's suspicions, and due to be joined in marriage to a prominent lass. He never dabbled in any kind of magic, yet, as he observed the nocturnal group, he could not deny something about them was preternatural.

He never knew his parents and grew up hearing stories of his father's skills with the dark arts. Tales told at his brother's knee suggested his dead father, the old Earl, rose once every seven years on New Year's Eve and sang in the holiday as he danced a jig. If he was born of a man suspected of shapeshifting to a bird and flying away, why couldn't he believe in creatures of the night?

Mass was endless that night. The rain recently let up after two days of downpour, and Rick caught some fresh air sitting on a bench before the chapel. Absently, he honed his personal weapon while his thoughts turned to memories that were anything but pious. He recalled with relish watching Tsura bathe in the full moon's light.

The glowing moon reflected off the water that caressed her and continued in sheets down her womanly form. Soft dimples sat over two luscious buttocks that drew down into strong thighs, and then shapely calves. She washed with her head up, eyes focused on the full moon, sweet lips wide open, drinking the rainwater. When she turned, Rick saw her exquisite breasts, ample and creamy smooth with rose-toned nipples honed hard and erect in the cold rain. One graceful hand lifted a plentiful bosom while the other ran slow circles around it with a bar of soap. She obviously enjoyed her own touch, and he found himself steely hard as she moved the soap over the dark bush of hair at the junction of her thighs. Rick shuddered. How he longed to move over that forbidden junction himself!

Lantern light shimmered along the surface of his gold and silver dirk. He found the play of light mesmerizing, especially when it danced along the facets of the bejeweled grip. Pulling his thoughts from Tsura, he considered he might need to use this weapon against his King soon if things went badly. It was not an option he wished to entertain.

In the few days, he knew her, he often felt Tsura was privy to his most personal thoughts. She tapped into the tensions of Erne Castle, the hints of the King's displeasure and rumors of traitorous deeds.

"You dwell on imaginings, your Grace. Do threats of a trial affright you?" She asked gently when she came upon him. She sat beside him without permission. "They could hang you. Why do you not flee?"

Rick shrugged. "My name and countenance are known. If I tried to flee, I would be held fast at the first border. And…" he heaved a resigned sigh, "to flee would be an act of cowardice." Still, he resolutely sharpened the ornate but deadly weapon.

"I see no heroism in needless death," Tsura countered, but then she was a woman, and women did not understand honor.

Rick could pretend indifference to himself, but he could not hide his true feelings from Tsura.

"Your generosity will be rewarded, my Lord," she promised, placing a consoling kiss on his cheek. It was an unheard-of thing to do, and Rick could only stare at her in disbelieving gratitude.

"Reward will have to come in the next world, it seems."

Tsura's dark eyes gleamed in the moonlight. She stood tall, with a raucous mane of ebony curls. Her flesh was translucent under the fine linen blouse falling off her shoulders. Coins trimmed the hem of the scarf around her luscious hips, and their clatter sang her invitation.

"You understand this is imminent, don't you?" Tsura circled him, in the way a cat circles its prey.

"Is it that evident?" The young Rick stuttered out. He had scant experience with a woman this formidable. He only knew the attention of the jejune milk maids or the cook's daughter in the haylofts. His length grew harder as Tsura's circles drew closer. Her heady musk did not wash away even though she bathed in the pouring rain last night.

She strode toward Rick, and he felt she owned him. The difference between her aura and that of other women was her power. She embodied raw supremacy while looking every part an enchantress. She bent toward his ear, her breast brushing his shoulder and whispered, "Think of my cunny, deep, pulsing, nakedly marking you."

Rick's entire body stiffened, his back ramrod straight. His ear tingled at the chill of her breath. Did she know or even sense that he could think of little else? Rick's fantasies of making love with the possibility of being caught in the act with a milkmaid, had been prominent on his forbidden list. Where on the list would he place this siren?

Rick drew in a centering breath. He yearned to take her hand and wend their way up to his bed. Hopefully, the staff would be bedded for the night, too content to rise at the sound of footsteps.

"Can you feel the way my body aches at the mere suggestion of your naked flesh, nothing between us, the promise of our immortal fusion?

Rick rose to face her. His rising softened her stance for a moment before she stepped into his embrace. She ran her hand down his linen shirt, seeking the center slit. Furtively she slipped within the soft linen to find his pecs, then lazily drew her nail around his nipple, finishing with a gentle pinch. He gasped as she pressed closer and ran her tongue at the seam of his lips.

"Do you taste my primal hunger for your seed filling me, dripping from my womb, streaked hotly across my lips and tongue and pale skin?"

That was it. Rick dropped his dirk into its sheath and caught her up over his shoulder. He made haste up the curved back stone staircase past the fewest of family bedrooms.

Tsura forbade him to light a candle as she drew back the heavy draperies. "Do you see how I crave you and long to possess no other?" As she stepped from window to window, Rick thought her eyes glowed in the moonlight.

"Can you see the need wrenching me from the peace of my rest? Your spirit called to me."

"My…my spirit called to you?" His sac constricted at the thought. Rick watched his chamber brighten in the shafts of the full moon's glow. Wasn't he about to be joined in marriage till death do part? Shouldn't he exercise his education of the female body before his wedding night? What if he was carried off in shackles and beheaded and there was no wedding night?

Rick held an inviting hand out to her, "Was it a word, a gesture, a quality, a look?" His head tilted, and she grinned and began to remove the coin-lined scarf at her hips.

Her lips curled as her soft voice declared, "It was your mind, your body, your face, your desire."

Rick reached for her skirts, his tone doubtful. "My mind? My desire?"

"Am I not your fantasy?" Tsura seemed crestfallen at his question, although she allowed Rick to undo the ties at her blouse and her skirts.

This illicit real-life experience certainly surpassed his fantasy. Surely, it would assume such tremendous stature, it would steal him from an otherwise routine existence.

"Are you aware, your Grace, that you have overtaken my erotic imagination and yearning absolutely?" Now she moved with a lyrical gate, dancing between the shafts of moonlight, "And when you touch me, the pleasure will ripple across every inch of my body. You will mark my wanton desire indelibly, as I will mark yours."

Then, in his chamber, she stood naked as she had when she'd bathed the night before. Yet she did not stand still, she quickly began dispatching Rick's opulent garb, peeling layer after layer off his broad shoulders and slim hips.

Tsura reduced him to only his braies, as his cock strained to be released to her hands. It was a slow reveal that left him breathless.

Tsura's saucy grin encouraged Rick to release the tie and drop his final piece of clothing. She let out a bit of a giddy cry at their joint nakedness, bounded onto the sumptuous feather bed and threw back the bed linens. She lay there, spreading her thighs, arching her back, leading his hands to her luscious gaping sex.

Rick drew her into his lap, face to face with him, her legs coiling his hips, his turgid length pressed between them. Her arms rested along his shoulders while her hands finger-combed his coarse waves. He began to perspire, encouraging damp ringlets to gather around his face. Rick's heat only increased as he pressed his face between her ample breasts and inhaled.

His hand found a place atop one full, fat breast. A moan escaped him as his other hand weighed and molded her other breast. Not since Archimedes weighed gold, had anyone enjoyed weighing something so much. Her nipples were rose-kissed and rigid, her breasts full of desire.

Rick regarded her with curiosity. What engendered his fascination? Was it the deep and accented voice laced with carnal passion and erotic yearning? All angst evaporated, all guilt vanished as Rick devoured her bouquet. He forced her breasts together and suckled both her rigid nipples at once. Tsura's head fell back and rolled from side to side in ecstasy.

This was their connection, their chemistry. Her womanly curves invited his hard, muscled body to mesh in a carnal dance. His inquisitive sexuality invited her overwhelming presence and strength.

There was the insistent brush of her mouth, followed quickly by their sensual and ravenous kisses. They unfolded, lying alongside each other, trading kisses. Tsura trailed her cool tongue along the curve of his neck, continuing down his perfect torso to the line of his throbbing sex. She was ravenous to taste his uniquely masculine essence and consume his mortal warmth.

Pinning Tsura proved too easy for him, it felt as if she had truly surrendered to his sex. Lying there, she moaned as Rick's fingers mischievously plotted the richness of her wet inner lips. Every word she panted emboldened him to taste her honeyed cunny. And he did, with relish. He praised the pearl of her womanity, his lips commanding her body. His hands clutched her writhing hips as her legs encircled his head. Her thighs began to tremble, her entire body stiffened in ecstasy, as her feral cry crescendoed to her Creator.

Triumph coursed through every vessel, nerve and fiber of Rick's body. He knelt between her trembling thighs, amazed at his own phallus. His flesh had grown exceedingly hard and thick, throbbing its need to go hilt deep into her wet silk. Tsura's cool hand gripped his sturdy girth, endangering his control.

"Fill me, your Grace, fill me to the hilt, now."

*How could a woman, so soft and supple, be so compelling?* And what else could he do? Rick was desperate to comply. Before the moment of their fusing, he dipped his lips to hers, engaging her in delighted tongue play. Then, as passion demanded, he thrust his hard, thick cock into her.

Sweat poured in rivulets down his muscular chest as he committed every sensation to a blessed memory. With each thrust, fire burgeoned along his spine, driving down determinedly, as if euphoria could actually erupt from his sac. His cry announced his sacred relief.

* * * *

He was lost in his orgasm, and Tsura flipped him on his back without losing his spitting flesh from her the fist of her sex. Dominance radiated from her as she sat astride her prey. Tsura caught his wrists in her hands and forced them outward with incredible strength. Her throaty moan caused him to tremble.

She felt herself change. Her lips opened to reveal unmistakably long ivory canines. Her brown eyes silvered-over as they bore into Rick's. She pounced, sinking deep, squarely over his carotid, delivering a slaying bite. Then, all was silence.

* * * *

That night Rick was fascinated by the physical transformation of two complete strangers into the intimacy of lovers. In that night's union, he ran the gamut of emotions from awe to confusion. He ached for Tsura from the very beginning, and his heart unexpectedly clamored for more.

Emotionally exhausted and physically spent to the point of quivering, Rick felt out of his body. He recalled their sex play and her penultimate bite. Hazily he watched Tsura furtively pick up her clothing and hastily dress. Before her hand caught the doorknob, Rick asked weakly, "Tell me, Tsura, did you ache to taste the sunset in my blood?"

Tsura wiped his blood from her lips and touched an emerging tear. With a bitter-sweet smile, she sighed. "No. No, I longed to taste your spirit." Then she stiffened her spine and leaned against the tall mahogany door. "Giani will spend the rest of the night with you. You will grow hungry, and he will feed you. Initially, you will be weak. Obey his directions, lest you hurt him."

Rick drew an assessing hand across his throat and winced at the blood on his fingers.

"You have been born to a new world. I will return after sunset to begin your baptism." Tsura turned and opened the door to slip out, as her mortal familiar slipped in.

Giani stepped into a shaft of moonlight, his shadow falling across the bed, making Rick wonder if he was a giant. The gentle bear of a man padded to the pitcher and bowl in the corner of the room. He wrung out a cool cloth and then crossed to the bed cautiously.

"Your, Grace, be at peace. I have ushered many mortals through this transformation." Giani held out his peasant's hands. "These are large but gentle hands."

Resigned to his conversion, Rick had allowed Giani to bathe him. Feeling weightless in his bed, the transformed Duke surrendered to the night.

* * * *

*Los Angeles, Present Day*

What began as a whisper in Rick's ear, stirred him to awareness. From the day he was turned until the mid-eighteenth century when she was slain by a vampire hunter, Rick craved Tsura like a drug. As he showered and prepped for the day, he wondered for the umpteenth time if his attraction to domination in the present day was a remnant of their torrid passion. One night of watching her bathe turned him on forever. For a solitary vampire that was a very long time.

Rick filled his nights with amusement where others found passion. As a Dom, he traded human thrills for food, even as his spirit withered. The further he journeyed from his time with Tsura, the fiercer his sexual dominance became. Ultimately, he reached his tipping point. It was time to surrender or fight.

"Everybody I love dies," he brooded to his reflection in the mirror.

*That's life. People die,* his reflection hurled back.

"Not if I can help it."

*Yeah, cuz you're everyone's hero, right? Because now you're gonna use your domination powers for good?*

"Well, at least I can be Cupcake's hero."

Rick's reflection was mute.

He dropped his fangs. "No smartass retort?" Rick left the bathroom counter and flipped off the light, over his shoulder, he shot back. "I didn't think so."

# 4

Slayer wasn't a bad dog, really, Anna thought as she unloaded a huge bag of dry dog food from her car. He was neurotic from being alone. Dogs were social animals. They belonged in a pack, and if Sterling was going to leave him without human affection, he should at least have a companion dog. She hoped Rick wasn't afraid of dogs. If you didn't know Slayer's behavior was neurotic, you could read it as aggression.

She looked around the neighborhood. It was dusk. The sun, though not totally set, had gone down behind the hills, and the resulting twilight should be ideal for Rick.

* * * *

When he pulled up, Rick found Anna burdened by a bag of dog food nearly as big as she was. He hoped that asswipe Sterling hadn't dumped the cost of the dog food on her. Obviously, this was not a toy poodle they were feeding.

"Hello, Sir." She smiled broadly in greeting, trying to juggle the enormous bag.

Rick jogged to her and threw the bag over his shoulder. "Hi. You can stop 'Sir'ing me. We're not at the club."

"Oh, okay." He waited a beat as she took that in. "So, you're not a Dom all the time?"

"Twenty-four/seven would be a heavy time commitment, don't you think? Most Doms don't adhere to that kind of protocol away from the club. Now, sexually, that's maybe a different thing, but socially, it's tedious." Rick flashed a boyish grin and then playfully elbowed her. "It would make people look at us funny. They'd think I was your commanding officer or something."

"Yes, Sir…" she began and was cut off by his slanted glance. "I mean, yes, that would be kinda odd."

"This is the house, huh?" He looked it over. "Doesn't seem too sinister." He gestured her forward. "After you."

"Now, before we go in, I want to warn you about Slayer. He's pretty big—a Rottweiler—and he's kinda neurotic. Not mean, but, some people are scared by him."

"So, you like dogs."

"Yeah, I do. I like all animals."

"You need to know, vamps have no trouble with aggressive animals. They're more afraid of us."

"Oh."

Anna opened the bolt lock and turned off the alarm. The house was obsessively immaculate in its gothic clutter. Not a thing looked like they were in sunny Los Angeles. Rick half expected to see a skeleton fly out at them on a zip line.

As Rick wended his way behind her into the kitchen area, he could see a broad expanse of concrete leading to a neglected pool, and in the back corner, an eight foot by eight-foot cage of chain link fencing, enclosed on all sides and over the top. *What the hell was he housing*, Rick wondered, *a mountain lion?* A massive dog house dominated it, a doggie water fountain, but no doggie toys evident. Inside the dog house lay a forlorn-looking black and tan behemoth.

The dog barked and shook ecstatically from head to toe when he saw Anna. However, when Rick walked out behind her carrying the bag of food, the dog tucked his stubby tail under and cowered in the corner, howling his distress.

"Oh, my god!" Anna exclaimed. "He's so upset! Oh, I've never seen him do this before…"

Rick preceded her to the gate and unlocked it. "Don't worry. It's because he smells me. He'll be okay."

"I don't know, Rick, maybe you shouldn't go in, you know what they say about wounded animals."

Rick flashed a confident grin. "He's not wounded, he's intimidated. Don't worry, Cupcake, you just fix his food and water. Let me get to know him. What's his name?"

"Uh…Slayer," she mumbled, clearly embarrassed.

"Slayer?" He laughed. "Well, that's stupid."

"I know, right?"

He handed her the bag of food and strolled over to the cringing dog.

"Hey, big guy." Slayer let out a pitiful howl that had other dogs in the neighborhood barking in sympathy. "Now that's a little extreme, isn't it? Come 'ere, lad, let's get acquainted." He reached out his hand, and the dog drew back as far as physically possible. "I know." Rick soothed, even as he picked up the enormous beast as if he were a puppy and carried him to the middle of the enclosure.

"You think he's getting any better?" Anna asked, concern edging her voice.

"He will. Be patient." Rick encouraged in that same soothing tone. He laid the dog down on his back and held him with a firm grip on his throat. The dog whimpered pathetically. "Now, that's as bad as it gets, fella," Rick reassured. "See there?" He moved his hand down and gently rubbed the dog's massive chest, soon he was using both hands to rub his belly, and the dog panted and kicked his back leg in delight. "Now we're gettin' somewhere, aren't we boy?"

"Look! He likes you!"

"Sure, we just had to get to know each other, that's all. This poor dog needs some play and exercise."

"Yeah."

"Well let's take him to the front and let him run to chase a ball or something."

"I don't know…" Anna hedged. "What if he runs away?"

"I wouldn't blame him." Rick scratched the dog behind his ear while the giant leaned against him as if he was a puppy. "Look." Rick pointed to him. "He's leaning."

"That's a Rottie trait." They said together.

"You like Rotties too?"

"I love them." Rick's smile was relaxed. "I had one when I was a lad."

"You must miss him."

"It was a long time ago. Anyway, don't worry about him running off. He won't leave me." He walked to the gate totally unconcerned, and he was right, the dog shadowed his side all the way.

* * * *

Out on the lawn, Rick broke a sturdy piece off the branch of an orange tree and threw it, sending Slayer soaring over two hundred and fifty yards to retrieve it. Anna's heart warmed watching them.

If a dog could immediately warm to Rick as Slayer had done, that must mean there was goodness in the man. Right? Surely if Slayer could trust him, she could. Something in the way he loved the dog told her that, despite his cynical exterior, Rick Hiatt might be able to love a woman as well. *Don't do this*, her heart warned. *Do not crush on another vampire.*

Jerking her thoughts away from the perilous prospect of loving a member of the undead, Anna cheered on man and dog as back and forth they went, throwing, wrestling for the stick and generally having a wonderful time. Finally, the athletic dog flopped down at Rick's feet and whined, his tongue lolling.

* * * *

Rick laughed. "Time for dinner?" He invited, and the dog sat up and cocked his head in expectation. "Oh, man," Rick shook his head. "This dog is too great. I'm not sending him back to that…that…cage, that's not a life."

"I agree." Anna crouched down to rub Slayer's cheeks while he happily licked her face. "It's too bad…"

"It doesn't have to be. This dog is about to be stolen."

"Rick!" Anna was shocked, she looked around for witnesses.

"What? He'll never know you were in on it. I'll make it look like someone broke into the backyard and took him. Of course, I'll have to change his name…"

Anna giggled. Rick was in the right mood to love that sound. "No more 'Slayer'?"

"How about…Player?" Rick decided. "Yeah, Player suits you fine, right boy? C'mon, let's go back in, and you can eat while we're looking around." The dog followed them docilely back inside, obviously overjoyed to be in Rick's presence.

"Down to business," Rick urged while the dog scarfed up his dinner. "Where's this 'vampire room'?"

* * * *

Anna led the way through a California dream home perfect for Rock Hudson and Doris Day. Incongruously, the walls were painted hideous black, dark purple and indigo. Heavy velvet drapes of the same hues hung in every airy window and hallways were narrowed by shadow boxes of gothic relics.

Rick surveyed it all with a critical eye. "I take it back, it's a good thing he houses Player outside. This whole damn house looks like Gothorama. I'd be afraid they'd use him as an animal sacrifice."

"Here we are." Anna indicated a doorway, and Rick took an instantaneous trip back in time. With the echo of each footstep, Rick returned to his mortal years.

Everywhere he looked, there was imitation Tudor décor. The walls were covered in vivid scarlet moiré vinyl wallpaper, a sad replica of the opulence Rick had been born to. In a castle, rich crimson velvet wall hangings were fitting, but in the smallish room, the effect was claustrophobic. The hideous wallpaper competed with reproduction sixteenth-century portraits in baroque frames.

"It's a little over the top," Anna noted needlessly as she looked around. "Seemed more malevolent when he was in here telling his gruesome stories."

"It's a little something, alright. Looks like his designer was going for early demon hunter."

Ceramic salt cellars, along with a hag stone and a grouping of witch balls were displayed along the wall.

Anna studied them with interest and flipped on the overhead light in the dim room to get a better look. "What do these do?"

"They were used for warding off witches and other evil spirits."

"How?" she asked incredulously, and Rick laughed.

"I didn't say they were successful."

The obligatory strings of garlic hung on every wall beside framed prayers of protection on scraps of parchment. One tall, heavily carved bookcase contained antique advice for vampire hunters, written mostly in German or Latin along with old English. Rick's eye caught diaries—old, beaten, leather-bound books stuffed with personal notes. They were shoved tightly into the highest shelf. Rick sublimated his fear about what those diaries contained. *Information about vampire hunting in L.A.?*

"These must have been dear," Rick mused, running his finger along the spines of the antique tomes. "How could Sterling afford them? Is he independently wealthy?"

"Not that I know of. I think he works as a stocker at Macy's."

"Hum. Maybe they were inherited?" He moved along the room. "Now, this is amazing. A gold chess set on a marble board. I might have played on one of these as a boy." He walked to the small, heavy wooden table where it sat, a chair on either side."

"Oh? Was your family wealthy?" Rick looked up expecting to see guile in Anna's question, but there was simple curiosity in her eyes, nothing more.

"We did alright."

* * * *

Anna walked to his side and caught herself inhaling the scent of the room with all its antiquities, then catching the scent of the man. First, she caught the starch of his crisp white shirt, then the citrus high notes of cologne that finished with a beloved fragrance—clean riding tack. Unbidden thoughts of her first riding instructor, all lean and dark and tall, crowded in as she stood beside the formidable vampire. Her heart's loyalties warred within her. Hadn't she wasted her tween years vying for her instructor's praise and approval? Now she was aflutter and feeling thirteen again. She hastily crossed her arms over her sundress to hide erect nipples. *Pull it together!*

* * * *

"I've never seen things like this." Anna waved her hand at the curiosities. "How do you know what they are?"

Rick thought for a second, she might be putting him on and slanted a glance down at her. Clear green eyes met his in return. "Cupcake, how old do you think I am?"

Anna wet her lips nervously during a long pause. "I hate these age-guessing games," she demurred. "I'm never any good at it."

"Give it a shot." He almost enjoyed putting her on the spot.

"Oh…thirty?" She hesitated at his shocked expression, followed by a crooked smile. "See, I told you I'm no good at it…twenty-eight?"

He blinked at her.

"Older? Younger?"

Rick gave a short laugh. "A little older. It doesn't matter. Anyway," he changed the subject adroitly. "These are remarkable examples."

Player appeared at the doorway, licking his chops from dinner. He whined and sat but refused to enter the room. *Probably doesn't like the wallpaper. With all the delicate items in here, it's just as well.*

"Okay, now we're talkin'!" He enthused as he led Anna to a carved chest. It sat open, faded red velvet padding cradling its contents.

"What is it?"

"What do you see?"

"Um…well…is that a wooden stake?" She touched it tentatively.

"Yeah, there are a couple of different kinds of stakes here. So, it's a…" No response. "What else do you see?"

"A small gun with curlicues carved in the metal…"

"That's probably a one-shot silver Derringer, ivory handle, I'm guessing with a silver bullet. I'm not gonna touch it to find out, though."

Anna nodded comprehension. "A Crucifix, and is that a vial of Holy water?"

"Yep."

"And those look like vials of herbs and spices. I don't get those."

"Yeah," Rick picked one up carefully and examined it. "Folks thought spices deterred the undead."

"But that's not true?"

Rick opened a vial and sniffed. "Guess not." He shrugged and replaced it, then turned to Anna with a clever grin. "So then, that makes this box a…"

She looked at him vacuously.

Rick took a step back from her, tucked his chin and hid his face in his hand as if in contemplation. "It's a vampire hunter's kit!"

"Oh!" She shuddered. "Oh."

He gave her a teasing glance. "What do you know about vampires?"

"Um…not much? I thought I did." She sagged. "I'm not thinking as clearly as I should. I need to eat."

"You need tutoring, Cupcake!" *I'm just the vampire to do it!* "Now I feel guilty for not feeding you. Let's finish up here, and I'll take you and Player to my place."

"Your place?" she began uncertainly.

Rick was already on to his next concern. "I don't see any dagger, here. Do you know where it is?"

Anna nodded. She walked to the mantle of the faux fireplace and lifted the shelf. From a hollow section, she raised an object wrapped in lambskin and carried it to a table, carefully laying back the wrapping.

Rick had to grab a high-backed chair to keep his knees from buckling. There, among all the cheesy imitations and bogus antiques, lay his family dirk. Rick stared at the nine-inch double-sided blade plated in silver and gold. It had a three-inch grip elaborately encrusted with jewels, most notably the seventy-seven-carat emerald, carved with the Fitzjarrald family crest. Rick regained his composure and stepped forward to peer at it.

"I can't touch this. It's silver. Will you please hold it up, so I can see the emerald?"

"Emerald?" Anna snorted. "That can't be right. My God, it would be worth a fortune."

"Please, just hold it up." When she did, Rick got weak-kneed all over again. Yes, this was definitely his blade. There was the Fitzjarrald night bird, quite clearly carved above the jousting helmet. There was no question, it was his dirk, and the only weapon, it was said, that could prevail against him. "Anna," he said in a restrained and solemn tone as if she was holding a bomb, "will you please wrap that back up in the lambskin and put it in a bag of some kind? I need to take this with me."

"Oh, but Rick," She shook her head in protest. "The dog and the dagger? I mean, he'll think…"

"He'll think he was robbed," Rick agreed implacably. "That's exactly what I want him to think. In fact, I'm coming back here with a team to comb over this place. We'll take a variety of things, he'll think it was a simple robbery. But Anna…" He drew in a deep gasp, almost as if he couldn't catch his breath. "This was pre-eminent."

"Pre-eminent?" she wondered, her eyes wide with bewilderment.

"Important, Cupcake." He sighed heavily. "You may have saved my life."

# 5

Anna didn't know what she expected when they stepped off the penthouse elevator into Rick's home. Maybe his 'dungeon' should have given her a clue. She always thought of him as ultra-modern/ultra-hip, but his home was…for want of a better description…modern-medieval. If Sterling lived in cheap imitation Goth, Rick had real, obviously priceless antiques. Any reproductions were painstakingly crafted. The place was breath-taking, with stone walls, dark, heavy woods polished to a lustrous sheen, and fine-textured, time-muted fabrics. Any prince of the realm would feel perfectly at home. She turned a circle, noting the balustrade that ran along the high ceiling of one wall, and led, she assumed to bedrooms. The opposite wall was floor to ceiling windows allowing a spectacular view of downtown L.A. but flanked by heavy curtains, undoubtedly, to exclude sunlight.

"Wow!" Anna breathed. "I can't wait to see the bathroom!"

"Down the hall to the left," Rick called over his shoulder as he led the dog into another room.

Anna followed shyly. "No, I don't mean I have to use it. I just want to see it."

"Ah." Rick laughed, and rocked on his heels, looking awkward. "I forget people find this," he gestured around the kitchen area, "unusual."

Anna took in the stone and plaster walls, heavy wooden beams on the ceiling, thick marble countertops, and appliances secreted behind gleaming carved wood.

"Well, the dog fits, anyway. You know, guarding the manor house."

Rick laughed again and fidgeted. "You said you were hungry. Let me call down to the grille and get you something to eat. Steak okay?" He punched a code into what looked like an elaborate intercom system.

"Sure, but if it's a bother I could slap together a sandwich here." She gestured to what she assumed was a well-hidden fridge.

"Uh…" Rick rubbed at the bridge of his nose. "I'm afraid you won't find anything in there. Vampire," Rick grinned wide and clicked his teeth. "Remember?"

Anna slapped a hand over her mouth and closed her eyes in embarrassment. "You know, I actually forgot."

"Yes, Mr. Hiatt?" A voice crackled to life on the intercom.

"Bobby, send up our best steak, medium rare, with all the trimmings…I have a guest. A bottle of fresh AB negative and Everclear for me, please."

"Yes, Sir. On a cart?"

"No, use the dumb-waiter. As quickly as you can, please, the lady is hungry. Oh, and," he looked down at Player who sat at his side. "Send us a big bowl of chopped sirloin, raw."

"Yes, Sir…" Bobby's disembodied voice sounded dubious. "Right away."

"That's convenient." Anna teased.

"Yeah. So, I need to put that," he pointed at the bag containing the dirk, "in the safe." He picked the item up almost reverently. "When I get back, you want a tour?"

* * * *

After a dinner of what must have been some kind of rare premium beef, the likes of which Anna had never tasted in her life, Rick led her onto the balcony to finish her wine. She gaped. Rough travertine led to an exotically curved edgeless lap pool with transparent walls. A heavy all-weather bamboo couch in a semicircle overlooked the pool and the whole of the city. Rick handed her onto the couch and sat beside her.

Anna was starting to feel intimidated by the sheer scope and drama of everything she saw in Rick's life. She could feel herself withdrawing into that shy remoteness she so often employed to stay emotionally secure. Thankfully, her retreat was broken by Player who ignored all the ostentation and splashed down the stairs of the pool to slurp up some water.

Rick chuckled. "Okay, you need a water dish. Point taken." He turned to Anna with an amiable smile. "More wine?"

She guarded her goblet with her hand. "No thanks, it's outstanding wine, but if I have more than one glass, I'll never be able to drive home."

"You're a cheap date." He deftly removed the empty glass, sitting it on a nearby table. "So, a few nights ago, I asked why you wanted to come back to the Gaoler. Do you think you can tell me now?"

"Oh…" now she wished she hadn't turned down that wine. "It's…" she fretted. "It's embarrassing."

"Give it a try. I'm a pretty good listener."

Anna snorted, which was totally unlike her, and blurted out a reply. "Yeah, right! A Dom who likes to listen!" *Okay, maybe just that one glass was the better idea.* "Oh!" She covered her mouth with her hand. "That didn't come out right…"

Rick gave her a searching look. "I think you said exactly what you meant. You think Doms are only interested in themselves."

"I—"

"But the truth is, a good Dom is always listening to his sub, he's always reading her and trying to anticipate her needs."

Anna's skepticism showed on her face.

"You don't believe me?"

Reluctantly, she shook her head.

"That tells me either you've never had a proper Dom, or you never understood the Dom/sub dynamic in the first place. If you think all a Dom does is bark orders and mete out punishment, you're wrong. But it makes me all the more curious to know, if you find that idea objectionable why do you want to come back?"

"I…um…" She couldn't get the words out.

"Do you have friends at the club? Is that it? Girls, friends you miss?"

"No!" She startled both of them with her vehement reply. "I don't miss any of the women there. They were horrible to me! They made me feel like I couldn't do anything right."

"Cupcake!" Rick murmured sympathetically. "Don't you understand they were jealous of you?" He smoothed a stray lock of hair behind her ear with a gentle touch.

"Jealous?" She scoffed. "Why?"

"You had Matt, and they didn't. They had no idea what he did with you. And…" he sighed, "I'm sure they had great imaginations. Matt would never say anything about you to anyone. They probably thought you had wild kinky sex with him every night."

Anna blushed from the roots of her hair to her toes.

*What would I have to do to get her to blush like that over* me*?*

"Now, I happen to know Matt wouldn't and didn't do that. Matt never had sex with a donor. But, from their perspectives, the most eligible guy at the club had chosen you over them."

"I thought you were the most eligible guy at the club."

Rick waited, not saying a word until she finally raised her gaze to his. "Right?" her word floated like a feather.

His eyes twinkled, he smiled, moved in, and took her lips with a soft kiss. "You are an innocent." He scrutinized her with those warm whiskey eyes. "Tell me."

"I…I like the bite."

"You like the…" He paused. "You mean, you like the sensation?"

"Nothing else feels like that."

"You like the orgasm."

"What?"

Rick paused and considered, "Cupcake, haven't you ever had that feeling before?" He waited. "Never had that feeling with a guy?"

"No." Her reply was hushed, and Anna had the dawning notion she was completely out of the loop.

"Okay." Rick nodded decisively. "I get it." To her surprise, he leaned in again.

His lips started out cool, the expected chill of the undead, but as he worked her lips with his, they began to soften and warm. One arm circled around her waist, drawing her close to his side, the other reached in to caress her neck and angle her where he wanted. Anna felt her will bend to his. A slow burn kindled within her. He licked gently along the seam of her lips, coaxing her to open and when she did, he surged within, driving the kiss deeper to possess her. Anna trembled, her heart pounded wildly, and that feeling she always got from Matt seemed twice as intense with Rick. He drew back, a look of delight suffusing his handsome face, and bent forward to kiss her again.

The phone rang. *Damn! Not now!*

He retrieved the cell from his breast pocket and snarled into it. "This better be good." He listened for a moment and surged to his feet. "Excuse me," he apologized curtly. "I have to take this."

Anna bounded up from her seat, teeth gritted, hands clenching to straighten her clothing. She paced and fidgeted with her hair, peering into the great room to read Rick's body language. He hunched over the cell phone, a mass of tension, exchanging short bursts of conversation. *Whoever is on the other end of that phone needs to die!* She thought peevishly. She was exasperated, stunned by her own need. It felt as if she were riding a euphoric rocket that fizzled and was now plummeting back to earth. Rick Hiatt kissed her, and his kiss was damn near as good as Matt's bite. *Wow! Oh, I'm in serious trouble now.*

* * * *

"Cupcake, I need to take you home." Rick watched the color drain out of her young face.

"Home?" He scented sexual arousal draining as her disappointment filled the room.

Rick bent his head in thought. There was so much going back and forth between them now, maybe a cool-down was a good thing. Maybe they both needed a little distance? *Nah! The devil on one shoulder told him to drop trou right here and take her.* The mature vampire on the other shoulder argued the long game. *Make her safe, take care of the distractions and then make it a monumental communion.*

Rick sensed her dejection and held out his reassuring arms. Anna flew into them. He welcomed her warmth, trailing kisses from the top of her head to her ear, to her cheek and finally her waiting lips. His restraint was sorely tested by her ardent response. He felt every curve of her sweet body pressed against him. But no, if he took her now, how could he leave her? *Restraint, man, have some restraint. Where's that Dom discipline when I need it?*

They rode the elevator in tense silence broken only by Player's pacing and whining. Rick smirked. He knew the dog was picking up on the sexual tension. The doors opened to reveal a sleek, black limo. Anna cast an inquiring gaze his way.

"I'm sorry, Cupcake, this won't be a romantic ride, I need to make some calls. I promise to make it up to you."

Before Rick could make the first call, Player snuggled up to Anna on the back seat, apparently sensing her need of comfort. Rick watched fondly from the jump seat as he dialed.

"Get me the President, please." He put the phone on speaker. He smirked at Anna's astonishment. With a hand over the phone, he explained, "It's not who you think."

"What can I do for you, Sir Richard?" Came a lilting European voice.

"Mr. President, we have a situation."

"Is this related to Barranquilla?"

"Yes, Sir, I've received confirmation the Barranquilla massacre is directly related to Veronique Moreau."

"We were curious as to why this banquet took such a bloody turn. We've got to put these addicted vamps down before the news agencies start reporting."

"Well, we also have something in Los Angeles we need to quell."

"Humanité related?"

"No, Sir. Possibly a vampire hunter. The violence in Colombia could raise our profile."

"I agree, Sir Richard. Since you're well acquainted with the parties involved, may I assume you're calling to take the reins on this?"

"I'm ready, Mr. President, with your support. I'll need the usual equipment, troops, and resources."

"Your troops can be in Colombia, ready for an assault, by 1800 hours tomorrow."

"Adam Lachlan is already in-country. He'll act as my Second. Assuming we can capture Veronique, he'll escort her to Court."

"What about your local vampire hunter?"

"The responders are doing a walkthrough on the suspect's home."

"God's speed, Sir Richard."

"And to you too, Mr. President," and the call closed.

Anna watched in awe.

"You're *Sir* Richard? From which country? What President was that? This sounds really serious. What's going on?"

"There are more things in heaven and earth, Horatio, than are dreamt of in your philosophy," Rick quoted with a grin.

"You're Shakespeare now?"

"No, he was a few years behind me in school."

Anna stared at him in a daze, and Rick suddenly considered, *is she ready for all this?*

"You know, Cupcake, I am very old, and with age comes certain responsibilities."

"How old, exactly?"

"Matt never covered the basics with you, did he?" *She doesn't know what she doesn't know*, Rick realized. If she were to be part of his world, it would be up to him to educate her about the undead, starting with himself. "I was born in 1513."

"Oh, stop it! That's impossible."

"Anna, you know what Matt and I are." His voice was low and serious.

"You drink blood," she agreed with a nod.

"Drinking blood is more than a sexual thrill. For us, the club is a trade-off we make to stay alive. Blood is our food. Mortals get a rush, and the undead keep existing."

"Undead?" Anna shrank back behind Player, her eyes wide.

*How is she not familiar with all this? This is Vampire 101.* "I'm not trying to frighten you," he continued gently. "Nothing has changed. Nothing is any different between us than it was in my apartment."

Anna moved hesitantly out from behind Player's huge presence.

"I need to be sure you understand exactly what we are and how all this works. I'm seriously concerned that your vamp education lacks depth."

"You bite us, we get off, and we go home." She frowned and added glumly, "With any luck, we don't fall in love. I wasn't that lucky."

"You fell in love with the sensation. You don't know the whole story. After you know the depth and breadth of it, if you want nothing more to do with me, I'll understand."

"This doesn't sound like a short story."

Rick checked his watch. He was not so much concerned for the length of his tale, as for what her reactions might be. He sighed. Well, at least they were headed for her home. If need be, he could thrall her, leave Player with her and say goodbye.

* * * *

Rick covered the basics in detail by the time they pulled up at her Laural Canyon address. Anna didn't freak out, and she was frankly mystified Rick thought she might. She may not be aware of all the details, but Anna always got the gist of vampire life.

The non-descript stucco bungalow could have been found on any street in the city. "I have a private entrance around back." Anna fished for her keys.

"You and Player go ahead, I'll be there anon."

As she reached the back hedge, Anna cringed at the foul language, and drunken slurs of the men gathered on the patio she shared with her landlord. *Damn it! He and his slimy friends are at it again.* She only lived there three weeks, and already this guy was making a nuisance of himself. Anna peeked over the hedge and spied the six men in patio chairs around the fire pit. With her head up high and her gaze fixed on her door, she hurried Player along the flagstone path, hoping to avoid conversation.

Her landlord staggered to his feet at the sight of her. "Here's the sweetheart of a renter I found," he slurred to his buddies. A bevy of crude retorts echoed behind him.

Anna winced, and Player hunkered low and growled. Rick observed from behind, wanting to do more than growl.

* * * *

The drunken man ambled his way over to her, keeping a respectful distance from the dog. "Hey now, you didn't pay a deposit for a dog. If you wanna keep him, that'll be an extra fifteen hundred dollars."

"I…"

"That is unless you want to work it out between us, sweetheart." His compatriots egged him on. His smarmy side overtook his drunkenness. He sidled closer, trying to wrap his arm around her shoulder. Player's growl grew fiercer. "Tell your doggie to pipe down. We have negotiations…"

Vamp speed being what it was, Rick darted in between the two of them and placed his arm firmly around the spot the slimebag was aiming for. There was an immediate startled silence from the peanut gallery.

"Holy crap! Who the hell are you?" The landlord staggered back.

"Her guardian angel." Rick turned to Anna. "Go ahead, Cupcake." He nodded toward her door. "I'll take Player." Anna handed the leash over with a dubious look.

Rick turned back to the riff-raff, intent on thralling them. "Your renter is moving out, and you're gonna be fine with that. You and your boys drink a few more shots, get nice and drunk. No one will remember me or the dog in the morning." He looked around the men, observing their glassy stares and slack jaws as he compelled them with his mind. "When the moving company calls and says they're coming to pack and move Miss Curley's things, you'll be cooperative and polite. You'll decline their offer of a check to pay off the balance of the lease." Rick pressed a firm hand on the man's shoulder to reinforce the suggestion. "Got that, boyo?" Slimebag nodded slowly. "Good. Now, go start some serious drinking." The men seemed momentarily dazed by his thralling and then commenced more shots.

* * * *

Anna stood in her tiny studio apartment and glared at him. "I'm moving out?" She demanded, hands on hips.

"Yep. There's an open apartment at the Consort building."

"C'mon, Rick! I couldn't afford the electric on one of those units!"

"Well, yeah, maybe, but you'd be doing me a favor, keeping the place occupied and in shape for now…" He started to cajole. He didn't want to have to thrall her.

"I'd feel like a kept woman! I can't accept that."

"Besides, it's more convenient for you, right across the street from work, you wouldn't have to drive so much and…" This argument clearly wasn't working, so Rick switched tactics while she shook her head.

"Look, the truth is, I didn't think this thing through with keeping the dog, you know? I mean, Player needs a mortal to look after him. I can't take him to the park in the sun. I can't take him to the beach to play. I want him to have a good life…"

Rick could see her softening and moved in for the kill.

"Listen, how much do you pay for Lothario's garage?"

"Thirteen hundred dollars a month."

Rick was incredulous but pressed on. "Plus utilities?"

"Well, yeah."

"Great! Thirteen hundred. Just the cash flow I was looking for and utilities happen to be included. What a deal!"

Anna shook her head. "Rick…"

"So, pack whatever plate you've got and let's get outta here."

Anna knit her brows. "My dishes?"

Rick chuckled. "It's an old expression. It means, pack your valuables. The moving company will pick up the rest tomorrow."

Anna opened a duffle and tossed in her makeup bag and a few clothes. "You know this is crazy, right?"

Rick stood in the doorway, rocking on the balls of his feet, arms crossed over his chest. "This is gonna work out great, you'll see."

Anna threw the duffle strap over her shoulder and met him toe to toe at the door. Her eyes twinkled. "So, plate—is that something a Duke would have?" She flirted.

"Let us alight to my carriage, and I'll tell you more."

* * * *

Player barked and pulled them toward the limo. Once inside, it was clear the atmosphere had swung from business to affairs of the heart. Anna laughed watching Player, his head happily hanging out the shotgun seat window in front. Passersby in adjoining cars pointed at him and commented. Anna turned to Rick, his intense appraisal stopped her.

"You're beautiful, Cupcake." He whispered huskily. "I don't know how I'll bear to leave you."

Anna melted. The light jazz on the sound system invited romance, and suddenly the soft leather seats became a sensuous playground. In her world, Rick had slain the dragon, stormed the castle and won her heart.

<h1 style="text-align:center">6</h1>

Rick wasted no time. He hadn't been this eager for a woman since Tsura, and this time he was the experienced lover. Rick's heart opened as he sensed every unexpressed emotion within her. He'd surpassed the point of infatuation long ago. How could he return the devotion he read in her eyes? He would worship her body. He was as hungry for her as she was for him. He drew her closer, her face upturned, eyes closed in anticipation of his kiss. She was his sleeping beauty, her sexuality waiting to be awoken with his kisses. Rick's lips glanced along her forehead, taking time to caress each eyelid. Hearing her catching her breath, he ran the tip of his tongue down the bridge of her perfect nose, making her giggle.

"Oh, Cupcake, you are delicious," he whispered as his lips claimed hers with unbridled hunger. Anna arched up to him, her heart thundering in Rick's ears. She was so receptive. Rick longed to give her more.

"I wish you could feel what you do to me!" Anna confessed breathlessly.

Rick grinned down at her, his nose tracing her hairline to her ear. "Cupcake, I do. I feel every quiver." Rick's arms tightened around her. "I scent your arousal." His palm slid under her skirt to hover at the juncture of her thighs. "I know you're ready for me."

Anna shuddered. He had to feel her touch. Her fingers fumbled at his shirt buttons. Rick upped the ante and, pushing aside her restricting panties, he caressed her anxious clit. Her back bowed instinctively, and she tore his shirt open. Buttons flew everywhere, and looking down at her, he chuckled. Her hands found a playground in the light dusting of golden hair over his solidly muscled pecs.

Rick hit the intercom button to alert the driver. "Take the long way home."

Rick's lips met hers in a blistering kiss, his tongue driving into her mouth, mimicking the rhythm of his fingers breaching her panties.

Her hands slid under his shirt and around his back. She moaned, "Too many clothes…"

"I can fix that!" He growled, grabbing the silky impediment of her tiny bikini panties and tearing them from her in one impatient motion.

Anna squealed and giggled as she spread her legs in invitation. Abruptly, giggles turned to keening when his insistent fingers drove inside her.

"Oh my God!" Anna panted as he rolled down the elastic top of her sundress and dove into her waiting breasts.

"Is that a prayer?" Rick turned his face away momentarily and returned icy-eyed. His fangs dropped long and hungry. "Because I've been known to answer unholy prayers."

Anna moaned. Rick's sharp fangs glanced along one quivering breast, savoring her exquisite bouquet along with the glory of her surrender.

* * * *

Anna's hand grew bold at the chance to caress his length through his fine trousers. Rick's breath caught. His fangs pierced the velvet softness of her breast, as his thumb danced on her clit. The hair-trigger of her climax roared within her as he drew in the full bloom of her blood. Anna's hand reflexively gripped his pulsing erection, and Rick's hot climax met hers measure for measure.

The two of them rolled in dazed response to the limo's turns and braking. Anna's heart sank at the thought of leaving the shelter of his arms. They sighed with relief when the limo accelerated onto the freeway.

"You don't play fair," Rick whispered huskily, gazing down at her with a lopsided grin.

"*I* don't play fair?" Anna's eyes widened. "You're the one with the buttons and zipper."

Rick sighed regretfully. He sat upright, bringing her with him. Attentively he dug for her scrapped panties and pocketed them.

Anna rolled up her strapless sundress, only her swollen lips betrayed her new-found appetite. It was obvious they would soon be yanked out of their nest and back to reality. "Let me see the real you." Her sweetly serious face turned up to Rick's.

* * * *

Rick watched the limo pull into the C.G.I. portico. "*Can* you see the real me?" He averted his eyes, his feelings too raw. *This is not the hour and place for that confession.*

The car jarred to a stop, Player barked, rescuing him, and Anna clenched her teeth. Rick cast an irritated look at his driver and finished pulling himself together. He glanced at his watch in dismay. "Anna, I truly regret I have to leave you. I have a team waiting for me at Sterling's house. You know I won't dally." He released her and stepped out of the limo.

Anna whimpered low in her throat and followed him out. "Player and I will wait up for you."

"I have no idea what we'll find at Gothorama, and I have to prepare for Colombia." Rick smoothed the gathered frown across her brow. "Anna, I want another first time. One that won't be interrupted." Rick drew her bright hair behind her ear and left a kiss there.

"Yes, I want to be everything you've ever dreamed of."

"Aw, Cupcake, you are."

Anna sucked in a sigh. They were suddenly bowled over by the insistent Rottweiler vying for their attention. The building doors opened, and they followed the dog in.

"I'll have Helen get you settled in your apartment tomorrow. You and Player will bunk up at my place tonight."

"Will you kiss me goodbye before you leave for Colombia?" Anna nearly begged.

"I'll be your wake-up kiss. How do you drink your coffee?" Before the elevator door opened, Rick caught Anna in a swooping embrace, bent her back over his arm and gave her a firmly definitive kiss.

The doors slid open, and she and Player stepped into the car.

"Until morning."

* * * *

It was 12:35 in the morning and a nearly moonless night. Rick threw the Hummer into park and listened as the engine ticked while it cooled. When all was silence again, he flipped the dome light off and opened the door, stepping from darkness into darkness. The alarm code Anna had given him was in his pocket, Rick pulled it out and headed to the front door. He nodded to the four responders tacking back and forth down the side of the mountain behind Sterling's home. It took only moments to get to the back door and let them in.

"Just when you thought it was cool to be a vamp, you see this crap!" Rick gestured at the bizarre accouterments of the house.

The four vampires seemed appropriately aghast at the excess. "Bloody oath!" agreed Reggie, a vamp from down under. He shuddered but looked about for anything of value.

Arne, their Viking vampire, raised his eyebrows nearly into his blonde hairline.

Rick turned to the two second-story men in the group. "Once we're done, it needs to look like a standard home invasion. Got it? Until then, look for hidden compartments, secret rooms, loose floorboards. In fact, check that fireplace," he pointed, "top to bottom. He had an extremely rare artifact hidden there."

Each vamp struck out in different directions. Rick stood at the bookcase, thumbing through the journal he found earlier. The entries looked like notes and newspaper clippings made by Sterling's grandfather. The writer had apparently met an exotic woman in Haiti who was mysterious and had the bad luck to be in the vicinity of several murders.

*Veronique? The time frame fits, and she wouldn't hesitate to rip out a slayer's throat.*

On the last few pages, Sterling's rambling impressions were an example of pathetic prose. Brett's staking was noted there. *Sterling has a new diary to break in, how unsettling.* Rick was disappointed by the absence of a computer, though dust on the desktop outlined where a laptop had sat.

"Rick, I've got something!"

Rick followed Cary's voice into a bedroom where a gun safe the size of a refrigerator stood agape inside a closet. "This glass case is sealed." Cary gestured to an item he carefully placed on the bed. "The documents inside must be ancient. I wouldn't open it until you get into a museum-protected environment."

Rick bent closer, peering at the leather cover with faded stamping. "These are the journals of Silvu Mares, Vampire Slayer, the year of our Lord 1699," he read aloud. He straightened abruptly, seeking Cary's reaction.

"Any more like this in the safe?"

Cary gestured his flashlight beam to reveal at least eight more archival document cases. "Want them all?"

"Take everything in the safe. Lawrence can sort it all later."

Efficiently locating and packing up everything a crook might cart away, the four vampires worked silently while Rick returned to Sterling's office. The trashcan overflowed with crumpled papers. Smoothing out the sheets, Rick discerned Sterling's itinerary. Yeah, he was headed out of town for three weeks, but he wasn't going on a cruise. Sterling was headed to Barranquilla, Colombia.

Rick's curses became shouts at the name on the smudged itinerary: Carl Black. The bastard was related to Ramsey Black! Probably the dead slayer's grandson. Why change his name? Sterling must have sounded more seductive to the local coeds.

Rick gathered the papers and tied up the bag of trash. Who knew what other confessions he would find printed on twenty-pound white paper?

"Those document cases need to go directly to the museum," Lawrence advised, speaking in subtones to avoid waking the neighborhood. "I'll review and record what I can before you leave town." He loaded the last of the precious loot into the cargo area of the Hummer.

Rick rattled the car keys nervously. "Want a ride over, Larry?"

"Sure, it beats running behind the car!"

Rick looked at the others. "How about you fellows?"

Cary shook his head. "No, our van's at the top of the hill."

"Okay, gentlemen, I owe each of you. Drop by the club whenever you want." In seconds the street was as quiet as before they arrived.

# 7

Lawrence pushed the cart bearing nine archival boxes to the Historical Documents Room. Rick felt faintly ridiculous in the Tyvek suit Lawrence insisted they wear—still the preservation of the documents was paramount.

"Let's begin by putting the journals in chronological order." In the end, the journals spanned the years from 1699 to 1975.

"I already have the last journal, 1976 to present. It ended when Brett was staked."

Larry stepped back and surveyed the cases. "This is a lot of material to review."

Rick became uncharacteristically somber. "Will you please open the case containing 1740 to 1780?"

Larry shot him a surprised look. "Sure." Larry handed Rick white cotton gloves after he unsealed the box. Rick stared at it, fearful of the revelations it might contain.

"Would you like some time alone?" Larry asked moving toward the door.

Rick pulled out a stool and nodded. "That would be great."

Alone with just the sound of the negative airflow, Rick opened the book to its center, finding the entry dated 1755, Hungary. It documented a series of slayings, possibly related to the Hapsburg dynasty. He and Tsura lived in Hungary at the time. Rick remembered the violence of the day well, it had prompted them to immigrate to Bologna, Italy. There, Rick passed as a physician and Tsura as a midwife. They prospered within the growing medical education community until she was suspected of being a witch.

He read in the journal:

*Fall, 25 October 1759. There come rumors and tales, told by mistrustful families, that infants born of barren mothers, who were prophesied to be stillborn, were delivered hale and hardy. The greater part of these infants having been delivered by a midwife known as Tsura Sylvestro, wife of the physician, Ricardo Sylvestro. These have been most reported in Bologna.*

*29 October 1759. This servant of the Lord, charged by God Almighty with hunting the savage vampire, has followed the trail of increased baptisms. I have found myself in the small village of Saenza, where I have met in secret with the Parish Priest, Father Lorenzo. He avows the healing arts of this couple to be unnatural. He warrants they fail to associate with accepted society, they neither garden nor pay for food or livestock. Staples given to them by townsfolk find their way back to villagers untouched.*

*31 October 1759. I sat vigil in the home of Anthony and Isabella Piero. Her labor began today after Mass. Her eldest son being unable to summon the Midwife Sylvestro to Isabella's bedside, her husband requested that I try. I traveled to the Sylvestro home seeking abidance for a difficult birth. I encountered only their manservant, who insisted neither were available until after dusk. I tarried along in prayer for good Madam Piero, climbing up the mountain pass where I came upon a cave. Blessing myself, I entered therein and found a blocking stone, as for a grave, barring my way. Believing I had found a vampire's lair, I returned to my lodging to retrieve the tools of vampire destruction. Distrustful of the village, who had been enchanted by them, I silently hurried to return, armed against the undead demons.*

Rick blinked back tears. Their time as healers was a triumph for them, and they reveled in saving mortal lives. He fondly recalled the mortals who did not find their nature to be either foul or sinister. He and Tsura celebrated centuries of explosive love, harmony, and companionship. He would never have guessed their parting would be so violent after two hundred and twenty-five blissful years together.

Though nearly three hundred years had passed, Rick recalled the happenings of that day as if they were yesterday. He'd arisen before dusk to harvest a restorative herb Tsura kept ready in her midwife's case. It was his nature to do these small things for her, and his heart was light, thinking of her thanks when she realized he found an unusual amount of the precious herb.

Mateo, their mortal familiar, sought him out in the depths of the forest. Rick did not expect Mateo's disturbed demeanor. The word that a stranger in the village was prying into their habits was as alarming as it was unexpected. Unconcerned for his own welfare, Mateo forced Rick to accept their emergency haversack and urged him to roust Tsura and flee.

Rick was brought to his knees when he stepped behind the partially unrolled funerary stone and found Tsura's decapitated body. There was no time for grief, his tears had to wait, for he was in mortal danger. All he could do was flee. He knew one alert vampire slayer could marshal a torch-bearing mob. He found the first ship sailing for the New World and boarded it, never to return.

Now, staring at the frank words of a long-dead vampire slayer, the grief of three centuries was unleashed. Rick balled his fists into his eyes and felt the rolling emotions of extreme loss pour from within.

The unearthly keening wail brought Lawrence to the doorway at vamp speed. "Rick, whatever it is, man, what can I do?"

# 8

Rick stepped out of his loafers before the elevator doors slid open. His return home was later than he intended, and he wouldn't have time to give Anna her well-deserved goodbye. Yes, Player did lift his muzzle off the pillow to see the source of the mechanical *whoosh*. Rick needed to glide in and then out again and get to the airport. He silently padded through his penthouse. His reward was the moments he spared to watch his Cupcake asleep on the deeply padded sofa before the fireplace. Rick winked at the behemoth and raised a finger to his lips, "Shhh," and the dog returned to his happy place beside his new friend.

Rick threw together his black tactical gear and personal weaponry. This time, he would take the limo to the airport and leave the Tesla for Anna. In long, silent strides he moved to the coffee table and left the key ring where Anna would see it when she awoke. He regretted missing the chance to serve her coffee as he promised, but his driver idled on the street, and they were wheels up in thirty minutes.

* * * *

The ding of an incoming message, along with Player's insistent nudging, rousted Anna from her dream-filled slumber. Weren't Rick's strong arms around her moments ago? *Oh, no, that was a dream.* The sun was fully up. *Didn't he say he'd bring me coffee? What time is it? Am I late for work? Oh, wait, it's Tuesday, my day off.* Player pawed at her again, and she could read the desperation in his eyes.

"Okay, time to go out, right?" She fished for her shoes under the sofa. "Get your leash." By the time the dog brought it to her, she was up. "Let me grab my phone." She pressed the elevator button. "Oh, there's a message." She let Player pull her along as she read. It was a video voice mail.

By the time they reached the lobby, Rick's video was playing. "Cupcake, I'm sorry I couldn't say goodbye in person. We struck gold at Sterling's. I have a suspicion he's in Colombia, and not to see Juan Valdez. Speaking of coffee, color me guilty. I wasn't there to bring it to you this morning. I promise to make it up to you. Don't let Player wear you out..." *That was supposed to be your job*, she groused. "...that's supposed to be my job." Anna laughed at their mutual line of thought. "Till I see you again..." He held up his index finger, then all four fingers, then three fingers. "...hope you know what that means." The video ended.

"What *what* means? What is that?" She looked down at Player. "Who does that on a phone message?" Player looked back and yawned. "Your concern is underwhelming." Anna sighed deeply. "Well, I don't know about you, but I'm hungry, and I *do* need coffee. I'm gonna have a little fast food." Anna set off down the block, her sense of unease growing by the moment.

What if Sterling was in Colombia laying the perfect trap? What if Sterling ambushed him? He could kill Rick. It would be her fault, and Rick would never know she loved him.

* * * *

The 'bedroom' on the jet was dark thanks to the heavy blackout shades, there was stone cold silence except for the distant drone of the engines. It was just right for a vamp's rest, but all Rick could do was count the perforations in the jet's leather headliner.

*What genius*, Rick asked himself, *breaks into a home and carries out millions in antiquities when an innocent like Anna is the one holding the alarm code?* In the event of his untimely demise, he hadn't laid any plans for Anna's future safety. Now, at thirty thousand feet, and hurtling toward Barranquilla, his undead heart lay heavy in his chest. In the midst of his irrational pity party, the phone rang.

Rick glanced irritably at the clock. There would be no rest. He snatched up the phone. "Hiatt."

"This is Larry. Not interrupting anything am I?"

"Just my guilt trip. Thanks for returning my call. Do me a favor, I stored a jeweled dirk in my safe. Would you pick it up and appraise it?"

"Sure."

"I have a guest, I'll text her to expect you." Larry signed off the call, and Rick texted a short message.

* * * *

Rick dispensed with his usual telephone courtesy the moment Helen answered the phone. That was just as well since she lit into him as soon as she read the caller I.D.

"Didn't I tell you, if I were her mother, she'd never come through the front door? What is she doing in your apartment with that beast?"

"And didn't I tell you, you're not the boss of me?"

"I may not be the boss, but I keep track of the boss's things."

"Are you objectifying her?" Rick smirked.

"Aren't *you*? Remember, forty-some years ago I fed you. Don't tell me what—"

"And *then* you were delightful. Not so much, now. This is different, I'm being serious now, Helen."

"Oh."

"She's put herself in harm's way for the Family, and it's the Family's job to protect her."

"What do you need, boss?"

* * * *

Anna returned to the penthouse with Player dragging her back to his water bowl. Once inside she unsnapped the leash and felt suffocating stillness.

*What if this is it? What if I never see him again? What if all that remains are his collections, his shirts and socks, and sweaters? What if all I can sample is his cologne or brush my hair with his hairbrush?*

Anna stripped down and made her way to Rick's shower. She snorted gently at its splendor. Well, she should have expected it. She'd never seen so much marble outside a museum. Standing under the rain shower, she grasped for his washcloth, and the tears broke. She cried into it. He hadn't even said goodbye.

She came of age within this vampire culture. She crushed so hard on Matt, and that was all for nothing. Oh, for months she was alone unable to share her heartbreak with anyone. How could you tell your best friend you'd been thrown over by a vampire? Even if she'd had a best friend. It was pure irony that the vampire she had feared most was the man who'd won her heart.

In numb mourning, she memorized the scent of Rick's soap and shampoo. She lavished each of his bath products on her body as if his hands were holding the cloth. When the water ran cold, she reached for his fluffy bath sheet and let it embrace her as she sank to the bathroom floor in quiet sobs. Player, sensing her distress, leaned into her, and showed his best 'puppy eyes.'

"Player, we can't let them do all the heavy lifting. We need to do something."

Anna dragged herself up, dried herself off and headed directly to Rick's vast closet. Although Rick wasn't there now, the shadow of his presence lingered in his wardrobe. Pulling on the softest wool socks and a pair of navy silk boxers, Anna turned from side to side in the floor to ceiling mirror. Her fingers lightly danced over a stack of cashmere sweaters until she found one the color of his milk chocolate eyes. It smelled like him. If she held it to her nose, she could almost feel him. She inhaled until she was forced to exhale. Every token of Rick was with her, everything except the man.

Player snuffled through the bespoke English leather shoes from Crocket and Jones. At last, he let out a deep doggie moan of pleasure and sank onto the recently worn shoes Rick hadn't put away. He picked up what was surely the costliest wingtip in the bunch and cradled it between massive paws. He was just about to taste that fine leather when Anna glanced around and caught him.

"Oh no, no, no, noooo!"

Player looked at his mistress with eyes of innocence.

"Let's get a bone!" she exclaimed over-enthusiastically.

* * * *

Anna's back was turned to the elevator while the opener ground the top off a large can of dog food. "It's time you had meat. Shoes are bad, meat is good." Anna exaggerated her admonitions until she delivered the bowl. She was bent over, with her silk-clad ass in the air when two rather large leather shoes suddenly approached her. Slowly, her gaze rose past lime green and cobalt blue argyle socks to sharply creased charcoal trousers. Those trousers seemed to go on forever. Then there was his face.

*What the heck is Lawrence from the museum's research department doing in Rick's apartment? Are they checking up on me? Did they GPS my company phone? How did he gain access to the penthouse elevator?*

"Lawrence! What are you doing here?"

"Mr. Hiatt asked me to check on something."

*How does he know Rick Hiatt?* Anna retreated to the dining nook. "Are you checking up on me?" She was about to launch into an interrogation when she got a look at herself in the wall of mirrors. *Why are there so dang many mirrors in a vampire's home?* She could barely keep from laughing at Lawrence must see —a slip of a girl in man-sized clothing.

"On weekends I always go for comfortable clothes," Lawrence said affably. "The boxers are a nice touch."

"My clothes were dirty...I... haven't done laundry yet...the dog got mud..."

"The building does have laundry services. I mean, why do laundry on your day off?"

"Yeah, thanks, so, how do you know Rick?" Every permutation of that question rushed through her head. *Is he a member of the club? Sub or Dom? Donor or Vamp? None of the above?*

"We share an interest in antiques. He has a piece he's asked me to appraise."

"He's out of town today." Anna hedged.

"Yeah, he told me he had a guest. I came by to see the piece wrapped in lambskin."

She dropped the nonchalant act. "It's in the safe, I don't know where that is."

"I do. No problem." Larry headed toward Rick's office, and Anna fell right into step, with the dog behind her, sniffing suspiciously.

"Oh, good! I would so love to hear what you have to say about that thing."

Larry was already working the safe's keypad and opening the door as she cleared a space on the desk.

"Please, would you unwrap it for me?" He asked.

"You can't touch it either?" She untied the ancient leather wrapping and let the jeweled dirk twinkle in the LED light. "Rick says this is real." Anna tapped the humongous emerald in the hilt. "That just can't be possible."

Larry produced a jeweler's loop and penlight from his pocket. "Let's take a look." He scrutinized the stone. "I'm checking for air bubbles. Real emeralds don't have them. Also, inclusions—real emeralds do." He continued his examination for a moment, looking at different angles. "Yep, it all checks out."

She was incredulous. "But it's carved! Why would anyone carve an emerald?"

"People do." Larry straightened and removed the jeweler's loop. "These giant stones typically have irregular cuts to catch the deepest color."

"What's the sculpture?" she asked, pointing to the jewel's relief.

"It's the Fitzjarrald coat of arms." Larry was matter of fact.

"Who are the Fitzjarralds?" Her nose scrunched up, remembering Rick's conversation in the car. "Are they a royal family?"

"They are, to this day."

"And is Rick a Fitzjarrald?"

"You'll have to ask Rick about that." Using the lambskin as a buffer, Larry turned the piece over to count the diamonds. "There are easily a hundred and fifty carats of diamonds here. This is priceless."

"You mean these are real?" Anna gawked and drew back her fingertips.

"They look real to me."

"Would it help if I researched this in connection to the Fitzjarrald family?"

"If you do that, you should be discrete. This is a sensitive piece of history."

Moments of time with Rick flashed through her mind like pieces of a puzzle. His announcement that "You may have saved my life." The President's send-off of, "Godspeed, Sir Richard." The fact that Rick walked in daylight and lived surrounded by mirrors. His existence laughed in the face of vampire superstitions.

# 9

The airstairs of Rick's jet dropped shortly after six in the evening in Barranquilla. Night already enshrouded the city in staggering humidity. Rick drew in his customary 'reading' breath to gauge the city's vibe. The scent caused him to grab for the railing. The coppery tang of blood combined with the stench of fear and violence permeated the city.

*What level of Hell is this?*

Once he steadied himself, he took the stairs two at a time to reach the safety of the heavy-duty SUV waiting on the tarmac. Vamps were definitely being hunted here, and probably for a good reason.

Rick ducked into the back seat. A grim-faced, but no less handsome Adam Lachlan greeted him, "Welcome to Hell."

Adam's uncommonly long legs seemed cramped, even in the generously leggy vehicle. The parking lot lights made the silver in his burnished gold hair shimmer, and his pale aquamarine eyes flashed with irritation.

"Good to see you too," Rick grumbled.

"This time tomorrow, remember you said that."

Within moments the sleek SUV powered toward the hangar. The C17 sent by the Vampire Council birthed a series of armored SUVs and a platoon of troops assembling equipment and weapons. Rick and Adam alighted their vehicle, bringing the hangar occupants to attention.

The most muscular of the group approached them, his valor evident by the rows of colorful slides on his chest. His height nearly met Adam's at attention, and he threw a sharp salute.

"Good evening, Sirs. I'm Lieutenant Jan Kulczyk. I'm your point man on this mission." He flashed a thousand-watt smile. Standing together, he and Adam looked like gigantic opposites. Where Adam was fair, Jan stood equally comely, but jet-haired, with cobalt eyes.

Rick returned Kulczyk's salute, looking up at him with a wry smile. "Thank you for your discretion on this black op, Lieutenant."

"Yes, Sir, proud to assist." Kulczyk pointed toward the three Apache helicopters parked outside the hangar. "The Apaches depart at 22:00. We'll drop the computerized weaponry within thirty minutes and return by 23:00."

Rick gestured toward a squad in camo pairing Bluetooth controllers "What's your confidence on the wireless pieces?"

Kulczyk held a set in his hands, "First, it is a guided armament. It has the necessary weight to lay down where we want it, and it answers when we call." The lieutenant smiled confidently. Adam picked up a canister and shook his head in disbelief. "I'd never question your judgment, old man, but Vamps handling white phosphorus and benzene?"

Rick slid his hands in his pockets and nodded toward the Lieutenant.

Kulczyk answered crisply, "Yes, sir. We're targeting vamps, so we're going with SIP's."

Adam winced at Rick, "This stuff is unstable as hell."

"That's the fire-breathing dragon I know and love." Rick thumped him on the back. "You could save us all a trip with a quick fly by, there's still time for me to annoy you into a shape-shift."

Adam glared at him.

"Your mother wears army boots!" Rick arched a brow, "That do anything for you?" Adam turned his back, resolutely ignoring him. "I get it. Don't go away mad, just go away."

Adam continued down the aisle, "We need certain destruction of the pharmaceutical plant. It's far out in the boonies, surrounded by ten-foot razor wire fences and the like, which discourages mortal villagers from getting curious."

Kulczyk nodded, "These weapons are efficiently spaced for internal building damage as well as the surrounding perimeter."

"Jesus, man, we don't want to take out the whole countryside!" Rick turned and twisted the tablet to view the area's geography.

"No, sir. These devices hit, flare hot and burn out fast." The Lieutenant assured them.

"Now that we have the barbeque planned, any location on our guest of honor?" Rick nervously watched the civilian activity outside the hangar. The city's vibe was disturbing, an awareness apparently shared by both vamps and mortals. Small jets were leaving the private airfield in steady succession.

Adam herded his distracted friend back to the SUV, noting Rick's unaccustomed nervousness. "C'mon. I've got surveillance set up back at the hotel. Veronique stays holed up at Lust for Life." He knocked twice on the car's roof to signal the driver to move out. "After she settled Papa's goldmine of an estate in Haiti, she apparently decided to run what was left of the Dias Cartel from the resort. That includes the pharmaceutical plant. They're manufacturing high-grade Oxycodone as well as Humanité. The National Police are starting to sniff around the Oxy, though, so what she lacks in diplomacy she makes up for with cash."

Rick rolled his head to loosen uncommonly tense muscles. "It's been a week since the massacre. When I got off the plane, the scent of violence and tension smacked me right in the senses. What else has been going on?" Rick scowled at the emotions in the atmosphere.

Adam handed him a tablet. "Read for yourself." Adam nodded at the device. "Here are the regional headlines from the past week. We've suppressed the truth on over a dozen savage feedings. These are the ones we couldn't suppress."

Rick scrolled through the headlines, *Hospital ICU Demolished by Blood Thirsty Fugitives, Blood Bank Emptied in Unprecedented Break-In, Morgue Raided by Unknown Vandals.*

"Shite!" Rick exclaimed. "This is the *unsuppressed* news?" He dropped the tablet in his lap and threw back his head. It took him a few moments to recover.

Rick's hand propped his face toward the street lights. "I need you to make some crucial arrangements for me, arrangements I'd make myself, but I can't know the particulars. Make them tonight, please, before we leave. I know her family lives in Columbus." He leaned against the car's tilt as it turned out of the airport and hit the pot-hole-strewn road. Rick passed a scrap of paper to Adam, "She needs to take the item in lambskin with her. Make funds available, plenty of money. She's young, if anything happens to me, I want her set for life." Rick's words were met with stunned silence. "Understood?"

Adam nodded and looked down at the name in graceful Spenserian handwriting—Anna Curley. He slipped his phone out of his pocket and thumbed Rick's directives to a trusted third party.

* * * *

Anna juggled Larry's admonition for a discreet investigation of the dirk in the back of her mind. He declined an early lunch but threw on a baseball cap and large sunglasses to face the bright and sunny day before he left. *Dollars to donuts, Larry is a member of the undead.*

Opening the floor to ceiling draperies covering the wall of tinted windows, Anna approached Rick's massive mahogany desk. *This is bigger than my bed!* She bent down to admire the artistry and ran her fingers along the heavily carved friezes on the ends and serpentine front. *Where have I seen these images before?*

Rick kept his desktop immaculate, which she was beginning to understand was his nature. Still, she couldn't imagine he actually got any work done here. She pulled out the executive chair, sat in its highly upholstered full grain leather and sighed. *I don't need a bed, I'll just sleep in his chair.* Rubbing her cheek against the soft leather released remnants of Rick's scent. *I am not going to get anything done if I sit here.*

She snapped out of her reverie and refocused on finding a legal pad and a pen. Reaching for the night bird-shaped drawer pull it hit her, the carvings were from Rick's family crest. *What's the deal with all the night birds?* The center drawer glided open to reveal a stack of custom legal pads. The contents of the drawer were as inherently neat as the desktop, but no pens. She glanced about, and there, sitting casually at the corner of the leather blotter, stood a distinctively etched clear glass beer stein. Even without lifting it to see the trademark, Anna knew this piece should have been in a museum, not holding a dozen fountain pens.

She hesitated to reach into the stein to retrieve one. Those fountain pens were probably worth more than the home where she grew up. *Go ahead* she mused, *live a little!* She figured if they weren't to be used, they wouldn't be available. So, gathering her gumption, Anna peered into the beer stein and chose the pen with a snake styled clip. *Finally, something without night birds!* She recognized the stylized snowflake logo because Mont Blanc was a brand familiar to even a member of Generation Z.

Returning to the coffee table and her sleeping roommate, Anna opened her laptop and employed a virtual private network to begin her research. Finally, her Art History degree was worth something!

One consuming hour later, Anna discovered Rick had come to manhood in Tudor-era Ireland, as Richard Fitzjarrald. By the time he became Duke, his was a house divided. His oldest half-brother, Ian, was a Separatist, fighting against the English Crown. Richard was a Loyalist, fighting alongside Henry the Eighth. It was Ian's ill fortune to be tried for treason and sentenced to hang. Ian's resulting hatred of all things Fitzjarrald, and his knowledge of black magic, so unnerved his guards that their recollections were noted in history books. He apparently cast a spell that was heard through the window of his cell. "Rise from your old thrones once more and accept the soul I offer. May my family dirk be chained to this curse; may the weapon's spell serve for all eternity."

In the hours before his sentence was carried out, Ian was allowed to see his wife and daughters, who were escorted by Richard, the current Duke. Despite the disgrace, Ian brought to the family, his youngest brother could not bear to see his brother die in agony. He petitioned the King to allow Ian to be beheaded instead of hanged and privately paid for the kingdom's best executioner. It would be a far quicker and more merciful death.

In an emotional parting, Ian repented of his evil curse, and according to witnesses, called for a priest to join him and his brother. During prayers he was heard to plead, "I retract and declare void the curse and condemnation I knowingly projected onto this object." Afterward, among tearful embraces, the brothers parted.

The only Fitzjarrald to escape death in either battle, decree, or plague was Richard. He mysteriously disappeared a few weeks after Ian's death, just prior to his nuptials. His fate was never known.

Anna was dumbfounded to see Rick's beloved face staring back at her over a stiff white ruff. Holbein painted him as the Duke of Erne, Earl of Mayo in 1534. Anna giggled as she noted the prominent codpiece, colorful clothing, and nestled on his hip, the gold and silver scabbard. It held what was unmistakably the dirk that was now wrapped in lambskin and secreted in Rick's safe.

Though to all intents and purposes the curse had been broken, the family's losses became legendary. The dirk was priceless. Still, believing that as long as the dirk—or any monies received from its sale—remained in the family, every member was subject to the curse, the weapon was secretly buried in 1798, after a child of the reigning duke died in infancy. Anna's head hurt from the sheer volume of information and its import.

* * * *

Helen had her phone on speaker as she googled information about Barranquilla, Colombia. "You're sure he wants her in Colombia? That's kind of a hot spot right now."

"Yeah, that's what Mr. Lachlan texted. He said to get her and this thing, whatever it is, there as soon as possible. He said I should have the jet standing by."

"Okay, I guess. It wouldn't his first strange request. I'll get on it. What are we looking at in Colombia? Are we going in under the radar?"

"Totally."

"Right. I'll call you with the flight time."

Helen tapped her pen against her desk blotter. She reached for the phone and drew her hand back three different times, finally standing with a sigh. "He's been prickly enough lately, I'm not gonna question my orders."

* * * *

Anna rang for the elevator, and while she waited, went to the refrigerator to fill a water bottle. Player was still enough of a puppy to want to run. *Maybe I'll take him to the dog park. But I'll take my car. I don't want him to dirty up the Tesla...*

The elevator dinged, and there stood Helen. "Hi!" Anna exclaimed delightedly. "I haven't seen you in months, Helen!"

The former donor from decades ago stood at the kitchen island with a black leather folio. She plopped it down on the marble countertop and, hands on hips, glowered, "I'm not putting this in your hands."

Anna looked at her askance. "O...kay..." Anna reached across the island and picked up the document case. Scanning the papers inside, she read the directions "take the item wrapped in lambskin and board the company jet to Colombia at once."

"I should probably light a candle for the two of you, you'll need it," Helen grumbled worriedly.

* * * *

Anna had never flown anything more sophisticated than economy. Rick's private jet with its butter-colored leather and rosewood was a revelation about how the one percent lived. Ensconced in the luxurious Recaro recliner, Player at her feet, she felt as if she were in an opulent living room rather than a jet. Acoustic modifications made the ride quiet and soothing. She refused the offering of Champagne but did take advantage of a delicious Panini sandwich served by the uniformed flight attendant.

In the midst of her newfound affluence, a shiver overcame her at the thought of Helen's warning. *Why would Rick bring the dirk into such a dangerous arena?* She looked over her travel documents. The flight would be about eight hours. A limo would meet her when she arrived to escort her to Rick at the hotel. Anna was excited. She'd never been outside the United States, this was an adventure of unprecedented scope. She opened her laptop. What else could she discover about the mysterious Rick Hiatt?

* * * *

A power nap during the flight left her more alert than the hour indicated, it was eleven in the evening Barranquilla time. The air was hot and humid when she stepped off the jet, and the wind blew fiercely, whipping her long, glorious hair across her face. There was no limo on the tarmac. She stood waiting, buffeted in the gusts for fifteen minutes before she headed for the small, exclusive terminal building. *I'm a self-sufficient woman, I can find my own transportation.*

The terminal staff assisted her with a town car, and within a half hour, she arrived at the lobby entrance of the hotel. She waited for the driver to bring her carry-on from the trunk while she juggled her backpack, purse, and Player. He danced around her feet anxiously, overstimulated by the myriad sounds and smells. Anna was a little overstimulated herself, trying to see everything at once. The precious backpack containing the carefully wrapped dirk, hung precariously from one shoulder as she tried to control the agitated dog.

* * * *

Anna never saw Sterling poised in the lobby bar, watching the exotic Colombian upper-class stroll by. Their nightlife didn't get started until midnight. His elbows slipped off the bar in surprise when he saw the girl who was supposed to be watching his house, emerge from a luxury sedan with his dog. *Flying monkeys! What the fug is she doing here?* He noticed the backpack she'd sloppily thrown over one shoulder. Even more alarming was an unmistakable swath of lambskin that was supposed to shelter his ceremonial dirk. The time for questions was passed, he wanted his dirk back now.

Pulling his hood up over his head, Sterling decided to reclaim his property. He darted between incoming guests, causing grumbles as he pushed, then broke into a run as he got within grasping distance of Anna's backpack.

* * * *

Anna felt his impact like a body check, her shoulder felt as if it was dislocated. She dropped her purse and the leash. She could only stare after the scoundrel who escaped with Rick's most precious possession.

"Miss, are you alright?" The driver asked urgently in accented English.

Shaking, Anna regathered her purse, Player's leash, and tried to calm the fiercely barking dog. "Yes, I'm unharmed. I want to go inside."

The desk clerk was pleasant but impersonal. "Is Miss checking in? Your identification, please?"

"No, I'm here as a guest of Rick Hiatt. I need to be shown to his suite immediately, please." She answered breathlessly.

"A guest of Richard Hiatt?" She had the clerk's attention instantly.

"Can we hurry this along, please? I was just robbed outside your hotel."

"Of…Of course, Miss. Is Miss injured? May I call the authorities for you?"

"I just need to see Mr. Hiatt." She said emphatically.

"At once, Miss," he rang the bell. "Front, please."

# 10

Within moments Anna was whisked through the opulent lobby and up to Rick's suite. The bellhop knocked. When there was no answer, he opened the door and let her inside. Anna released Player's leash and let him trot ahead of her. It sounded like a war film coming from the back room, and then the sound of two men high-fiving.

Anna reached for her rolling carry-on bag. "I guess they didn't hear your knock. I'm fine from here, thank you. Can you take American dollars?" She handed him a gratuity, and as she shut the door, heard Rick's surprised exclamation.

"God's bollocks! Player?" Rick stood over her at vamp speed. "Anna? Bloody hell, why are you here?"

Anna stood dumbfounded. "You sent for me."

It was Rick's turn to be dumbfounded. "No…I didn't…I sent you away. Far away from here." He blinked, appalled.

"Oh, yes you did. Look." She held out the travel portfolio. "See? Colombia. With the dirk."

Rick sighed heavily, reading the note. "No. You were supposed to go home to Columbus with the dirk." Rick pointed angrily in the general direction of the States. "I wanted you safely away from all this."

"Rick, I have to tell you…" Her voice trembled.

He looked at her closely then, concern evident in his coppery eyes, and his voice gentled. "What is it, Cupcake, what's wrong?"

"The dirk was in my backpack, wrapped in the lambskin. It was just stolen."

"Saints in Heaven! How long ago?"

She watched him. "About fifteen minutes ago, maybe. I was getting out of the car out front and suddenly, from nowhere, this guy…"

"Well, it's too late now." He drew a hand down his face. "Are you okay? You're really pale, let's get you a drink…"

All at once, Anna's legs went weak. "I think I need to sit down."

"Here," he guided her to a chair. "It's just the adrenaline wearing off, you'll be okay." He brought her a drink of something that smelled strong, and took her chin in his hand, raising her face up. "You're okay? He didn't hurt you?"

"It felt like he pulled my arm out of the socket." She drew in a ragged breath. "Rick, the dirk is gone, I'm so sorry."

"The most important thing is, you're okay." He reassured with a pat on her back. "We'll worry about the dirk later. It's strange, though, that this guy would target your backpack. I don't like coincidences, they make me twitchy."

Adam appeared in the doorway, followed by Player who jumped up and down on his hind legs, trying to lick Adam's face. "What is this?" he asked irritably.

"This is a dog," Rick lectured patiently.

"I know it's a dog. What's it doing here?"

"Good question. What is she…" Rick pointed at Anna, "doing here?"

Adam looked startled. "I don't know. Last I knew she was headed for Columbus."

"Apparently not. It seems there was a mistake."

"Well, crap." Adam turned to the leaping dog, and in his best Dom voice commanded, "Get *down!*" Player whined and shrank to Anna's side.

"Adam." Rick reached up his hand to the nearly seven-foot shape-shifter. "Let me see your phone."

Adam's large hand dwarfed the phone and Rick's as he relinquished it, embarrassment written over his face. "The keyboard is too small for my thumbs."

Rick took the phone and scrolled through a day's worth of messages, finding the offending text. He held it up. "Does this say Columbus?"

"Er…no…but it doesn't say Colombia, either."

"It would have been definitive if you said Columbus, *Ohio,*" Rick groundout. He shook his head. "So now that Cupcake is here, protecting her will be your responsibility. She and Player," he gestured to the dog, "will be your new little buddies."

"Hey! I can take care of myself!" Anna protested.

Rick turned a skeptical look her way. "Aren't you the woman who was just robbed in front of the hotel?"

"Well, yeah…"

"No arguments."

Adam glanced down at a flashing alert on his phone. "I'm afraid this is a moot debate. We have a situation."

"God's nightgown! What now?"

"We've got a mayday on the third copter. It's gone down."

"I'll be a three-penny upright!" Rick swore. He darted into the back room. Adam and Anna followed and found him pacing before the violent images on the monitor screens. "This is my deuce-hitting-the-fan moment!"

"A rescue team is on the way. Unfortunately, this blows our covert op."

Rick rubbed his forehead. "Well, if we're blown anyway, let's decide how we're going to handle Veronique now."

Anna narrowed her eyes. "Who is Veronique?"

Adam saw her expression and his guffaws burst the tension. "No one you need to worry about."

Rick keyed some strokes on the computer and brought up the camera in Veronique's suite at the Lust for Life Resort. "This," he gestured, "is Veronique. And, she is pissed. I don't even need the soundtrack to know that."

They watched as the quintessentially perfect brunette ranted at several men standing haplessly before her. Item after item hit the mirrors in her suite, racking up centuries of bad luck.

"Emm. She does look upset." Adam agreed. "The trouble is, she's on alert now. She'll never leave that damn suite."

"Well, not unless she's spooked enough to want to leave the country."

Anna swirled her drink and watched the strategists at work. Rick glanced her way. "You've gotta be worn out, Cupcake, and you don't need to listen to this. Why don't you take the third bedroom…"? He nodded toward its location. "Get settled, sleep if you can, I'll come and say goodbye before I leave."

"Like the last time?"

"I need you to go. Now, please." It was his Dom voice. That didn't mean she wouldn't give him a hard time later.

* * * *

Anna found the lavish bedroom more than a pleasant place to sleep. The view off the balcony enticed her with swaying palm trees, ocean breezes and an endless parade of revelers. The leather guest-services book next to the phone invited her not only to dine in her suite but to sample the wines and liquors from their cellars. It urged her to enjoy a shopping spree from the hotel's smart designer boutiques and take advantage of their spa amenities. While Player sat obediently on the balcony, Anna made some decisions. She picked up the telephone to dial room service.

"Good evening. This is Mr. Hiatt's suite. I'd like your largest Chateaubriand, rare, with a baked potato, a salad with onions, a bottle of your best Merlot, a bottle of Grand Marnier, and an entire mango and coconut flan." She paused, then asked. "Do you serve garlic bread? You do? Can you make it with extra garlic and lots of butter? Wonderful!" Anna's gaze went back to her wallet, and she shook her head at her reflection in the mirror. "Just charge it to the room, please!"

Anna kicked off her ballet flats with a vicious toss, watching them fly across the room. She rolled her carryon to the closet. *Send me off to my room like a child! I'll eat and drink you right out of the castle!* Anna opened the small suitcase and realized how huge the closet was. It dwarfed her paltry wardrobe. *I'll bet Veronique travels with trunks and trunks of shoes alone!*

Anna set her toiletries on the long granite vanity and thought about the raven-haired beauty she saw on the monitor. Even in grainy black and white, she was probably the most beautiful woman Anna had ever seen! She vaguely remembered Veronique's name mentioned by Rick when he was talking to that President. *President of what?* She couldn't remember the context, but in any context, there was absolutely no way she would ever be able to compete with that woman!

She turned and gasped at the jetted tub. *It's the size of a small pool! I could teach Player to swim!* Anna resisted the urge to draw a bath in favor of exploring the television channels while she waited for dinner to arrive. She wondered if she could tip the concierge to walk Player? She was still a little unnerved by the robbery. The big dog obviously hadn't deterred the thief, so she'd just as soon not take him out by herself. Anna stretched out on the chaise and clicked on the television. Everything around her was unnervingly elegant. *Rick wants elegant? I can be as elegant as the next girl!*

She fell asleep, and when she opened her eyes, she saw Rick standing behind the gracefully draped room service cart, a serving towel over his arm. His expression confused her until she caught a glimpse of herself in the mirror. *Oh, great! Now that's an elegant look!* Her hair was matted in an unbecoming lump, her makeup resembled a panda, and drool pooled at the corner of her mouth. Jet lag did not an elegant lady make. She sat up in a rush, hurriedly wiping at the circles under her eyes and finger combing the matt in her hair.

"Room service, Madam." Rick bowed. "Planning a party?" Anna bit back a grin as he set the table and she tried to make herself presentable. Rick opened the wine and removed the cover from her entrée. He bent within inches of the hefty piece of meat, inhaled and narrowed his eyes at the rare blood. "Who's the vampire in this room?"

"I like my meat like I like my men, a little bloody." *Omg! I can't believe I just said that!* "Um…most of that meat is for Player."

He raised an amused brow. "Well, that's nice of you. I'll bet he doesn't get that much Chateaubriand. I'd go easy on the wine on top of jet lag if I were you. We can't have you heaving over the balcony like a girl-gone-wild at Mardi Gras."

"I've never been to Mardi Gras," Anna confessed wistfully.

"I can change that." He grinned charmingly.

*Who could resist that grin?*

"We'll put it on our list. Right now, I have to slide out for a while."

"Are you coming back?" Her tears erupted.

"I aim to." Rick held out his arms. "I've got a lot to come back for."

Anna leapt into his arms and embraced him fiercely. "Please come back to me." She dotted anxious kisses over his face.

"Don't worry, Cupcake, I've ridden out to many battles. I've always returned."

"Sometimes you'll have to tell me about that."

"Whenever you want." He glanced around the room. "Is this room okay? Seems like you found the guest-services book easily enough. Make yourself at home, order whatever you want."

Adam's footsteps echoed on the polished wood floors of the living room. "Rick, we've got to bug out. Now."

Rick sheepishly repeated the mime from his video message. Then, at vamp speed, he was gone, and she was alone with the closed-door reverberating in the quiet space.

"What the heck does that *mean*?" she yelled at the door.

* * * *

Rick and Adam strategized over what to do about Veronique as they drove back to the private airfield. They could see the fire raging in the distance.

Colombian Naval helicopters equipped with enormous buckets ferried ocean water to drop on the flames.

"I hope our rescue was successful." Rick sighed. "That's an inferno. With luck, it didn't get close to any residents."

"Yeah, the National Police are gonna be rankled. You know they'll be all over that downed copter looking for the registration."

"I know," Rick said with a sly smirk. "Wouldn't it be terrible if was registered to Veronique?"

Adam took his gaze off the road for a moment to stare. "What are you thinking, Rick?"

"How's your Spanish?"

"As it happens, I have a talent for languages."

"That'll come in handy."

They pulled into the hangar, and Lieutenant Kulczyk was standing at attention before their vehicle stopped. Rick opened the door and returned his salute. "Your men okay?"

"A couple of minor injuries, Sir, they'll be fine with a little extra blood."

"Good." Rick nodded. "Well, we screwed the pooch on this one, gentleman."

"Yes, Sir." Kulczyk looked embarrassed. "It was mechanical failure. We did accomplish the mission, Sir. The factory was leveled."

Rick looked over at the rows of packed gear. "What's their body count?"

Kulczyk nodded. "The vamps working there are dead, along with a handful of civilian drug runners. I think it's safe to say we've broken their back."

"That's excellent work, Lieutenant." Rick acknowledged with a nod. "Now to damage control."

Adam walked the room's perimeter scouring for evidence of their presence. "It goes without saying you've got to get the remaining copters out of here before the sun comes up. You, your men, and all your gear need to disappear ASAP."

"Yes, Sir," Kulczyk agreed. "The remaining copters have already landed in Venezuela. We're loading the rest of our gear now, and we're wheels up in fifteen, Sir."

"Before you go, Lieutenant, we need to make some modifications to the registration and flight plans of the choppers," Rick said.

Kulczyk laughed. "I thought President Koehl told you, Sir?"

Rick shook his head.

"He had every copter, our troop carrier, flight plans, everything, registered under Veronique Moreau's name, just in case there were questions. He anticipated just such a complication, Sir."

Adam chuckled.

"That sly old fox." Rick laughed. "He doesn't miss a thing.

"Okay, Lieutenant, there's one more operation we need your assistance with. Get on your secure satellite phone and find us your best hacker and forger. Mr. Lachlan, here, is about to become a member of the Colombian National Police." The Lieutenant pulled a tablet from his pack and began a search. Rick continued, "We need a work history on him as Colonel Raul Martinez—commendations, performance reports, the whole show, right down to fingerprints and pictures. Veronique is bound to have him checked out thoroughly."

"Yes, Sir, I'm sure we can create that."

"Do any of your men speak Spanish?"

"Well, Sir, as it happens, two are actually from Spain originally. Garcia is from Cuba, and I studied languages at the Academy."

"Perfect." Rick rubbed his hands together. "You're all recruited to the National Police. We need police gear—uniforms, badges, weapons, a couple of their vehicles, the works. Can we count on you for all that?"

"Yes, Sir, once the info on "Colonel Martinez" is in their computers, everything should be easy enough to request."

Rick grinned. "Here's the hard part. We need it in two hours at most. You know it won't take the Colombians long to figure where Veronique is. We have to get to her before the real police show up."

Adam turned to him. "What about you? Are you going to be the puppet master, pulling strings from above?"

Rick put his hand over his heart. "You wound me, old man. When have you ever seen me duck a good fight?" He punched playfully at his friend. "I need a news crew."

"A what?"

"A news crew. Colombia must have the equivalent of Celebrity Tonight or TMI? Let's get 'em out of bed. I'm about to buy the Lust for Life Resort in the splashiest possible way." Adam and Kulczyk shook their heads. Rick gestured to Adam. "By the time you're done scaring the starch out of

Veronique, she'll know I'm virtually next door. If she doesn't reach out to me, I'll prod her." He stared into the distance. "Where can we get a gold limo?"

* * * *

As it turned out, rousting the computer hackers out of bed in Geneva was harder than rousting a film production company in Barranquilla. Disgraceful. After all, it was seven in the morning in Geneva. Still, the hackers did a great job putting together an authentic looking resume for Adam and his squad. The film producers couldn't jump fast enough to supply police uniforms and weaponry. A quick trip to the police motor pool and they were set.

* * * *

Rick watched the drama unfold in Veronique's suite from his tablet. The jet circled the city, appearing as if he was newly arriving. He had press greeting him and falling in line behind his limo all the way to the resort. They craved splashy spectacles passing as news. For now, Rick ate up Veronique's attempts to evade speaking with Adam.

* * * *

Rick sat forward, gleefully watching the screen as Veronique finally allowed her men to open the door. Rick wished the sound was more distinct, but lip reading would suffice.

Adam clicked his heels in the epitome of an old-world courtesy bow, and Veronique staggered back at the sheer size of him. If Rick knew her at all, she also appreciated his Nordic good looks.

"Madam Moreau, I am Colonel Raul Martinez of the Colombian National Police." Adam flashed his fake badge.

"Colonel! You don't look Colombian."

"My family moved here in the 1940s." He clicked his heels together again. "I'm here to investigate the fires outside town."

"Yes, Colonel, you know, my factory was the primary target. It's been burned to the ground."

"Along with several of your workers," Adam said pointedly.

"Well, yes, of course, the workers…" Veronique murmured in mock concern, and Rick laughed at her predictability. Count on Veronique to consider property before lives.

"This happened under suspicious circumstances, Madam Moreau. Our Fire Inspector tells me accelerants were found."

"That's preposterous! My factory employed many locals."

"Our records show something quite different. In looking into your employees, we notice many of the managers are international, and some of your workers have suspicious ties to the Dias drug cartel."

"Inaccurate."

"I don't think so." Adam towered over Veronique, invading her personal space to further intimidate. "Can you please explain the helicopters seen flying over your factory in the early morning hours?"

"Why ask me?"

"Perhaps because their I.D. numbers were registered to you."

Veronique stared at him in horror. Adam snapped his fingers at Kulczyk who handed him a short stack of pictures.

"This picture," he threw a blurry police photo onto a table, "is of the helicopter that crashed. It was a miracle it ditched in a pasture and not a more populated area. What do you have to say for yourself?"

"I...I...these are lies manufactured by my competitors."

"And I'm sure you'll be able to prove that in a Court of Law. Here in Colombia, as I'm sure you know, one is presumed guilty until proven innocent."

Rick snickered, watching Adam cross his fingers behind his back at the lie. A lot depended on Veronique buying that before she called for an attorney.

"I'm a Haitian citizen!" She sputtered, clearly daunted. "I have powerful friends in Europe."

"Your powerful friends will not help you now," Adam drawled. "Arson is a serious crime. You have killed or injured many Colombian citizens, destroyed property—"

"I demand to speak to the Governor!" she interrupted.

"Very well. I would suggest you call one of your powerful friends. I'm happy to wait." Adam made as if to sit in a nearby chair.

Kulczyk stepped up from behind him, touching an earpiece as if being given information. "Colonel, we have been summoned to confer with the Governor."

Adam clicked his heels with military precision and bowed stiffly. "It seems I must leave you, Madam Moreau. I urge you not to leave the premises. There will be guards, and I will return, perhaps with the Governor." He swept grandly from the room, his "guards" following behind him.

Rick rose, ready to land and meet the press. "Great job, guys."

# 11

Veronique could not fight, so she rushed to take flight. Throwing her jewelry roll and makeup bag into her Louis Vuitton keepall, she wrapped a scarf over her trademark brunette Veronica Lake hairdo and donned her Jackie-O sunglasses. Anything for a disguise! She snuck down the resort's staff elevator. Her anxious escape was thwarted in the hallway by a sea of press clamoring for entry into a swamped ballroom.

"What fresh hell is this?" Veronique shrieked at the common photographers jostling each other.

"Some hot shot from L.A. just bought the place. Are you somebody?" A squat guy checked his lens setting, anticipating her answer.

Veronique struck a pose and lowered her sunglasses. "Little man, your camera is out of memory, and you need to leave. You didn't see a soul here."

The photographer stood for a few seconds, scratched his head and let the camera hang from his neck. Mumbling to himself, he headed for the exit. Veronique stepped into his place at the door and felt her undead heart quake.

Feedback whined from the sound system, and a harried-looking hotel executive stepped forward. "Ladies and Gentlemen, may I introduce to you the new owner of this singular resort, Senor Richard Hiatt."

Veronique watched Rick advance to the podium, his body language boyish and purely American. She always hated the cocky son of a bitch.

"Thank you, Señora Leon, for your gracious welcome to this spectacular resort. The Consort Group International has led North America and Europe in supplying the ultimate in vacation experiences. We look forward to creating the very same quality ambiance here at Lust for Life." Veronique, head down and pushing through the shoulder-to-shoulder crowd, stopped dead at his next words.

"This venture could not have come to fruition without your government's generosity. Before sunrise, the Governor and I will meet in this very room to sign papers and discuss employment opportunities for entertainers, staff and suppliers."

There was appropriate light applause from the audience.

Veronique checked her watch. *Will that odious giant of a man return with the Governor? Should I try to bamboozle Rick out of a jet ride to Haiti, or should I try to thrall the Governor?* The factory was a total loss, perhaps escape was the better plan. She could regroup safely in Haiti.

Veronique glanced at the three entrances to the ballroom. All were guarded by a member of the National Police. Martinez wasn't exaggerating, she was being watched. She needed to talk to Rick. She had no choice, so she'd simply charm her way out, using the arrogant prick. With her mind made up, Veronique propelled her way to the front of the podium and made sure Rick noticed her.

Immediately after stepping down from the stage, Veronique cornered him. "May we go somewhere private? I need to speak with you urgently."

"Of course, Ronnie." He gave her a benign smile as he blithely signed autographs handed to him by the crowd. "It's good to see you. I'm sure we can arrange a private meeting after the Governor—"

"Now, Rick! This can't wait. I need to speak with you now. I…I'm being hunted!"

"Hunted? Oh no." He drew out signing an autograph and stopped for the man to take a selfie. "Well, they can't follow me into the toilet. I'll post a guard." He motioned to one of the hotel staff and led the way into the men's room. He leaned back casually against the porcelain sink, arms crossed over his chest. "Now, how can I help you, Ronnie?"

Veronique stood shoulders hunched, her fingers white from pinching her nose closed. "I've got to get out of this country, right now." She glanced around at the urinals with obvious distaste.

"I see. Why the rush? Who's hunting you?"

"The National Police! My pharmaceutical plant burned down hours ago, and they believe I committed arson. Can you believe that?" She glanced around in a furtive state.

"That does seem harsh." Rick feigned sympathy. "Can't you reason with them?"

"Not with that brute who interrogated me this morning! He wasn't the reasonable sort. He'll throw me in jail and ask questions later. And Rick, you know vamps don't do well in jail."

"Well, maybe if you feed up beforehand, surely it will only be a couple of days before your attorney gets you out?"

"You know very well I can't count on that!" She shook her head vehemently. "I need to go now! Please, Rick, let me borrow your jet. Haiti is only a few hundred miles away. You'll have it back before you need it again."

Rick shook his head. "I don't know, Ronnie, I don't want to be accused of aiding a fugitive."

"But I'm not a fugitive!" she cried and continued conspiratorially. "At least, not yet. They haven't arrested me. You could say…" She grabbed onto his suit coat lapels. "You could say I tricked you! That's it! I…I…told you a relative was dying in Haiti. I tricked you, and you were only helping a friend…"

"Hmmm." Rick pretended to consider. "If we do this, we'll have to act immediately, before the Governor arrives. I can't miss my meeting with him…"

"Yes! Now! Let's go right now!"

"All right, I'll have an SUV pulled into the underground service entrance. I'll go with you, chances are good they won't stop me."

"Oh, thank you, Rick!" She groveled. "I just can't thank you enough!"

"That's alright, I don't need your thanks, Ronnie. What are friends for?"

* * * *

The SUV was waiting for them, and Veronique was in such a panic she didn't even take a moment to look at the driver. Had she, she might have noticed a chauffer's cap covering Adam's flaxen hair. For his part, Rick was relieved they pulled onto the street as a genuine cavalcade of National Police cruisers pulled into the resort's portico, sirens blaring.

Veronique's gaze stayed riveted to the rear window until they were well on their way to the airport. Rick made a big show of ordering the jet to be fueled and ready for takeoff in thirty minutes.

At last, Veronique turned around to converse. "I don't think they're following us."

"So, Ronnie, what exactly was this dust-up over Humanité? Seems like you were getting some bad side effects?"

"Oh, the fuss they made over those few silly incidents! Honestly, those mortals would probably have died in poverty if the feedings hadn't gone awry. I mean, really, progress always comes with sacrifices."

"Progress. I see." He watched her with a cold stare, then brightened as they pulled into the International Airport's private transport area. "Ah, here we are. You'll be on your way very soon."

"You are too kind, Rick. Really, if there's anything I can ever do for you…"

Rick smiled tightly. "Let's get you aboard." He glanced around as if it were an afterthought. "No luggage?"

Veronique shook her head. "No time." She waved a dismissive hand. "No worries. I have plenty of clothes and personal items elsewhere. I may simply resume travel on my yacht. International waters. I'll be safe there."

Rick led her aboard the jet. "Please, make yourself comfortable. The staff will be out to greet you in a moment." Rick lingered at the jet's doorway.

* * * *

*If he doesn't look like a model from a 1990's Vogue photo spread, then I'm not the most anxious vamp on the planet!* Veronique thought petulantly. She squirmed, trying to find comfort in the seat. Rick flashed his megawatt grin, killing time. Veronique returned it with a silent tepid smile. *Don't roll your eyes at him, not until the plane departs.* Rick shifted his pose to another confident posture. Veronique's eyes widened, she hated the bastard, but he was her only hope. *Keep it together, girl.*

Uncomfortable silence brewed Veronique's terse question. "What was our departure time?"

Rick nodded accommodatingly. "I believe we have one more passenger to board, Ronnie."

*I hate when he calls me Ronnie.* "Oh? I won't be traveling alone?"

Rick pulled his phone from his pocket, read a message and nodded to someone behind her. The flight deck door opened, and a uniformed responder stepped into view. When Veronique heard footsteps from behind, she gripped the armrest desperately. Rick handed his phone to the responder.

"Veronique Moreau, under the Uniform Code of the Vampire Council, you have been cited for the following infractions: Endangering the concealment of the vampire Family, squandering mortal lives, the manufacture and sale of harmful substances, consorting with known criminals, destruction of vampire property and crossing international borders to perpetrate all of the above charges. Anything you say can and will be held against you in a court of law. You have the right to an attorney. If you cannot afford an attorney, one will be provided for you…"

Veronique's eyes paled in a slow transformation. "I wave the remainder of the reading." Her fangs dropped. "I demand to speak with my attorney, I have nothing further to say." Her gaze darted to Rick. *You son of a bitch! When did you turn into a Boy Scout like your buddy Matt?*

Rick was somber, his voice implacable. "Ronnie, how many times have you been cited?"

"And how many times have I been found innocent?" She shot back defensively.

Rick raised a brow and turned to the responder. "She's all yours."

The gloved responder stepped forward, pulling silver cuffs from his weapons belt.

Veronique groaned. "Not the *silver* cuffs." She felt large hands resting on her shoulders. It wasn't the gentle pressure they imposed, it was the dread of how those hands could inflict agony.

Adam bent to her ear. "Oh, don't worry, if the cuffs bother you…" He slid those menacing hands under her arms and lifted her from the seat. "…we can always stake you." The responder charged forward with a polished wooden stake and thrust it cleanly into her heart. Veronique sank back into Adam's arms.

Rick flew to the seat with a thick blanket and spread it on the chair he adjusted to recline. Adam shook his head. "You think she needs a blanket?"

Rick looked at him askance and scoffed. "I just had these seats reupholstered. I don't want the cabin to reek of staked vampire!"

Adam lowered her body into the chair and straightened. "Prudent point, old man."

* * * *

Rick arrived back at his suite absolutely bone tired. He hadn't rested in over thirty-six hours, and even with vampire strength, he still needed downtime. He couldn't wait to crawl onto his slab and get at least five hours of uninterrupted oblivion. There was just one complication—Anna. She needed his attention after coming all this way to help him. He hoped she would be happy to amuse herself for a day while he took a break.

Apparently, he needn't have worried. When he walked into the suite his vampire senses told him immediately, he was alone. It was 8:30 in the morning. He sighed, where was she? A note on hotel stationery stood tented on a table with his name across the front.

*Dear Rick,*

*I thought you might be gone for a while, so I decided to treat myself to a spa day. Player is in doggie daycare. I'll do a little shopping after the salon, so I should be back sometime between four and five. I hope you're back by then.*

*Love, Anna*

That fit his plans perfectly. He wasn't even going to shower before hitting his slab. All he wanted to do was close his eyes.

* * * *

Anna floated into the suite at two o'clock, feeling like a million bucks! Enough could not be said for a body scrub and facial followed by a massage, a steam shower, shampoo and hair conditioning, cut and blow dry. She was stopping back in her room to change into comfortable shoes before she went shopping. The salon offered a makeup demonstration, and Anna allowed it, happy with the natural look. She wanted to get some loungewear and dresses in silky, luxurious fabrics. Men liked silky fabrics, didn't they? Liked to touch them? She wanted Rick to touch her. She couldn't wait for him to see her polished look.

She glanced at her note and noticed it had been read. The maid? She didn't hear a sound anywhere in the suite. Maybe he was in one of the bedrooms. Well, she didn't want to disturb him if he was sleeping. She'd check on him before she left.

Anna felt beautiful! Boy, if she'd known a spa day could make her feel like this, she'd have gone years ago! A ding sounded on her smartphone and she opened the message to see doggie daycare sent her a short video of Player romping with the other dogs. He looked like he was having a ball. Anna sighed with contentment. All was right in her world!

Tiptoeing up to what she assumed was Rick's bedroom, Anna cracked open the door for a peek. She was not prepared for the sight. The latch slipped out of her suddenly numb fingers as she stared in shock. A blast of frigid air hit her. The room's velvet drapes reduced the afternoon sun to dim twilight. There, at the other end of a spacious bedroom, in place of a bed, Rick lay naked atop a marble mortuary slab. *Dear God!* She resisted the urge to cross herself. Despite the loud thunk of the door when it hit the wall, he didn't stir.

Anna crept closer. He wasn't breathing, he looked...dead. Anna shuddered. His skin, normally pale, was now waxy and colorless. Well, colorless except for the faint blue tinge around his fingers and lips. His mouth was slightly open in repose, and he looked nothing less than cadaverous. Oh, how she longed to hear just one gentle snore telling her he was alive, just one rise and fall of his chest. But there was nothing.

Her teeth sank into the fist she had thrown against her mouth to stifle a scream, but the scream squeaked out anyway. She turned away with the sudden certainty that she was going to be sick and ran for the bathroom. Halfway there Anna realized she just needed to escape. She wanted to hide. Yes, she should hide, hide where this corpse in Rick's place would never find her! She sought the cover of the drapes that partially hid the farthest corner of the living room.

How could he look like that, Anna questioned in a panic? Yeah, he's a vampire, undead, as he always said, but this, *this* was wrong! This was unacceptable! This was atrocious! There had to be some explanation. The body in that room was not her Rick.

* * * *

Rick rousted, sensing horror in the air and unsure of the source. As a vampire he always awoke in a rush, no more gentle partings from Morpheus. Vamps were thrust into wakefulness, just as they surrendered to death when they 'rested.' But something unusual had forced him up early. What was it? He threw on his robe and noticed the door to his room was open. *Oh...this can't be good.* By the time Rick went to investigate the living room, Anna was already out of the corner.

* * * *

Anna wiped furiously at her tear-drenched face. *What am I doing here crying like a baby? I know he's a vampire. End of story. And what the hell am I doing falling in love with a vampire? There are plenty of normal men out there, men who don't turn blue when they sleep.*

She lifted her carryon to the bed and opened it. Careless of hangers, she threw what little she had in the closet into the case. *I simply need to get on the plane and get out of here. Maybe I'll go home to Columbus for a while. That's what Rick wanted me to do. He was right.* Her thoughts tumbled out in a flight of ideas. *Player can stay in doggie daycare until Rick's ready to leave. I have a job, I could stay in L.A., but I'll have to find a new apartment...* She began emptying the dresser drawers.

"Cupcake?"

Anna froze at his voice, his use of that nickname. She looked up, a classic deer in the headlights.

"Anna." Rick's voice grew firm. "What are you doing?"

"What does it look like? I'm packing."

Rick waited two beats before replying. "Right. So, you're leaving?" He edged carefully into the room.

"Yes." Her voice was flat. "I'm leaving."

"Mind telling me why?"

"We're not suited to each other, Rick. You know, Matt told me months ago that mortal/vamp relationships didn't work. He was right. I'm ending this before…before…" Anna started to shake, and the tears she'd already forbidden swamped her.

"Before…" Rick encouraged.

"Before one of us is in too deep and can't get out."

"One of us? I see." Rick edged toward her, she backed up. "Which one of us?"

"Don't be obtuse! Me, alright? Me. I don't want this! I don't want…"

Rick edged closer. "You don't want me?" His voice was unbearably gentle.

"I…I…Of course, I want you!" Anna doubled over with tears, she shrilled. "I want you, okay, I love you, but you're…dead!"

Rick sighed and sat on the bed, giving her some space. "That's true, I am dead, or undead, anyway. You knew that before. What's different?"

"I…" the tears were coming so hard now she could barely speak. "I saw you sleeping. I saw how you sl…sleep…" She shook her head violently. "It's unnatural."

Rick inhaled deeply and blew out a breath. "Okay, you're right. Not everyone can accept what I truly am. I'll understand if you can't—"

"Why?" She flew at him, catching him off guard. "Why? Why? Why?" She demanded beating at him. "I love you, damn it! I love you and I can't have you!" She dropped her hands piteously, racked with sobs. "Why would you do this to me when you know I can't have you?"

Rick took her hands gently and guided her to sit beside him on the bed. "Well, see, I think you can have me." He smiled boyishly. "I think we can work this out. Say, you were fascinated by a man from, Britain. You would think because you both speak English that it would be a breeze to put your shoes under his bed and have some fairy tale of a life. But the first time Prince Charming asked for elevensies you'd wonder what onesies through tensies were."

Anna screwed up her face and cocked her head.

"Anna, would you be ready for Tea and Supper or choosing dessert or pudding?"

"What does all this have to do with how you live?"

Rick drew in an unnecessary breath in an effort to appear mortal. "Everything, Cupcake. If I were a foreigner, all my habits would show you we were different. I'm different because of some extreme dietary requirements."

"Extreme dietary requirements? You sleep on a slab!"

Rick continued, "Also, I have an allergy to sunlight, and I need a very cold bedroom…"

"You sleep on a slab!" She accused in exasperation.

"True, you've seen something even my enemies haven't seen." Rick rose and ran a thumb over a still chilled bottom lip. He stood back from her and studied her body language, "That slab seems to be your breaking point?"

Anna shrugged, "I've seen Vampires do everything just like us," Anna gestured to herself, "It was a rude awakening to see the man I love…dead."

Rick retightened his robe and nodded his head. "There are times when vamps need extreme rest, or deeper rest—just like mortals—times when I may look to you as if I'm dead." Rick watched her for a moment, reading her emotions. His voice was reassuring. "Today was one of those times because I hadn't rested in a couple of days. It's not always like that. Usually, I'm simply still."

*I've really put him on the spot. I've never seen Richard Hiatt sweat. Do I mean that much to him?*

Rick narrowed his eyes. "Look, is any of this due to your past appraisal of me? I've been called a few names in my five hundred years. S.O.B., jackass, and even the poetic 'a little wicked,' but, Cupcake, that's what they call me because they've never been as close to me as you have."

Anna gazed at him silently, her heart battling with her mind.

Rick leaned toward her in a conspiratorial way. "You know, I have the most amazing king-sized bed at home."

"I've seen that movie too."

"Cupcake, you're too young to be cynical." Rick returned to the point, "My bed has one of those Evercool mattresses, and the sheets are out of this world. If you ever found your way into that bed, you'd never want to get out."

She gave him a dubious look.

"I'm not being egotistical about my prowess in that bed." Rick finished his sales pitch on his knees in front of her, "and bonus! If we shared a bed, you'd never have to worry about me stealing the covers." Anna saw a wicked gleam of hope in his eyes.

Rick caught her hands in his as they shared a grin; he leaned in to assure eye contact. "There are lots of rewards to living with a Vampire."

"Oh?"

"First of all, no cooking involved!"

Anna felt a wash of humorous obstinacy, "What if I like to cook?"

"You saw my kitchen, I've thrown some killer parties with top chefs entertaining my mortal friends. I'm sure you'll find something to like in all that stainless steel."

"Maybe. You said my vamp awareness was superficial, go on, educate me." Anna flipped her head and smacked Rick in the face with a wave of titian hair.

Rick rose to sit beside her, "I can show you all the best nightlife! You like art history? I've lived art history!"

"Yeah, I noticed that just looking for a pen at your place."

Rick reached under the curtain of her hair to fondle her neck and draw her into him. His lips rested against hers as he assured her, "And I'm inexhaustible in bed." He kissed her soundly.

"Is that a vamp trait or a Hiatt trait?"

"If I told you it was a vamp trait, you might run off and look for another vamp." Rick played the crushed suitor.

Anna's gut twisted as she tried to separate the romance from the truth. *We feel it all; we felt the rise before this fall.*

"Aw, Fitz, talk is cheap. As an art history professional, I believe I need a challenging examination of this historical artifact." Anna ran one arm around his back in a sweeping caress while she slid her hand into the front of his gaping robe. Rick's eyes widened when her fingers danced lightly over his nipple. His grin was huge.

"How in depth is this examination?"

"Skin to skin, I'll leave the depth up to the artifact." Anna dropped her hand onto his waiting flesh and smiled slyly as their gazes met.

They rose together, and Rick's gaze drank her in. "You look delicious, my Cupcake! I didn't even shower before I rested. I'd hate to wash all that pampering away, but I cannot bear to leave you for a shower."

Anna giggled, "You know the spa is open seven days a week. I can always go back…"

Rick caught her hand and nearly dragged her to the master bathroom. He began the job of adjusting all the shower controls, fragrant steam rolled out of the stall.

*I thought I had a humongous bathroom, good golly, I've never seen a shower with so many gadgets.* Anna's hands began to unbutton her shirt and Rick flew to her assistance.

"A gentleman never makes a lady work." Rick began to bless her flesh with light kisses as each button opened. Anna luxuriated in the heated rush only his lips engendered. Her back arched, throwing her body into his petting. Her wrists rested on his broad shoulders where her hands could caress his strong jaw.

Rick peeled back her blouse, dispatching it with grace. He moaned at the sight of her ripe breasts, flushed with arousal. Rick drew his index finger from her navel straight up her tingling body and raised her chin to taste those inviting cherry lips.

Anna fell into his embrace breathlessly, and his hands deftly released her lacy brassiere. Finally, they were breast to chest.

*How can I leave his embrace to lose the rest of my clothes? His arms are too heavenly.* Anna nuzzled into Rick's neck. This isn't a dorm room, this isn't the back of a limo. This is the real deal. Her confidence fell away with her bra. Between them, there could be no failure. Would she be a worthy lover in his skilled embrace?

"Oh, Cupcake… you are such a naughty little temptress. I'm drawn to your scent. I'm so turned on." He placed her hand around his pulsing erection. "I taste your lips, and you make me hungry for more."

Anna searched her limited experience and failed to find any man who had claimed her body and her heart. Had any man ever spoken to her like this?

*Is this his Dom act?*

"No games, Rick." Her forehead fell on his shoulder.

Rick's hand froze on the drawstring of her linen pants, he frowned. "Do you want me to stop?"

Anna heard the unmistakable disappointment in his voice. Her hands fell to his chest, separating them by half an arm's length. "Those dangerous lips, that magnificent equipment of yours…"

Rick grimaced. "Your words sound complimentary, but the message I'm getting isn't a good one." Stepping back, he re-wrapped his robe, tying it tightly. His hand ran through his hair before he spoke, and he licked his tongue slowly over his bottom lip. "Go on…" He stood stiffly, hands on hips, waiting for her verdict.

In a sudden stroke of modesty, Anna covered her breasts with a bath towel. "Your first rule to Matt was don't get involved romantically with mortal women. Am I some kind of five-hundred-year itch? Do you want to find a steam grate, so I can stand on it and titillate you?" Anna's pain resonated through every word.

"Is this about trust?" Rick's head fell back, looking anywhere but her face. He leaned over the vanity to watch Anna in the expansive mirror.

Anna watched his tense, wounded posture from the back, as well as his reflection. "Partially. You're trouble in trousers, or out of them. Rick, you know your game, your role as a Dom. A year from now—"

"A year from now? How about five years from now?" he interrupted.

"It's your nature to feed and fuck and forget mortals. Who will I be to you in a year?" Anna pulled at the end of the towel to wipe her tears away.

Rick spun to face her. "Anna, you need to know a few things about me. I'm particular, I'm opinionated, I can be exceptionally covetous, and I don't suffer fools. But one thing I can say about myself after five hundred years, I know my own mind."

Anna let the aspects of his self-appraisal pinball in her brain. Her brows knit as she tightly closed her eyes, breathing deeply to gather her words, "And this affects me how?"

"When we met, our worlds collided. Since we've been involved, I've not had the urge for those past predilections. In Heaven's name, Cupcake, you've changed the behaviors of a five-hundred-year-old vampire."

Anna felt his sincerity, yet her inferiority floated to the top of her reasoning. "When the conquest is over, am I enough for you, Fitz?"

"That's what you think? I'm here for another notch on my belt? Do you know how long it's been since I stopped counting those?"

Anna shook her head, beginning to feel chagrined.

"You call me Fitz? I guess I deserve that… I do seem to be giving you fits. Since we met, has anything been easy? No, but we've been shoulder to shoulder fixing the things that some malcontent fouled up."

Anna sighed deeply and shook her head, "I don't want to play Dr. Watson."

"I don't need a Dr. Watson, Cupcake; I need you for the rest of my eternity."

Anna began to tremble. *Is this a proposal?* She was suspicious that love found too easily would be of little value in the long run. Could she trust their mutual trials to make her a prize in his heart? Anna's head rose seeking his gaze. "Your eternity, with me?"

"You bring so much life to me, Cupcake. I can't exist unless I'm living with you." Rick words were emphasized by a nod. Anna flew into his powerful embrace, the protective towel long forgotten. "I'll love every particular, opinionated day with you and we can be fools together."

Rick released her just enough to pull that drawstring on her linen pants, "Cupcake, I'm up to bat with two strikes. Pitch the next ball, so I can hit a home run, okay?"

* * * *

Rick held Anna in a wicked embrace standing in the middle of the humongous shower stall. He lapped at the water sheeting off her soft shoulders. Anna's sighs syncopated with the motions of Rick's tongue against her quivering flesh. He pressed tightly against her flat belly. He took a half step away from her, and she gasped at the loss of his close throbbing. Anna delighted in Rick's questing tongue along her shoulder and the lithe length of her arm.

The steely silk of his length bobbed at her as Rick's lips moved from thumb to finger to finger to finger. Anna fell under his wicked charm as his nibbles turned into sensual suckling of her index finger. His gaze mesmerized her. Anna's body quaked and arched boldly into Rick's. The sensations were delicious.

Rick released her finger. "I can't slow down. I can't hold back, I wish I could." At vamp speed, he caught her up in a spin and rapidly pressed her back against the marble wall, catching her wrists in his hands high above her head.

"Let me wash you, Rick, let my hands roam over your entire body."

"How can I turn down that request?" Rick's brow arched playfully, then grabbed for the velvety washcloth and soap. Despite his assertion otherwise, Rick was reluctant to rush her.

Anna assumed a dominating posture and wondered if she could pull this off. "Stand back, don't touch me while I'm washing you."

"Yes, Mistress," Rick replied wryly, standing feet apart, his fists resting on his hips.

His reply empowered Anna to begin at the top of his head, standing on tiptoe. Her breasts bobbing in his face, "No playing with me, Mr. Hiatt." Her lips fought her emerging smile. Fingertips massaged Rick's head and neck, her soapy fingers swirling around his ears. Pleasure burned within her belly as her hands skated the curves of his muscled torso. Soap bubbled in the dusting of golden hair on his pecs and flowed alluringly down his treasure trail. Running circles around his navel, she debated about how long to tease him. Once or twice? Maybe four times?

"Turn around, Mr. Hiatt." Anna's hands on his shoulders pivoted the tall man before her. *I've got to get that tremendously inviting naughty bit out of my face or I'll be tempted to end this all too soon. Must... take... time...*

Anna sucked in a calming breath. Rick loomed large, palms flat above his head, feet spaced wide on the mosaic marble floor. Sheets of water sluiced over his athletically broad shoulders. Bravely, Anna stole the hand wand off the holder, plotting to tease Rick with the pulsing stream. *There ain't no rest for the wicked 'til we close our eyes for good.* She leaned within an inch of his long torso, close enough for Rick to feel her heat. Dashing the stream over his head, she read his pleasure as he arched his back seeking her breasts and hips against him. *Did it tickle him under the arms? Is he sensitive there?*

"Anna…"

"Patience, Mr. Hiatt!" Anna's admonition was for both of them.

One hand circled the soapy washcloth down Rick's spine as the other rinsed away his tension. *Did he growl when I soaped up his bum?* Anna tested with the other cheek. *Oh, yes, I do hear a bit of a rumble from that damn fine chest.*

"Anna… I appreciate your stepping up the discipline, but I really do need to ravish you soon." They laughed together as Rick spun around to grab his prized woman. Anna's legs wrapped around his trim waist.

"I thought you'd never ask…" Anna confessed with a kiss on his ear.

* * * *

They tumbled together into bed. Wrapped in the bath sheet, they rolled to and fro, drying themselves. Rick savored the feel of her damp, fragrant skin as much as he enjoyed the warmed bath sheet's velvety texture. He sank into her silken embrace. The truth of his love burned within him. Time had freed his mourning heart. He was a vampire reborn to love again. Anna's devotion deserved only his most fervent and worshipful touch.

Rick threw back the comforter and tenderly drew her face to face on the fresh sheets. His lips gravitated to her breasts, kissing first one, then the other. She moaned under his touch then caught her breath as his lips embraced her aching nipple. He worshipped that succulent flesh, licked it, stroked it with his tongue, drew on it like the hungry soul he was. At the same time, his fingers danced along the lively flesh of her hips.

"Is this really happening?" she whispered dreamily. His hands stroked the long column of her back, setting a fire in her flesh.

"Finally? Yes, it's really happening." Rick's hand slipped slyly to lovingly cup her firm buttock.

"Please, don't stop!"

He chuckled low in his chest. "What makes you think I could?" Rick asked as he rolled her onto her back.

His eyes adored the slopes and plains of her luscious body. His palm rested softly on her belly, a touch away from her mound. Rick inhaled deeply, savoring the punch of pheromones his touch elicited.

He whispered in her ear. "Tell me what you like." He punctuated his question with a soft inhalation.

Anna shuddered in expectation. "Everything you do."

Rick's confession was a throaty growl. "But I haven't even gotten started." His clever fingers probed at her slick sex, and he withdrew them to taste her. "My God, you're spun sugar!"

Keening, she grabbed his hand and pressed it back to his loving task. "Cupcake, don't forget to breathe, I don't want you passing out…yet." Rick left her embrace to slide to the end of the bed. "I want to see you."

Anna sat up, knees to her breast. She rolled her eyes and sighed. "Rick…"

"Shh. It's okay. You can't deny me this." Rick reached for each foot and slowly drew them apart. He realized she'd never had the satisfaction a lover should give.

"What is this? What do you want?"

Rick scented her fear. "I want to see your beauty close up. I want to taste you. I want to drive you mad with ecstasy." His gaze hungrily caressed her hidden prize, when he suddenly realized there might be more to her hesitation. He looked up at her. "Has anyone hurt you there?"

Anna blushed furiously. "No! But why would you want to look at me?"

Rick leaned up on his elbows and smiled boyishly. "You are a delicate flower. You have drawn me in with your enticing fragrance." He drew in an appreciative breath. "I told you, you taste like spun sugar. Did you think I fibbed?"

Anna stared, awestruck, as Rick softly stroked from her feet to her knees. "I want to see you because this old heart of mine doesn't get many opportunities to race." He inched further up the bed and stroked from her knees to her thighs. "You know you make my dick rock hard. I want to see the part of you that's going to strangle me into submission." Anna relaxed into the mountain of pillows, her gaze riveted on his sensual advance. Rick reverently parted the folds of her sex. He held perfectly still, drinking in her beauty. Anna shivered. Deliberately, he lowered himself down to her.

* * * *

Rick placed teasing kisses away from her sex. Anna moaned, surprised by her disappointment. He persevered; his lips making their way back up again. He did it again, down the other leg, making sure he touched her sex with the lightest glance of his lips. Anna's entire body tensed with need. *This is exquisite torture. When will he just do it?* Rick turned on the action with one strong lick from her center to her clit. Rick lifted his head. "Do you like to watch me?"

Anna flopped her head back and giggled. "All the time."

"Can you see how much I enjoy you?"

Anna smiled girlishly. "Do you know how much I enjoy you?"

Rick's crooked grin grew. "Well, let me get back to us enjoying each other." He found her clit with slow, harder strokes and sped up gradually.

Anna arched with need fully into his mouth. "How do you know exactly how to touch me?" She moaned, breathlessly.

Rick's moan vibrated through her sex. She ground back into him at the sensation. Rick got straight back to that hardening clit.

Anna fisted the bed sheets, her knees widening in invitation, her eyes clenched shut. His tongue dove into her, heightening her excitement. Her fingers released the sheets and slid into his hair holding him exactly where his tongue could stroke her hard. She was so close to something unknown. Sweat beaded on her chest. A tornado spiraled within her.

Taking her to the next level, Rick slid one long finger into her tight, wet, flesh. With a come-hither motion on her g-spot, her eyes popped open. Their gazes met, and her thighs tightened, evidence of her rising orgasm. Rick moved with her, his cool mouth delivering a steady beat of his tongue. Anna hung on to him, as his lips nibbled on her clit.

"Don't let go! Don't let go! Don't. Let. Go!" Anna's screams became a mantra. The symphony of their bodies working together, came to a crescendo. Anna's mantra became an exultation, "Rick! Rick! Rick," growing softer and slower with each exclamation. Her total satisfaction, a low moan, played out on her lips.

* * * *

Rick watched her unwind into loose-limbed relaxation. Brimming with pleasure at her response, he pulled the sheet with him as he crawled up to her side. Embracing all the wonderful aspects of her humanity, he held her and savored her racing heart. He kissed at the beads of hard-earned sweat and coveted her flush of color. Listening to the music of her quieting breaths, Rick held her along his body, stroking and kissing her heated flesh. She was almost asleep, and that was fine with Rick. His turn would come in the next round. Right now, he gloried in her surrender to his touch. This was tender, this was mutual and profoundly hot. *This is not vanilla.*

# 12

Adam stood behind a mirrored viewing window, watching Veronique, seated at the interrogation table. She was flanked by her high-powered attorney. Adam's job was technically over, but he couldn't resist watching Veronique's circus unfold. He had refrained from flaming her. He'd rather the Council draw out her suffering.

George Bellamy, Veronique's attorney, made his living off other's tears. George sat as tall as his below-average height allowed, sausaged into his forty-six regular Hugo Boss suit. What George lacked in style and grace he made up for with courtroom cunning. Like sharks, George never slept.

The Vampire Council Attorney, Elena Keller, was tall, lean and extremely blonde. Elena was as fastidious as George was slovenly. Tonight, she discounted her opposition as a nebbish. She had no idea George lived for war, and she could be courtroom cannon fodder.

"The charges against you are extreme, Ms. Moreau," Elena threw down her opening gambit. "Your cooperation could affect your sentence."

"What are you offering?" George asked as he gestured for Veronique's silence.

"It could be the difference between life and termination."

"You'd never make a case for termination; no judge would go that far."

Elena shuffled out pages of Veronique's record. "Your client has a jacket going back to 1699 for a string of rape turns."

George lowered his voice to control the room. "My client has paid her debt on any charges for which she was not acquitted."

"What a proud day," Elena sniped, distributing copies of victim statements from the twenty-seven rape turns while Veronique and George remained aloof.

Elena fumed over their dismissive postures. "Only five of those twenty-seven victims survived. Twenty-two fledglings went feral and had to be put down. The five survivors were rescued by Richard Hiatt." Adam's ears perked up at his employer's name.

"Of those five," Elena continued, "only one made it past five decades. This, Mr. Bellamy, is an atrocious rate of carnage. If I had my way, we'd terminate her right now."

Bellamy clenched his jaw in mock affront, "I'd like a few moments to confer with my client, alone."

Elena stood and strode from the room. While client/attorney conferences were held, the mirrored viewing window and sound were suspended, giving Adam a chance to digest what he'd heard. He knew from scuttlebutt around the club that Matt Brenner's turning had been against his will. He never knew Matt's sire, which would never be discussed. Now he understood, Rick had step-sired his best friend and business partner. No wonder they were so close. Without Rick's fostering, Matt would have ended up torched. It explained why Matt tread carefully around mortals. Catherine Temple, his new bride, had inspired Matt to break all his own rules.

Adam watched Bellamy signal the guard for the negotiation to continue. Elena approached the table cautiously.

"Although Ms. Moreau feels remorse for the events at Lust for Life, many other factors came into play. As a gesture of healing, she would like to offer compensation to the donor's families."

"Well, isn't that generous?" Elena sniped. "How does she expect to compensate for endangering the concealment of our vampire Family or consorting with known criminals?"

Bellamy answered with silence.

"Mr. Bellamy, what monetary payment erases crossing international borders to perpetrate heinous crimes?"

Again, Bellamy and his client sat in stony silence.

"How do you go back in time to compensate those twenty-seven rape turns?" Veronique pouted. "Matt Brenner has had a bad attitude since the night he was turned."

* * * *

Vampires do not sleep. How, then, did Rick explain the warm rapture of the sex-scented sheets twisted around them? Rick could only explain it as their love's spell. He floated between light and dark, recalling each of the sensations he provoked in Anna. His grin was dashed by the discordant jangling of the room phone. His euphoria evaporated at the sound of the voice on the line.

*"Anna? Anna Curley?"*

"Who's calling?" Rick clipped his response. He knew damn well it was Sterling.

*"A friend. I heard she was in town."*

Rick sat up abruptly.

Anna shook herself from sleep and saw Rick holding the phone. "Who is it?" She lip-spoke.

He covered the receiver and whispered, "Sterling."

Anna winced. "Should I talk to him?"

"See what he wants." Rick held out the receiver, but Anna crawled over his lap to sit on the side of the bed. Rick lip-spoke, "No fair," as he slid to the warm side of the bed that radiated Anna and sex. *Anna's husky voice is wasted on that bastard.*

"Who's this?" Anna challenged.

*The slimy cur who got us out of bed!*

*"The owner of the dog and the dagger you stole,"* Sterling growled.

Rick and Anna exchanged curious looks, suddenly on alert. "You got me, and obviously you have the dagger. Did you pick Slayer up from doggie daycare too?"

*"What do I want with a dog? What's your game, Anna?"*

"I needed money. He offered me *so much money,*" she drew out dramatically.

*"Who offered you? For what?"*

Anna winked at Rick. "You know, that dagger turned out to be kinda valuable."

*"You took my dagger!"* He accused.

"Well, I had to get it down here because that's where the money is for stuff like this."

*"How much money are you talking about?"*

"It was a lot." She answered breathlessly. "I don't know how high he'll go."

*"You've got diddly without the dagger."*

Rick scribbled a number on the notepad and handed it to her. *One hundred thousand dollars.*

"You don't have the contact; I don't have the dagger. Can't we meet in the middle and split the hundred-K?"

There was a moment of silence, and Rick could almost hear Sterling calculating in his head. *"I'll tell you what, I always liked you, Anna. That's why I asked you to watch my dog."* Rick rolled his eyes. *"You're staying in a nice hotel. Why don't you order us up some dinner, I'll come to your room, and we can talk about it?"* Anna clapped a palm over the receiver and silently gagged.

"Will you bring it? Will I be able to see it again?"

*"No, it's in a safe place. You can't let that dagger hang out of a backpack. Somebody might grab it from you."*

Anna gritted her teeth. "I'm meeting with the buyer tomorrow night, so I'd need to see it no later than noon. Why don't you come up for lunch? I'd love to catch up."

*"Lunch is good!"*

Rick nodded approval.

*"Anna, don't fuck me over,"* Sterling threatened. *"See you then..."*

Anna re-cradled the receiver with a defiant *thump*.

Rick lay back in a nest of pillows, the comforter pulled up to his hips. One leg was out of the covers, knee bent, his wrist resting casually on top. His adoring gaze followed Anna's heart-shaped backside around the bedroom. He ran his hand over his stubbly jaw and finger-combed his bed-head. "That slime-ball did have one solid idea." Rick ran his hand back and forth across his six-pack, and Anna arched a questioning brow. "You could order some dinner..."

Anna cocked her head quizzically. "But you don't eat..."

"Well, if you dine on liver and spinach, I could snack on you."

"Ewww. No liver."

"Fielder's choice. May I still snack on you?"

Anna launched herself at the bed, landing beside him and delivering a sound smooch. "I thought you'd never ask. Am I your one-course meal or are you calling for takeout?"

Rick grimaced. "No. I packed my lunch."

* * * *

Anna wheeled the room service cart to the table by the window. Rick exited the master, fresh from a shower, a towel slung low around his hips and another at his neck.

He transferred the covered dishes to Anna's side of the table. After a trip to the suite's kitchen, Anna returned with a crystal tumbler. Rick pulled out her chair and bid her, "bon appetite."

"Well, where's yours?" Anna asked in surprise. "I brought you a glass. You can have some of my lemon for a garnish."

Rick raised a brow. "Oh, yeah? What are you eating?"

"More than a lemon. I have a spinach salad, and a filet, and..." Anna lowered her head. "And another whole flan."

Rick suppressed his discomfiture over feeding in front of her and elected to use his travel mug. "Anna, the tumbler idea is sweet, but I'd feel more comfortable using a mug."

"Here's a straw. It's blue. I can't see through it." Anna held out a wrapped straw.

Rick could feel her sincerity. She obviously wanted to include him in her dining. He supposed that's what normal couples did. Didn't they share an evening meal and discuss their day? *I'm an asshole. Here she is, trying to engineer a romantic evening for us, and I'm tossing up roadblocks. If I throw out enough hurdles, I can be alone for the next millennium, too.*

"Thank you, but the travel mug will keep it cold." He disappeared into the kitchen and came back with the mug. "I know you want that wonderful steak warm, but my meal is better served chilled."

Anna nodded acceptance as she attacked her steak with relish. "You made me hungry!"

Rick smiled at her with a little fang showing. "Eat up, you're gonna need it." He took a sip from the cup and lamented the taste of bagged blood. He hoped his conversation wasn't as flat as his dinner's flavor. This was beginning to feel like the world's longest blind date.

Anna raised a fork full of spinach salad to her lips, only to put it down. "What's it like to be a vampire?"

"Mostly, it's great."

Anna cocked her head.

Rick could see she wasn't satisfied with his reply. "Have you ever been on vacation away from all your favorite food? It's like they don't serve O positive here." Rick managed to coax a smile from her. This could be the beginning of a discussion he didn't want to have yet.

"So, other than the food…" Anna prodded.

Rick paused, considering. "Imagine your senses times one thousand. Imagine what we did this afternoon sang in your blood. Imagine you could scent my arousal across the room."

Anna's eyes went round as saucers. "The night in the parking garage, I was freaking, thinking you could read my mind!"

"In a way. Every vampire has heightened abilities as part of our survival skills. Each of us is as different as mortals."

Anna was thoughtful as she chewed a bite of salad.

Rick couldn't read her mind but knew she was coming up with a full slate of questions. "So, if you had actually gone to Columbus, where I thought I was sending you, where would we be tonight?" *Good diversion old man!*

"We'd be on a hayride. If my parents weren't around, I'd be drinking hot buttered rum. You'd just be drinking rum…and hopefully, me…" She waggled her brows and smiled. "Speaking of which, why haven't you done that yet?"

Rick shook his head at her, his fangs lengthening even more. "You are a bad girl, Anna Curley. If you don't stay on topic, how do you expect me to get to know you? You don't want me to know just the naughty parts, do you?"

"Um…is this a trick question?"

"Bad girl. C'mon, answer my question."

"All right, we'd be snuggled under blankets, in the hay at the back of the wagon so we could neck."

"You know, that's funny, my Family considers necking to be something else."

Anna looked up at him, chewing, and winked. "You can show me that later."

Rick shook his head. "What if your parents *were* there?"

"My little brother would be sitting between us, and I'd be drinking spiced cider. At one point in the evening, my father would have you behind the barn with the rest of the men, discussing tractors."

"Thank God you added the bit about the tractors, I was starting to get worried."

"My mother would be pressing me about your education, and your job, and your family, and—"

"Oh. Is your mother a Knights Templar?"

"No, she's a member of the Inquisition. Oh, the tortures I've endured!"

"I see where you get it!" He nodded wisely. "The female is the deadliest of the species. I'll have to look out for Mama."

Anna stopped chewing, set her fork down and stared at him.

"What is it, Cupcake, did I misspeak?"

She smiled with tears in her eyes. "You're talking about meeting my parents. You realize that, right? Do you understand what that means in today's society?"

Rick stretched his hand across the table to capture her fingertips. "How can I know the woman I love if I don't know her family?" He drew her fingertips to his lips and nibbled gently. Anna giggled. "You know, Cupcake, I run a multimillion-dollar conglomerate, and the majority of my consumers are mortals, but you're the mortal I've spent the most time with."

Anna smiled slyly. "So, Fitz, how long do we have to wait before this dinner gets in my bloodstream?"

*And…we're back to that subject! I'm beginning to worry vamps are only appreciated for our bite.* Rick answered her question with a question and a sly smile of his own. "Is this the science portion of tonight's quiz?"

Anna laid her napkin aside with great deliberation, strolled to him and melted into his lap. She gently tongued the shell of his ear and dawdled a kiss over his lips. He let her explore his mouth with her tongue and prayed she'd linger there a moment longer. Something she probably would have done had there not been a knock on the door.

Anna pulled back, and they looked at each other in alarm. "Could that be Sterling?"

Rick narrowed his eyes and sniffed. "Nope. Not Sterling. Player."

Anna's eyes went round in horror. "Oh my God! I forgot him!"

Rick shook his head in mock disappointment. "Bad doggie mama!" He headed for the door with Anna following close behind. He opened it to a uniformed attendant who handed off Player's leash. Rick dropped it to look at the card he was handed. "Is this the bill?"

"No, Senor. It is Player's report card."

"I… see…" Rick frowned in confusion. "Was he a good boy? He didn't flunk, or something, did he?"

"Oh, no, Senor. He was an exceptionally good boy. He is very social."

"Well, that's a miracle." Rick slapped at the towel as if it had pockets. "I'm sorry, I don't have any cash on me. Could you add a tip to the room charge?"

"Si, Senor, if you wish."

"Great. Give yourself twenty American."

"Thank you so much, Senor Hiatt, we will be happy to have Player back with us at any time."

Rick and Anna waved the attendant out and turned to find Player swallowing the filet and starting on the bread basket. Rick looked at him sorrowfully. "Look at you, you're such a little carnivore. Taking all the food from your poor mama…" he threw Anna a grin "…who forgot you."

Anna swatted his shoulder. "I was distracted!" She glanced around the room. "You think if I make him a bed with a blanket, he'll sleep in here okay?"

Rick slanted her a chiding look. "He'll be fine. Turn on the TV and toss him a shoe."

"Not on your life." She slanted a look back, "And, you don't know how true that is." She frowned. "Seriously, though, if we leave him here alone, do you think he'll cry?"

Rick growled low in his chest and Player raised his head in alarm. Rick smiled with satisfaction. "He wouldn't dare."

He laughed at her disapproving look and caught her up in a fierce embrace. Raising her to his lips, he rumbled low, "Why don't you relax on your balcony, I'll be right there."

Anna sucked in a deep breath. "'Kay…" She sank back on her feet and shook off his spell. "He's more potent than he thinks!" she whispered to Player.

Rick stopped, turned, and gave her a grin. "For your sake, I hope so!"

Anna grimaced. "He could hear a fly fart!"

"The worst part is the smell."

Anna laughed all the way to the balcony. The night was fragrant and black when she stepped barefoot across the terracotta floor. The silence was perplexing. "Where has last night's music gone?"

Rick slid behind her, his arm wrapped around her waist. He nuzzled under the curtain of her hair. Feeling thwarted, he slowly drew the thick, red, mass aside, letting it tumble in a fan across her breast. "There's music all around us," he whispered huskily. "Listen to the ships calling to each other as they move on the river." He slid his tongue along the tender flesh behind her ear. Anna squirmed against him. "There's the rhythm of the traffic below us, notice it's slower at night?" He nipped at her earlobe with his lips. "Close your eyes, can you hear my heart beating?"

"Would you hate me if I said I couldn't?" Anna tucked her head. Rick felt her frustration. "I can feel you pressed against me. I can feel a slow thump…"

"Oh, Cupcake, this isn't a test, it's just an example of our differences. I can hear your heartbeat." Rick slid his hand around to rest over her heart. "I can feel your pulse." Rick trailed a string of wet kisses down her neck to her shoulder. "And I can feel it race faster as I kiss you." Rick turned her smoothly to face him.

She leaned into his embrace, his thick length resting against her belly. "I can feel your pulse now…" she said impishly.

"I'll bet you can." Rick's fingers wove into her hair, capturing her. The truth of their love sparked between them. His lips descended on hers, within seconds he was love-drunk, dizzy with passion.

"I can feel the heat building within you." Rick murmured huskily. "When you're turned on, your blood is like a beacon to me. It rushes here." Rick slid his hand into her robe to caress her clit. "And when your body is ready for me," Rick's finger descended further between her legs, inside her. When he withdrew, she cried out at the loss. His tongue lapped his finger and Anna watched, mesmerized. "I taste your arousal like honey."

"Ahh." She sighed. "I wish I could do that." Longing rang in her voice.

Rick paused. *Should he mention this?* "As a matter of fact,…" He paused again.

"What?" She waited. He stayed silent, considering. "Don't do this to me, what?"

"There is a way for you to feel some of what I feel, short term…" He bit his lip in indecision.

"There is? How?"

Rick's soul searched Anna's. "You could take a little of my blood. It would join us, temporarily."

Anna stood, stunned. "Really?"

"I've never done it before." Rick confessed. "I'm not sure it isn't an old witch's tale." *Would sharing his blood give her fleeting ecstasy, or would it lead to disappointment?* He knew vampire blood had healing properties, would it allow her to share his experience? "I wouldn't force you to do this."

"Of course, you wouldn't. But it would be so interesting. What could go wrong?"

Rick shrugged. "It would either work or it wouldn't, I guess."

"Is it a lot of blood?"

Rick sniffed, thinking of a mid-nineteenth century battlefield when he stepped in with a cup of blood-fortified wine to save a comrade. "Just a couple of drops."

He turned his face away from her to hide his transformation. Anna caught his jaw gently and pulled him back to her. "I love you so much." She whispered. "I want to know all of you."

Touched to the core, Rick allowed her to watch him transform. He felt his flesh pale to translucence. His vision sharpened as his eyes became opalescent, and his fangs descended.

Anna reacted with pure acceptance. "I love you." She stood on tiptoes, her hands on his shoulders and kissed his jaw, his cheek, his lips. "I love you." She reiterated softly. Rick basked in her total approval.

His voice was deep, gruff, animalistic. "I love you, too, Cupcake. I want to share everything with you." He bit his lip with one razor-sharp canine, and blood pooled immediately.

* * * *

Anna felt herself suddenly lifted and drawn against him. His kiss was soft at first. She licked the few drops of blood from his lip and tasted the salty, coppery tang. His hand at her hip drew her closer. Her heart pounded in her ears. His hands tangled in her heavy mass of hair and he pulled gently, deepening the kiss, demanding her surrender, and she gave it.

Anna was swept into his arms as if she were light as a zephyr. Still kissing her, Rick laid her gently in the center of the bed. The scent of this afternoon's lovemaking lingered within the bedclothes, titillating her senses. It inspired a fullness between her legs, a tingling that spread up into her abdomen and down into her thighs. Her toes began to curl. She moaned. Rick chuckled. What a delicious fire was igniting within her!

Rick's skin, already so smooth and appealing to her, now felt like the most exquisite silk. The ridges and chords of his muscular abdomen sang a siren's song to her sex. His kiss tasted like the finest bittersweet chocolate.

She arched hard against him. "Take me! Take me now!"

"Not yet," he coaxed. "Have a little patience."

"No patience. Patience is dead. Now."

"Cupcake…"

Anna had no restraint, she was consumed by carnality. With one quick motion, she flipped Rick onto his back and straddled him, her knees on either side of his waist. Rick followed her lead and caressed her breasts. He raised his head until he could trace the delicate skin over her breastbone with his tongue.

"More… Harder…" Anna commanded, her voice husky and low to her own ears. "I need you inside me." Her thoughts ran wild, sensations were in the driver's seat. *Is this what angels feel, or is it demons?*

Rick gathered her in his arms, drawing her to him in a vice grip. "Take it easy, I'm an old man." Anna felt his pulsing sex pressed between them. Her heart thundered in her ears. Slick with sweat, Anna ground against her captive lover. She sought the sweet touch of friction.

Rick growled low in her ear, "I think we need to dial you down a notch."

"I'm ravenous for you, give it to me, Rick."

"I want you too, Cupcake." Rick rumbled. He flipped Anna onto her back, held her, arms outstretched. "We both need a good fucking." Rick released her wrists and slid down between her thighs. "And I'm the primitive beast inspired to deliver it."

Anna caught his thick erection, holding it firmly in her delicate hand. He was hot and hard as heated granite. She stroked him at her cleft, aching to feel him inside her. Her own feverish flesh opening to coat his crown. She pumped him, once, twice, a third time. He growled his desire.

"Does that make you want me, Fitz?" Anna purred.

Rick arched into her grip with a strangled guttural moan, "Oh, yeah."

Nothing could have equipped her for the exquisite sensations he aroused. His hips rocked his hard sex in her soft hand, his motions slow and deliberate. She would break that iron control, she determined. She would drive him as wild as he had driven her. Even as the thought crossed her mind, the carnal excitement aroused by her virtual vampire senses drove her higher. She teased him, goading him to rut with her, mindless as a stallion and his mare.

Her strokes sped, inviting his delirium. Rick fell forward, hungrily consuming her kisses. "Cupcake, I'm gonna fuck you." It was an inhuman growl. Pulling back from her plump lips he thrust hard into her, gripping the firm curves of her ass in his hands. She moaned into his mouth as he clutched her. Anna's legs reflexively rose around Rick's waist, pulling him deeper. Rick followed the motion of her hips, "Talk to me," he commanded, their gazes intent on each other.

"Take me like an animal, make me scream." Anna gritted. Her body strained against him, the hot, pink flush creeping from her chest to her face and throughout her body with every untamed stroke. "You, devil, oh, Fitz, you…you feel so…!"

Looking up at him, she caught his feral intensity. He thrust into her powerfully, his jaw tight in concentration. Somehow, without asking, he knew what she wanted.

"I want you to come with me." Rick snarled. His eyes had already silvered. She felt his tremendous length increase.

His fingers pinched her nipples, and she gasped. "Yes! Yes! Make me come!" She pleaded. Her inner muscles rippled to draw him deeper.

Above her, Rick's hands and tongue and fangs drew sensations from her she thought impossible. His pressure on her nipple increased, welcome torture alongside the divine relief of his cool mouth as he suckled her other needy peak. His fangs rode the slope, ending with a teasing nip that sent fire shooting down to her core.

Rick tilted her hips up to him with a jerk, allowing him to sink deeper still. The perfectly pleasing curve of his phallus hit every erogenous nerve within. Her greedy sex fisted his heavy flesh. Her clit ground against his root until a climax swept her like a torrent, rolling and sustained. She glowed with a fine sheen of sweat. Her tight flesh rippled with her release and her breasts heaved as she shrieked his name.

She watched Rick labor above her, his face hard and dark with passion. His fierce strokes fed their still escalating fire. His fangs elongated, piercing his lip again. Unconsciously, he licked the drops away. Just the act of sucking those crimson drops reminded her of his tongue between her legs. The vision drove her into another orgasm, higher and brighter than the one before.

* * * *

Anna writhed beneath him, arching up, baring her throat, begging for Rick's bite. He focused on the ravishing woman beneath him, so eager to meet him passion for passion and stroke for stroke. It boggled his mind that a few drops of his blood permitted his little bonbon to overpower his six-foot-two muscular frame. The revelation washed over him. His blood had fostered her endurance and erased her inhibitions, yet Anna's lustful abandon was purely her own. *The hunger wants what the hunger wants.*

A few hundred years of being either a Dom or a sub had taught him the protocols of the dungeon. Rick had the discipline to play the roles, and that was all there was. Wasn't it? He now realized how wrong he'd been, and little Anna Cupcake taught him. Being in this bed, her total attention on their lovemaking, was the only thing on Anna's mind—not rules, not games. She challenged him to forget all artifice and plunge into pure emotion. They were in a duel for their hearts, and it was no contest. He'd concede the field of honor right now. She won. His heart was hers.

The root of Rick's spine tingled, his toes curled, and his sac drew up tight against him. He needed the bite, he was desperate to bite her. With swift determination, Rick's fangs sank into the sweet spot of her neck. Light exploded from behind his eyes and his ears rang with the percussion of her heart. He felt his muscles twitch and spasm, flooding her as she held him in her intimate embrace. He welcomed the undulating pressure of her sex as she came again. They panted together as they melted into bliss.

# 13

Silence… or so it seemed to be. Consciousness trickled back to Anna, and her eyes opened slowly. She felt compelled to stretch muscles she didn't remember having. A pleasant ache subsided as she curled into Rick's warm body, kept warm under the fluffy comforter. She fit perfectly into the hollow of his arm stretched across her pillow. Her sleep-heavy eyes savored the sight of his face in peaceful rest.

She watched his eyelashes for any sign of movement. Although he lay utterly still, he was perfection to her. If a Greek god walked this earth, he would be Richard Hiatt. Forget the fabulous muscles and slender physique. Forget the handsome, chiseled features and long-lashed whiskey eyes.

She sighed pensively, toying with the thought of waking him. Looking over his chest to the French doors, she vaguely recalled their talk on the balcony and Rick suggesting she take a few drops of his blood. Then, a total body rush, and…nothing. Just looking at the extra bed pillows cast pell-mell across the room, told her it must have been a wild night. The bath towels hadn't been scattered on the floor when she went out on the balcony, and there had been no empty champagne flutes next to the bed.

She was in such a delicious state of satisfaction—*um, they had certainly enjoyed each other*—so why couldn't she remember any of it? She couldn't see a clock as she lay still listening for cues from the traffic. *Is it three in the morning or is traffic building for rush hour?* Anna licked at her dry lips. Rick was still resting deeply. Obviously, he needed it. *I'll just close my eyes for a few more minutes…*

* * * *

The next time Anna awoke, she felt a warm presence along her back. Had Fitz changed sides? When she heard gentle snoring, her brows knitted together, and she flipped over. It wasn't the bedmate she'd expected. Player lay happily asleep next to her, stretched out with his large square head centered on a pillow. *Fitz must have let him in early this morning.* Rising up on her elbows, she surveyed the dim room. Sunlight hid behind closed balcony doors and drawn drapes. The clock's face glowed brightly 8:51.

Player's head inched its way under her armpit nudging her to get out of bed. "You probably need a walk." Anna groaned. "I don't want a walk." She picked up the phone to dial the Concierge. "Good morning. This is Mr. Hiatt's suite. Will you send someone up to walk our dog, please?" While the concierge arranged Player's morning, Anna noticed the note leaning against the bedside lamp.

> *Dear Cupcake,*
> *Last night was unbelievable! You know how to hold up your side of the bed! Forgive me, I'm poorly practiced at pillow talk. I count the moments until this insanity with Sterling is over, and we can retreat back to our lover's bed. Yesterday was physically draining for both of us, I'm sure. Please excuse my need for some slab time before we have to deal with that fool-born, lout, Sterling. I've scheduled a wake-up call for you at ten. Feel free to wake me once you're up and about.*
> *You are my sweetest Cupcake!*
> *Love, your Fitz.*

Self-conscious about what the maid might see, Anna pondered what must have happened. *Where am I going to start?* Empty champagne flutes sat next to the bottle, turned upside down in the chiller. A path of damp bath towels trailed across to the credenza where the flat screen TV was pushed off center. Her memory did not budge when straightening the lampshades. The large oil painting over the credenza hung crookedly. If the room looked like this…Anna cautiously opened the French doors and sucked in a breath. The balcony chairs were pushed into a jumble and the tiny table toppled over. Their robes lay in puddles on the tile. She slammed the doors closed and turned, leaning against them, hoping the room would talk to her.

Anna rubbed at her temples, head in her hands, wishing she could blame last night's oblivion on the Magnum of Dom Pérignon White Gold. But no, physically she felt wonderful. Why then, was a chapter of her night missing? Anna prayed that restoring everything to order would download her memory.

Starting with the towel in front of the credenza, she bent and picked them up one by one, making her way to the bathroom. They were still damp, meaning they must have been used late into the night. She held them close to her, hoping for a revelation. They smelled invitingly of grapefruit bergamot.

A flash of memory assaulted her—*Rick, deliciously naked in the doorway holding a bath sponge and a bar of soap.*

*"You've been a dirty girl. You need a bath." What did I do?*

Anna startled at the sight of the tub full of bathwater gone icy, Fitz's sponge floating aimlessly. *Well, it is a huge tub...*

Balanced on the edge of the tub, a plate held bitten strawberry tops and a pared apple core. The knife on the plate seemed as old as Fitz's dagger. The blade tapered to a pinpoint. Two brandy snifters and a bottle of Grand Marnier shared the ledge behind the tub. Remnants of the liquor dried, and one snifter held a markedly deeper color haze. Anna stared at the pinprick on her left index finger. Had she flavored Rick's drink with her blood?

Slowly, a photo developed in her mind. *Fitz's head thrown back against the edge of the marble tub, his face a mask of ecstasy.* Somewhere in her faulty memory she knew she had been the impetus for his rapture, but how? What had she done, and most importantly, could she do it again? She clenched her teeth in frustration, a moan of pure defeat escaping her lips. She stared into the mirror over the tub and saw only her befuddled self. Anna dropped the towels on the mosaic floor and darted to the balcony for fresh air.

The sun was gloriously risen, as if to taunt her hazy start to the day. Anna took several calming breaths as she reached for their robes. Belatedly realizing she was naked, she wrapped herself in the first. It was Fitz's. His cologne was like a beacon. Wrapped in the robe's velour embrace, her back stiffened as memory assailed her.

*She stepped toward the railing, her hands reflexively outstretched to grasp the wrought iron. In her mind, Anna felt the chuff of his breath at her neck, the pressure of his fine form smack against her, his rhythm fierce and unrelenting as he drove hilt deep into her.* Flash and the pixels exploded to nothingness.

She hadn't been drunk—she wasn't hungover. Anna cursed her elusive memory. The last thing she vividly remembered was his kiss. What if this was the result of their unequal vamp/mortal life energies colliding? Are all mortals this disadvantaged? Would it always be like this?

There was a discrete knock on the hall door, and Player came running in, stubby tail wagging, body shaking, drawing Anna from her reverie. The here and now called to her more urgently, and she went into the kitchen to prepare Player's breakfast and focus on their upcoming meeting with Sterling. Fitz still hadn't explained the threat the dagger held over him, but he certainly seemed eager to have it back. Since she was the one who'd allowed it to be taken, she felt it was her duty to reclaim it.

* * * *

By ten, Anna was showered, dressed and appropriately made up to greet Sterling. The front desk rang with the wake-up call she'd forgotten to cancel, and she could hear Rick pick it up behind his closed door.

He emerged from his bedroom, wrapped in a light silk robe, hair tousled from the night before and an unmistakable hickey on his neck. Anna was mortified! She'd never given a hickey in her life, nor could she remember giving this one.

"Hey, wild woman!" Rick caught her up for a robust hug and morning kiss. "You look no worse for wear." He smoothed her hair back. "How do you feel?"

"Fine." Anna forced a bright smile. "Great. Never better." She returned his kiss enthusiastically. He touched her differently, she noticed. Somehow, more familiarly. "Ah…" she ventured. "Was there maybe an earthquake last night? I…"

Rick laughed. "An earthquake? Not that I'm aware of. Why do you ask?"

"Oh, it's just that furniture was moved, the pictures were tilted on the walls…"

He laughed uproariously and squeezed her in his embrace. "Well, the earth moved, but I don't think it was a natural disaster, just our own personal quake." He nuzzled and nipped at her neck.

"Oh…yeah…" Another bright smile. She resolved not to mention her unfortunate memory lapse, at least not now. There would be time after this threat from Sterling was resolved to talk about what happened last night.

* * * *

Anna opened the door to Sterling, every sense on alert. She didn't trust the slimy weasel one bit. She would do her best to follow the plan they laid out an hour ago. She knew she was safe. Rick was watching them from a camera discretely hidden in the wall clock. He'd burst through the door at any sign of trouble. She hoped Sterling wouldn't have a gun. It was hard to outrun a bullet.

"Please come in, Carl." She stood aside, wanting to avoid any show of affection. He entered the suite to Player's growl.

Sterling looked at the suspicious dog. "I can't believe you brought the dog. You can have him if you want. I inherited him from my Dad, I should have sent him to the pound." Player's growl became marginally more aggressive. If she didn't know better, Anna would believe the dog understood every word.

"I would love to take him," she acquiesced quietly. "I hope you like chicken. I ordered Sudado de Pollo."

Sterling shrugged. "Sure, whatever."

"Really, you're too kind," Anna said coldly.

He surveyed the suite. "This is a pretty fancy place. You have the dough to fly in with a dog, stay in a suite at the classiest hotel in town? I don't get that. How does that work, exactly?"

"I have a credit card, and a friend with a private plane. I figured once I'd sold the dirk…"

"Ah, yes, the dirk." Sterling rounded on her with a dangerous gleam in his eye. "*My* dirk. Just how did you figure you were going to sell it without me?"

"I always intended to give you some of the money, Carl," she lied smoothly. "I would have contacted you, but I couldn't find you. You weren't on a cruise as you'd said…"

"Right." Sterling countered sardonically. "You were going to cut me in."

Anna headed for a chair and sat shakily. Sterling started forward and would have towered above her if Player hadn't stood and placed himself between them, his lip curling warningly.

Sterling changed course and sat in an adjacent chair. "You know I could send you to jail for grand theft. I could probably tack on another charge for stealing the dog, and I'm guessing there's no record of you at Customs, so…"

"I don't understand, Carl. You want to sell the dagger, you stand to make a lot of money from it, and yet, you threaten me? So, I call off my buyer and you have no money. You do have the satisfaction of sending me to jail, but it seems like a bad deal to me."

"That's just it, Annie," Sterling sniped. "I've been considering this fifty-fifty split and *that* seems unfair to me. If you found a buyer, chances are I could too. Maybe I'd even get more money." Sterling's look turned sly. "Or, maybe I'll just keep the deal and give you a smaller cut. I think a finder's fee of two thousand dollars would be sufficient reward. Well, that and my promise not to call the Feds."

Anna frowned. She repeated the number just to stall for time. How should she play this? If she gave in too quickly, he might get suspicious, come on too strong and he might decide to call the cops. "I'm willing to negotiate." She said at last. "Two thousand is way too little cash. Let's say ten thousand, but you have to show me the dagger now."

"Show you the dagger?" Sterling snickered cynically. "So, you can hit me over the head or poison my lunch and take it? I don't think so. It's in a safe place away from here. Once you introduce me to the buyer, if I like the deal, I'll take him to it."

* * * *

Rick stood in the hall, not two feet from the suite door, watching the action from his cell phone. A grin cracked his handsome face. Anna was good, man, she didn't choke, and she thought on her feet. He was proud of her. Sterling had the dagger with him, alright. Rick was sure of it. He'd been playing some version of poker for five hundred years. He knew tells when he saw them, and if Sterling wasn't bluffing, he deserved to lose his seat at the World Series of Poker. He guessed the dirk was either secreted on Sterling's person—may be in one of those ridiculous cowboy boots, or maybe in the rucksack. The likelier would be the boot, closer to his person, harder to steal.

* * * *

Anna spent the rest of the time before lunch counter-offering the amount of money she'd accept as a finder's fee. It kept Sterling occupied. She was frustrated in her efforts to get him to produce the dagger, but she felt certain Rick would be able to get it, one way or another.

Sterling didn't blink an eye when Rick entered the suite wearing a hotel uniform, towel over his arm and announcing, "Room Service," in his perfectly accented Spanish. No, Sterling had been too preoccupied with threatening Anna to notice the tall, beautifully presented waiter.

Rick displayed their lunch with style. He stood behind Anna and to her left when he was finished.

"…then where will you be?" Sterling finished his latest round of threats. "A fifty-year-old crone straight from the slammer. Too young for social security and too tainted to work in bars. Poor little Annie."

"You always did have a flair for the dramatic, Carl."

"Yeah." Sterling stopped talking and eyed Rick standing behind her. "Why hasn't the waiter left?"

"I imagine he's waiting for a tip," Anna sniped. "Since you're the one with all the money now, why don't you pay him?"

* * * *

Rick watched Sterling surreptitiously reach for the unsheathed dagger in his right boot. He took a large step forward as Sterling grabbed Anna's hand and yanked it across the table, palm down.

"It would be a shame," Sterling gritted, poising the dagger directly over her hand, "to leave Annie with a crippled hand over a few thousand dollars, wouldn't it?" Sterling looked up at Rick.

"Senor…" Rick began, halting where he was.

Sterling rose and made the mistake of taking the dagger away from Anna's hand as he tugged her forward. It took Rick a millisecond to close the distance between them. *Put your hands on her? I'll kill you!*

Anna tugged back with all her weight, hurling herself into Rick, projecting them both back onto the floor and throwing Sterling off balance. Sterling supported his weight on his left arm, aiming the dagger at Rick.

Rick fought the irresistible inclination to turn and let the vampire have its way. *Don't turn! Not in front of Anna.* Though Anna saw his vampire-self released in passion, rage was a whole different animal, and one she might find horrifying.

Sterling defended himself with wild gestures, slashing the air within a centimeter of Rick's thigh, momentarily halting his advance. A bestial growl escaped Rick's lips. Sterling jerked the blade back, sliding away from the man who'd served his lunch.

*I could kill you with a snap of your neck*, Rick fantasized. Sterling spun, knees bent, with the priceless dirk held as if he were a gang member in a knife fight.

Rick saw Anna hesitate and move toward them. "Get back, Anna," he hissed. "Get into the bedroom and lock the door."

"How chivalrous," Sterling taunted. "Protecting the little woman when your plan goes sideways."

Anna stepped between them, her hands outstretched, palms forward in a calming gesture.

"Dammit, what are you doing?" Rick gritted.

Anna's voice was low and soothing, trying to de-escalate the situation. "If we wind up killing each other, what good is the money?"

Rick ground his teeth and turned his attention to Sterling. *Give me a reason.* "That's the best you've got? Gang style choreography? C'mon. You're the one with the knife. You just gonna crouch there?" Rick jeered at him over Anna's shoulder.

Sterling snarled, watching Rick straighten, ready for an onslaught. "No, you want this thing so badly, you come to me, pretty boy."

Rick was tempted. He glanced at Anna and saw her face was a mask of concern. *Not in front of Anna.* There was nothing he'd love more than to finish this guy right now. His brain burned, his fangs ached to drop. Reflexively, Rick dropped his chin to his chest. *Do not turn.*

Sterling began circling, thrusting, trying to back out the door. *This could be over in a heartbeat,* Rick reasoned. *Take your time and defeat him as a human.* Rick had a mental picture of the worst possible outcome in front of

Anna. *One moment I'm her lover, the next I'm the dead-eyed vampire, fangs bared, claws unsheathed, murdering a helpless mortal.*

"So, pretty boy," Sterling jeered, inching around the lunch table, "too gutless? Afraid I'll mess up that pretty face?"

*Don't turn!* Rick grimaced from the pain of repressing his nature.

Sterling danced in Anna's direction. Rick saw the impending strike and caught her by the shoulders, spinning her away from harm. *Just one quick move.* Rick narrowed his gaze in Anna's direction, calculating. *Do I have the cover?* Anna crawled away from where she'd landed on the floor and Rick knew instantly he'd never be able to hide the kill-punch from her.

In the seconds it took Rick to stay his hand from murder, Sterling jabbed repeatedly at his chest and gut, making contact but not deterring him. He gave Rick a look of pure consternation. *Kevlar vest, asshole. Don't turn!*

Rick punched his fist into his palm and spoke in perfect English. "For a dickhead, Sterling, I gotta say, you really piss me off!" Rick swung a pulled punch, his vampire reflexes missing Sterling by millimeters. He watched the guy's face pale. *That felt good.*

"Too bad, cuz I can do this all day!" Sterling snarled as he alternated stabbing and dodging.

Rick could hear his labored breathing. He gave Sterling a doubtful smirk. "Really? Did you bring your inhaler, Sterling? Rick danced from one Ferragamo to the other as he watched in amusement.

Sterling barked back, "This isn't a game, pretty boy." His breath wheezed.

Rick was at a breaking point. The internal fight with his vampire was more taxing than the duel with Sterling. His snarl was guttural. "You come in here, threaten my woman, dance around with my dirk?"

"*Your* dirk?" Sterling pulled the dagger high and away from Rick. "I don't think so."

"You try to stab me and think you'll get away with it?" Rick lunged forward, lightning fast and slapped Sterling's face.

At this point, Rick had done all he could to suppress the vampire. He needed to dial this thing down to done. Sterling gasped for breath. *Heart Attack? Well, that would end it.*

"You want to end this alive? Drop my dirk and bugger off." Rick ordered.

Sterling clutched his chest, the dirk in his fist. Rick froze, listening for heart sounds. *It's still beating—too bad.*

Sterling grimaced, dropped to one knee and sank toward the ground.

"Well isn't this convenient," Rick chortled. "I don't have to kick your ass, you're gonna kick it for me." Rick eased in, reaching for the dirk.

Sterling countered with an uppercut. Anna shrieked as Rick felt the dirk pierce his chest under the armpit.

Silence.

Rick's strangled roar shook the floor.

"You son of a bitch!" Anna swept a marble obelisk off the end table and swung it with all her might against Sterling's skull. He fell in a limp heap at her feet.

She stood stock still, hands shaking, eyes wide at the sight of Rick, panting on the floor with the dagger embedded deep in his chest. "Get...it...out..." He gasped. "Anna!" His urgency galvanized her to action. "Get it out, now!"

"You're not supposed to remove an object from a puncture wound," Anna objected with her farm-learned first aid.

"Get...it...out! I can't do it myself." Rick's eyes glared wide with desperation.

"Are you going to bleed? Will you gush?" Anna turned her head away but found the dirk easy to dislodge. It emerged thick with black-red blood. She grimaced at the sight and gagged. Rick slid away from her, toward the wall, holding his shirt tail to the open wound, trying to clean it.

"Are you bleeding?" Anna's words shook as hard as her shoulders.

"It burns, it's the silver, it hurts." Rick grimaced as the silver burned its way into his heart.

"Tell me how to help you." Anna leaned over him, her hand outstretched but hesitating to touch.

"Get away from me, Anna." Rick directed curtly, feeling his skin chill as it paled. "Get back." Anna stumbled a few feet away then stood gaping as Rick's field of vision narrowed. She shifted foot to foot in indecision. "I need all the blood." Rick repositioned, trying to evade the pain. "In the fridge....my...room, all...of...it." Rick gestured vaguely.

Anna fled to his room. Rick teetered on the edge of reason. *If Anna couldn't handle me sleeping on a slab, how will she deal with a dying demon?*

Anna drew up short when she returned, obviously aghast at what she saw. "Fitz, can vampires die?"

Rick pushed himself back up the wall. "I look that bad?" He rubbed his painfully dry eyes. His claws gouged a track across his eyelid to his cheekbone. The flesh peeled back as he blinked, trying to relieve the dryness. He reached out a desperate hand for the blood.

"Rick, you're blue." Anna shrank away.

"The blood, Anna! Toss me the blood!" His reach ended in split-skinned blue claws. "Don't come any closer…toss it, toss the blood to me."

Anna slid the three bags across the wooden floor.

One greedy hand grabbed the first blood bag to his aching chest. His hands fought to remove the plug. He shook as he lifted it to his mouth.

Anna sank to the floor leaning toward him until Rick halted her with a deep growl. He tilted the bag up and sucked it dry, "Close enough. Stay there."

"What?" Anna objected, even as she did as she was told.

"Don't make me talk." He panted, and she was immediately contrite as she registered the pain in his eyes.

"I'm sorry, I'm sorry. Just tell me what to do to help!"

Rick pulled the plug from the second bag and gulped it down more easily. He gasped with the last mouthful "How many left?"

"I brought them all, there were only three." Tears filled her eyes.

"Not enough." He murmured shakily. Rick pulled the plug on the last bag, in his unsteadiness, spraying precious drops everywhere. He raised his head. "Anna," His voice was stronger, commanding with his last ounce of strength. "Take my phone." He spun it to her. "The directory…an international number…Responders. Got that? Responders." He enunciated. "Go to your room, tell them who I am…where we are…I've been poisoned…silver."

"What…" She picked up the phone. "Rick, no. Take it from me…"

Rick downed the last pint, "You're crazy!" He snarled. "Never take you. Get out…lock the door…call. Tell them…emergency. Get here…fast. I swear to God, Anna don't make me show you…medieval…"

He glared at the wasted blood covering him. "I need more." Rick lowered his lips onto his forearms and hands, hungrily slurping every drop. He gritted his teeth and writhed in pain before finishing the last precious bag. "Call. Now. Get here quick…I need living blood."

"It's you or him, Rick." She looked at Sterling, still and deathly pale on the floor. She wasn't entirely sure he contained living blood. And oh my God, what did that mean? She'd killed a man? Well, in defense of another, but… "Do what you have to do."

"Call," He gasped as he slid toward the floor. Anna backed out of the room.

* * * *

Anna sat obediently on her bedroom's chaise. A responder named Raquel trooped in looking for all the world like an Emergency Medical Technician.

She leaned over Anna, professionally calm, questioning her in a soothing, accented voice. "Did you hit your head? Did you lose consciousness?" She felt Anna's head for bumps.

"No," Anna gazed dully at her medic insignia. "I hit him."

"No, he was never here. Rick went to the meeting alone." Raquel softly caught Anna's face and met her gaze. "You're feeling numb right now, Anna," she said firmly.

Anna's gaze seemed to fall deep into Raquel's unblinking ebony stare. "I'm floating."

Raquel held that unblinking gaze. "That's right, you're floating. You feel so comfortable, so relaxed, so peaceful…"

* * * *

"Senor, this is Senorita Moreau, please make an evening appointment for me at the bank. I've arrived at the Waldorf, I'm cash shy…" Veronique rolled over in the sumptuous bed and hit the button on the drapery's remote. The Panamanian night fell and headlights on Avenida Balboa darted as spasmodically as her thoughts.

She was a free woman. She'd paid her 'dues'. The Vampire Council had accepted Attorney Bellamy's offer of restitution. The billions she paid broke her financially. She did regret she hadn't hidden Papa's estate. Veronique's last hope was the contents of the safety deposit box in an obscure Panamanian bank, but she was hungry, and she couldn't think straight when she was hungry…

* * * *

Well, that was embarrassing. The contents of the safe deposit box was a parcel of damned emeralds, a deed to five acres of vacant desert in Bombay Beach, California and the spare keys to a 1999 Bentley Azure.

The emeralds were iffy, she'd have to sell them and to sell them she'd have to deal with mortals. *Uhh.* The property was a joke, it was an undeveloped desert. At least she could use the Bentley to perpetuate the image she exemplified.

Everyone she trusted was gone, dead. The architects for her destruction were Matt Brenner and Richard Hiatt and she would spend eternity to exact retribution.

* * * *

It took three emeralds to pay the storage on the Bentley. It took more to have it shipped, which was just as well as she could not afford jet airfare. When the ship docked in Long Beach, Veronique was worse for wear. Emotionally drained, nutritionally starved and a hundred percent travel weary, Veronique impatiently tapped the toe of her last pair of Louboutins as the car was uncrated and driven before her.

* * * *

"Ms. Morrison, we've reviewed your portfolio. I have good news and bad news." The real estate broker parsed out his words, attempting to gauge his new client's attitude.

Veronique hunched over a vodka martini in the country club lounge. With a sneer, she raised the glass to her suicide-red lips and sighed, "Lead with the bad news, Mr. Snyder."

The gangly man spread out the real estate specs, "I realize you haven't been to Los Angeles since you were a child and I'm sure your parents didn't discuss property values…" The man edged on her last nerve.

"Mr. Snyder, I apologize, I have a dinner date, could you be expedient?" Her nail tapped the empty martini glass in her hand. The thin man gulped and fast forwarded.

"Your property, Ms. Morrison, has seven to ten thousand dollars of value. Unencumbered as it is, we could acquire a mortgage, and you could bank the proceeds. There is no real estate in Los Angeles within your budget."

*If he gets out of here alive, it will be a divine miracle.* "So, what's the good news?" Veronique exhaled her tension.

"Well, uh, we do represent a concern expressing interest in parcels of this size for cash. It would be a lump sum, and we could close within fourteen days."

Veronique held out her hands and tilted her head, "How much?"

* * * *

Richard Hiatt and Anna Curley checked out of the hotel early. The sun hadn't revealed itself, as if to give the vampire his preferred cover of darkness. In the limo they avoided conversation, taking turns speaking to Player as if he were a three-year-old. *Was she recounting the whirlwind hours with sensual regard?* Rick wondered. Rick needed Anna, yet he turned away from her. His anxious fangs dropped to their full length, craving her.

His eyes grew heavy and although he was attended by the most renowned responder healers, he felt emotionally burdened and incomplete. It was a familiar feeling after dealing with an 'incident.' *Our survival was worth it. Yes, it's all worth it,* Rick convinced himself. In due course the physical healing would be complete. Emotionally, they needed time to reconnect.

* * * *

The Fitzjarrald dirk lay in Anna's lap. Since boarding the jet, her awe was reverently evident. "It's more beautiful than the portrait portrayed it."

"The portrait?" Rick cocked his head at her. "You saw that?" Rick ran his tongue over his lip, wondering exactly what else Anna discovered.

Anna's eyes widened, "You don't think I'd stay with someone unless I did my due diligence. Do you?" Anna carefully rewrapped the weighty dirk in its lambskin case and then she handed it to Rick.

She sought his gaze as he accepted the package. Rick's generally polished, metrosexual persona transformed since he brought back the historical masterpiece.

Now Anna's tone changed. "Fitz, did Sterling say if he was returning to L.A.?" Anna leaned back and adjusted the seat. She casually watched out the window as the ground crew completed their pre-flight routines.

"Sterling?" Rick's pause was a beat too long. "L.A.?... I doubt it. He looked as though he was headed anywhere but L.A." Rick fussed today, moving from place to place until he was satisfied with the right storage compartment for the dirk.

He returned to his seat next to Anna and caught her hand in his. He mirrored her watching the ground crew, "We expect to arrive around sunset, Cupcake." He brushed his lips across the palm of her hand, "I realize you're dressed, and you're ready for the day, is there any way I could entice you into the back?"

Anna softened within his touch, "Oh, Fitz, there are so many ways you could entice me, and probably a few ways we haven't discovered."

The aft cabin's ambient lights reflected deep blue. The turn-down service had left robes and slippers at the foot of the generously sized bed. Rick ushered Anna toward the bed and blessed her eye-lids with whispers of kisses. She shivered at the thrill as he simultaneously undressed her while his lips journeyed downward.

Once he knelt before her, he slipped off her ankle boots and slid down her pencil skirt. Standing barefoot in the peachy silk panties and bra she'd chosen at the hotel boutique, she felt she was the physical embodiment of her nickname. Like a groom, Rick caught her up and carried her to the center of the bed.

* * * *

"Don't you want me to undress you? I can handle those suspenders …" Anna sighed and stretched on the fluffy comforter. She'd flown down to Colombia a confused and curious girl and flew back to L.A. with the man she loved.

"You could dress me when we land, hum?" Rick offered, and Anna wiggled in the downy covers at the sight of Rick's particular style of disrobing, a striptease, treating her to the music of the snap of his necktie. Anna chuckled in surprise at his precision toss of cufflinks into the padded leather tray on the valet. His shirt waited like a faithful servant hung over the valet hanger.

Anna adored his well-built back as he sat at the foot of the bed to slide off his loafers and trousers. Preternaturally graceful, Rick stood and pivoted to face her, then slid his thumbs into the band of those deep blue silk boxers he favored. "What have I done that I get every part of your magnificent body?"

Rick shrugged, "And all my parts move." Just past his slender hips, the boxers fell to the floor leaving Rick gloriously naked.

* * * *

Sometime during Rick's undressing, Anna's hands traveled to find her nipple and her clit through the flesh-colored silk. Rick felt her heart thunder the second their lips touched. Now standing before her in silence, Rick posed offering himself. As Rick felt the figurative burn of her gaze, the curve of his phallus became more distinct. It rose from the inviting flesh at his thigh to the able and satisfying cock he hoped she held in the vault of her desires.

In the past forty-eight hours Anna ripened. Although the weekend's focus was based in espionage, Rick salvaged their time together with the best of food. His Cupcake wore the finest of those sumptuous dinners on her hips and in her breasts. The rose of her cheeks carried all the brilliance of the bottles of wine they shared.

Rick longed for her, his fangs itched to trail down her neck and take delicious advantage of her. She wiggled out of her panties and shot them directly at his cock. Rick shook his head at her as he stood, hands on hips, with silk panties hanging off his thick member like a game of chance. Even in her playfulness she was beautiful. *She sings to me, sings a melodious song of passions untapped and desires undiscovered.*

* * * *

The Captain's announcement that they had begun their descent jarred Anna from reading an article on her iPad. Rick playfully suggested she redress him before the flight landed and he hadn't opened the door as an invitation to play. She glanced at her watch and calculated he was horizontal over seven hours. Popping off the seatbelt she called ahead, "Fitz, this is your wakeup call, you promised I could dress you…"

No response. Her hand on the door, she peeked around it before entering, "Fitz? You up, baby?"

Anna knelt by his bedside, and saw he was every bit as ashen as the afternoon she'd discovered him on his slab. This evening he was markedly greyer. His lips were distinctly bluer, coordinating with his hands. Anna laid the back of her hand on his forehead, he was frigidly cold. She caressed his face softly and got no reaction. She pulled his hand into hers and chaffed his wrist until his bluish eyelids slowly lifted and he turned toward her. In a middle European accent, he drawled, "Good evening."

"Fitz, that's just wrong. If you're over five hundred years old, you must have better vampire humor than that."

There was a whisper of a smile on his pale lips, "Where do you think Bela Lugosi got it? It's a classic."

"Now you're going to tell me you were a film consultant?" Anna reached for his clothing.

"A story for another day, Cupcake," Rick deflected, as he rolled to put his feet on the floor. He held that position, his forearms on his thighs gathering strength. Anna handed him his socks, he rolled them back into her hand, "You promised you'd dress me." With that, he fell back onto the bed, his feet on the floor.

"Did Sterling slip you a mickey when you met with him? You look hungover, bad…" As she put his socks on, she noticed very blue toes and his feet were icier than a dog's nose in January.

"Like I'd drink with that minnow? He kept the meeting on point, and we parted ways," Rick answered curtly.

Kneeling before him she rubbed up one calf and then the other, "Do you feel cold?" She exhaled warm breath onto his thigh and rubbed some color back into him.

"I haven't been 98.6 in a long time, Cupcake, but if the plane wasn't about to land, we could do a fierce sixty-nine."

She was on her knees with him making bad sex jokes. It would serve him right if he had to take her licks. "If you're just going to lie there, I'm getting you dressed." Anna slid the boxers up his legs, and when he didn't sit up directly, she extended her hand to his and tugged. She stood to pull him with her and he stayed seated. His eyes unfocused, he blinked and reached out for the nightstand.

The jet lurched slightly, and Rick overbalanced and caught himself landing back on the bed. Anna returned to the bed with his trousers and scrutinized every aspect of his behavior. "Fitz, you weren't like this when we boarded the jet. There's something wrong with you."

He bent over, shoving one foot at a time into the pants. This time he stood up slowly, one hand on the nightstand, "You wore me out." His sly smile melted her worried heart.

She blanched at the thought of another night she couldn't recall. What about the other night's gymnastics? Now, last night was a complete wash on any carnal highlights. All Anna could recollect was their tuning in Casablanca and opening a bottle of wine. Player kept her company stretched out in the king-sized bed, his cold nose in the small of her back.

Rick sleepwalked into his shirt as Anna held it out to him, "Cufflinks?" she queried offering them in her palm.

"Not tonight." Rick pulled on his suspenders as Anna lovingly buttoned the waist and zipped up his fly, "Cupcake, you dress as well as you undress." His arms encircled her tenderly, and she noticed his stance widen to compensate for the jet's descent.

Anna held on tight, *Take my breath, do you need it?* She pressed into him, her head burrowed into the hollow of his neck, hoping to tease his earlobe with her fingertips. His lips found her neck as he brushed her hair away. "Hold me closer," Rick did, "Closer still." His kisses were unhurried, his lips dry and cold. *Fitz, let me breathe some life into you.*

* * * *

Before they could rise from their seats Adam loomed large in the doorway. Anna startled at his abrupt entry. "Hey, old man. I got a head's up on a serious note."

Rick narrowed his eyes and stayed seated. If this was about Veronique, they might have to file a flight plan for another trip. "Good to see you too, Adam."

"We've got the SUV set up." Adam directed his comment to Rick, and then thoughtfully turned to Anna. "We're going to get Rick comfortable, and I'll be back for you in a few." Adam's hand rested on her knee as his gaze homed in on hers. "Give us five or ten minutes." In an instant, he was up, his arm under Rick's and they were out of the jet.

Stunned, Anna sat, her palms sweating. *For certain, Rick isn't well. Do vampires get sick?*

The steward stood at the doorway, watching the SUV and Anna. Time crawled before the steward approached her and extended his elbow to escort her off the jet. She was uncertain about the past few days. *What am I walking into?*

# 14

The SUV's engine hummed as a trio of black autos waited. Adam held the rear passenger door open, yet no light illuminated the interior. He flashed a penlight and assisted Anna into the seat. Her seatbelt was locked, and the door closed before her eyes adjusted to the ebony interior. A gurney replaced the seat behind the driver, from which an IV hung. As the SUV moved from street lamp to street lamp, she identified Rick with a needle taped into his forearm.

Even with his eyes closed, he reached for her hand and softly squeezed it. "Have you ever gone on vacation and eaten really rotten food?" Rick joked.

The SUV pulled to a red light, and she saw the IV bag was blood.

Anna's breathing hitched, "You've been away from living donors. I told you I wanted you to snack on me." Her heart broke as the pieces of the puzzle began to make sense.

"It wouldn't have been enough, Cupcake."

Adam turned around from the shotgun seat, "We were alerted this morning. We didn't want to land the jet in an unfamiliar airport, so we gritted our teeth and hoped you'd make it this far." Anna sank back against the seat, edified her intuition was on point. *Why didn't I force him to feed? If he was ill, could he have taken too much?* Her brain nearly imploded with the possibilities, so she simply held his hand in silence and waited for the shafts of street light to illuminate his resting face.

"So, we didn't get much time to talk in Barranquilla, how did you enjoy yourself?" Adam asked pleasantly, as he watched the Rottweiler make a place on the gurney at Rick's feet.

"Why didn't you admit you were sick? I could tell, you know." Anna shook her head as Player slithered further from Rick's feet to his hips.

Rick answered above the static in the SUV, "If I were human, they'd have medicated me. Just consider this an oil change."

Anna reached her limit, "Rick, they're transfusing you. I'm no vampire M.D., but even Player is concerned." The dog rested his head on Rick's shoulder.

Adam shook with laughter at the sight of big, bad Richard Hiatt under one hundred and forty pounds of dog. "I didn't know Rotties were lap dogs." Player rose and licked Adam's face.

* * * *

The elevator door slid open, and Player lurched out of Anna's grasp. Barking and loping the dog sped toward the living room. Anna played with the IV pole rollers to lead Rick out of the elevator. The bark echoed over the penthouse's hard surfaces.

"Player's hungry, that jet wasn't ready for him," Anna remarked as his barking escalated.

Rick inhaled and shook his head. "He's barking at Matt."

Anna checked herself, she felt she carried a day of travel on her face. She wanted a shower, she wanted to take off her shoes, she was hungry. *It's too much to see Matt again.*

The three of them rolled in to find Matt in his usual spot on the overstuffed sofa. Anna recalled his customary manspread, with his left arm along the back of any sofa he occupied. *Why is his body language inviting when he enforces hard limits on Vamp/Mortal relationships?*

Tonight, Matt leaned back with the massive Rottie standing between his knees, a broad paw on either side of his quarry's neck. Matt was nose to nose with the inquisitive dog.

"What is this?" Matt asked mildly. Player barked an unintelligible answer.

In unison, Anna and Adam replied, "It's a dog."

Rick shook off Adam and Anna to stand alone with the IV pole, "Player." The dog obediently returned to Rick's side. "Player, this is your new friend, Matt Brenner."

Matt knelt and extended the back of his hand to Player. The dog moseyed around Matt actively sniffing every possible inch of the dark-haired vampire. Matt chucked under the dog's chin and established his dominance, and Player answered with a wide yawn and a string of slobber.

Once Rick and Matt's handshakes and embraces had concluded Anna slipped behind Rick and silently guided him to the nearest chair. She felt Matt's inspection as she rolled the pole closer and Adam adjusted the flow on another pint of blood. When Adam and Matt pulled chairs closer to Rick, she turned and automatically asked, "May I get you gentlemen refreshments?"

Out of the corner of her eye, she saw Adam and Matt exchange looks.

Matt smiled politely as he got comfortable on the sofa, "Lots of changes around here. Do you have a list of talking points for me?"

Rick winked at Anna, and then spoke directly to Matt, "Anna's off the menu now. Adam, could you find us a beverage or two, please? Perhaps a coke for the lady?"

Rick rose from the chair to move to the opposite sofa where he patted a spot next to him. Anna burned inside. *Of course, I'm off the menu. Matt banned me months ago.* She would do anything for Fitz, even stand up to Matt Brenner's scrutiny. She sat beside Rick and evidently not close enough. He extended his free arm around her shoulder and slid her closer, his hand caressing her gently.

Anna was determined to keep eye contact with Matt. He nodded to Rick and then Anna, "So, how did this happen?"

Rick shook the IV pole and laughed, "Bad South American food." Anna knew what Matt meant, and she wanted to hear it from Rick's mouth.

Matt clarified, "How long have you two been a couple?"

Anna felt Rick's gaze from her knees to her eyes, he was comfortable next to her, "One night we ran into each other in the garage."

Matt ran a hand through his hair and prodded. "The garage, at night?"

Adam returned with a decanter and four glasses, a bottle of cola in his pocket, "Matt, I've got to take credit for this."

Anna prepared to be mortified.

Adam poured drinks while he spoke, "We had a bit of a situation, and we were already in Colombia. Rick gave me instructions and spell-check flubbed it."

Rick butted in, "It would be those paws you call thumbs. Anyway, Matt, she arrived at my suite with the dog. What could I do but fall in love with her?"

Rick caught her hand and kissed the back of it before placing it on his thigh.

Matt answered too quickly, "Who can argue with love?"

Anna took slight offense at the cliché, thinking it a blanket statement dismissing his friend's involvement with a mortal. Anna wanted out of there. She extracted herself and reaching for Player's leash, spoke to Rick in a whisper, she knew they all heard anyway.

"Fitz, you have important things to catch up on. I'm taking Player for a walk, and I'll get something to eat. I might be gone a while." Rick reached for his money clip, and she waved that off. She'd be damned to take something from him in front of Matt Brenner.

As long as she was in their sight, she walked purposefully erect. Once behind closed doors, she furiously stripped off the clothes Rick chose for her. Out came her yoga pants, tank top and her UCLA hoodie. She found a few dollars and her ID and slipped out by the service elevator.

* * * *

"Well, Player, that was the longest ten minutes of my life." The Rottie looked somberly at his mistress as they approached the fast food window. "A large Butterfinger shake, chili cheese fries, a double bacon cheeseburger and one triple burger, plain." She stood, seeing herself in the security camera screen, and barked at the image, "Don't judge me, I've had a bad day."

Player danced around the heavy bag of food, sniffing for his reward. Anna found a table under a broad swath of park light and spread out her calories for the month. "Somebody probably should have mentioned the elephant in the room." Player followed the fry she gestured with. "There's something wrong with Rick and none of them would say it!" The Rottie snapped at the next fry she wagged.

Anna squirted the ketchup packet and dropped it angrily. "Matt spoke like I was…!" Anna sucked an inch of milkshake down, and then bit her burger. While she chewed, she unwrapped Player's dinner. The dog ignored her tirade as long as he had food. "…Insignificant! How can I be with his best friend and partner if Matt won't speak to me?" The more Anna ate, the more scattered her thoughts became. "Forget I'm there with Rick, Matt didn't even mention his wife."

Matt Brenner drew a line between mortals and vampires. He was aloof, and the mortal women loved him even more for it. Anna, the donor, had been banished and Anna, Rick's girlfriend, took her place. *If I'm with Rick, there will have to be a truce.*

* * * *

Once Anna was gone Matt jumped Rick with what was really on his mind. He gestured to the I.V. pole. "What happened here?"

Rick rattled the pole and nodded, "I'll give you the Cliff Notes. A mortal, a guy who saw himself as a vampire slayer, had property of mine. Cupcake and I set our sights on retrieving it. There was a skirmish, and when the bastard came in for the kill, he missed the vest and got me."

Matt grimaced in sympathy. "Silver poisoning?"

Rick nodded. "The funny part? Anna swung the home run."

Matt looked around the room. "Does she generally carry a baseball bat?"

"A marble obelisk. Killed him. Saved my life."

Matt leaned forward. "Did he know what you are?"

Rick expected Matt's hyper-concern. "The guy wouldn't know a vampire if he was at Comic-Con."

"Who handled the cleanup?"

"The responders. They did disposal, cleanup and thralled Anna."

Matt sprang to his feet, anxiously pacing the length of the sofa. "You've got too many loose ends, and that thralling thing, does it ever work?"

Rick tapped his foot and drew Matt back in front of him, "Let's not borrow trouble. They've been doing this for hundreds of years. They're professionals."

Matt dug both hands deep in his jeans pockets, "Right, because that worked so well with Cat."

Rick quieted. "The subject is closed." He smiled briefly to soften the sting of the abrupt dismissal. "Look, Adam has been trying to get his news out since the jet landed."

Adam sat straighter on his chair and took the floor. "The Council convicted Veronique on all charges." That earned him Rick and Matt's full attention.

* * * *

Adam continued. "However, they declined termination or jail time, and levied restitution."

Rick groaned in disappointment.

"They know how money driven she is. They broke her financially."

Matt shook his head in skepticism. "Did they believe this type of punishment would reform her?"

Rick joined in disapproval. "As long as she can make Humanité, that's like printing money. She won't be broke long."

"No, they outlawed Humanité and made selling or using it punishable by immediate termination."

"Nothing reforms a psychopath," Rick observed bitterly.

Adam nodded agreement. "The ruling gave money to some of the survivors. Matt, you're on the list for one point five million. They took billions. She's supposedly destitute."

"Less money means fewer resources to cause chaos, I guess." Matt turned to Rick. "Don't you own all her sire's land in Haiti?"

"Yeah, well, I have the signed document, but I've never executed it. If I did, I'd have to pay one hundred million for essentially worthless land, and she would know I was the one who killed Papa." Rick considered. "I wouldn't trust that Ronnie is ever destitute. If I know her, she's got diamonds hidden in an anthill or something. Where did she go when she was released?"

Adam rubbed at his forehead. "That's just it…she seems to have disappeared…"

"Well, Zip-a-Dee-Doo-Dah." Matt exploded. "I guess I can use the million and a half for enhanced security."

"Yeah. She's out and about, and we don't know where."

Rick's exasperated, "Son of a scandalous cur!" Broke their stunned moment of silence.

"All bets are off, and that psycho bitch could be anywhere planning anything," Matt said grimly. "Since she's not the forgiving sort, I'm guessing she's heading for us." He glanced at Rick, sat back and crossed his arms across his chest. "How serious are you about this mortal?"

Rick's face went stony, and his movements became precise. He removed the IV from his forearm and slid the pole aside. His hands fisted one inside the other as he leaned forward, forearms resting on his thighs. He felt aggression rising within him and struggled to dial himself back one degree to assertive. "Call her that again. See what happens."

Matt drew a calming breath. "I'm not looking for a fight, she's your business. I need to know where we all stand. If Veronique's coming, we've got to have a plan."

"You know the target's on your back, Rick." Adam nodded.

"And, Veronique won't come at you head on," Matt deduced. "She'll head for your soft spot." Matt's summation hit the mark he was aiming for and weighed heavily on Rick.

"I watched the questioning, Matt, she still has you in her sights, too," Adam parried. "In fact, I'm guessing Rick is her last target. She's going to pick us off in order of vulnerability. She wants all the destruction laid at Rick's feet. Then she'll go in for the kill."

Rick stared at his hand, folding down fingers as he spoke. "Anna will be the first, because she's my weakness." He nodded at Matt. "Then Cat. Then you, Adam, because you witnessed the massacre, then Matt. By the time she gets to me this is going to be up close and incredibly silent." Rick stared at the bottom of his empty glass. "We have to protect the women."

Matt reacquainted himself with the L.A. nightscape out the window, his back to the others. "How do we do it without scaring the crap out of them?"

Rick slid back against the sofa and nodded. There was a silent beat as they drained their glasses and passed the decanter for another. Adam declined a refill. The testosterone settled and became grim contemplation.

"I guess I shouldn't have taken credit for getting you two together?" Adam made an obvious effort to break the tension. Matt and Rick chuckled wanly. The huge man rose. "I'm gonna go wrap up a few of the security details I've been handling while you were out of town, Matt. You couldn't be back at a worse time, but I'm sure as hell glad you're here." Adam left them to deeper discussions.

Matt rested his glass on his thigh and pointed to Rick, "Cupcake? Fitz?"

"Cupcake, yes. What?" He smiled wryly. "She never struck you as a cupcake?"

Matt snorted. "Helen called her a bonbon. Yeah, so ah…" Matt started awkwardly and frowned.

"Look," Rick interrupted, "anything that happened between the two of you before we met is history. We …don't …speak…about it."

Matt nodded silently and stared into the bottom of his glass.

"How are you going to break it to your wife that Veronique is afoot?"

Rick watched Matt's unmoving silhouette at the window.

"Tonight, while we're getting settled downstairs. Of course, I'll have to include her when we have these discussions. She doesn't like second-hand news."

"We need more cameras, more trip sensors, self-defense classes. When Brett was staked, he couldn't discern voices or the mortal's scent," Rick thought out loud.

Matt spun on his heel. "When did this happen?"

Rick stretched out on the sofa, his chest beginning to ache again. "About a week ago. The guy from Colombia staked Brett in an alley."

Matt paced closer. "What's happening to the Los Angeles vampires?"

Rick chuckled. "You go away, and shit happens." Rick read Matt's alarm, "Calm down, it's all been handled. We got lazy and we had a wake-up call. The threat has been contained. He worked alone, and he's been neutralized." Rick knew he baited Matt's curiosity with that concise comment.

"The threat has been neutralized? That's a little sanitary for your vocabulary, buddy."

Rick sat back up, crossed one ankle over his knee, and threw up his hands. "Once a cop, always a cop."

"Wasn't there a reason I handled these things?" Matt lifted the decanter and figured the contents were about one last serving, he poured it into his glass and drank it down.

Rick parked his hand over his heart. The pains were coming around again.

"Have you found evidence—"

"Stifle it, Matthew."

Matt threw his hands on his hips and shook his head, "Have you lost your mind?"

"Unless you plan on departing tomorrow evening for an extension of the love boat, may we table discussion for now? Detective Brenner, did you notice my entrance with the I.V. pole? It wasn't my dance partner. This evening we need not fear vampire slayers—the Cupcake took him down." Rick swelled at the satisfaction of repeating that news.

Matt cast a sideways look, "Tomorrow night, we talk. We talk in depth over the myriad of questions I'll have by then."

"Because you will," Rick mumbled as he struck his chest over his heart, "I'll stake a c-note on that. How about a change of subject? It's been months since we've had a heart to heart."

Matt ran his tongue over his bottom lip and his eyebrow arched. He walked over behind the sofa and leaned into Rick's ear. "A while back I told you, Anna's a nice girl." Matt straightened, hands on hips. "So, I'm asking you again, how serious are you?"

Rick enflamed at the question. "Don't throw that wedge between us!" Rick rose to face his friend over the sofa, "Don't I deserve nice? She's more than a nice girl." Rick circled the sofa to meet Matt toe to toe. "She came here to warn you about the vampire slayer. She accepted you were gone, and she wanted to make sure we knew about a threat to the Family. When it all came down, she took care of us, all of us." The tension rekindled.

"I…just…want to know how serious you are… Is this 'now serious' or 'forever serious'?"

"Well, you tell me! It happened to you and Cat. How did you know? One night with the girl and you were cashing in your chips and heading out of town. I prefer to stay here and figure it out with her."

"Are you ready to turn her?"

"If she wants it…" Rick's hand sliced the air in frustration. "When is anybody ever 'ready' to turn? You weren't, I wasn't." Rick's boyish smile erupted, "It's like buying an R.V. or getting a spray tan—it happens when it happens."

No amount of bad humor stopped Matt's grilling. Truth be told, Matt was the only one who could strip bare Rick's emotions. "You love her." Matt declared.

Rick frowned. *Love is a long-lost word.* "Yes, and I'll do whatever it takes to protect her."

Matt nodded. "I've still got renovations going on at my…er…*our* loft…"

Rick smiled at his friend. "It's different when you have to remember 'we' and not 'I', isn't it?" He laughed wryly. "I'm stumbling myself." He walked to the desk drawer and pulled out two key cards. "You can stay in your playroom, but I think you'll be more comfortable in the unit below. It's clean and the linens are fresh. Make yourselves at home."

Matt accepted the cards. "I agree. I'll have to talk it over with Cat."

"You two can't stay at the Biltmore, what's the discussion?"

Matt laughed and pocketed the cards. "There's always a discussion, Buddy." The two men walked toward the elevator. "Would tomorrow night be a good time to introduce the ladies?"

"The sooner, the better. Anna knows you're married to a vampire, but she doesn't know any details. By the way, she's living here with me."

Matt raised a brow and disappeared into the silent elevator.

* * * *

Rick stripped off his travel clothes and showered. He welcomed the peace inside these four marble walls. Toweling off, he decided it was time to feed fresh. Under his regular close inspection in the mirror he saw his color returning. Rick threw on virgin wool trousers and a cashmere sweater. Checking his watch, he stepped into his loafers, sans socks, and headed downstairs. Shortly he'd feel a hundred percent.

* * * *

Anna led the dog into the fashionable lobby. "Now that I've eaten enough for the week we'll go upstairs and get you settled. I'll bet Fitz has two hundred channels of cable to watch." She nodded at the cherubic guard, he touched his cap's visor and the private elevator door opened.

She saw the empty decanter next to the three Baccarat old fashion glasses. The men were gone. *When did normal become picking up after two vampires and a shapeshifter?* "Fitz, are you here?" Her call echoed back. *No, he isn't.*

She ran out of reasons to stay upstairs. It was way too early, and she was conflicted. Anna wound her hair into a messy bun and turned on Animal Planet for Player. Her linear logic told her Rick would naturally gravitate to vamps. As she left the penthouse she called, "If you find a shoe, have at it…Unless it's mine!"

* * * *

Nervously, she flipped the key card. *Will it work throughout the building?* Mortals were food and Rick had to feed. *He left the penthouse for fast food, too.* She had to see what dazzling dishes were on the menu. With trepidation, she slid the key card into the reader and pressed "G", for Gaoler, not for Ground. The forty-some floor drop began.

Anna hovered near Rick's dungeon. She slid off the hoodie and tied it around her neck, pocketed the key card and let down her messy bun. A bare neck was an invitation she didn't extend. His dungeon was dark, he had to be elsewhere. She felt invisible. Couples passed her deep in conversation and groping.

Thinking he might be meeting with Helen, Anna headed to the office, past the demonstration area. Couples gathered to watch the demo in the subtly lit room. The usual erotic paraphernalia was gone, leaving the feeder centered onstage, back to the audience, on a simple wooden chair.

The donor entered from the side of the stage. The feeder laid back into the slight angle of the chair, his knees spread offering a wider seat for the woman in the diaphanous jumpsuit. She was statuesque, perhaps because of the piles of dark curls stacked on her head, leaving her neck deliciously available.

Anna had never watched a couple feed. The demos, performed in near darkness, were to titillate the undead. She squinted to see the feeder's hand beckon the donor. Her lips moved, but there was no sound. Anna saw the crowd multiply. A woman sidestepped into her personal space, they brushed shoulders briefly.

"Please excuse me, did I step on your foot?" The blonde beside her was flawless. Her open smile and clear blue eyes drew a smile to Anna's face.

"Oh, no. It's okay," Anna replied, not taking her eyes from the arena.

The blonde whispered, "I want to see this. Sometimes I feel clumsy when I'm feeding."

Anna felt she was hearing confession. That got her attention, "Feeding? You're…" Anna couldn't tell, the girl looked so *west coast.*

"Just a few months." The confession continued.

"I'm a donor." *Shut up, she can tell from my cheeseburger body spray.* Anna sneaked a sniff of her clothing.

The donor strolled to the feeder's shoulder and their heads tilted together for a second, and then she presented her wrist.

Anna leaned her head toward the woman. "Is it attraction that makes it hotter?" The feeder drew the donor across his lap, supporting her back with one arm. His head bent reverently, scenting the length of her arm.

The vamp shook her head, "If there was an attraction, it could be problematic to a vamp's personal relationship. For him?" She nodded at the vamp on stage, "I think it's his natural elegance." Anna guessed that wasn't learned within a few months.

Abruptly, the feeder rose, embracing the donor as if she were air. Her arms wrapped around the feeder's neck, as he caught her behind the knee and swung her legs around his waist. It was executed as sharply as a ballet's pas de deux. The donor's head fell back relaxed, her lithe, pale neck exposed.

The crowd gasped. The feeder lowered them both to the chair where her high-heeled feet rested on pegs on the chair's back legs. Anna's breath caught as the donor's knees tightened around the feeder's hips and she ground her perfectly shaped ass into the feeder's lap. "I'd imagine it's a little different for you, hum?" Anna whispered as she became further mesmerized by the dance.

"Hmm, yeah. Roles reversed aren't quite so…Come this way, this is his third feeding tonight. I want to see his face." She caught Anna's hand moving to get a better view of the vampire's face.

As the feeder and donor were in full profile, Anna froze. Rick was the feeder. Anna didn't know the donor, but she was the most zaftig donor she'd ever seen. Now, watching from the side, it was too close, too personal. Rick's fangs dropped as he studied the donor's décolletage. When he caught the woman's neck in one hand, Anna's stomach churned. His lips parted to reveal hungry fangs and her heart jumped. He nuzzled at the donor's neck, chose the vein and struck. Vampire and mortal melted together as the donor swooned to orgasmic completion. *This is damned near pornographic!*

Anna stepped behind her new friend, hiding when the donor's moans escalated. The ingénue vampire fisted her hand, drew her knuckle to her own fangs, and sighed. It was more than Anna could watch, "I gotta go…" and she darted toward the elevator.

"Don't go, yet." The blonde vampire caught up to Anna. "Please, would you want to have a drink….? Not you… I mean in the bar."

Anna was horrified to admit this ingénue was possibly the perfect match for Rick. In that light, she examined her reluctance to drink with the vampress. Her insecurities about attracting men were deep-seated. *How can Rick prefer me to some of these stunning mortal donors?* That alone left her self-doubting and when she looked at the new competition that feeling rose even higher. Now, she realized, she faced rivalry with flawless vampire women, as well. Rick had so much more in common with them, what could she offer that the woman in front of her couldn't top in every way? Her qualms soared to the moon.

"It's been such a long time since I've had a girlfriend to talk to," the blonde implored. "I'm Cat, what's your name?"

"Anna…" She couldn't help smiling at the vivacious vampress before her. *Wow, I never thought about female vampires before."*

* * * *

A server made his way to the booth Anna chose, the same one she shared with Rick. "Ginger ale, please," Anna ordered.

Cat folded her hands on the table, "Oakheart and a splash of O positive." She settled in the booth and gave the room a scan, "I hope I'm not keeping you from anyone. Do you have a date?"

"No, my friends are busy tonight." Anna played with a strand of her hair, pushing it behind her ear. *What do you say to a Gen-X vampire?* She needed a girlfriend in the worst way. It was hard to experience all she had in the vampire world without sharing it. Cat had to see things from a slightly different perspective but surely, if she was recently turned, they shared similar experiences. Maybe this warm, engaging blonde would be her friend? Perhaps even a confidant?

They stared at each other's manicures for a beat. Anna noticed a humongous diamond ring on her new friend's left hand. *A married vampire. Good, not competition!* Cat tapped her nail at Anna's tapered manicure. "That is unique, what style is that?"

Anna giggled but self-consciously curled her nails under. "You won't believe this, they're called coffin nails."

Cat clinked her glass in a toast. "How apropos."

They laughed and sipped.

Anna crossed her arms on the table and leaned toward Cat. "What do you think about that demo? Do you think he's hot for the donor?"

"I asked my mate the very same question when we got down and dirty about feeding. I was so jealous." She shook her head and waved a dismissive hand. "Now, I know its sustenance. We need blood like you need food. It's not personal."

"So, feeding's never personal?" Anna felt deflated.

Cat reached over and put a reassuring hand over her new friend's. "Here, there are definite lines between feeders and donors. It's a business. It all depends on the context."

"Did you feed anyone before you were turned?"

"No. I started off feeding from my sires."

Anna's jaw dropped. *Sires? I don't know her well enough to pry into that.*

"… and also bagged blood. I've only recently started feeding fresh and being a newbie, they started me on the wrist."

Anna knew she got off when she fed Matt from her wrist, "It's good for us, it is. In fact, that's the only way I ever fed vamps." *And I only fed Matt Brenner.* "Does a vampire get off on feeding the way donors do?"

Cat grinned mischievously, "Well, you know vamps have to bite before they come. Now, that doesn't mean they orgasm every time they feed, it's not the same thing…"

Anna's mind flew to her lost night. She knew Rick bit her, she had the marks. *I missed his orgasm, Dammit! So, if Rick feeds from me…*

Cat's glossed lips wrapped around the straws, "I'm not exceptionally strong yet, that will come. Right now,…. Oh, you don't want to hear tales of the most awkward vampire in Los Angeles…"

Anna's eyes widened at the thought of picking her brain. "Oh, yes I do!" They shared the laugh.

"Well, okay, I'll tell you what I can. What do you want to know?"

"In the demonstration tonight, you mentioned there was something about that feeder's natural elegance?"

"Oooh, that's Rick Hiatt! He's one of the owners of the club and probably the most proficient Dom here. He's several hundred years old, he's schooled, and I hear his gift of empathy gives a donor the most exquisite experience."

Anna squirmed in her seat. *Nothing like talking to a cheerleader for your lover. Nice to know he's held in high esteem.* Anna fought the urge to moon over the romance of it. She had to get off the subject of Rick. "I'll need a few viewings to process the sight of a vamp feeding live."

"Ah, you know bottle vamps?" Cat had a sense of humor. "The first twenty years are the worst, the way one of my sires described it. I've been lucky my mate has paid a lot of attention to my adjustment. I'm sure I give him fits. He isn't ancient, so we're making our way together." Cat ran her finger in the wet circle on the table, "I've never seen a place like this in action. We've been solitary since my turning, I've had to pick up feeding tips here and there."

*Stop nodding at her like a ninny.* "Do you think it would be harder if your sire was a few hundred years old? You know, like you have to catch up?"

Cat shrugged, either thinking it unimportant or without an answer. "In Los Angeles it's a young town. While my mate and I were on the coast of Spain and Italy, the vamps were positively ancient!"

*She's giggling like a sorority sister dishing about the nearest frat house and I want answers to a final exam.*

"Trust me, the feeding is just food. Your man wouldn't get upset if you smiled at your server at a steak house, would he?" Cat prattled on.

"Your face just lit up when you mentioned steak." Anna narrowed her eyes suspiciously, "do you miss eating?"

*She's certainly hungry for conversation,* Anna thought as she unconsciously touched her right wrist and flashed back to her last feeding. Matt's bite left her wet for hours. In fact, she extenuated the sensations in the locker room shower when she touched herself. Although she prized Matt's bite, Rick's kiss blew through every scintilla of her body, mind and heart.

* * * *

Rick felt phenomenal, physically. He gave three superb bites in a row and carried each of the donors to comfortable chaises in the next room. The living blood was the ultimate cure for what ailed him. The trade off? His mind ran laps faster than the Indy 500 anticipating Veronique's power play.

# 15

"Cupcake? Player?" Rick entered the brightly lit penthouse and found Player curled on the sofa opposite the flat screen watching Puppy Planet. "Son of a nutcracker, great watchdog you are. I could be robbing this place." Player raised his large head off his paws and cocked his head, nonplussed.

Rick checked the time, unclipped his watch and placed it carefully on the burl wood tray of the sofa table, next his money clip and phone. 5:41 in the morning. Unless Anna found an all-night, all you can eat burger joint, she should be home. Okay, he spent time chatting up folks visiting from the London Gaoler, but where was Anna? Cupcake should be home with Player.

Urgently, Rick tapped commands to bring up security cameras. *She wouldn't go to the ...* Rick gasped. He laughed and dialed the apartment below. "Dear boy, why don't you flip on security camera twelve and watch a bit of I Love Cupcake?"

"Not on your life, why would I want to watch the two of you make out in the bar?"

"Oh, I'm not in the bar. Your wife and my girlfriend have their heads together down there."

* * * *

"Listen," Anna dropped her volume for confidentiality. "Have you ever heard of a vamp and mortal having sex, but the mortal not remembering it?"

Cat looked around the bar, took in a sensing breath, and slid closer to her new friend. "I wish I could say I had more experience with vamp/mortal relationships. I'm sorry Anna, I just don't know. Did that happen to you?" Cat thought for a moment. "You know, I could ask Rick, he'd certainly know."

Anna groaned. *How in the name of God is this new vampire on a first name basis with Rick Hiatt?* "Rick who?"

"Hiatt, of course."

*Of course. Why not? Kill me now. Hit me in the head with a shovel and bury me below this building.* Her green eyes met Cat's blue eyes. "So, you know Rick."

"Sure. He's one of my sires."

*Life with Rick Hiatt is like dating an octopus. I'm pulled and pushed in every direction. His life is certainly complicated, especially with the other sex. There was Veronique, tonight's donor, and this perky blonde who claims he is 'one of her sires.' Is this vampire status quo?*

Anna's hands fell to her lap and she placed them protectively over the sinking feeling in the pit of her stomach. "So… who's your other sire?"

"Matt Brenner." Cat smiled dreamily. "He's also my mate," she added with delight, as she caught his scent entering the bar. Cat waggled her fingers at Matt and Rick. In a heartbeat she was out of the booth and greeting Rick with a baby bear hug. "Hi, Dad! Come meet my new friend!"

Rick's lips curled boyishly. "Hello, Cupcake."

Anna waggled her fingers like Cat and winced. "Hey, Fitz. Have a seat, there's room for two more."

Rick checked the time where his watch had been. "Well, you must be one tuckered cupcake. You've been up for twenty-four hours…"

"Oh, that's okay, I've recently heard news that has me wide awake."

He stood, rubbing the back of his neck. "News? Huh, well, does everybody know everybody?"

Matt shifted uncomfortably from foot to foot. "Looks like they're getting ready to close. Why don't we adjourn this party upstairs?"

* * * *

In the elevator, Rick wrapped a protective arm around Anna, which she removed, to stand stiffly by his side. Matt wrapped his arm around Cat, who looked at him questioningly, not understanding the cause of the underlying tension permeating the air. Rick ripped the band aid off. "So, Cat, I guess Anna told you she was Matt's donor before he met you?" Matt had nowhere to look.

Anna closed her eyes in mortification and exhaled. Cat's bewildered gaze swept them all.

*If looks could kill…* Rick thought accurately.

Matt ran his hand down his face, trying to think of something to say that would cut the tension.

Cat spoke up. "Why didn't you tell me you knew Rick and Matt?"

Anna shifted uncomfortably. "I didn't want to throw Rick's name around. You didn't say who your sires were. I figured that was private." Anna turned to Rick. "We haven't had vampire Family protocol classes yet." She poked a finger into his chest and rolled her eyes, a gesture Matt and Cat couldn't see. "I guess the proud sires don't send out 'turning' announcements." She turned to Matt. "Congratulations are in order." She extended a hug to Cat. "And best wishes. I can tell you're both over the moon about each other. Fitz is ready to hit the slab, so perhaps tomorrow evening you and I can have drinks by the pool and get to know everything about each other?"

Cat clapped her hands around Anna's "We just got into town. We're in the apartment beneath Rick until our place is ready. I have to pick up a few things. You wanna go shopping? I haven't shopped in months."

"Come get me when you're up. I just moved in with Fitz. I'm sure these two big lugs…" She threw an acid glance at Rick and Matt. "…can take care of themselves for a few hours."

The elevator door opened, and Matt and Cat exited. "Tomorrow then!" Cat called excitedly.

"Bye!" Anna waved, while Rick and Matt exchanged stony looks as the doors closed. Anna pivoted on her heel into Rick's chest. "Make new friends but keep the old…"

"You've gotta watch out for the silver," Rick snarked.

Anna turned a sad look of betrayal to Rick. "Why didn't you tell me?"

Rick frowned. "It all happened so fast. I intended to tell you Cat was here. You didn't come home. Why would you go to the Gaoler alone?" The elevator doors opened on the Penthouse, and Rick drew her to the sofa. "I need to be serious. You left before Adam shared his news."

"I got some—" Rick placed a silencing finger on her lips.

"This is bigger than all of us, just listen for a minute." Rick watched darkness and confusion color Anna. *This mortal has been through too much in the past week.* Rick poured a brandy and put it in her hands. "We have some enemies."

"Who is 'we'?" Anna whispered as she held the glass up to her mouth.

"Well, it's really Matt and me. Unfortunately, you, Cat and Adam are in the crosshairs too."

"Who's the enemy?"

"You heard us talk about Veronique Moreau in Colombia."

Anna nodded.

"She was tried, and they've taken away the majority of her power, but she's crazy as a bag of snakes. We don't know how long it will take for her to mount an assault, but she'll be coming for me and anyone close to me."

Anna steadily sipped her brandy, all emotion drained away, leaving only her desire to be with Rick. "So, this could happen next year for all you know?"

"Ronnie has no impulse control. She'll strike at the first opportunity." He poured himself a brandy. "That's why I don't want you going anywhere without protection, and never to the Gaoler without me."

Anna nodded. "Okay."

Rick read the wariness in her eyes. "Cupcake, if all this seems too daunting for you, too foreign to your mortal life, I want you to know, I can relocate you. The financial package Helen gave you is still good. We can even change your identity. You say the word, and I'll understand."

Anna's lips pursed for a second. "What will you understand?"

Rick shrugged, his dark eyes warm with pained compassion. "I'm not worth the danger."

Anna's hand sought his. "Three nights ago, in Colombia, did I tell you I love you?"

Rick was confused. "You know you did." He watched curiously as relief spread over her face.

"Well, that's your answer. I love you. I'm not leaving."

Rick smiled and pulled her into his embrace. He nuzzled her into a smoldering kiss. "Bear with me a little while, Cupcake, and this will all be behind us."

Her arms tightened around him as her teeth plucked at his neck. "You told me you've ridden out to many battles and you always came home. You promised to tell me about those one day. I want to know everything about you."

"Aren't you the curious historian?" He softened in her arms, falling back against the sofa.

Anna ran her finger down his nose to play at the bow of his top lip. "Yes, and right now I'm an exhausted historian. What about that Evercool mattress you're so proud of?"

"I could use some horizontal time myself." Rick stood and threw her over his shoulder. "Let's go to bed."

"You know I can walk, right?"

"This is more fun. Indulge my inner caveman."

"Tomorrow, I want to hear the 'tale of Cat and her two sires'. In detail."

Rick sighed. "I suppose I can't get out of that one?"

"Not on your life."

* * * *

"Anna was your donor?" Cat asked sharply. "I mean, *your* donor? Your personal donor? She never fed anyone else?"

Matt frowned—he was doing a lot of that lately. He put his hands on his hips and drew in a hissing breath while he tried to formulate an explanation Cat would understand, or at least buy. "She was a really nice girl. We don't get many of those." He looked up at Cat from underneath his eyelashes. "She didn't belong at the Gaoler."

"So, the Gaoler has a diversion program?" Cat crossed her arms over her chest and waited.

"Uh…not exactly…although Rick has said I have to stop rescuing the donors."

"Oh. You're a serial rescuer, now?"

"Uh…no…uh, not exactly…"

"Well then, what name would you pin on it?"

"Basically, this is about Anna. And uh…I was afraid she'd get hurt."

"So, what did you do about it?"

Matt puffed out his chest. "I banned her from the club. For her own good."

"Then what is she doing with Rick, if *you* banned her from the club?"

"I'm a little iffy on that whole thing." Matt scratched at the back of his head and ran his tongue over his lip. "I had the same question earlier this evening when Rick walked into his penthouse with her on his arm."

"When was this? While I was setting your toiletries out on the bathroom vanity? While I was hanging up your collection of Hawaiian shirts? You were getting reacquainted with Cupcake and Fitz?"

"It wasn't like that." Matt held up a hand. "She took off five minutes after they arrived. She had to walk the dog and eat…"

"Walk the dog?" Cat was incredulous about a canine in the building. "You told me animals didn't get along with vampires?"

"I don't know, I didn't ask. We had more important things to discuss. She left Rick, Adam and me to talk, and by the way, I have news we need to discuss."

"Oh, the little lady wasn't included?" Cat ground her heel as she leaned into him.

Matt shook his head, both hands up in surrender. "They flew straight in from Colombia. The dog needed to be walked and she needed to eat. This is not a conspiracy. But there is one brewing and I need your attention."

* * * *

Veronique rested her chin in her palm as she stared at the alcohol coating the martini glass. She had two to three months to regain her financial footing; her college girl persona was counting on the trendy apartment near Wilshire and Hauser to supply her with a steady flow of UCLA college boy blood. She made her rounds of cut rate forgers, avoiding the vampire Family of services. Rick Hiatt and Matt Brenner didn't need to hear about her, yet. She would be Vivian Morrison, a French major from Miami, Florida. A dilute amount of Humanité daily allowed her to navigate daytime hours when she scouted. If she chased the big men on campus, they might just enjoy a pajama party with her.

* * * *

Helen looked down at Player, it was not yet quite eight in the morning. "You're a good boy, but Auntie Helen doesn't have the time or inclination to babysit you every day. Starting today, you're going to the Beverly Barkshire, the best doggie daycare in town. Won't that be fun?" Player looked up at her and drooled.

"Helen?" Brett called from the lobby. "I've got Randy from the Beverly Barkshire here to pick up a dog?" Brett sounded non-plussed.

"Oh, good. I'll be up in just a sec. I guess Rick didn't tell you he adopted a dog?"

"I knew we were on alert, I didn't think it would come to that."

"We wouldn't send a watchdog to daycare, Brett." *And he's our guard.* "Randy will pick up and deliver daily, so make sure he can get into the penthouse elevator."

"Whatever you say."

* * * *

Rick watched the cocoon he presumed was Anna, as the late afternoon light filtered around the edges of the blackout drapes. He lay on his side, his head propped on his palm, searching for more than her pert nose. He touched the tip. It was cold. *That can't be good.* He peeled back the covers to reveal fluttering eyelids. He drank in the sight of her copper eyelashes and the delicate dust of freckles over the saddle of her nose. Clearly, half of this bed has to be warmed up for her. *How long do I have to stare at her before she wakes up?* He blew a chilly breath at her eyes. They fluttered again. He could stare at her all night, but that wouldn't accomplish anything. He dropped the coverlet back over her eyes, laid back into his pillow, arms folded under his head. "Cupcake, are you awake?"

"I am now. I guess." It was an inhuman growl. Rick slid an inch away from her as the cocoon wiggled and unwrapped. Anna sat up, pulling the coverlet close. She frowned. "We have to talk about this mattress. Cupcakes aren't meant to be stored on ice."

"On your little shopping extravaganza with Cat, you can buy a heated mattress pad and an electric blanket for your side of the bed. Meanwhile, I'll be happy to get your blood flowing."

"Do you think you can make that happen?"

"I have before…"

Anna frowned. "Tell me about that…"

Rick smirked at her. "You just want me to tell you what a hot, wild woman you are when I get you going."

She hesitated. "You remember our romantic night in Colombia?"

"I sure do!" Rick rolled over and kissed her cold nose.

Anna wrapped her arms around him, ignoring the increased chill. "Tell me all about it."

Rick cocked his head back to see her expression. "I can show you." He rolled her under him and leaned on his forearms.

"Maybe you should tell me, first." She wasn't meeting his gaze.

He caught her chin with his index finger. "What's going on, Cupcake?"

"I don't exactly remember that night."

"Any of it?"

"I remember we were on the balcony. And I remember you gave me a little of your blood, and…that's it." Devastation oozed from every pore. "Have you ever heard of that happening between a vamp and a mortal?"

"I know when we fed blood to soldiers on the battlefield, they never talked about their recovery. It never occurred to me they might not remember it." Rick rolled to his side, considering. "Wow, so our first big night is a blank for you?"

"I don't know what to say. Except, I was embarrassed that I gave you a hickey. When I saw that I was mortified."

"Well, the transfusion kinda took care of that. Believe me, you have nothing to be embarrassed about. I'm sorry you can't remember it." He reached out and meshed his fingers with hers, and then they were forehead to forehead. He whispered. "Ah, this is our first time all over again, isn't it?"

"Just for grins, how was I?"

He smirked boyishly. "Pretty athletic." He wiggled his brows. "Good times."

"What if I can't do that again?"

"You just be yourself, and no more vampire blood for you!"

"How about more of you?" She wiggled her slim, arched brows.

"There's no time like the present!" He swooped in to nibble her neck, eliciting giggles and wrestling under him. "You like that?" His flesh, pressed between them, stiffened, and she giggled into a moan.

His lips found hers in a searing kiss, filled with erotic promise. *She's warming her side of the bed now!* She looked into his eyes for a moment, and then smiled when their eyes met. Rick pushed her up slightly and moved his lips to her breasts, kissing first one, then the other. She sighed under his touch and caught her breath as his lips embraced her aching nipple. He worshipped that succulent flesh, licked it, stroked it with his tongue, drew on it like the hungry soul he was. At the same time, his fingers danced along the lively flesh of her thighs.

"Oh Fitz, do that again!" she whispered, as his hands adored her breasts. "You set me on fire!" His hands left her breasts and stroked her back, raising gooseflesh, and darted daringly into the cleft of her buttocks. Rick's long, clever fingers enjoyed the silk of her slick sex. Keening, she thrust back into his touch and bucked up to kiss him. *How can a mortal be this seductive?*

Rick's arms treasured her gentle body as he paused to consider her fragility. He flipped her on top of him. "I think this would be the right time for me to lie back and let you take the lead." He watched as her hair spread out, enclosing the two of them in this moment. "What a goddess you are, Anna, you're so sexy."

"I'll do my best." Anna rose up and straddled him, her knees on either side of his waist. Rick masterfully moved his hands back to her breasts and raised his head until he could trace the delicate skin over her breastbone with his lips. With a slight nudge, she positioned him at her wet cleft, teasing him.

"You minx, you're so ready for me this evening! Do I make you wet? Do you want me to fill you up?" Anna's head fell back as she continued her assault on his forbearance.

*She's going for the throat right out of the gate. How much more can I take before I throw her down and take her hard?* Rick's hand slipped between them, and with unerring accuracy he circled her clit. Her thighs tightened at his waist and her vibration played the tune of her excitement. "How long are you going to make me wait?"

"Is this what you want?" She lifted slightly and hovered over his cock. He could feel her heat. "You want in there right now?" He bucked his hips just enough to coat his crown with her dew.

Even as the thought crossed his mind, he heard her breath catch. His vampire senses read her blood rushing with every touch they shared. "I'm being a very patient man right now."

She lowered further, only to rise up again. She slid to his knees and cupped his sac as her tongue laved her juices along his turgid length. He reflexively arched into her mouth, drawn into her heat. "Cupcake, wait. Cupcake, Wait! Wait!"

"Yes?" She gave him another lick that flicked the head of his cock. With that sensation, Rick was up, and she was under him. "What was that?" Her eyes went wide.

"That's what happens when a mortal plucks all those undead sensations in just the right order! You're going to make me have to bite…"

"About that bite thing…I can't wait for that!"

"Yeah." His eyelids dropped dramatically, and his boyish smile grew knowing and sensual. Her hands held his handsome face as she sought his transformation. He notched into her. "If I get too rough," he drove hilt deep, "stop me."

She bucked up to meet his thrust. "Why would I stop this?"

It was yin and yang and every other symbiotic move. They danced over the sheets with heated abandon. Sighs and groans melted into each other's mouths as they rode their consuming passion. Rick tilted her to a well-practiced angle and depth, one he knew would hit her g-spot. His soul opened to the song of her sexual exhilaration. Looking down at her, he watched her face bright with pleasure, and felt her fingers tremble on his nipples.

"Harder!" she cried, her eyes were intent on his.

*Well, I think I will.*

While their bodies clung to each other, his desperately hard cock drilled in more deliberate strokes. She held him tight-fisted, deep within her. Her legs around his hips rising to his strokes, answering his deep rumble with sighs and cries, begging for more. It was a horizontal tango, brewed from their need.

Anna cried out. "So close! Don't stop!"

"Fu…, no!" Rick flipped her over on top of him.

* * * *

Anna leaned into the curve of his hard cock. She drove toward her orgasm. Below her, Rick's hands, tongue and lips danced on her skin, awakening sensations in her flesh she had thought impossible. He was back at her breasts, now, working her rosy nipples. His free hand pinched the other nipple, and she gasped. Her inner muscles clamped down on him. She caught his shoulders in her hands and fought for the last bit of friction as she drove herself home. Her moan vibrated, and she collapsed onto his chest.

* * * *

Rick shared a brief kiss and sought the florid flesh of her neck. He felt his length increase, and the fire burgeoning in his balls. Her flesh was fresh and sweet as his lips found home, his fangs dropped with sensual ferocity and he bit. He drew her bliss with his bite, whipping her fading orgasm back to life. He tasted her love singing from her veins. Rick felt the fireworks within twitch in her velvet grip, and he released into her. Her blood and his cum were their climatic exchange.

* * * *

Anna continued her gentle rise and fall against him, savoring their electric union. His upward thrusts continued to meet hers as they returned to earth. Tears of joy shimmered on her cheeks.

"You gave me my heart," he said softly, as they lay entwined in the aftermath of their coupling. Her head lay on his shoulder, and his hand lazily stroked her hair and back, bringing her to a shudder of sensual pleasure.

"You gave me mine," she replied. He kissed the top of her head. "You can read minds?" she asked.

"What? Oh…" he thought, dimpling as he remembered his response to her passion. "I can read people in ways mortals can't, if their emotions are clear and their minds are open."

Rick knew from their first evening together, Anna's heart was wide open. Kissing her nipple, his cool tongue stroked the rising pink flesh. Receptively, she rolled onto her side and placed a warm, gentle hand on his cool, muscled thigh.

"Cupcake," he said and laughed softly. "You are unlike any delight I've ever tasted."

"Why that nickname?" Anna asked and snickered, hand rising to cuddle his intriguing flesh.

Rick nodded. "Sweet, creamy, flavorful." His fingertip traced down the bridge of her nose to glance off her plump lips and the dimple in her chin. Rick's brow rose. "Little did I know you have a voracious sexual appetite."

"You bring that out in me…" Anna blushed. "When that hunger emerges inside me…" she trailed off and shifted dreamily, nipples peaking with arousal, unashamedly sensual. "It's as if you drew me out of a deep sleep."

"I have totally relished that awakening."

"Me…too…we're so unequally matched, what you are… That night in the garage, you could have taken me without asking, without respecting me, you could have killed me."

Rick closed his eyes as his lips thinned. "It was in my initial interest to thrall you and turn you away."

Anna ran her fingertips through Rick's hair, combing it to one side, then the other. "What changed your mind?"

Rick caught her hand and kissed her palm before placing it over his heart. "You want me to tell you all my secrets?"

She drew lazy heart shapes in his chest hair. "Just the ones that concern me."

"Don't you have to get a shower before your shopping date?" Rick slid toward his side of the bed.

"No. I want to feel this way until I get home and we do this again." She pursued him to his side of the bed.

"You know Cat will smell everything we've done." Rick made an 'ick' face at her.

Anna shook her head. "I don't care."

"Yeah, but Matt is coming up with her, and his sense of smell is far more honed than Cat's."

Anna grimaced and reluctantly pulled away from him. "I think I need a shower and I'll probably even wash my hair."

Rick laid back and stretched. He hadn't used some of these muscles in a few days. He supposed it was wiser not to mention this building crawled with vamps, and a shower would actually disguise nothing. *She's marked with my scent and every intercourse will amp up the pheromones of my possession. If our initial coupling was wild, and "athletic" and today was uninhibited, will we ever get to the point of a slow, comfortable screw? And what did happen in Colombia? Who do I know that's knowledgeable about sharing blood with mortals? Does it always come with a period of amnesia?*

Rick wandered to the kitchen au natural, seeking a quick juice glass of A positive. He checked the messages on his phone and flipped on the evening news. The hairdryer droned from her dressing room. Before the night began, a shower was in order. He needed to check on Veronique's whereabouts. The responders needed to be sent over to Sterling's house. There were checks to authorize, and charges to dispute. There were self-defense classes to be scheduled, and then a memo about the mandatory meetings. The Tokyo market had been open for two hours, he was behind…

* * * *

Anna, dressed and ready to shop, thought she'd better grab a quick smoothie in the kitchen before Cat arrived. Los Angeles was an open-minded town, but it was still hard to find a vamp/mortal bistro outside this building. She pulled out the blender and began dumping in the fruit, yogurt and almond milk with a cup of shaved ice. *Wow, this blender is loud.* She pulsed the mixture to a creamy texture. She stood, bobbing her head and humming along to her iPod as the blender whirred.

* * * *

Matt stepped from the elevator and followed the sound of the blender. He hesitated and read the room. Rick was probably the one in the shower, and Anna would be in the kitchen. Head down, he stepped into the room. Her back was to him as she jauntily moved to the tune she hummed. Hands on hips, he watched her amber earrings sway to her beat. Her luscious red hair was wound up and held by an ornate comb. She wore a silk scarf wrapped twice around her neck, undoubtedly hiding the evidence of Rick's orgasm. Matt fought the inclination to read her. She was dressed in jewel tones rather than pastels. Her perfume was an exotic blend of lush florals and rich spices, definitely not the sweet girlish fragrance she used to wear. She tapped a booted foot as her hips swayed. Her hand reached out to the cabinet for a sports bottle and her nails were painted a vivid coral. Sometime between the day he'd cast her out and this evening, Anna Curley had grown from a girl to a woman.

He watched as she poured the smoothie into the sports bottle and capped it. Then the show began. She bent her knees, ground her hips, and growled out the lyrics into her sports bottle 'microphone.' *"I must admit I can't explain any of these thoughts racing through my brain. It's true. Baby I'm howling for you."* Matt silently moonwalked backward into the hallway. He looked around for something to brush into, and finally decided on calling out, "Anna? Rick? Are you two decent?"

"I'm in the kitchen." Her tone was the soul of innocence as she leaned back against the counter, sucking on the sports bottle.

If the back view was telling, her face cemented his impression. Her vivid green eyes were smoky dark, and she wore a flush of excitement. Her well-kissed, swollen lips sucked breakfast through a fat straw. Although Matt fought the inclination to read her, he didn't have to. *This is in my face. She is a new and confident Anna, and the difference is Rick.*

"Hi, Matt. Where's Cat?" She stood draining the bottle.

Matt shifted, watching her cheeks hollow. "She…uh…said she had to measure something before she came up. Where's Rick?"

Anna shrugged. "Shower, I guess. I'm really going to enjoy getting to know Cat."

"Oh, yeah?" Matt looked at his shoe, and then, belatedly, "ah…that's good."

Anna tilted her head at him. "Are you okay?"

"Sure, why wouldn't I be?"

Rick walked into the kitchen. A towel slung around his hips. "Because this is awkward?"

"Awkward? I dunno." Matt's nose twitched, he raised an eyebrow at Rick who smiled smugly.

Anna looked back and forth between the two men and shook her head. "I'm gonna get my purse. Should I get my keys? Who's driving?" She disappeared down the hall.

Both Rick and Matt piped up. "You have a driver."

Rick frowned. "Safety first, Cupcake." Matt shook his head and widened his eyes. Rick licked his lips. "It's that May/December romance thing."

Matt chuckled. "More like January/December romance thing."

"She might surprise you." Rick looked down at his towel. "I need to get dressed. Make yourself at home. There's some fresh A positive in the fridge."

# 16

Rick squirmed for the umpteenth time in the horrendously uncomfortable theatre seat. He looked over at Matt and spoke in sub-tones. "This has been the longest hour of my life."

Matt peered sideways. "You keep track of that stuff? I mean, old man, you've racked up a lot of hours. But yeah, this is tedious." Now Matt shifted, it was contagious, like a yawn. "Isn't it time for this thing to end?"

"Don't you want to see how we're perceived?"

Matt grimaced and gestured subtly at the actor. "I've got more swagger than that." He and Rick were startled to hear echoing applause from the sparse audience. "I guess we're on. How do we get backstage?"

* * * *

Behind the curtain, drones struck the sets. Well-wishers and admirers mostly thinned out as Rick and Matt circulated. The buzz from the male performer's dressing room centered on which actress was the easiest, versus who was the unattainable hottie.

"No poontang without a little starter fluid," Barry, the salt and pepper Dracula observed as he tissued off his artificial pallor. "Six weeks of priming the pump, I need sheet time. Isn't Hank a bar back?" He looked over at the twenty-something preening in the mirror. "Hank, couldn't we scam some hospitality prices?"

Hank finger combed his hair into place. "Nope, they frown on that. How about we go to Slammers?" The whole room groaned.

Rick and Matt, who eavesdropped, gave each other decisive nods. Rick knocked on the half-open dressing room door. "Excuse me, I'm Rick Hiatt, this is my partner, Matt Brenner, we're with the Consort Group International. We've had an eye on your production, we're thinking you might want to up your game." Rick stepped aside to let his words sink in.

Matt stepped forward and scanned the cramped dressing room. "Would a gig at the Pantages interest you? Something you might want to discuss over drinks?" He held out their cards.

Barry stepped forward. "Sure, worth a discussion."

Rick drew their attention. "Would the cast enjoy a small after-party? We could talk?"

Hank said what everyone was thinking. "If it's on you? Sure."

"The address is on the cards." Rick handed several more around. "Just show them at the door, let the manager know you're with me." He turned and faced Matt with a superior grin and wagged his brows.

* * * *

The Mercedes G65, though difficult to climb into, was luxurious inside, and the safest ride possible. The girls strapped in and turned conversation to domestic matters.

Cat fastened Anna with a serious look. "It's not like converting to a new religion. There are no lapsed vampires." Street and headlights strobed past them as they drove to Box and Bed at the Galleria.

Anna considered Cat's grave words. "How did you make your choice?"

"It was made for me. Matt and Rick did it to save my life. Technically, I died in front of them."

"You remember that?"

"Oh, yeah. It was a slip and fall. You know, the deadliest accidents happen within three miles of home. I would never have survived it."

"You seem happy. Are you okay with it?"

"You have to learn how to make your own way in this life. I want to be with Matt forever, but circumstances change, you know, just like in mortal life."

"What you're saying is, if I moved across the world for a man, how would I go on if something happened to him?"

"That's right, understanding you can never go home again. That's your choice, Anna. So, if there are reasons, beyond Rick, that you would want to join the Family, then it's something to contemplate. But if your motivation is only to be with Rick, take a long time to consider."

Anna stared unseeing out the window and thought for a beat. "No lapsed vampires, right?"

Cat reached over to squeeze her new friend's hand. "That's right."

* * * *

Thelonious Monk once remarked the function of a bridge is "to make the outside sound good." Rick made sure in double time new patrons drank in the 1930s ambiance in the bar he named The Bridge. He took pride in curating the original art hung over the long copper and mahogany bar, probably a good deal more elegant than anyone at Vampire Roleplay ever enjoyed. Relaxing deep blue leather bar stools dotted the undulating bar. Rick loved to see people in clustered groups enjoying his liquor. Dynamic art deco sconces illuminated gold etched wall coverings and cast a candlelight glow that softened many a complexion. An impossible array of the finest spirits graced the mirrored back bar as the staff charmed their guests.

Matt spoke with the Chef while Rick instructed the bar manager. "Ray, I have a party of twelve coming, comp their tab."

The bar manager groaned. "Comp their tab?"

Rick shrugged with a smirk. "I doubt these kids drink Johnny Walker Blue Label."

Ray's eyes lit up. "How about pitchers of Planter's Punch for the ladies and Manhattans for the men? They'll think they're drinking with Jay Gatsby, and it won't break our bank."

"I like it! Thanks, old sport." Rick turned with a spring in his step.

* * * *

Anna skirted the higher-priced bedding in front of the display. She knew clearance and out of season goods would fit her budget. Finally, she laid her hands on a king-sized bed warmer and electric blanket. She juggled back and forth at the two price tags, shaking her head at the investment.

Cat silently swung around the corner with a cart of dramatic red bath sheets. The sales clerk pounced.

"Are you finding everything today?"

Anna arched her brow. "Three hundred dollars for infrared technology in a mattress pad? I'm not keeping burgers warm."

Cat elbowed her in the ribs. "It would keep your buns warm."

Anna frowned as the sales woman gave her a sour look. "Well then, may I suggest Sunbeam? They sell them at Sam's Club." The clerk turned and headed for the couple hovering around the wedding registry.

Cat smirked. "Guess she thought she told you!"

Anna blushed with embarrassment. "I can't afford this stuff, even if I needed infrared technology."

Cat caught the bed warmer from Anna's hands and held it up. "How long do you think you'll use this? A month? A year?"

Anna read Cat's subliminal question and sighed. "I don't know."

Cat nodded. "Good answer." She put the pad into her cart.

"I barely know you. You can't buy that for me."

Cat put her arm around Anna and touched forehead to forehead. "I'm not buying it, Rick is."

Anna took a centering moment. Life had sky-rocketed to a whole new income bracket, bringing with it a touch of altitude dizziness. She watched Cat head to the register, picked up the deluxe electric blanket and trotted to catch up. "Spending Rick's money makes me thirsty."

Cat looked behind her. "Have you been to the Bridge at the Consort Building? We should go there."

* * * *

Rick was on the phone when the theatre troop piled in. "Send up whatever Monitors we can spare, and Adam, would you join us too? I need some guys to charm the ladies while Matt and I pump the fellas."

Matt was already greeting their guests and guiding them to strategically-chosen seating, primed for separating the men from the women. Rick joined them with full watt vamp appeal radiating charm. "Ladies, I hope you don't mind, I know some backers who are admirers of yours, who begged to meet you. They should be here soon."

One skeptical beauty asked, "Just for drinks, right?"

Rick nodded. "Of course. This is all upright, just getting to know you."

Matt ushered the servers toward the men's table with four generous pitchers of Manhattans and the bar's largest martini glasses. As the servers placed the beverages on the table Matt hovered. "If you prefer them on the rocks, here are other glasses." Another server put down a tray of sixteen-ounce tumblers with a small ice bucket. Rick recognized the look of men facing an alcoholic challenge.

"You must be hungry. Some appetizers are coming." Rick stepped aside to let the tall server deliver an iced crystal tray of deviled eggs and stuffed mushrooms. The men's eyes were on the alcohol.

Rick offered the first toast. "To vampires!"

Matt tossed his back in one gulp, hoping the others would take the challenge. "Drink up gentlemen."

When the volume at the men's table rose over the jazz trio's, Rick moved into the cluster surrounding the pitchers. "Whatever happened to that guy who used to play Van Helsing? What was his name?"

Barry blew a raspberry. "Ugh, Sterling. He went to South America on a cruise. That was two weeks ago."

Hank raised a silencing hand. "It's been fourteen glorious days since we've had to deal with that blow hard."

Even the silent actor working his way through the deviled eggs spoke up. "I'm surprised you haven't kept track of the hours."

Rick noticed the testosterone in the troop. "So, he was the lady killer?"

"More like the cock blocker." Barry grumbled.

Matt pushed a chair closer and lamented. "Just what the world needs. Less cock."

"You wouldn't believe this douche!" Renfield's portrayer exclaimed. "He actually thought vampires were real." A chorus of snickers broke out among the progressively drunker men.

Rick did a spit take. "No shit? How did that work for him?"

Barry gestured with his glass. "I dunno, but he had all this vamp crap at his house. And he told the chicks he hunted vampires. Can you believe that? The dumb shits bought it!"

Hank nodded sorrowfully. "They pretended to."

Rick insinuated himself next to Barry and commiserated. "Did he only tell the stories to women?"

Barry nodded. "Who the fuck else would listen to that crap?"

Matt lifted another glass. "Well, then, wherever Sterling is, may he stay there."

The men hoisted their glasses as Rick confirmed, "and so say I!"

* * * *

Matt watched the women's flushed faces, relaxed body language and easy laughter as the Monitors entertained them with booze and flattery. *Two pitchers down should loosen those pretty lips.*

Matt swaggered to their table and smiled charmingly. He didn't know their names, so he went with the character's monikers. "Ladies, are these gentlemen treating you right?"

Mina giggled. "Who knew the last night would be the best?" The actress winked. "They're all so handsome."

Matt gave them the once over. "They're okay."

Lucy batted her eyes at him. "None of them are as handsome as you."

He deflected. "Don't let my wife hear you say that. She'll have your neck."

Adam shook his head and turned a thousand-watt smile on her. "Guess you're stuck with me."

Lucy nearly had the vapors. "Poor, poor, pitiful me…"

Matt took a knee between the actresses. "So, what's with the name Black Heart Players? Have you done other productions that aren't vampire?"

Lucy's maid waved her glass and Adam topped it off. "That was Sterling's stupid name. We used to be the Red Curtain Players, and we used to do repertory theatre. He came along with the vampire stuff, which I think has played itself out."

"I thought people found vampires sexy?" Matt kept a straight face.

Mina grimaced. "Meh. That was Sterling's thing."

"Has anybody heard from him?"

The girls looked at each other and shook their heads. "Maybe we'll finally get our creative freedom back."

"I heard he threw some crazy parties?" The girls gave Matt guarded looks. His voice became conspiratorially deep. "I have a friend who said he led a secret society of vampire hunters."

Mina's Maid stared at him wide eyed. "How did you find out?"

"Is it true?"

Lucy waved a dismissive hand. "I hung around that jag-off for three weeks. He kept promising he was gonna show me something. It was bullshit. He just wanted to get laid."

Mina and her Maid blinked at her. "Ewe."

Lucy nodded. "I know, right?"

Matt grinned. "Nothing to him?"

Mina cracked. "I hope he falls overboard."

Lucy winked. "I was hoping they'd make him walk the plank."

"Into a school of sharks," Mina's Maid concluded.

Matt lifted a toast. "To sharks everywhere!"

* * * *

By the bottom of the pitchers, the men were lit, and the ladies were giddy. Matt and Rick stood at the bar with Ray. Rick surveyed the room and shook his head. "Call the car service and get these shiny, happy people home."

Matt beckoned Rick over with two glasses and a bottle of Everclear. "I think it's safe to say the menace of Ramsey Black, enacted by Carl Sterling, is over. The slayer has been slain. The museum can enjoy the diaries as a point of fiction, along with all the memorabilia."

Rick stared pensively into his glass. "I'm relieved to get the Fitzjarrald dirk back. I wish I could be certain the curse was broken."

Matt frowned at him. "You don't believe in curses, do you?"

Rick circled the glass in his hand watching the legs of the alcohol. "You live another couple hundred years, dear boy, you might believe in a lot of things."

* * * *

*Being a vampire is cool twenty-four/seven when you're a billionaire with assets accrued over three to five hundred years*, Veronique thought. *But being a vampire sucks when you're looking at less than a ten-thousand-dollar bank balance.* She couldn't bear to part with the Bentley convertible. *I need transportation, don't I?*

Veronique labored under a new set of rules with the Council's zero tolerance policy on Humanité. She didn't regret parcels mailed to her California address while Colombia cranked out several thousand capsules a week. She needed to function in daylight and at least mimic eating food. She played with the dosage until she found the exact amount which would meet her needs. Even if she thought of peddling her few hundred capsules, her new milieu got their thrills from surviving in L.A. on middle class standards.

It was nearly impossible to survive as a vampire off the grid, away from the Family and the communal feeding resources. She hadn't fallen into the 'dine and dash' feeding method in Echo Park. She could still pick up a guy or gal and tap a pint.

She dialed back her singular glamour, to minimize the chance of being remembered. Luckily, an emerald was enough to finance a cut-rate pixie hairstyle and a heavy frosting job. The contact lenses were next, and her peridot eyes were instantly altered to deep espresso. A few hours of hunting through second-hand boutiques netted her an entire BoHo chic wardrobe. In one day, Veronique Moreau's transformation to Vivian Morrison, a twenty-one-year-old coed, was complete.

Vivian would normally have been limited by the cost of drinks at the trendier night spots, but the male patrons proved to be more than generous in picking up her tab. The management was always pleased to see her walk through the door, it almost always meant increased sales as well-heeled suitors bid for her attention.

She dawdled at a bar between a couple of studios when a new revenue stream suddenly occurred to her. Two casting directors drank and bemoaned the scarcity of actresses with 'natural' assets. Well, she had natural assets if you overlooked her paranormal existence.

"Good evening, ladies..." The two women looked up in surprise. "I couldn't help overhearing your discussion. I've always been interested in entertainment, but I don't know how to get a foot in the door. I wonder if you could give me some advice?"

The salt-and-pepper-haired woman on the left peered over her half glasses. "Honey, a girl who looks like you could do well if you can handle lines. Do you have any training?"

"No." Vivian pouted prettily.

The bleached blonde looked her up and down. "No matter, acting can be taught. You have natural presence and a pleasant vocal quality, if you can read lines, you could do well. Do you have head shots? A resume?"

"No, and I'm a student, I just can't afford a photographer." She upped the pout.

The gray-haired woman dug into her Birkin bag. "This is my card. I'm writing the name and phone number of an agent on the back. You call him, tell him I referred you and make an appointment. If he likes you...

*Oh, he'll like me.*

"...he might spring for the cost of head shots with a really good photographer. I'll call him and tell him I'm sending you. What's your name, sweetheart?"

Like a snake, Veronique Moreau shed her skin, and Vivi Morrison was born.

* * * *

"Thank you so much, Miss Morrison," Tommy, the choreographer, patted Vivi on the back as she left the set. A delicious B negative chorus boy waited for her. This music video for the latest hip hop star would increase her notoriety. It was all too gratifying to circulate in an industry where kink was straight and body fluids of all types were generously given.

Next week she would start shooting her cable television series, Mystical Therapies. In which she played, of all things, Lilith, a vampire who was a practicing hematologist. Vivi had no idea what mysterious elements created a hit show. *But the money will be good while it lasts.*

Luis Rocca had a great body which was all he'd developed. Luis had already showered in Vivi's Star Wagon, in expectation of her return. Now he struck his best manspread pose on the sofa, cold beer in hand, waiting to make his next conquest.

Vivi opened the trailer door bringing the commotion of the striking set and breaking camp of Star Wagons along with her. She looked him up and down. "You look good enough to eat, Rocky, but we need to adjourn to my apartment." He rose to his feet, letting the towel fall to the floor.

"For sure, Mama, cuz I'm no minute man."

Vivi folded her arms over her hardening nipples and grinned. "I know, once you get that beer can of a dick going, it wants to play all night!" She smacked him on his hard ass as he headed for his clothes. *I might just have to turn him.*

* * * *

Mortal work was hard. Even in Hollywood, even if you were a minor star. She'd held this position, lips pursed against a bottle of sun screen, for half a day. She wanted to scream in frustration as the grips fussed with the lighting and prop placement. Thankfully, they were about to call a lunch break and she had to confer with the gentlemen from Flask Brothers Investigations. She should be more grateful. The endless shoot was funding her surveillance of Rick and Matt's love lives.

She let the Flask brothers ogle her before she got their names. Robert's eyes barely moved above her décolletage while he pumped her dainty hand. The visibly older brother, Joe, was married and settled from the looks of his shoes. *You can tell a lot about a man by his shoes.*

"How can we help you, Ms. Morrison?"

Vivi spread a series of photos she collected from Consort Group's promotional pages. There were staged images of Rick shaking hands, Matt presenting ceremonial keys and lots of random candid shots. "These two gentlemen, Richard Hiatt and Matt Brenner, are your targets. You can find their bios on Google. What I want to know is, how they spend their private time? Who do they see? What's their status?"

Joe nodded to his brother and began. "Well, ma'am that would be our standard rate plus expenses. You're probably looking at thirty hours of work." He slid a notated contract across the table to her.

Vivi swallowed at the hourly rate and possible expenses. "Couldn't this be done in less than thirty hours? I mean, I gave you where they work…"

Joe negated that idea with a firm shake of his head. "No ma'am, that's what it takes."

"Well," Vivi began coyly. "Maybe we could work something out in advertising? Maybe I could do some free ads for you?"

Robert frowned at his brother. "It's more work than it looks. Otherwise, you could do this yourself. If we return with photos and sufficient dossiers and we haven't used thirty hours, we'll only bill what we worked."

Joe sniffed. "What exactly are you looking for? Do you have home addresses, jobs, backgrounds, out of town relatives?"

Vivi did the math. "I want to know who the gentleman are bedding." Vivi's long nail tapped Rick's photo. "You might have a lot of work for this one."

The brother's exchanged a curious look. Robert pushed the paperwork closer along with an agency pen. "When did you want this?"

Vivi hesitated to say she was on the last flight out to Hawaii. *They'll charge me more.* "I'll be out of town shooting for about ten days. Can you have it ready when I return?"

Robert slid the pen closer to touch her hand. "That'll be a one-thousand-dollar retainer."

Vivi signed on the dotted line and slid an envelope to Joe. "Do I get a receipt?"

Joe nodded as he gave her one of the three carbonless forms.

Vivi held up the blue ink pen. "May I keep this?"

Joe smiled. "That's why we have them. Tell your friends."

* * * *

Rick opened the express package in the privacy of his office at the Gaoler. Leaning on his elbow he spread out the photos in an arc with the oldest black and white images up close. "Helen!"

"Rick!" *Age hasn't sanded off your edges has it, honey?* He heard her chair screech and then the rhythm of her clogs from her office to his door. She knocked and waited for his answer. *It's been this way for thirty-five or was it forty years?*

"I called you, didn't I?" *This is our back and forth, I love it.* The door opened, and Helen peered over the top of her readers. "Have a seat, I have an idea I want to run by your mortal mind."

Helen's potential for sarcasm was strong. She slid gracefully into the chair in front of his desk and tapped her thumb and index nails, waiting…

"I was expecting a crack about the mortal mind…"

She arched her brow and pursed her lips.

"Okay." Rick gathered the photos and handed them to Helen. "I'm bringing my family's castle into C.G.I. It's in Ireland—Erne Castle. We're turning it into a resort."

Her tongue moved over her lip as she squinted at the oldest images, and then flipped through to the newest and brightest photos. "And how can my mortal mind contribute?"

"If I offer Anna a position curating the art, I don't have to share her with the folks across the street. If it were you, would you travel back and forth to Ireland for me?

Her soft face brightened. "If you asked me forty years ago, I'd say yes. Old Helen might be the wrong mortal to ask." She placed the photos back in his hands. "What about that exit strategy you put in place? You've given her enough money to set her up for life, if she chooses to leave."

*Go ahead, Helen, ask…Am I planning a different exit strategy, am I planning to turn her?* He followed Helen's gaze as she scoured the photos of other clubs on the wall, many including donors through the decades. There she was, between Matt and Rick at the Palm Springs opening. *She knows vamp/mortal romance has a sell by date.* She said a lot when she said nothing at all.

"Okay, point taken. Point considered." Rick ran his thumb over his bottom lip as he stared blindly at the photo of the master's quarters without raising his eyes, he sniffed dismissively. "You have my package for the Cincinnati trip?" *Of course, you do, Mistress of Efficiency.* "That's all. Thanks, Helen."

* * * *

The Old Kitchen was a moderately priced restaurant with Colombian cuisine conveniently located by the museum. Although Anna insisted her co-workers go to no trouble on her behalf, they planned a gathering at the restaurant. Once they heard of her romantic trip with Rick, they wanted to celebrate. She'd tried for the past seven weeks to blend her work hours with

Rick's upside-down routine. It simply didn't flow, and Anna was getting further and further behind on her sleep. It was set, her friends were throwing her a 'retirement' party!

* * * *

Lawrence led Anna through the ornate gates of the restaurant's patio. Gay lanterns and decorations hung over the long table laid heavy with Colombian delicacies. To the right, a table heaped with gift bags and cards awaited her attention.

She was seated as the guest of honor and a Colombian beer was shoved in her hand while the other party members joined her. "Rick sends his regrets," Lawrence began, "he's opening a club in Cincinnati, so we have Anna all to ourselves." There was a round of applause as Anna lifted her mug in a toast.

"You guys didn't have to go to all this trouble!"

Her best work friend, Barbara, gestured to the food. "What are you talking about, we get to sample new foreign cuisine and drink."

"Here, here." Mugs of beer were raised all around as she opened her gifts. The very first box held sterling silver Claddagh earrings.

"Lawrence, can you begin a thank-you list? Will you get a look at this, Sterling silver!"

Lawrence held out a wicker basket. "You leave it to me to record each thing, we can't let you leave town without getting your thank-yous written."

The family style meal was served by colorfully dressed staff. Sudado de Pollo, deep fried plantains stuffed with cheese and milanese. Anna was thoroughly enjoying herself until the tureen of chicken was set before her. One whiff of what should have been the fragrant aroma of onions, peppers, tomatoes and cumin brought on a wave of anxiety.

Barbara passed her a basket of bread. "I'm glad you liked those Sterling earrings."

Anna stiffened. "Sterling? Earrings?"

Barbara pointed to Anna's beer mug. "Are you used to drinking?"

Anna blinked. "I generally don't drink. I'm overwhelmed, Barbara, and this chicken stew is making me a little nauseated. I'm sorry."

To Anna's right, Sammie looked at her closely. "Oh, sweetie, are you and your pretty boy…"

Anna picked up her water with a shaking hand and gulped it sloppily. Lawrence flew to her side. "Are you okay, you're really pale? Are you sick?"

A happy voice shouted from the other end of the table. "She's pregnant."

"Noo!" Anna held up her hands. "I'm definitely not pregnant. But I might be a little sick. I'm sorry guys."

Another voice rejoined. "Yup, she's pregnant." Then the table was abuzz.

Lawrence leaned down to her. "Do you need me to take you home?"

"I think I'll be okay if I'm not near this chicken. I must be sensitive to one of the ingredients. Would you please move it to the other end of the table?"

* * * *

The elevator opened to the penthouse and Player ran to greet them. Lawrence followed her to the kitchen with her basket of parting gifts. "You still don't look right. Is there anything I can get you?"

"Thank you, Larry, I know Rick charged you with my care while he and Matt are out of town, but I think I can manage a sick day on my own. Player and I are going to climb into bed and watch T.V."

Player herded her into the bedroom where he stood at Rick's side of the bed. "Do you want the bed warmer on your side, too?" Player barked and jumped onto the bed. She put her fingers to her lips. "Don't tell Daddy!" *As if Rick can't smell a Rottie.* "Let's go to bed, you can watch Puppy Planet." She clicked on the T.V. and the dog cuddled next to her.

* * * *

The Colombian air nearly suffocated her. The limo's air conditioner hadn't cut the humidity. Player whined incessantly, pawing at her backpack. When the vehicle jerked to a stop, the hotel was disappointing. Paint peeled from gaudy carved surfaces. As she stepped from the limo, the pavement heaved under her feet. In slow motion she fought to balance her bags and the dog. Why was Player so needy? Lights flickered under the portico and then flashed out. She squinted to see. A voice extenuated behind her. She turned as though she was slogging through mud. The man stood dressed in a black sweat suit. The hoodie was tied down around his face, obscuring him from her vision. "Killl herrrr!"

Anna jumped to avoid the attacker, almost dropping her backpack. She fell against the limo and the dirk dropped into her hand. The man advanced glacially, both arms reaching with cadaverous fingers clutching the air. She raised the dirk in self-defense when his face came into focus. Sterling's death mask laughed at her. "Killl herrr." She broke out of her mire and slashed at the specter. He dissolved into thin air.

* * * *

Anna bolted upright in the bed, shrieking. Player climbed into her lap, licking her face with a sad whimper. "Oh, baby, I'm so glad you're with me." She kissed his broad flat head as he offered doggie comfort. "We need a diversion, let's go for a swim."

* * * *

When Rick challenged his architect to create an oasis of luxury, the trend-setter played with clear materials. Standing tall above The Miracle Mile, the thirty by fifty by ten feet deep cantilevered pool juxtaposed his serious Elizabethan penthouse. If vampires existed on the fringe of life, Rick wanted his guests to swim along that fringe.

Bands of clouds obscured the sliver of the moon. Anna caught sight of it as she padded out to a lounge chair beside the pool stairs. A mist hovered over the shimmering water. Player shadowed her devotedly as she dropped her towel on the chair and shook out her hair. Together, they stepped into the cerulean radiance of the warm pool water. It was heavenly. She dropped down the steps as it caressed her and held her as she pushed off from the bottom step. Player paddled in circles around her, shaking his head enjoying the buoyancy of the water. She swam over to the outside wall and marveled at the clarity of the eight-inch-thick transparent glass shell. Through the undulating water, she could see the city below, and she shivered at the thrill of being so many stories high and floating.

She remembered summers as a child when she would swim the length of the pool on the bottom like a mermaid. Of course, Player hung back at the center of the pool and howled at the thought of swimming off the edge of the world. *Let's see how far I can go.* Anna dove to the bottom and took graceful strokes. *What a feeling!* She reached the wall, did a kick turn and headed past Player. *I can do another lap.* She kept rapt attention at the night sky to her left through the glass wall. She heard the pool filter, Player's splashing and her steady heartbeat as her strokes continued. *Ah, peace! I wish Rick were here with me.*

She considered what vampire pool parties would look like with the softly colored lights outlining their toned bodies. She would enjoy watching Rick at play tossing a beach ball to Matt. Maybe Adam and Lawrence would join them. Cat would be there and…A page sounded through the water. "Mr. Pretty Boy, paging Mr. Pretty Boy." She broke out of her stroke and bounded up out of the water's depths searching in a circle for the source. The night was mockingly silent. Anna made for the stairs, the words echoing in her mind,

*Mr. Pretty Boy, paging Mr. Pretty Boy* it looped irritatingly again and again. A chill ran down her spine to her toes as she stumbled up the steps toward the chair and her towel. Player shook the pool water off as Anna scrutinized the dimly lit living room from the patio. Eerie shadows played games inviting her back into the room. *This is silly, if there was an intruder Player would be having a fit.*

She stood dripping at the threshold summoning her wits. Firelight danced behind the Elizabethan fire screen, casting a reflection on the imposing ceramic dog on the hearth. As Anna approached the sumptuous wing chairs flanking the mantle, shadows played cruel games with the static dog's expression. She tiptoed across the deep carpet, past Arthur, Rick's standing set of armor. She stopped and pivoted toward the dining room and peered down the hall to the foyer. The freezer dropped a load of ice and she shivered under the beach towel. "Mr. Pretty Boy, paging Mr. Pretty Boy". Anna spun on her heel and shrieked at the standing armor. With two steps back, she was lifting the faceplate, "Who's in there?" Player joined her side and barked. *This is ridiculous, Rick has security cameras everywhere. I couldn't be safer in a bank vault.* The phone on the sofa table shrilled. She jumped.

The trill repeated, and she extended a shaking hand to pick up the old-fashioned receiver. "Hello?" She was taken back at her own weak voice.

"Anna, what's wrong?" Rick's warm solid voice comforted her.

"Oh, ah, nothing. You woke me. You know us silly mortals. Sometimes I doze once the sun sets."

"Larry said you got sick at your party, are you okay?"

"Did he tell you what those hens said?" Anna shifted with pool water dripping down her legs.

"No, I heard you got plenty of Sterling Silver."

"They think I'm pregnant."

"Well..."

"Well, what?"

"Well if you are, we have to talk."

"Nothing to talk about, Fitz. It was that damn chicken stew. Ugh... After Colombia I never want to see chicken again."

"Really?"

"I don't know, babe. It was warm today, I had beer. I miss you. It's complicated."

"If you're lonely you can go downstairs and knock on Cat's door. I'm sure she can make up an entertaining story about me."

"I like that idea! When are you coming home? I have to change the sheets…"

"What?"

"Player claimed your side of the bed when I napped."

"Right… We'll be back around two in the morning. And by the way, Player is guarding my side of the bed. I love you, Cupcake."

"I love you, Fitz." Player barked. "And Player loves you too."

* * * *

Anna arrived at Cat's door wearing lounging pajamas and her fluffiest robe, carrying a liter of tequila, a salt shaker and a bag of limes.

Cat opened the door holding a bottle of nail polish and an orange stick. Her toe separators were bright blue, they matched her romper set as she balanced on her heels. "Hi! What's up?"

"Tequila."

Cat's eyes danced. "I can see. That's a lot of tequila."

"Want to play a game? We can play while your toenails are drying."

Cat shuffled backwards to let her into the dramatically modern apartment. "What kind of game?"

Anna went directly to the wet bar in the living room and spread out the salt shaker and limes. She instinctively knew where the cutting board and paring knife were. The TV remote was on the coffee table, and she walked over to pick it up. "It's called Show Me Your Hands." Cat cocked her head in confusion.

Anna flipped through the channels and found a procedural cop show. The star of the show stood stalwart, gun in hand, shouting, "Show me your hands!"

She gave Cat a significant look. "See there, the game is afoot!" She poured two shots and Cat nodded. "Ah, I get it. Set 'em up."

* * * *

Cat was prepared for their appearance even before the elevator dinged, Matt called her from the car. She gestured the men into the room. "Entre."

Rick peered over her shoulder. "Is that my Sleeping Beauty?"

"Yep. Two shots and she was out."

Rick's lips curled at one side. "I guess it's a good thing she isn't pregnant."

Matt's eyes went round, and Cat gasped. "If she is, it can't possibly be yours."

Rick gave her a sardonic look. "She's not pregnant. Do you scent any HCG? Increase in estrogen? Of course, she's not. One little virus and her hen friends are crocheting booties."

Cat shrugged. "That's what mortals assume when a girl is swept off her feet and returns from an exotic vacation."

"They have no way of knowing you're a vampire and vamps are sterile," Matt pointed out.

"What about all those kiddos we've fostered over the years?" Rick winked. "We've kept a few colleges in business over the decades."

Cat crossed her arms over her breasts. "Boys *and* girls?"

Both men turned in complete innocence. "Of course."

"Okay, then, but it's still not the same as having a baby of your own."

Matt turned to her. "Do you regret that?"

She shook her head. "It is what it is. There are tradeoffs for everything in life. So, no, I don't regret it. And, if I have the yearning to mother, I always have you."

Rick made gagging sounds. "T.M.I. newlyweds. It's time I get my little princess to bed." Rick bent and gently laid Anna over his shoulder—she never stirred. "See you fine people tonight."

* * * *

Player greeted him with his usual doggie excitement when the elevator opened on the penthouse. He spoke to the dog as he walked through the apartment. "Yes, I missed you too. Let me put your mom in bed and I…" He stopped dead at the scent of Player on his sheets. "God's nightgown, Player, Mom is sleeping on your side today, I prefer Eau de Cupcake." Anna mumbled in her sleep and cuddled into the pillow as Rick covered her with the electric blanket.

Rick watched the dog circle three times, and then lay on the rug next to her. It was good to be back in his sanctum. *Nothing like a bedtime snack to promote peaceful rest.* He strolled to the kitchen and along the way, noticed the glass wall to the patio was left open. Pouring some O positive, he thought, *it would be relaxing to enjoy a few minutes by the pool.*

Predawn, the multicolored pool lights shifted as he stretched on the lounge chair and closed his eyes. The sky began to lighten, the tension on the street below radiated upward. *Time for this party to move.* He swallowed the last of his blood, and headed inside, picking up Anna's wet towel, dropped at the threshold.

*I didn't realize she enjoyed the pool...she might enjoy the Malibu beach house...* when Matt and Cat left it last year, he remodeled it to be vamp friendly as well as a vacation property.

* * * *

Larry was up late today, but it was worth it to see the manufacturing process of Yamamoto's Custom Jewelers. They were the only ones he would trust with the Fitzjarrald family dirk. He watched as the dirk was measured by the computer-aided design software. Painstaking measurements insured the historical piece would be reassembled in newly cast yellow and white gold, exactly as it looked today in the cursed yellow gold and sterling silver.

Mr. Yamamoto pointed to the image. "Lawrence, after this process, we will extract each jewel, clean it and mark it for resetting. The rendered images of your design will give you a clear sense of what the finished piece will look like. I must say, this carved emerald is exemplary use of a precious stone. I know you said it was seventy-seven carats, but we measure it at eighty-two."

Larry moved in for a closer view. "It is glorious, isn't it? An associate asked why anyone would carve an emerald, but I think the artisan did an inspired job. There will only be one revision to this design. On the blade, please engrave these words." Larry handed Yamamoto a typed notecard. *Lord, clothe me with the robes of innocence.*

Mr. Yamamoto accepted the card and then gave him a puzzled look. "It is not my place to ask why you would go to such expense to recreate an object already in perfect condition. However, this is a costly project."

Larry nodded. "Sir, do you believe in fables?"

The elderly Japanese man thought for a moment and nodded knowingly. "This piece means many things to your client. It is in good hands. Each of your requested steps will be performed to the letter."

"One last thing. We'd like the old gold and silver sent to this address." Larry handed a simple business card to the artisan. The card read, Tectonic Diving Consortium, with a San Francisco address.

"You realize you could off-set a great portion of your expense by selling me the discarded gold and silver?"

Larry nodded resignedly. "Each step of this process is to be carried out as my client has specified."

Mr. Yamamoto bowed. "Your project should be completed within three to four weeks."

Larry shielded himself from the now fully risen sun, and thought with satisfaction, that Rick's family heirloom would soon be something he could handle with impunity. By the time the dirk was in Rick's hands, the original gold and silver would be thirty-six thousand feet below the ocean in the Marianas Trench.

* * * *

Rick was home from Cincinnati a week, and Anna tried hard to overcome her natural biorhythms and sleep during the day when he rested. Rick wondered if that could be the cause of her preoccupation. She didn't behave like her usual upbeat self. Maybe some time at the beach over the holidays would improve her spirits. He ordered the house opened and decorated for Christmas and planned to surprise her with a getaway.

"Cupcake, are you awake?"

Anna cuddled into him, running her hands down his treasure trail. "Why? What did you have in mind?"

Rick hated to turn her down, but, "Ah, ah, none of that, we're going on an adventure. Pack for a couple of weeks away."

"Oooh. Pack what? Where are we going?"

"Pack layers and a swim suit."

"This sounds intriguing."

"Well, it is me talking, here. Don't I bring the party?"

"You sure do." She fondled him again. "Are you sure we don't have time for…"

Rick leapt from the bed. "Nope! Plenty of time for that shortly."

Anna sat up and drew her knees under her chin. "Aw. You're getting tired of me already?"

"No, we have a time schedule to keep so, get up, shower and pack, we're out of here in one hour."

"You're so bossy! Is Player coming too?"

"We can't leave Player alone for Christmas. Yes, he's coming too."

Anna squealed. "Oh, this is exciting." She jumped up and headed for the shower.

Rick watched the pep in her step as she tossed a few things into a duffle. *Yeah, this'll improve her mood.*

# 17

Rick had Anna navigate as he sought the lighted house numbers in the gated Malibu beach community.

"How can you enjoy the beach?" Anna's gaze swept from her phone to the horizon and back to Rick.

"A few vamp-friendly improvements, and a beach house becomes welcoming to mortals and vamps alike."

"Is that guaranteed at one of the travel sites?"

"Are you wearing your smarty pants?" His hand crept up her thigh.

"Nope!" She spanked his hand. "You made me wait. Now you have to wait four more houses."

The car slowed as it approached a striking Mediterranean modern home with split garages. The barrel tile roof capped a generously deep wrap-around porch. L.E.D. luminaria outlined the circular bricked driveway; evergreen wreaths decorated the massive double entry doors and a twelve-foot Christmas tree twinkled merrily through the shutters of the front window.

"Oh, Rick, this is gorgeous! I've never been anywhere like this. This is heaven! I never guessed we could share the beach."

Rick bit his lip. "I don't want you to miss out on anything because of me. If there is ever an activity you think I can't do, I can arrange for you to enjoy it. Promise me you won't miss anything in your lifetime."

Before they got out of the car Anna's eyes glistened. "That's why I love you!"

Rick's head fell back onto the headrest. "That's the only reason? Damn! I have to try harder!"

"C'mon Master Dom! Show me your pleasure palace."

They alighted from the car and Player bounded in front of them. "Oh sure, now it's all 'pleasure palace'…"

"This is a vacation! It's all pleasure, all the time!" Rick looked over his shoulder as he keyed the lock code. "I've got your pleasure right inside!" He swung the door open. "Okay, close your eyes!"

Before his hand descended over her eyes, Anna caught a glimpse of snow-white linen, fine china and glimmering goldware. Christmas music performed by some symphony orchestra played low on the sound system.

* * * *

"Do you trust me?"

"Trust you?" Anna nodded. "I trust you with my life."

Rick stepped away from the table to tie a blindfold over Anna's eyes. She shivered in anticipation at the sound of foil and the turning of a cork screw. She jumped when the bottle popped.

Rick held the glass to her lips "A taste?" Anna approved the sip and he fully lifted the glass to her mouth. He placed the glass in her hand and poured his own. She held it out for him to touch in a toast. "May we kiss whom we please, and please whom we kiss." The toast's notion wasn't lost on Anna. Leisurely, they sipped in unison. Her head began to swirl with the inviting scents, wondering what complex dishes were waiting. Rick watched her and then began to play out his plan. The sounds of china and glass overrode the music.

"What did you just do?" she asked. She held her wine glass before her lips, as if hiding.

"The food is complex, and I thought you might enjoy something different. You were concerned I would get bored not eating, so I thought you'd allow me an opportunity to spoil you." He beat around the subject, evading her direct question. The cheerful music relaxed her as she convinced herself to go with his flow. Rick was a man to follow, she was still getting used to that.

Her head spun as she considered beginning a conversation. *What do we talk about when there's a five-hundred-year gap? Do we talk about his trip to Cincinnati?* Previously, they discussed art.

"So, who recommended this chef?" *Clever, a vampire food critic,* Anna mused as she sipped her wine. The wine glass was bulbous and large in her hand.

"I use him lots for entertaining." Rick pressed a kiss to her cheek. Anna's eyebrows rose above the blindfold at the thought of who might have been entertained here in the past, and what might have gone on between vamps and mortals.

"You know so much about me, Rick; I read there was some kind of spell or something on your dirk. Tell me about that." Her voice trailed off as she found a breadstick and lifted it to her lips. She had Rick's full attention.

"It was in the family for generations before me." He took a sip of his drink. "Tell me about your family."

"Rick! You do this every time I ask about you! Mom and Dad like to dance. We're Irish, and Dad sometimes wears his kilt. My brother is in high school, ugh."

Rick held his napkin in his hand preparing to spread it over his lap. Anna heard his movements and realized the first course was up. Rick's right hand held the wild Brown Gulf Shrimp by the tail while his left held a lemon wedge.

"Lemon?" Anna's nostrils flared as he squeezed the juice over the chilled prawn.

"But there's more. Allow me." The sound of his voice ran over her like silk, smooth bass plucking a chord in her heart. His near whisper drew Anna to slide closer and turn her open mouth to him. She felt the firm flesh of the chilled shrimp on her lip first, and then she caught a tang of the cocktail sauce with her tongue and bit the shrimp in half.

"Tell me how it tastes, describe it to me, please." Now Rick's voice was commanding a woman who beheld art for a living to describe the food he was smelling and seeing. He had no sense of the flavor.

"The shrimp's firm, chilled, it has a delicate flavor." She was caught up choosing words, all she could think of was the next bite. He dragged the shrimp through the cocktail sauce and then drew it over her lip. "I taste coarse cut horseradish mixed with tomatoes." She nibbled as he moved it closer, right up until she felt his fingers. She couldn't help it, she puckered slightly and kissed his fingertips, tasting a bit of spice. She caught his hand in both of hers and licked the red sauce off his fingers.

"You make my vampire want to play." Anna licked torturously slow. "Keep it up, and you won't finish dinner." She felt Rick's hand tremble as he guided the shrimp to her lips.

She heard Rick move away a plate and return. Anna wanted to ask about Rick's life before the vampire's bite, however he selected the right forkful of textures and flavors to keep her mouth full.

"How is the salad?"

"The apples are crisp, sweet…The cranberries bite back. The walnuts are rough from being sugared, they're so fresh they crunch into nothing." Anna's calm was shaken, she moved indecently close to Rick. Suddenly there was no space between them. His arm found its way across the back of the chair and she found herself insinuated into his side. The fork in his right hand caught the next bite as she described the crisp greens and the piquant dressing.

If Anna stopped to dab at her mouth and angled back just so, she noticed a gap in the blindfold. She froze at the expression on Rick's face. His eye-lids were half closed in ecstasy. As she described the blue cheese, he bit slightly on his bottom lip. He sat tall, hanging on her words, then put down the fork and ran a finger around the inside of his shirt collar. Was it Anna's imagination or was Rick turned on by the food's description, or by feeding her?

Turning her face within inches of his, she released a mouthful of warm breath toward his cheek and his eyes sprang wide open. The tip of his tongue darted over his bottom lip. He froze at her proximity. "Anna, are…you…ready…for…your…next bite?"

Anna swiveled in her seat and drew her hands to Rick's thigh. "Are you?" Anna slipped off her shoe and ran a bare foot up Rick's pant leg. Her heart beat through her chest, she knew he could tell.

"Are we going to get through dinner, Fitz?" Anna's voice was thick with desire. He hesitated to answer while he regained his composure. His gaze fell to her hands on his thighs, her fingers gripping tighter.

"Of course, we're just two people enjoying a meal." Rick sat back. Anna smoothed the tenting dinner napkin in his lap. Something told her he was headed for sheer torture while she ate. Rick's finger traced Anna's profile as he whispered "However, my seductress of the most dangerous type, all innocence and charm, I suggest we continue your meal, you'll need the strength."

Rick drew in a long unnecessary breath and she heard him run his hand over his face. Anna waited patiently. If there was a bit of salad dressing on her lips, she could feel him brush it aside with his thumb or bend close for a disarmingly chaste kiss. The salad was reduced to shreds and she squirmed. Then she was overwhelmed by the aroma of steak.

"New York Strip with an espresso rub, grilled rare, served with pan-roasted fingerling potatoes and garlic buttered broccoli."

Anna laughed, "Garlic buttered broccoli? You're a brave vampire."

"I'm tougher than a little garlic. You're going to love this. It's sauced with demi glaze."

"Is the glaze bloody?"

* * * *

He sliced the delicate cut of beef and the juice ran red. "Oh, yes, it is…" His undead heart hiccupped its sluggish rhythm and the subtle smile returned to his face. He took her hand and drew her finger in the blood. "This will be divine." He gently suckled her finger long after the beef blood was gone. Boldly, Rick, pierced her fingertip with his fang and drew a drop of her blood onto his tongue.

His head dropped back, in the ecstasy of tasting her without a sexual preamble.

"What took you so long?" Anna reached out to him and he caught her hand, kissing the back of it.

"You know I didn't intend to do that," Rick said as he grinned boyishly, shook his head and gently placed her hand on the table.

"I wanted you to." Anna removed the blindfold. "You know, we've danced around the subject of my feeding you."

"Cupcake, you're not food."

"So, every woman who feeds you is groceries?"

"In a way. Anna, if I fed from you every time, we made love, you'd be dead. The human body is quite remarkable at replenishing blood, but c'mon, there's a reason people are only allowed to donate every fifty-four days. We go at it at least once a day, and I always bite," he reached out and touched his most recent mark. Her heart skipped a beat as she flushed with the memory. "I always take a little of you. You don't seriously expect that I would choose to endanger you."

"Okay, I see…"

"My very serious question at this point is, am I giving you what you need? Am I enough lover for you?"

"As a mortal, I need to know you need me."

"Cupcake, you didn't answer me. I need to know."

Anna threw down her napkin and gathered her wits to flee.

Rick's vampire reflexes blocked her at the French doors. "We each have questions. We can't run from the answers."

Anna was surprised and embarrassed by the sobs and flood of tears that overwhelmed her.

"It's true isn't it, I'm missing my mark somewhere," he persisted.

Shaking her head and hiding her face in her hands, Anna choked out, "It's not you, it's me." She turned her back on him and faced the front doors. Rick came up behind her and placed a tentative hand on her shoulder.

"That's what everyone says when they're leaving a partner who doesn't meet their needs. Cupcake, either you've got to explain to me what you're feeling, or our relationship is going to die."

"You know, the other night when I met Cat, all I could think of was what a great mate she would make for you. I was relieved as hell when I saw the ring on her finger. But that could change too, right? You have your own kind all over the world. What's my sell by date, Fitz?"

"What's your… Cupcake, are you saying you're feeling insecure?"

"You may be a vampire, but the longer I know you, the more mortal you behave." Anna drew in a deep, calming breath and shook her head.

"Well, what does that mean?"

"It means, you big dummy, you're the world's greatest lover, okay? Every time you kiss me, I come. But good God, you're thick. I *told* you, it's not you, it's *me!* "

Rick dropped to his, knees, fists clenched in front of him. "What does that *mean*?"

"It means, I'm afraid you'll leave me. Because you're out of my league. And if I can't even feed you…"

Rick dropped back on his heels, "C'mere." He waved her down. "C'mere." She crawled into his lap, his arms comforted her as he whispered. "You are all I want." He turned her face to his. "We each need things from other people. We aren't foolish enough to think we can live in a bubble." He pressed his cheek to hers and then drew her chin back. "At the beginning of my night and at the end of my dawns, I only want to be with you."

Anna looked up through tear-laced lashes. "You do?"

He kissed her pink nose. "Yes, I do. But Cupcake, I can tell you that daily. Until you believe the truth of our love, you won't feel its security." He stood and drew her with him. "Let's go for a walk on the beach. I wanna tell you a story..."

He drew the cashmere throw from the back of the sofa and lovingly wrapped it around her. Player darted out the door ahead of them, and they walked close, his arm around her, their steps in synchronicity. Anna continued to sniff back the last of her tears.

"When I was a young Duke, I met a woman named Tsura..."

* * * *

The dawn was beginning to break when they headed inside. Anna was floored at his revelations. "Two hundred and twenty-five years with the same person? I can't imagine that!" She sank into the sofa.

"No, I can't expect you do. You have to remember that everyone lives in the now. We may have had two hundred years of experiences together, but we didn't carry every one of those days with us."

"The only comparison I can see is my parents together for twenty-six years. Only they've aged and slowed down."

"True, mortality does that. Immortality is a whole 'nother deck of cards."

"How do our two worlds mesh?"

Rick shook his head as he activated the shades. The house dimmed considerably. "Mesh is an optimistic term, Cupcake. Sometimes, those worlds collide."

He waited at the bottom of the stairs. Anna's thoughts were eating at her. She didn't move from the sofa. *Does she need me, or does she need space?*

Anna ran her hands through her hair and hugged herself. "It's all about the immortality."

* * * *

Adam snorted into the phone when he realized what she wanted. "You want me to have four donors eat boxes of our best dark chocolate, right?"

"Uh huh."

"Then, we draw their blood, and send it to catering?"

"Uh huh."

"And you want blood crafted petit fours?

"Uh huh."

"We haven't done that in decades. And you probably want it by sundown, right?"

Anna winced. "Uh…maybe…midnight?"

Adam capitulated. "That's completely different."

"And delivered to the beach house…"

"But, of course. Whatever Madame desires," he teased.

"We really should give the volunteers a nice reward for indulging me. After all, they don't get a bite this way…"

"Well, a gift certificate might take the edge off."

"Perfect! Would you arrange that, please, Adam?"

"What can we send for you?"

Anna hesitated. "Is any of the Stilton left that Rick flew in from Harrods? I could enjoy the rest of that."

Adam barked a laugh. "The rest of it?"

"At least a pound or two. A girl's got to keep her stamina up."

"I think there's a pound left. You want crackers with that, or just death by cheese?"

* * * *

Anna and Rick enjoyed a convivial evening with Matt and Cat. They savored fine drinks, conversation and present exchange. Santa and his elves were generous to each of them tonight, and they were replete with Christmas cheer. The men repaired to the upstairs covered lanai, where Rick and Matt traded chuckles as they lit their cigars and sipped their blood-laced vintage Armagnac. They stood and held their silence puffing. Anna and Cat sat below on the deck, each enjoying her own version of dessert.

Rick winked at Matt and spoke in subtones. "Don't you love to hear them moan?"

Matt shook his head. "Now…when she moans on my cock…I can feel it right there. That's what I like." He grabbed himself and drew hard on the cigar.

Rick elbowed him. "You, Sir, have a lot to learn about romance."

Matt shrugged.

Anna raised the pitcher of Margaritas to Cat. "More?"

Cat nodded. "You really like Tequila!"

Anna giggled. "It's good for you. It's probiotic."

Cat skeptically looked down at the fancy glass. "O…kay…"

Once the third round of drinks were begun, the subject of S - E - X came up, vampire sex. "When you and ah, ah Matt are ah, you know done…is he, ah, I mean, do you . . . cuddle? I mean, do vampires cuddle with other vampires?" Her hiccup twisted to a giggle and a stifled second deep hiccup.

Cat launched into the stats on how often Matt 'wowed' her and copped his post-coital cuddling versus the 'fantastic fuck and run.'

Anna leaned close, hanging on every word. Rick heard lots of 'a-huhs' and 'yeahs' while Matt made crowing facial expressions of pride, until Cat made the 'fuck and run' comment. Rick spun on his heel as Matt made one of his 'I have no idea what she means' looks.

"I mean, right now it's all well and good," Cat said and giggled at Anna's hiccups.

Rick choked on Cat's comment, "it's all well and good?" Was Matt just "well and good" in the sack? Didn't he just talk about her moaning on his cock? *What the hell?* Rick shook his head.

Matt leaned over the railing. "Well and good? This has to be out of context, I can't see her face. What does she mean, well and good?"

Rick stifled his laughter. He shook his head, wagged a finger at Matt and pantomimed shock.

Anna's voice rose to the second story. "Rick is all arms and spider legs while we're, you know, in the act. He's on top, he's on bottom, we're on our sides, and he has a…"

Rick caused a loud clatter from above, halting her comments. He pumped his fist and nodded to Matt.

Matt grinned vengefully. "Spider legs? Spider legs? Ewe. Top, bottom, side, aren't you the gymnast?"

The conversation ended in giggling, and girlish titters when Rick leaned over the railing to the two tipsy ladies. "Don't you just adore it when love sucks?"

The girls looked upward and toasted him with their drinks.

* * * *

Veronique sorted through the information from Flask Brothers Investigations. Matt and the dishwater blonde he'd mated were fairly insulated. Even though she was a fledgling, Catherine Brenner was a much harder mark than Anna Curley. The mortal was young and naïve and the only way to her was through layers of Rick's good intentions. There was no way to take her head on, but with a little ingenuity, she would wreak just as much havoc through the back door. She studied the last picture, Rick and the mortal walking the beach at twilight with a big black dog. This was something she could work with.

* * * *

Player danced at Anna's feet, anxious for his morning run. They enjoyed something of a routine now. He ran, she walked, and by the time they got back to the house after sunrise, she was ready to climb into bed with Rick, pleasantly tired and ready for sleep. Today, was windy, the ocean waves crashed onto the beach, signaling a storm ahead. It was hours away yet, but cool and windy enough to make a cup of hot chocolate a goal at the pier coffee shop. Once they'd warmed up a little, they'd head back home.

"C'mon. Leave Daddy's shoe behind, let's go for a walk." Player never required a leash anymore, and she was never concerned that he would run away or start a fight. As far as Anna could tell, and she'd grown up with every kind of animal, he was the perfect dog.

* * * *

Veronique posed behind a sunrise edition of the *Times*. Her oversized Jackie-O sunglasses masked her suspicious eyes. The beach business was slow this morning, and she was about to shove off when the bounding dog came into view. *I hate dogs.* The girl behind the dog fought with an impossible length of wild red hair. *How far has Rick Hiatt fallen? This is a child dressed in her mother's clothes.*

The redhead padded up to the cashier. "Hi Bobbi. No tea today. How about a medium hot chocolate?"

"Whipped cream or marshmallows?"

Anna patted her pockets. "How much is that?"

"Five forty-nine."

Anna pulled up a five-dollar bill and frowned. "How much for the small?"

Before Bobbi could void the sale, Veronique slid in front of Anna with her hand up. "Need fifty cents?"

Anna found herself looking back and forth from Bobbi to the stranger. "Oh, I couldn't. That's the Universe telling me I don't need a medium. Bobbi, make it a small."

Veronique's eyes fell into slits behind her sunglasses. *The Universe should tell you and that beast to curl up and die.* "You, my dear, have far more discipline than I." Veronique could not clamp onto this girl's attention. She watched Anna as she added chocolate powder and cinnamon to the cup and recapped it. The girl looked scatterbrained. Veronique gazed over the occupied tables. She was lucky to find the last open one, and she laid in wait. "Do you want to have a seat?" She gestured graciously.

"Okay, for a second." Player growled low in his throat. "Player, be a gentleman. Rick taught you better."

"What a charming dog." Player continued his low ominous growl punctuated by a *ruff* now and then.

"I'm sorry. He usually isn't like this."

Veronique waved a dismissive hand and motioned her to sit. "Are you a pro?"

"Excuse me?"

"Dog walker? I've been trying to get a gig like that on this beach for weeks."

"Ohhh. No. No, Player is Rick's dog."

"Oh. Rick is your husband?"

Anna looked at her left hand and dropped it in her lap. "No."

"My name's Vivi by the way. Do you want part of the newspaper?"

Anna shook her head, vainly trying to control her whip of titian hair in the gusty wind. "Too windy."

Veronique nodded and folded the paper expertly in two crisp movements. "You staying around here somewhere?"

"A little way up the beach." She nodded in the general direction. "In fact, Player and I need to get home. He's not himself."

Veronique bit in frustration. She hoped to gain better footing today, but her inner bitch just hadn't let up. She could be more agreeable tomorrow and win Anna over with a grand apology. Weren't girls suckers for apologies? Besides, she had an idea for a foolproof icebreaker.

* * * *

Rick had a business meeting tonight, leaving Anna on her own with the howling storm and a howling dog. She dutifully tried to stay on Rick's schedule, and spent the evening working the remote up and down the channels, only to flip off the set and browse online through Irish antiquities. Her ass went to sleep, and she opted to distract Player from his restlessness. When she got the behemoth focused on a knot of maritime rope, she returned to the movie channel. It had to be better than procedural TV.

The last thing she remembered was Captain Renault calling for "the usual suspects." She woke to a commercial for the next film series and decided to stumble up to bed. Player yawned and followed her.

Anna fell into the bed clothed and pulled the covers over her. At three in the morning she felt a jolt. She raised her head and listened for Rick's car or the garage doors. Nothing. Her head hit the pillow and she prayed for more than an hour's sleep.

* * * *

Ceiling fans turned lazily casting shadows across the dinner club patrons. The pianist played seamlessly from song to song. Rick paced the room, hand in his white dinner jacket pocket. From behind her, the door opened bringing a cacophony of uniformed men, only one advanced to her table. He sported a severe mustache and officious Nazi uniform.

She accused him. "You weren't on a cruise as you'd said."

Sterling's voice emitted from the Nazi's thin lips. "A fifty-year-old crone, straight from the slammer. Too young for social security and too tainted to work in bars. Poor little Annie."

Sterling whipped the Fitzjarrald dirk out of his gun holster and grabbed her gloved hand. She slipped from his grip as Rick bounded between them. "So pretty boy," Sterling jeered inching around the table, thrusting the blade toward Rick. "Gutless? Afraid I'll mess up that pretty face?"

The piano music rose in volume as the club's occupants left in droves, the room's light narrowed to a cone focused in front of her. Rick and Sterling thrust and parried at each other, as she screamed for them to stop. Darkness and light strobed, creating a macabre silent film. When sound returned, Rick's dinner jacket bloomed with broad flowers of blood, his bow tie hanging askance.

He held his bloody decaying hands out to her. "Don't come any closer. Toss the blood to me."

* * * *

Anna felt his hands on her. "I don't have any blood..." she shrieked. Rick flipped on the bedside lamp.

"Anna, Cupcake, are you having a nightmare?" He sat on the bed and gathered her into his lap, smoothing her wild hair.

Anna sighed with relief, she scrutinized his jacket. It was his charcoal suit. There was no blood anywhere. He wore a navy silk necktie with a gold clip. "The Nazi was trying to stab you."

Rick chuckled. "Well, they haven't tried that in a while."

"How can you laugh about that? It was real." Anna buried her face.

"No more World War II movies for you. Besides, they tried, but they just couldn't kill me."

Anna giggled. "Do you have war stories? Did you fight in the war?"

They spread out on the bed. Rick loosened his tie and grinned. "Have *I* got war stories for you!"

* * * *

Much to Player's displeasure, Anna had him on a retractable leash today. It unnerved her to hear him growl at someone, even if it was a rare occurrence. She supposed she should pay attention when she met someone the dog was wary of. They set off, leash extended to its ultimate, allowing the dog to chase the skittering water birds along the path. Anna walked the rain-purified shore and wondered idly if she might be losing her mind. She'd heard that phase "pretty boy" in the pool and the apartment, nothing less than hearing voices. She'd had those awful dreams about Sterling. What was going on? She was afraid to mention it to Rick. He would think she was crazy. Even talking with Cat was a bad idea. But what would she tell a counselor? Would they commit her?

In her isolating haze, she didn't see the dog bounding toward her until Player was involved in getting acquainted. Anna was amused. This had to be a female, she was a smaller, and more delicately-boned Rottweiler. *Player is a chip off the old block, fully engaged in Rottie romance.* Anna retracted the leash closer and the female followed. While she walked in circles keeping a careful eye on the strange dog, she didn't notice the woman jogging toward her. It was the coffee shop lady—Vicky? —Vivi? The woman stopped and posed a few feet away from the canoodling canines.

"Oh, my gosh! I need to get in better shape! I can't believe Ricci took off on me!" The woman bent over catching her breath, making a show of it.

Anna smiled tolerantly. "Ricky? She's a bitch, isn't she?"

Veronique stood flabbergasted and then her face registered understanding. "Ricci. R-I-C-C-I. Not like your boyfriend."

"Did you get the dog-walking gig you wanted?"

"Right after I met you yesterday, I got a call at home and I'll be walking Ricci for the next week. Its owner had foot surgery…"

Anna let her words flow over her head like the breeze. "Which way are you headed?"

"Well, before it saw your dog, I was headed the other way. There's a large dog park just past the pier."

"Oh. Okay." Anna tugged at Player and he fell into step.

* * * *

Veronique snapped to attention as her quarry strode on. She attached the leash on this bitch of a beast and trotted to catch up. "Why don't we take them together? When we get to the pier you take Ricci and I'll pick up coffees for us. Okay?"

Anna ducked her head into the breeze and retorted. "I'll pick up the coffees. You were so kind to offer me money yesterday. Player and I will meet you at the dog park."

*She's a tough nut to crack.* Veronique carefully hid her displeasure. "At least let me give you money for mine."

"Don't be silly, I'm prepared today."

*Are you?*

* * * *

Player uncharacteristically pulled as Anna tried to balance coffees, it was clear he was heeding a siren's song. The leash was retracted to the heel position, and Anna was relieved when they entered the fenced area and she released him.

Anna found—Val? —Viki?—Veronica? sitting at a picnic table. The crowd was sparse today, and they had the run of place.

"Thank you!" Veronique greeted her. "I guess we'll call this a Christmas present."

Anna smiled tightly. "I'm so sorry, I can't seem to remember your name."

"It's Vivi and you are…Anna, aren't you? And your boyfriend is Rick?"

Anna nostrils flared over her coffee cup.

"I remembered his name because of the dog…"

Anna's expression softened a degree. *Did I tell her my name? It was a boneheaded thing to mention Rick's name.* Anna tucked her chin down to her cup. *I suppose I must have, or am I paranoid too?*

"Do you two live here, or are you on vacation?"

For half a second Anna considered lying. "In a way we're on vacation. We came for Christmas." Anna watched the woman absorb her words. *I'm going for broke.* "New Year's he's flying us to the Maldives. Then if the weather isn't too severe, he's taking me whale watching on the yacht."

"You two are world class lovebirds…does he have a brother? I would enjoy a man like that. Who is this paragon of virtue?" Vivi's chin rested on her hand in full attention.

Anna sipped as she thought. *Bond, James Bond.* She cracked herself up and waved at the woman. "He owns his own business."

"I need to own a business I can leave like that. What does he do?"

*This woman should walk a pit bull, she'd have more in common with that breed.*

"What do you do for a living, Vivi?"

"It's complicated. I run the advance process for an international pediatric A.I.D.S. clinic. I go into these desperate countries and assemble the people, so our medical staff can come in and save lives."

Anna stared at her, open-mouthed with shock. This beautiful woman was laying her life on the line to help children. What the hell was she thinking to be so guarded? "Oh my God, that's, well, that's literally God's work."

Veronique waved her off. "Yes, these days at the beach are really a blessing. I find I meet the most interesting people. Just as we've met. And when I'm working in the jungles at night, I think about all the big things people are doing around the world. Like the Maldives!" Veronique smiled effusively.

Anna shriveled at her comments. "I know my boyfriend's company generously supports children's charities…"

"Isn't that gracious?" Veronique nodded benevolently at Anna's words, full of enthusiasm. "Perhaps I could put him on our list?"

"Oh, you should! He would welcome it. *And I need to sign over my first paycheck as a donation.* It's the Consort Group International. My boyfriend is Rick Hiatt."

Veronique's face fell. The air thickened. Veronique drew back, her head swiveled to scan their surroundings. "Rick Hiatt?" she whispered, his name a dirge. She called to the dog. "I have to go!"

"What? But—"

"I'm sorry, I forgot an important meeting. I'm late. I have to go." Her demeanor darkened, and her tone grew grave. The dog came immediately when called, and she left no time for Anna to gather her wits before she bolted.

Veronique had the dog running in an effort to keep up with her as she scaled the tall staircase to the parking lot.

John, her show's animal trainer, waited there for her to turn over the dog. "Was she a good girl for you?"

"She's a keeper. Tomorrow's Christmas. How about the same time on the 26th?" She slipped him a hundred-dollar bill. "Okay?"

Veronique returned to the cliffs overlooking the beach and watched Anna's slow march home. *Have a Merry Christmas, Anna. May visions of vampires run through your head…*

# 18

Her Christmas day dawned before sunset. Anna rose first to plug in the tree and fluff the bow on Rick's gift. Gaily lit boats trolled along the shore while the revelers sat around bonfires with their coolers. Down the beach, a guitarist strummed carols as the sparkling lights in the palm trees punctuated his tunes. Anna never experienced a Malibu Christmas night. She tiptoed back to the bedroom and threw open the French doors to the covered balcony. She put on her elf hat and crawled back into bed with the Santa hat. It was her turn to watch him rest, or perhaps stare him to wakefulness.

She assumed *his* usual pose, reclined with her arm under her head. Then she struck. "Fitz, are you awake?" she almost shouted.

He wiped his hand down his face and scratched the back of his neck as he rolled over. "I am now, Cupcake."

Before he could move from that adorable pose, she fitted the Santa hat over his bedhead. Rick blinked at the camera flash. His hands flew to his groin. "Some modesty, please."

"I got a wide shot, but it's not *that* big!" She shook her head. "This will be next year's Christmas card."

Rick rolled over to her and caught the phone out of her hand. "We don't need photos when we can make memories."

* * * *

Anna carried the cooler from the front porch. "Your care package arrived." By now she was comfortable serving Rick's sustenance alongside her meals. "Santa brought you an AB negative for dinner!"

Rick grinned with his hands out for the mug. "Thank you, ma'am, may I have another?"

Anna stored the rest of the bags and poured herself a coffee. "Mmm! Mocha chocolatta!" She wiggled her nose at him.

"Are you making fun of me?" He drained the cup and leapt around to grab her. With vamp speed, Rick lifted her onto the counter, and he was between her knees. "Drink up. I like mocha chocolatta!"

Anna wiggled his Santa hat on his head. "They didn't have that when you were mortal."

"It's in clause twenty-seven. 'On the twenty-fifth of each month, I get an A positive mocha chocolatta'."

"Clause twenty-seven? I'm afraid to ask about the other twenty-six."

"The most important clause right now, is Santa Claus." He lifted her off the counter and led her to the garage door. "Cover your eyes." He placed his hand at the small of her back.

"Cover my eyes? Oh Fitz, what did you do?"

Rick proudly threw open the door to reveal a tricked-out garage with black and white checkerboard floor tiles. A border of competition red tiles framed a large, shrouded shape.

"May I open my eyes now?"

Rick pressed her into his chrome and enameled fantasy garage. "Open them now…"

"This looks like a beauty parlor for cars. You got me a garage?"

Rick shook his head. "Cupcake, what did I say about your car?"

Anna hemmed and hawed. "That it's the cutest little cupcake box you've ever seen?"

"No. I said, it was a death trap, and you needed a real car to stay alive in L.A."

Anna saw the shrouded shape on the far side. "You got me the space closest to the door."

"Sweetheart, come with me." Rick caught her hand and led her to the shrouded shape. "Pull that blanket off."

"Okay."

The blanket easily slid off the highly polished classic Mustang convertible. The custom plate read 'CPCK'. The candy apple red paint job sported twin white surfer stripes on the hood and trunk, and the interior was a masterpiece of red and black tuck-and-roll leather upholstery. Rick dropped the keys into her hand. "This is the way I want you to enjoy yourself."

Anna's hands flew to her face as she circled the car. "It smells new!"

"Trust me, it should! They've worked double time to have it here today."

Anna stuttered her thanks. "Oh Fitz...this is just...it's just...too much! Can I get in it? Can we take a ride?"

Rick looked at her nightshirt and his lounge pants. "Let's get dressed. Driving topless is different from riding topless."

* * * *

"Oh Fitz, I haven't given you your gift yet."

Rick's eyes danced between whiskey brown and opalescent. His smile revealed the tips of his fangs. His vampire was coming out to play. "Enough about gifts this second." Rick dug through the closet and pulled out a rockabilly dress. "Wear this for me. No panties."

"You're a bad boy."

"Bad boys love fast toys. You know it!" Rick slipped into his trousers, and then her favorite pull-over sweater. She noticed he went commando.

"What are you planning, Fitz?"

Rick gave her a naughty, mischievous grin. "That car goes from zero to sixty in 5.8 seconds. Do you? I think I could drive you to that."

Anna fit herself into the cinched waist dress and tied the ribbon at her breasts. Shirred sleeves fell off the shoulder in such an alluring manner. She held out the wide circle skirt and wiggled under the tulle petticoat. With a twist she clamped her hair up and wrapped the black silk scarf just so. Rick snuck up behind her and pinched her bottom through the dress. "You sneak up too quietly! Stop that!" She puckered into the mirror and checked her lipstick.

"Don't bother. I'm going to kiss that right off you, first chance I get."

Anna slid his gift into her purse, and they were off on her first convertible drive.

* * * *

Anna keyed the ignition as Rick posed in the passenger seat. "Do you know where you're going?"

"Uh...no! Where are we going?"

"Let's see how she handles the hills." Even the breeze didn't wipe the smirk off his face.

Anna followed Rick's directions, thrilling at the engine's thrust as she powered through the curves, climbing into the hills. At the pinnacle, she beamed at him. "Okay, I'm officially lost, but I don't care, this car is so cool!"

Rick caught an errant ringlet and slid it back under her scarf. "I know a place. Take the next left."

*Of course, he does.*

The city below was a twinkling holiday tableau. There was a fresh crispness in the air, along with the tobacco and amber of Rick's cologne. It was getting harder to concentrate.

"Drive up that steep hill." Rick pointed two fingers above the windshield. The headlights pierced the darkness to reveal nothing there. Rick waved her on. "Really, there's a driveway. Go on, it's steep." And indeed, it was a narrow and precipitous driveway.

"Fitz, where are we? This view is heaven." She turned off the car as he moved in for a kiss.

"I've always loved it up here." He drew a deep unnecessary breath. "Everything is at our feet."

Anna leaned across the console for a kiss. Rick's whisper tickled her ear. "Don't you think we'd be more comfortable in the back?" Rick twisted out of the front and into the center of the back seat in a second. He fit gloriously with his mighty manspread like a king on his throne. He held out his arms. "Climb over, I'll catch you."

Her dress poofed as she crawled between the seats and clambered onto his lap. Her knees spread around his hips, nestling her center over his growing interest. They cuddled sensuously on the smooth upholstery.

"You made this the best Christmas ever. Thank you so much I can't begin to tell you…"

Rick cocked his head and placed a gentle finger on her lips. "You could show me."

"You are such a cad!" Anna shook her head and giggled. "Words are good too, especially on a night like this." She tucked her head on his shoulder and imprinted that second in her memory. "It's easy to be with you, we have to remember to make time for each other."

Rick's head fell back, and he let his arms rest along the back seat. "Well, I'm curious. What brought on your deep introspection when we're parked on the finest lover's lane in California?"

Anna turned her head to see his beautiful profile. "See, here we are…I'm driving you crazy and…"

Rick's arms rushed her into a crushing hug. "I am also here to drive *you* crazy." He nuzzled his unshaven face into her neck. "I believe the insanity should begin soon."

Anna squirmed and squealed within his grasp. Taffeta and tulle rustled a love song. "I liked it slow the other night."

Rick purred into her ear. "I can do slow."

Anna dotted dainty kisses all over his face. "I really like this view."

Rick observed wryly. "You can't see the view where you're sitting."

Anna couldn't bear to leave the tent of his trousers. "But if I turn around, we can't…"

Rick raised his brows. "Oh, can't we?"

"Fitz, we're in someone's driveway…"

"Do you see any lights?"

"That doesn't mean they can't come home at any second!" Anna gasped as she rocked on him.

"I know…so, let's be bad."

"This is all too much…"

"Not yet. Let me hold…" Rick caught her slim waist in his hands and spun her. "Hold on to the front seats." Her high-heeled feet hit the floorboards. He was right, the view was exquisite. She heard a zipper and felt his hands skating up her hips, his thumbs caught under her buttocks, so he could tenderly knead them. She felt the crinoline rise up to her shoulders and she felt his cool breath on her ass. "You're right, this is quite a view."

* * * *

Anna gave a shocked, breathy, "Fitz!" as his tongue lavished attention at her sex.

"Emm, most delicious thing I've eaten all night."

Anna stiffened and grabbed for balance as his fingers played her like an instrument.

"Cupcake, you're so wet. I'll bet I have to send these trousers for cleaning." Anna was incoherent. "I want you to touch your breasts for me, I'm a little busy here." He heard her peel down the gathered flounces of the bodice and smiled. She was such a good little submissive for him. "How does that feel—your fingers pinching your nipples while I finger you?"

He felt her thighs quiver. His grin widened as his flesh grew harder and broader. "Answer me, Anna." He insisted in his Dom voice and she was powerless to refuse.

"It's hea…hea…heaven."

"Not yet, I hope no one comes home before I'm done with you. We could be like this for hours. I want to taste you."

Anna's head bucked back as she arched into hands. "I'm…can't wait."

"Shush…. I'll take care of you." His arm snaked around her hip and his hand covered her mound, playing with the curls nestled there. His index finger circled lazily as he pressed kisses down the back of her spine. His vampire came out to play when he unzipped the back of her dress.

Anna gasped in true alarm and pulled out of the moment. "Rick, you can't undress me here."

"I just want to see you. Trust me, I won't undress you. Where else could I hide while I eat you up?"

"Oh, dear, God!" Anna threw her supplications to the heavens and shook her head at his reasoning when she felt him pitch her forward. She threw her hands out for balance, but the broad span of his hand caught her firmly and his tongue traced her crease completely. She wailed with pleasure.

"Do you see those lights on the next ridge?" He watched her bob as her moans drew on. "They'll hear us and think it's bobcats." Anna heaved forward nearly breathless with her moans.

His lips, tongue and teeth attentively worshiped her clit, and circled swollen lips. Anna's breathing hitched in gasps. "I'm so close, so close." Rick's tongue stopped, he withdrew, though his fingers continued those maddening circles.

"We better slow down, I don't want you to hyperventilate."

Anna shrieked a long, low, "Noooooooo." The dogs in the neighborhood below answered her. "Good, God, they're gonna call the cops on us."

"You think? I guess I was right to slow down. Let me try this."

Anna shook with anticipation.

* * * *

She heard Rick slip out of his shoes and then the fluid sound of his trousers sliding down his muscular legs. When they dropped, she heard the definitive sound of his wallet and keys hit the floorboard. She knew he was naked from the waist down. *If anyone comes home now…*

Rick bent over her, his sweater brushing her back. "Gee, I hope we're still alone by the time I…"

She cried out at the sensation of his stout cock spreading her. He settled back on the seat and grabbed her hips, grinding her down on his hard length. "You're so wet, it might be hours before I come."

Anna surrendered to his mastery. She allowed him to move her as he wished. Willingly submitting to his expertise, she giggled giddily, "This just gets better and better." Her head lolled back praying for his nibbles.

His hips delivered a flawless thrust at her g-spot and she bucked to replicate it. "That's a good spot, let's do that again." He teased.

Anna's voice was drowning in hunger. "Again, oh, Fitz. Again." With unerring precision, he did, indeed, do it again and again and again. "Cupcake, you have my permission to come." His hands held her fiercely as his hips left the seat. She savored every ripple and ridge of his fine cock. She felt him thicken and warm from her heat. His Dom voice commanded. "Come for me. Now."

The dark universe drew down into her, twisted and erupted in constellations of sensation. Her limbs were electrified, a fine sheen of sweat covered her body, her muscles shook with tension and then blessed release. All air within her exploded in an inhuman wail.

Then, Rick bit. It was a perfect bite. His fangs rebooted the magnificent sensations his hands and cock instigated. She came again with him. *Did his bite last a little longer? Is he taking a little more of my blood?* They shuddered with consummation.

They fell together, replete in their afterglow. His arms caught and held her as he nestled in the corner of the back seat. She felt him still within her as she dropped her head back onto his shoulder and surrendered to sleep.

* * * *

Rick smiled with thorough satisfaction before he allowed himself a few moments of rest. Anna didn't stir when he lifted and carried her into his cliffside home. He laughed to himself—it had turned out to be very convenient. The front door opened at his voice command. There was no need for lights, the glass and concrete house echoed the light from the city below. He stepped around the leather chaise and laid her down gently, slipping the unzipped dress from her sleeping form. He fell out of his clothing and brought the cashmere throw with him. For a moment, his mind took a picture of her breathy beauty and he savored tonight. Rick crawled onto the chaise and spooned her, wrapped in cashmere heaven. He wanted her waking sight to be the moon over the dragonfly lights of the city. *This is peace.*

* * * *

Anna stirred to wakefulness slowly, cuddling into him. He was gratified to hold her close and kiss the top of her head. He rained slow, gentle kisses down the side of her face to her lips and there he settled one, warm, long, seductive kiss that brought her fully awake. She moaned against his lips. His laugh was deep and resonating, the vibration shared between them. "Merry Christmas, Cupcake."

"Is it still Christmas?" She was buried under the cover in his embrace.

"It's Christmas for as long as we want to make it."

"You haven't opened your Christmas gift yet."

"Haven't I?" He kissed her nose. "You haven't given it to me."

"Well, let me get it…" Anna wiped the sleepy dust from her eyes and blinked at her surroundings. "Where am I?" She bolted up, standing and clutching the throw to her breasts. "Where is my dress?" Rick lazily put his arm behind his head ready for The Cupcake Show. Anna spun on her heel, providing an excellent view of her fine ass in line with his view of the moon. She moved toward the expansive glass walls and saw no flat space beneath them. "Where's my car?"

"You're so full of questions." He grumbled good naturedly. "In order: You're at my house. I think I dropped it over there somewhere." He gestured vaguely. "And the car is in the carport."

Anna looked at him blankly as she tried to absorb his answers. "This is your house? How many houses to you have?"

"In Los Angeles?"

"Go wild, total?"

Rick flared his nostrils as he considered. "I just closed on my twenty-fourth home last month. They're mostly investment properties, you know, like the beach house."

Anna stooped to pick up the dress and returned to the bed. She looked further for one last piece. "Where's my purse?"

"Small, red leather?" His gaze darted to a long low sofa.

"How many purses to you keep here?" She raised her hand. "Don't answer that."

"Is this a formal gift or may I stay here?"

Anna smiled impishly. "You stay there. I'm headed back to bed." She climbed in beside him and shared the throw, presenting a gaily-wrapped box.

"This is a treat, I don't usually get presents."

"Why not?"

Rick shrugged. "Matt and I usually celebrate New Year's in Vegas and Mardi Gras in New Orleans. Christmas isn't special without someone like you."

"Go ahead, open it!" She nudged him with her shoulder. He pulled the end of the fluffy bow and lifted the gold foil lid. Inside sat a jeweler's box." He sought her gaze. "What did you do?"

"You give me gifts, I get to give you gifts too. Open it."

Rick dropped the brocade box into his palm and flipped it open. Gold cuff links held rough-cut emerald nuggets. He held one up, then the other, comparing their shape and admiring the blue-green fire. "I'm blown away, these are… breathtaking. Thank you, Cupcake. I love them." He pulled her into a firm embrace, sealing another moment into his heart. They fell into silence studying the twinkling nightline. Reluctantly, Anna stirred.

"Are we going to stay here until this evening? Player is alone."

Rick frowned. "Yeah, we better dress and head back to the beach." They dressed and gathered their energy for the drive home. "But we're coming back here. I want to take you on every flat surface of this house."

Anna's head turned as they headed out. "There are a lot of flat surfaces in this house."

Rick winked as he pulled the door closed behind them. "Sure are."

* * * *

Anna stood in the bathroom doorway and watched Rick shower. She couldn't bear to wash away her mountaintop experience. Rick turned off the water and shook his head, the water flew, and his copper-brown hair stood spiked. *He's just adorable.* Anna popped open the door and handed him a fluffy bath sheet. "Did Player teach you that?"

"Sure, for my next trick I'll roll over and beg." Rick waggled his brows as he vigorously toweled the water off his handsome chest.

"I'm going to walk Player before I turn in, okay?"

"Player has a good Mommy because I was about to offer a little turn-in nookie." He looked at his reflection in the steamy mirror and smirked.

Anna smacked him on his damp ass. "I can barely walk from our backseat antics. How about tonight, it's date, right?"

She turned to leave when Rick caught her. "I forgot to show you something."

Anna made a screwball face. "I think I'm looking at the complete package here."

Rick tossed the towel in the hamper. "You're looking at my dick. I want to show you my dirk."

Anna's hands flew up, as if balancing a scale. "Dick, dirk they're both lethal with your guidance."

He bowed. "Thank you for noticing. Follow me." He led her to the bed and produced a polished wood presentation case. He opened the lid and the jewels shimmered with fire under the L.E.D. lights. "What do you think of this?"

"Did you have it cleaned?"

Rick shook his head and picked up the dagger. He hefted the weapon, testing its balance and held it out to her by the blade.

"I thought you couldn't handle it…"

"I had it recast."

"The stones have come alive. It's gorgeous."

He nodded and held it out further, "Take it. Hold it, feel the weight. They did an excellent job. I'm truly pleased with the craftsmanship."

Anna stared at the handle and then the engraving on the blade. She grasped the jeweled hilt and slid it from his hand. Squinting at the engraved quote on the bright blade, she asked, "What does it say?"

He raised his eyes upward and repeated it from memory. "*Lord, clothe me with the robes of innocence.* It's an old Irish prayer."

Anna gasped in understanding. "A prayer to erase a curse, right?"

Rick gave a relaxed smile. "That's right."

Anna gave him an impish glance. "I guess this is a little fancy for personal defense."

"It's a close-quarters weapon, perfect for boarding pirate ships."

"The only pirate around here guards rum at the pier bar."

Rick shook his head. "Sad it's come to that." He accepted it from her and wiped it with the chamois and then reverently closed the box. She gave him a quick peck on the cheek and turned. "Good thing you'll be protected while I'm away with the dog. I love you, rest well."

"I love you, too."

* * * *

Veronique sat at her usual table, an assassination bug waiting for her little redheaded spider to take the bait. She let Ricci run. She didn't care if the dog ran afoul of a car, another dog or a human, she wanted Player's attention on Ricci, and Anna's attention on her.

"Hi," she greeted innocently when Anna approached. "Did you have a nice Christmas?"

"Oh, yes, we had a wonderful Christmas! How about you? Did you get to your meeting on time? Did you have a happy holiday?"

Veronique feigned relief. "I wish I could say yes. The truth is, I was so upset when you told me your boyfriend was Rick Hiatt. I fretted about you all day yesterday, afraid of what danger you might be in."

"Thank you, Bobbi." Anna completed her coffee purchase. She turned and nearly spilled her cup when Veronique suggested she might be in danger.

"What in the world are you talking about, Vivi? Rick would never hurt me. He'd never hurt anyone for that matter. He's not that kind of man."

"I'm sure that's what he'd like you to think, it didn't work out quite that way for my roommate."

Anna stared. "What?"

"Oh yes, my roommate, Raquel, thought he was a wonderful guy. She was into that whole Dom/sub thing – you know DRWM or something? Anyway, Hiatt was her 'Dom,' and poor Raquel, he took her traveling just like you…"

"You mean, BDSM? And yes, I know Rick has been a Dom…"

"Whatever it's called. I don't know all the particulars. I was in Botswana at the time. All I know is, they came home from somewhere in Colombia, and I guess he was done with her. They went to a house on the beach, and she disappeared. Never seen again."

"Oh, that can't be. There would have been a huge police investigation."

"I heard, with his money, he can buy off anybody. He simply turned the police in another direction. He's dangerous, Anna."

Anna shook her head and took several sips of coffee while watching the dogs romp.

*Let it sink in… Think about it…*

"You don't really believe that? C'mon Vivi. Nobody in Los Angeles can buy off the police. And even if they could, Rick would never do such a thing."

"Really? Then why was that beach house raised to the ground and 'remodeled' within a week of Raquel's disappearance?"

"I have no idea, and I'm sorry about your friend, but I know Rick."

*But I knew him first…*

"He'd never do something to harm a woman. He'd be much more likely to hand her a pile of money and tell her to have a nice life."

"How do you explain the remodeling?" Veronique swung an inpatient leg under the table.

"Well, Rick has properties all over the world. It may have been scheduled for an upgrade long before…"

*I have plucked the web and the spider is emerging. She doth protest too much.*

"Look Anna, people, especially people with a lot of money, buy their innocence. They hide all sorts of terrible habits. I'm telling you, he's not a man, he's a psychological vampire living off the pain of others."

Anna stared at her appraisingly.

*That got your attention.*

"You look up Colombia, and you'll see – there were too many unexplained deaths while he was there—and one missing American named Serling or Sterling, something like that."

"He's not like that. But, thank you for your concern. Listen…" Anna glanced at her watch. "I have to get going." Veronique knew an excuse for escape when she heard one. "I have a couple of appointments of my own today, and I just took Player out for a short walk before leaving. I'll see you later."

*Got 'cha!*

* * * *

Anna dragged Player down the beach, furious at the way Vivi maligned Rick. *Who the hell does she think she is? How dare she say such things about him? I don't care how many AIDS babies she's helped. She has no right…*

Unbidden memories collided. Why would he maintain a bank of surveillance equipment in a hotel room? *Well, that was a military exercise requested by a President,* she heard about that in the limo. He didn't attempt to hide it.

Why was he watching one woman? *What could one little woman do to Rick Hiatt?* They said she was behind the Barranquilla massacre. Was that true? If he and Adam were there, couldn't they have been responsible too?

Why couldn't she remember her night of passion, with Rick? Five hundred years of vampirism and he pretended not to know she'd forget if he gave her his blood?

What else didn't she remember? Pictures coalesced in her mind. She knew Sterling was the thief on the sidewalk. She set a meeting with him and canceled it for a spa day? Suddenly Rick had the dirk, *why is that so foggy a memory? Why is she having horrendous nightmares about Sterling? Who is "pretty boy?" Why is that phrase haunting?*

Rick returned from Colombia terribly ill and no one would admit it. What was that about?

He had the dirk recast, supposedly to erase the curse—what if there was more? *Had it contained blood evidence? This is stupid, this is crazy. I watch too much forensic TV.*

He admitted he remodeled the beach house. *He couldn't even find it without me navigating.* That's not just an upgrade. If Vivi is to be believed, that's masking a brutal crime. Why would Rick do such a thing? It would be far easier to simply pay off a rejected lover. *He tried to pay me off.*

What if Raquel threatened to expose the Family? Rick would take drastic action to prevent that. *Would he kill to prevent it?*

Anna dropped the leash and let Player precede her into the house. She was too unsettled to sleep. She was unraveling. This house was an impediment to her refuting any of Vivi's claims. She blindly entered the kitchen and prepared a large mug of chamomile tea. If she could only think clearly. She needed to take her mind off this. A trip to the farmer's market would calm her down.

A note would be in order, Rick didn't need to worry where she was. The preternaturally clean kitchen didn't have a chalk board. Where did he keep notepaper? His briefcase sat on the bench next to the garage door. Surely there was paper and pen inside? She opened it to find an impossible number of contracts, emails and letters, no notepaper. She searched one of the pockets, and her fingers closed around a small notepad. Pulling it out triumphantly, she found a twice folded note wedged between its pages. The dog-eared scrap dropped to the counter with a single word visible – *Raquel.*

Anna's hand halted, it was the name Vivi mentioned. Was there bad juju in touching it? Hesitantly, Anna held one corner in place while she used the pen to spread the folds. She dropped the pen when she saw the confident handwriting.

> *Mr. Hiatt,*
> *The machine is in motion. You will be a contributor to*
> *either failure or success in this ruse. The effects of my work*
> *are in your hands.*
> *Raquel.*

What did this cryptic message mean, and why would Rick save it in an obscure pocket of his briefcase? *Was her intuition correct, was Raquel threatening him?*

Anna cautiously slipped all the contents out of the case and onto the large kitchen island. Carefully, keeping them in order, she skimmed the subject of each folio. The back folio held invoices. *Follow the money.* There, mixed within customs labels and value-added tax receipts was a half-page, hand-written receipt with Rick's hasty signature at the bottom. It was dated their last full day in the hotel and it was for 'extraction and cremation, one white male, mortal.' Anna's hand numbed, and the feeling spread toward her heart. Her happiness fell with the invoice. Hastily, she rebuilt the order of his papers and returned the case to its place. The home office was a better source of paper for the note she had to write. Where was the joy in picking up one of his fountain pens and custom legal pads? It was dashed on the rocks of her discoveries.

* * * *

Sunset darkened the mausoleum, triggering Rick's eyes to open. Reflexively, he scented his surroundings, and his awareness spread. The peace was unnatural. Disturbed, he made for the perimeters of the house, the doors, the windows, checking every lock and barrier. He turned in the center of the open floor plan and scented betrayal and despair. The air conditioner compressor kicked on and a top third of a folded piece of paper fluttered.

*One of the cornerstones of Dom/sub relationships is "Pleasure and pain is all the same; only the application of stimulus varies." I sublimated the extent of your domination.*

*I wish I never had met you, any of you. You had my heart, you had my body, my mind, my blood. I can't believe I wanted to offer you my soul.*

*I want a genuine relationship and you still want to play games. I want it all and I want it in daylight where I can see what's chasing me.*

*Go ahead and make your home, strengthen your fortress or whatever you call it and wait for your war of attrition. For me, there are no more tears. I'm done. The scars of our love, if that's what you call it, remind me to guard my heart.*

*The last thing a vampire needs is a dog, I've taken Player with me. I'll drop off the car in the city and leave the keys and your money there."*

The words assailed him without comprehension. Rick stumbled through the door into the bedchamber they had shared. The undisturbed bed mocked him. The closet was full, save for her boots and jeans. The lingerie chest drawers were open, her panties and bras were gone. The jewel cases and perfume bottles stood as silent witnesses to her hasty packing. With a feeling of deep dread inside his undead heart, Rick knew this wouldn't be the same place without her

# 19

Matt rang the bell and knocked without an answer. This was strange. They had a tee time for night golf, they needed to get a move-on. He punched the code into the door and expected the sounds of post-holiday recovery. Instead, he was greeted with mournful silence. With his vamp vision, Matt didn't need light to know Rick sat on the living room couch, unmoving, naked, a sheet of paper on his lap.

"What's going on?"

"She twinkled, she shone, and now she's gone."

"What?"

Rick held up the letter. "Anna left me."

Matt read the letter twice before he found the words to comment. "What did you do to her, Rick?"

"I loved her."

"Then what does this mean?" He held the letter out and quoted. "*...I want it in daylight where I can see what's chasing me.* What's chasing her?"

Rick silently shook his head and shrugged.

"Snap out of it. Somebody got to her."

"Do you smell anyone else here?"

Matt paced the edges of the rooms. "Brother, there are no points of intrusion, no evidence of break in. You didn't have a fight?"

"No."

Matt picked up the landline and scrolled through the week's calls. *Nothing nefarious.* He picked up a cell phone on the kitchen counter. "Is this Anna's?"

Rick nodded. Matt silently debated passwords.

Rick despondently said, "Liplock."

"What?""Her phone passcode is Liplock."

Matt scrolled through texts and messages and photos until his blood rose. One image angered him. He carried the phone and sat next to Rick. "If she cut and colored her hair, isn't this Veronique?" The two men dissected the candid image of two dogs and an awkward angle of their nemesis."

"She must be using Humanité. This was taken in daylight this week." Rick studied the shot.

Matt punched off the phone. "And she's back, the mistress of the mind-fuck."

* * * *

In cop mode, Matt recounted his assessment. "The garage door opened and closed at 7:27 in the morning. The Mustang was in a Consort parking space by 10:07. She entered and exited the penthouse in twenty minutes. Helen reported the Mustang's keys and a portfolio were left on the kitchen counter." Matt kneeled before his friend and asked, "Do you know where she would go?"

Rick's head hung. "She's got a twelve-hour lead on me."

Matt patted his knee. "Get dressed buddy." Matt slid out his phone. "Let's find out where she is. We'll call the responders."

* * * *

Matt carried a tall glass of O positive out to the dark penthouse patio. Rick floated in the water, eyes unseeing. "Hey, buddy. I got something."

Rick was upright and out of the water. "What?" He accepted the proffered drink and tapped his wet foot.

"Security cameras at LAX got a white female with a large black dog getting into a cab at noon. We caught up with the cab driver around nine and he remembered a girl with a big dog. He dropped her off at the train station."

Rick drained the glass. "Of course, because of Player. Which way did she go?"

"The Responders said, she bought a ticket for Vancouver."

"Where the hell, is she going?"

"We called Jerry Curley's home in a little town outside Columbus and they haven't heard from her since Halloween. Their birthday card was returned undeliverable."

"When was her birthday?"

"She was your girlfriend…"

"She *is* my girlfriend. So now we scared her parents."

"What's another log on the fire at this point, old man?"

Rick paced the patio, starting a sentence and halting. Shaking his head in private debate, then sitting back down on the edge of the pool. "I have to find out what happened, we had a fan-friggin-tastic Christmas. We were closer than we've ever been. And now she's gone."

Matt leaned on the glass railing. "I think that house is cursed. You need to burn it down."

"It's not the house, Matt. It's us."

"You and Anna?"

"You and I, the undead. We soulless night walkers. We're cursed."

Matt turned, leaning back at the railing. "Whoa. Did aliens suck you up to the mother ship? Who are you and what have you done with the poster child for Vampire Pride? Are you sure it's not foul play?"

"Whatever it is, it involves our favorite psychopath." Rick shuddered as he toweled off and switched on the evening news. "I need some background noise." Matt followed him inside and watched his friend. "I'm gonna pack a bag."

"For where?" Matt followed him through the loft. They ended up in the dressing room with the TV droning. Rick sat on the end of the bed, a duffle bag in his lap. Matt sat across the room on a hassock. "What now?"

Rick frowned. "You're the security expert, you tell me." They sat in uneasy silence staring blindly at the television.

A catchy instrumental island tune played over moonlight shining down on the ocean, rolling waves and torch-lit beaches. The voiceover announced. *"Premiering on the Supernatural Channel, "Mystical Therapies", starring Trevor McGonagall."*

Rick laughed at the square-jawed protagonist.

*"Lance Pak."* Matt nodded at the Asian practicing martial arts in the moonlight. *"…and introducing Vivi Morrison."*

The cafe au lait actress stood in a lab coat and assessed a test tube of blood. Matt and Rick launched to their feet.

"There's that freak of nature!" Matt curled his fist in agitation.

"Hidden in plain sight."

"Hollywood Confidential airs an exclusive backstage interview with L.A.'s own Vivi Morrison."

The two sat back down, riveted. The show's emcee set up the interview. "We were with Vivi Morrison at her modest Wilshire apartment tonight. We're talking with her about her breakout role as a Vampire hematologist in a new paranormal drama."

"Life imitate art much?" Rick dialed his phone. "Giles, I can tell you where to find Veronique Moreau, who you've been seeking all these weeks."

* * * *

Matt accessed the beach security footage. "Just because Anna drove away doesn't mean she wasn't stalked. I'm bringing up the pier footage and running the time frame when Anna walked Player."

Rick hovered over Matt's shoulder, hungry for the sight of Anna and the dog. "Looky who we have in the parking lot…this morning."

Rick rolled his shoulders back and drew in a deep unnecessary breath. "Did she touch her?"

Matt clicked through available cameras finally finding a long shot of Veronique and Anna in an animated conversation. "The responders hacked into the private security cameras to provide us with video of Anna's walk back to the house." They stood watching Anna's lips move. Rick squeezed Matt's shoulder. "Do you read lips?" Matt shook his head. Anna's face was angrily agitated, and she kept Player on a short leash, stopping periodically to stomp her foot or throw a piece of driftwood back into the ocean. At one point she walked out into shin-deep water, the dog resisting. Only after the dog raised hell, did she turn around. She wiped tears from her face and then broke off to run back to the beach house.

"Whatever happened, that artless wench is behind it."

* * * *

Matt's phone number appeared on Rick's caller ID. "What?"

"I have good—"

"Where is she?"

Matt let a second tick as he shook his head at Cat and put the phone on speaker. "A car rental desk at the Cincinnati train station rented a car to Anna Curley at four fifteen this afternoon."

"It's flipping two in the morning; how did this take so long?"

"Rick, we don't own the Midwest. I had to grease a lot of wheels with the Cinci club to get cooperation."

"…I understand."

"You're welcome…" There was a pregnant pause.

"And then?"

"The car's transponder registered at Anna's parents' home. You said she'd go home."

"What about the ticket to Vancouver?"

Cat closed her eyes and took the phone from Matt. "The ticket was used, she gave it to a woman. She doesn't seem to want you to find her. You have to consider this is really over."

Matt paced at Cat's delivery waiting for the explosion from upstairs.

"I have to find out what lies Veronique told her. If she still wants nothing to do with me after I've told her the truth, I'll let her go."

Matt took back the telephone. "I took the liberty of calling in the pilots." He rubbed the back of his neck and ran his thumb over his bottom lip.

Cat snuggled into his embrace. "Have you ever seen him like this?"

"Nope, he's got it bad."

"If he gets the chance to talk to her, they'll work it out. She loves him, and he loves her."

"When a woman really loves a man, they go through hell for each other."

Cat looked up at him and he savored the heaven he salvaged from their past hell.

* * * *

The rental car cut a trail down the half-mile road to the home she had known for eighteen years. Holiday greenery swaged across the window sills, the frigid night air carried wood smoke and burning pine cones. "You get to meet Bonkers. You don't eat cats, do you, Player?" Anna smiled at the dog in the front seat before she keyed off the ignition. She watched the porch light flip on and sucked in a fortifying breath.

Anna carried her one bag toward the two hundred-year-old brick farm house as a silhouette appeared in the leaded glass window in the door. It was her brother, he'd grown half a foot since she left after college graduation. He threw open the door and jumped down the snowy path.

"Anna Banana…You got a dog. Holy shit."

"Language, dork-pie." She dropped her bag in the snow and hugged him. He smelled like tacos. "Are you still working at Zapata's after school?"

"It's Christmas vacation, I'm pulling almost thirty hours, saving for a car." He popped a look over her shoulder. "What are you driving? Where's your car?"

"Wyatt, it's a rental. I left my car in L.A." *I left lots of things there.* "Where's the 'rents'?"

Player lunged toward the warmth of the indoors and they followed the dog as they caught up with each other.

"Dad's playing billiards at the VFW. Mom's taking water aerobics down at the Community center. Wanna pop a cold one while they're out?"

"I'm not even out of my coat and you want me to drink with you?" Anna hung her pea coat on the hall tree and dropped her purse and Player's leash. "What happened to 'a Scout is clean in thought, word and deed'?" Anna eyed the original part of the home with its high plaster ceilings and earnest woodwork. The breakfast table was covered with a quilted table runner and an unlit candle centerpiece.

"If I didn't ask, you wouldn't offer. Hey, I'm one project away from Eagle. I was just kidding."

Anna shook her head at her fifteen-year-old brother. "Has Dad turned my bedroom into a poolroom yet?" She waited at the foot of the staircase as the Rottie sniffed baseboards curiously.

"Nope, but they were pissed you didn't call at Christmas."

"I've been busy with a new job, I've been travelling," Anna answered absent-mindedly as she led the dog upstairs to her pastel lavender palace. The door opened on history with posters of Taylor Lautner and Chris Hemsworth. The full bed was an avalanche of stuffed kittens and eyelet pillows. She walked over to the historically small closet and looked at herself in the full-length mirror. Two days on a train, even in a sleeper, had wreaked havoc on her. She held out her hair and looked at all two feet of it. *Christ, I look like a child. I'm laughable. I need a radical makeover.*

Player circled and rested his head on a braided rag rug under the vanity table, he followed her with his soulful brown eyes as she stopped at the stations of her innocent years before she knew vampires were real. She stood at the poster of Eric Northman and spasmodically ripped it off the wall and into twenty or so pieces. *That felt really good.* Anna stuck her head out into the hall. "Wyatt, would you walk Player while I get a shower? I'll take you out to Rowdy's for pizza."

"Deal, Anna-Banana."

"Stop the Anna-Banana crap."

The clawfoot tub was the first of the things she needed.

* * * *

Rowdy's was her teenage hangout. Her high school heart throbs took her there after games or movies. It was flush with families and couples tonight. Anna checked her watch, only 7:45 in the evening. In the winter darkness it felt like midnight, she had to shake out of feeling it was 'noon'.

"Wyatt, over here." Anna led her brother to the two-topper in the corner of the bar. "I'm going to have a drink or two. I've earned it. Here's the keys for the drive home." Wyatt's eyes brightened as he caught the key ring. She ordered a tall Long Island iced tea and carried it back to the table.

"Nothing for me?" Wyatt snarked as he raised a finger to the server. "A large whole hog pizza, extra cheese. Garlic sticks, extra garlic butter and a pitcher of Mountain Dew. What do you want, sis?"

* * * *

After half the large pizza, six Buffalo wings and three Long Island iced teas, a familiar male voice called from across the bar. "Anna?" She pulled her baseball cap down and bit her lip. Her teenage dream, Mason Baker stood before her with a tall glass of ice water. "I was tied up with a private party but when I heard a redhead was ordering Long Islands with Grand Marnier I knew it had to be you." Without encouragement, the strapping farm boy threw his arms around Anna.

"What are you doing here, Mason?" Anna grimaced and sucked down an inch of water.

"I bartend on weekends, I got into the Master's program for Math at OSU. Are you back from the land of fruit and nuts?" Mason was six foot three of farm-honed muscle. His jet-black hair graced him with a five o'clock shadow by noon. If Anna hadn't dated him for a year in high school, she would have quivered for his attentions. *That was then, this is now.* "Are your parents doing the New Year's dance party this year?"

Purposefully trying to ward Mason off, she took a huge bite of pizza and chewed while she mumbled. Swallowing she admitted. "I just got in tonight, I picked up Wyatt and came over for a bite. Not sure about the…"

Wyatt washed down half a mug of Mountain Dew and piped up. "Bonfire at seven, dancing at nine, food goes out at ten. You coming over?" Anna glared into her glass.

Mason squeezed her hand. "Hope you brought your dancing shoes, Anna."

* * * *

"Mom, Dad!" Wyatt yelled as he pushed through the front door. "Look who I found on the side of the road…" Anna trailed into the house waiting for the blowback from not calling on Christmas Day.

"Annie, sweetheart…" There were hugs and tears and a few mugs of hot chocolate.

* * * *

The trouble was, Rick now felt isolated from everyone in his past, everyone he'd ever loved. And for the first time in a long time, he walked around with a lump of emotion, somewhere between his chest and throat. Generally, boarding his jet meant a phenomenal business deal or an exotic location. Tonight, he headed to the heart of snowy Ohio, and he hoped Anna's heart would thaw with his words.

* * * *

"Mr. Hiatt," The copilot tapped Rick's shoulder. "I know we've already been grounded once, but we've had word of a storm…"

"This is usually a five-hour flight. Bollocks!" Rick slapped the arm rest.

"Yes, Sir. We have to land in Northern Kentucky. The Columbus airport is closed. We've reserved a driver and a sport utility vehicle."

Rick frowned at the news. "Cancel the driver, I'll drive myself."

* * * *

Anna was in the safest of all places, her childhood bed. She held Bonkers on her chest. The huge cat purred as Anna stroked his bunny-soft fur. She spent the day weighing her options versus the weather. It was a matter of hours to days before Rick's gestapo found her. Now, instead of her home as a jump-off point it could become a siege point. What was she thinking leading at least one vampire right to her parent's door? She regretted endangering the people she loved most in the world. She had to get out of here.

She didn't want Rick's money, but damn, it would have erased her trail out of Los Angeles.

"You and I will stay in here away from that mean, mean, dog and the stupid boys, right Bonkie?" The cat slobbered and twitched. Then settled back down. She stroked both ears. "We don't need no stinkin' dance party! The New Year will roll right over us whether we like it or not."

She recognized her mother's light knock on the door. "Pumpkin?"

Through the door, Anna shouted, "What Mom?"

"Would you mind if I came in?"

Anna shuddered at what her mother could heap on top of tragedy. "Okay." She never got up.

Susan Curley, a honey-blonde highlighted with gray, who still retained her sense of vivacity, held a garment bag. "Pumpkin, your Daddy sent me in here with this. Would you dance a little tonight?"

Anna sat up resignedly. "Wyatt invited Mason. I want to kill both of them."

Susan hung the dress on the closet door. She sighed deeply. "Well, you two made a great couple. You wouldn't have won the Junior's Trophy if you and Mason weren't in step with each other."

"Mason was the only guy taller than me."

"It's not a New Year's party unless your Dad cranks up the tunes and we all take a spin. Don't think for a minute that he doesn't treasure the days you danced on top of his feet."

Anna rolled her eyes, awash in guilt at the soft peach chiffon dress her Mother unzipped. It was not the full-length gown Anna had cried for, it had a delicately pleated bodice with a cabbage rose at the waist. At least the skirt flowed when Mason spun her out. Anna rose from the bed and moved toward her Mom in a sad hug.

"Only if Daddy jitterbugs with me first."

Her Mom caught her daughter's sad young face in her hand. "Are you okay, sweetie?"

Anna brought her back to the bed and toyed with a pillow while she talked.

"I changed jobs recently and I've been seeing an older man."

"Older? Anna, he's not married, is he?"

Anna's smile broke out in relief. "Mom, he's thirty and single."

"Has he been married before?"

"She died, a while ago."

"Oh, sweetheart…I can't imagine what it's like to date a man who's lost a spouse."

"Mom, that's not the point, the point is, he's my boss and things have gotten messy."

"It's never a good thing to date someone you work with, especially not the boss."

"Lesson learned, Mom."

Susan frowned deeply. "Has he forced you into anything you didn't want to do? Because your father will want a piece of him—"

"No! I don't want Daddy to try anything. He's a charmer, a real lady's man. I need some clarity, so I came home."

"You know, if he'll cheat on you now, he'll cheat on you later. I'm glad you came home to think about things. You haven't had a break since equestrian camp before your senior year of high school. I have a little money put away. Quit your job and figure it out at home."

They hugged. "Oh, Mom, I love you."

"You get dressed and dance your little heart out. We'll share that tin of Buckeyes I was going to send to you."

"What's on the buffet?" Anna thought with dread of past menus.

"Your Dad requested a beef wellington this year, along with the pork loin."

"Who else is coming—it sounds like a lot of meat."

Susan laughed hard for the first since Anna's return. "About twenty of the usual party animals."

"And Mason."

* * * *

New Year's Eve was one of the few times of year when Jerry broke out the Clare family tartan. Susan adjusted his sporran with a wicked twinkle in her eye. "A lad can run faster in a kilt than with his britches around his ankles."

"And a lassie can be caught faster as well."

"Does the party have to start on time?"

"How well do you perform to the tune of ringing doorbells?"

Jerry turned to brush his beard and winked at his wife's reflection in the mirror. "It's good to have Anna home. She looks a little tired."

Susan straightened her tartan sash. "She's living the fast life in the big city, I expect it's tiring."

"After the house quiets down, we can celebrate properly." Jerry patted Susan on the ass as he left the bedroom.

* * * *

Curley family gatherings had long been assembled in the expansive, finished basement of the newer addition to the old family home. Jerry and Susan provided plenty of dancing space by arranging the groaning tables of Ohio comfort food along the walls. The preparation fragrances of pork and beef mixed with cheesy potato and ham casseroles upstairs. Appetizers, cheeses and fruits were displayed in the lower level next to the wet bar. A steady stream of guests filtered in and out of the walkout basement to the backyard fire pit where children and teens roasted marshmallows and s'mores.

* * * *

Better lubricated dancers bumped shoulders on the dance floor as the little ones twirled in dizzying circles. Jerry started planning his New Year's playlist in June. He calculated the tunes for dances from the twist all the way to rumbas and foxtrots that got grandparents on the floor. Once everyone was in a lather, he'd slow it down and enjoy a few ballroom moves with Susan. Tonight, he injected the music Anna and Mason had performed to when they won the Junior's Midwestern Ballroom trophy. If he had calculated right, their repeat performance would begin around 9:50 before the buffet opened.

* * * *

The navigation system blandly announced, "Your destination is three hundred yards to your right." Rick stared bleakly down a straight country driveway. A farmhouse's hospitality blazed against the brutal winter scenery. Snow banked under tall ice frosted windows, illuminated with single candles. Over the front door, greenery was bunched under bright burgundy bows. He rolled slowly toward his Waterloo. Did he have to march into her fortress on New Year's Eve? From the number of cars, it looked like they were entertaining. Rick took a long draw on his travel mug while he dialed Matt.

"Rick?" It was Cat's soft voice. Rick closed his eyes and gathered his senses.

"Cat, yeah. I wanted to let you good folks know I got here. Any words of advice from a woman of this century?" Rick adjusted the rear-view mirror and checked his teeth. Residual blood would not reflect well.

"Get in there and…be your charming self. You know she loves you."

Rick pocketed the phone and said a prayer. He knew he loved her, he only hoped she could love him.

* * * *

Rick Hiatt was a vampire who relied on information. He clicked through his accumulated data—Jerry and Susan farmed. Wyatt, their fifteen-year-old son was a freshman in high school and a dishwasher at a local Mexican restaurant. The closer to the door, the louder the music became. He raised his hand to the door knocker as the door flew open. He saw the back of Wyatt's head.

"Hey, what took you so long, Ha…?" Wyatt's greeting halted when he saw a stranger, not his friend. "Oh, crap. I mean, sorry, can I help you?"

"Yes, yes, you may, Wyatt?" Rick extended his hand toward the teen who stepped aside and motioned him into the foyer.

"Dad would have my head holding the door open. Man, your hands are cold. I'm sorry, you are?" The teen was age-appropriately scattered as he finished tucking in his shirt tail.

"Richard Hiatt, Anna's boss. Has she mentioned me?" Rick loosened the silk scarf at his neck and removed his flat cap.

"No, man. May I take your coat?" Wyatt reached for his coat and hat. "Everyone is downstairs, did you want to talk to her up here?" Wyatt hung the cashmere overcoat and hat on a hook.

"Would it be too much of an intrusion if I joined your celebration?" Rick's hands sought the warmth of his trouser pockets as he rocked on the balls of his feet.

"No, man…er, Mr. Hiatt, sure, come on down." The teenager ambled through the original part of the home and pointed toward the addition's staircase. It afforded Rick an opportunity to see family photos and Anna's origins. "Go ahead down if you're not afraid of being bored to death. We have a bonfire in the backyard too."

Rick hung back half-way down the stairs. A jumping playlist had half the room jive dancing while hungry and thirsty guests congregated over appetizers and tall drinks. Rick bent and inhaled. Anna was across the room laughing with another girl, mugging for selfies. Within her element, she was devastatingly fresh-faced.

"Mr. Hiatt, welcome to our home." Susan Curley quietly greeted him from the bottom step. "Anna didn't tell us to expect you." Susan moved up the stairs forcing Rick to straighten up. "May I have a word with you, Mr. Hiatt, before we join the party?"

Well, at least the missus inferred they would join the party, and she wasn't carrying a stake.

* * * *

Susan levied a Mother's suspicious eye over every inch of his six feet two frame. *Who does he think he is in that brilliant deep blue velvet blazer?* "What brings you all the way from California in this weather, Mr. Hiatt?" She stopped for a breath and revved up for more. "Private jet, chauffeured limo? I will allow you in my home, but I will not give you permission…"

"Mrs. Curley, I deserve your suspicion, I might even deserve your anger. Yes, I did use corporate transportation, however I drove myself from Kentucky in this weather to speak face to face with Anna." There was a beat of mutually assessing silence. "I hope you will give me permission to speak with Anna. If I upset her, I will immediately leave in that SUV." Her daughter's idea of an 'older man' pointed toward the front door then clasped his hands.

Susan reached up to Rick's collar and flicked off an errant hair. "Then follow me, I hope you're hungry. I don't feel like putting all this food away tonight." She spun on her heel and expected her corrected guest to keep up with her.

* * * *

"Mason, this is Richard Hiatt, will you welcome him and get him set up with drinks?" Susan grinned, straight-lipped as she headed toward the cheese tray and began to eat her feelings. Rick stuck out a warmed hand to the kid.

"Whadaya drinkin, Dick?" The taller youth asked as his gaze slid from Rick's.

"What do you have the most of?"

"Mr. Curley has his Glenlivet out for the holidays."

"Sounds good, neat." He couldn't miss Anna's scent, it was all over the kid. He ground his molars. He watched Mason snap the bottle over the old-fashioned glass, do a four count and snap it upright. "You do that like you've practiced."

Mason nodded. "I bartend while I'm working on my Master's." Rick felt scrutinized for the second time in three minutes.

"You go to school, Dick?"

Rick smiled kindly. "I finished my Doctorate at Oxford in Global Business and Languages a few years ago. I've never regretted my education."

Mason studied him slack-jawed. "I'll bet. You hungry? There's enough for everybody over there." Rick was concentrating on the bar mirror behind Mason. He tallied the number of young twenties women who must be Anna's contemporaries. They stood, planted in a group like colorful flowers in a garden. They were eyeing him back. There seemed to be a dearth of young men.

"I'll say there is, what's your type, Mason?"

"Huh?"

Rick gave him a look of consternation over his glass. He took a sip and swallowed ash—without blood the alcohol was tasteless. "Young ladies, what's your type?"

Mason leaned forward on his elbows conspiratorially. "Are you close to the Curleys?"

Rick met his lean. "Not particularly."

Mason ran his tongue over his bottom lip and hastily sipped a glass of clear alcohol. "The ones you never notice are the ones you have to watch."

Rick nodded encouragement. "Really?"

Mason nodded, and his gaze flew in Anna's oblivious direction. "That little peach," Mason took in a deep breath. "She's pleasant and she's friendly, but I've danced all around that one. If you're with her, you never know what she'll decide. I went home with her one night, she made me want to die."

Rick nodded wisely. "Blue balls?"

"How did you know?"

Rick pushed him further. "How did it turn out in the end?"

He leaned close into Rick. "Un-fuckin-believable. Fantastic."

Rick downed the drink and slid the glass toward Mason. Without a word he wiped his mouth with his thumb and turned his back on the little pissant. The girls were smiling and nodding his way. They were the perfect antidote to pissants.

He was halfway to the group when Anna stepped in front of him. "What are you doing here?" Her eyes flashed green flame.

"I had a short conversation with your Mother. Lovely woman. I had a drink with Mason." He grimaced his dislike. "Has he always been a pig? And I was on my way over to talk with the young ladies who were smiling at me."

"You stay away from my Mother and my friends. I don't care if you talk to Mason." She set her jaw. "What are you doing here?"

"I don't think this is the venue for…" He was interrupted by Anna's Father who clapped his hands for attention.

"Alright friends, you know how much we love to dance, and we are thrilled to have our baby back for New Year's Eve. Anna and Mason have agreed to grace us with their award-winning Paso Doble routine. So, won't you all get a drink and enjoy the show?"

"That pig is your matador?"

Anna pressed the flat of her hand against Rick's chest. Her touch was still vibrantly electric, and he wondered, *does she feel that too?* Their eyes locked but Mason stepped between them and caught her wrist, removing her hand from Rick's chest. *I was not done yet.* Rick's low growl rumbled in his chest and Anna narrowed her eyes as she allowed Mason to lead her to the center of the dance floor.

The pair moved into their first fixed position and the music began. Rick pressed back against the far wall, distancing himself from her perfection. For every mark she executed soulfully, Mason met them with cold, calculated steps. As they separated with Anna performing a caping walk, his right hand spanked her ass as she travelled around him. The audience gasped. Anna's demeanor stiffened, not appreciating Mason's improvisation. Her friends along the wall began to shake their heads in whispered disapproval.

*The matador does not spank the cape. Vampire reflexes be damned.* Rick insinuated himself in Mason's blind spot and whispered, "You're done." It appeared as though the newcomer had cut in with two innocent fingers. Anna stood, eyes closed, waiting for Mason to initiate the frame. Rick stepped in expertly embracing her, shocking her with the precision of his stance. His clutch drew her up on the balls of her dance shoes, her chiffon rose crushed between them as Rick stole her balance.

"What are you doing?" Anna seethed between her teeth.

"Actually leading." Rick's chest and head were held high with arrogance and dignity.

"Do you even know this routine?"

"If you wanted routine, you could dance with the pig. If you want a Paso Doble you need to be my cape, follow my lead, Cupcake." Rick's eyes registered his points as his hips steered her masterfully. His steps were silently sharp and quick. The sounds of Mason's dance shoes and the general crowd was replaced by the whisper of her silk chiffon and the gentle rustle of his wool trousers. Anna's breathing became the music of his soul as his mind counted the steps with the tune.

Sinuous twists wowed the crowd. Old women clutched their hearts as Rick's neat whiskey brown hair fell over his forehead. The crowd stood in rapt attention as the interloper spun and carried Anna on his hip. With a flourish he finished on one knee with Anna extended in a graceful line across his knee and shoulder. The music ended, and no one moved.

Rick remembered, the number one mannerism for appearing human: inhale/exhale, repeat. Besides, he had to read the room. Anna's breathing was the only sound he heard. He drew in a satisfied breath and relished that she followed his lead with unerring intuition. The room saw it, he saw it. Did she see it? Applause thundered throughout the crowd. They unlocked and stood. Anna dropped his hand and bowed. She turned curtly and walked him backward to his corner.

"What was that stunt?"

"I believe you did very well."

"I was in survival mode. I'm a trained dancer."

"Do you think I just picked that up tonight? Little girl, do you think this is the first house party I've danced at? I danced beside Henry VIII."

"In England?"

"Yes. The Paso Doble was introduced at Hampton Court. It's positively huge and I didn't have to cut my corners. You realize that's where I was trained."

"I suppose you danced with Catherine of Aragon?"

"She appreciated a good partner, although she was a little old for me."

Anna stood up under his nose. "Well, you're a little old for me."

Jerry, Susan and Wyatt circled around behind him.

Susan smiled a Mother's knowing smile. "Jerry, this is the man Anna works for…"

Rick turned on his vamp appeal; in 'meet the parents' mode.

<h1 style="text-align:center">20</h1>

Within ninety minutes Rick danced three rumbas, an Argentinian tango, a romantic samba, and three swing dances. On the Lindy, he nearly propelled his partner through the ceiling, but thankfully, caught her. The older ladies found their courage to step up for four jives. His swan song was the twist, with eighty-five-year-old Margaret Owen, from down the road. She seemed to have lost all inhibitions.

Susan watched with a smile on her face as she cupped Jerry's backside. Jerry slid his arm around his wife's waist and kissed her cheek. Anna walked by shaking her head. "We have innocent eyes here." Susan fell in step with her daughter as they moved to set up the flutes for the midnight toast. She watched the queue as eligible ladies exited the dance floor and got back in line. "Your father had stamina like that. Those were the days…"

Anna ripped open the plastic bag of disposable flutes. "Oh, Mom, T.M.I."

Wyatt lifted a case of champagne to the bar and made a face. "He dances like a boss, but not like, you know, a *boss*."

Anna nearly spit at her brother, "Shut up, dork-pie."

Wyatt rolled his eyes.

Susan wagged her finger. "Wyatt, I told you dancing is a great skill for a man."

The teen shook his head and began lining up the chilled bottles. "It's gay."

Anna arched a brow and nodded in Rick's direction. "Does he look gay to you?" Rick's vampire hearing caught the remark and he gave her an acknowledging nod. She grabbed the cardboard box and threw it out the basement door.

* * * *

Anna traded her dancing shoes for duck boots. In her woolly hat and parka, she held a long fork over blue embers. Blindly, she watched the jumbo marshmallow blister and burn. She could hear the television commentary replace the dance music. *Oh, good, Rick can finally catch a break, he needs one. Like a bunch of farm women can tire him out—and why am I thinking about him anyway?* She shook the ruined marshmallow off her fork and started again, feeling the air change around her.

"Cupcake, we have to talk."

"Ten… nine…" She heard the partygoers chanting with the emcee.

"I have nothing to say…"

"Three… two…"

Mason swooped in and caught her in an uncompromising embrace. He planted an intense kiss on her lips as the crowd indoors screamed in celebration. Anna broke the kiss. "Happy New Year, Anna Banana."

The tension between the trio boiled. Anna shoved Mason away, staring hard at the men. Rick arched his brow and shook his head. Mason stood, flummoxed.

"I'm done. Good night, gentlemen, and I use the term loosely."

* * * *

Rick returned to the farmhouse at dusk. The setting sun threw shades of gold that cast lengthening shadows on buildings. He stomped the snow off his boots as he walked up the wide porch steps. Jerry swung open the door. "Mr. Hiatt. Nice to see you. I hope you slept well after last night's celebration?" Did he detect a cool reserve in his host's greeting that had not been there last night?

"I didn't have the opportunity to speak in depth with Anna last night. I wonder if I may have a word with her now?"

Anna leaned over the staircase railing. "Let me get my coat. I'll be with you in a minute."

Rick rocked on his Chukka boots, jiggling his pocket change. Jerry stood impassively blocking the door.

*This is not the awkward I enjoy.*

Rick and Jerry stared at each other for uncomfortable moments until Anna appeared behind her father. "We'll talk in the barn, around back. I'll meet you there."

Rick circled the old house following the partiers' footsteps from last night. This was not getting off to a good start. Rick formulated and cast off a hundred versions of arguments for her return. In the end, they all boiled down to 'I love you.' It wasn't looking good for her loving him in return.

He walked from twilight into the darkness of the barn. The mixed scents of hay, earth and livestock greeted him as he waited. Rick loved this smell. It was home, family, grounding.

He heard the protesting squeak of the barn door as Anna joined him. She marched toward the tack room and pulled out a grooming kit. Dismissively, she glanced at Rick as she slipped into the horse's stall and began grooming Major. Rick followed.

"I'll ask you again, Rick, why are you here?"

"Your words stunned me. I don't understand what happened." Rick smoothed the horse's winter coat with his hand, following her harsh brush strokes.

"Those were hard words to write." She brushed furiously at the horse.

"Then why did you write them?"

She brushed harder. "It was how I felt." The horse shifted away from her, uneasy.

Rick caught the brush from her hand. "Don't take it out on this poor horse. Talk to me." His voice was low and commanding. The horse stomped. "If we talk and you want me to drive away, I will. At least give me the courtesy of an explanation."

Anna turned to face him, arms folded across her chest protectively. Rick scented her regret. At last, she spoke. "I can't live with a murderer."

"I haven't murdered anyone in eons. What are you talking about?"

Anna ducked under the huge horse's belly and put his bulk between them. "I heard about the murder at the beach house."

Rick ducked under the horse's neck to confront her. "Excuse me?"

"The murder, the cover-up. I had two days on the train to research public records on the reassignment of the house number. What carnage occurred there?" Anna ducked under the horse's neck again.

"There was no carnage. It was a dark night..." Rick followed her. She retrieved a hoof pick from the grooming kit.

"Aren't they all?" She picked up a rear hoof.

"Anna, I will tell you in confidence, but ask you to not speak with Matt and Cat about this."

"Right, because it's never Richard Hiatt's fault." The horse pulled his hoof away. Rick grabbed her wrist.

"Stop dancing around this horse and stop the goddamn sarcasm. You have something to say to me? Say it. You want an explanation, I've got one." He removed the pick from her hand, gathered the kit, and set it outside the stall. Anna brushed past him and headed for the tack room. By the time he caught up with her, she was shakily opening a bottle of water as she leaned against a massive trunk. Her angry complexion contrasted greatly with the white-washed walls.

"Enough with the passive aggression. Do I proceed?"

Anna nodded silently, dribbling water down her chin, her eyes huge.

Rick dialed back his irritation and continued his explanation. "That night at the beach house, we had what mortals would think was a terrible accident. Matt was on a drug that masked vampirism, you've heard us mention it before."

Anna nodded.

"The effects wore off and Cat was injured trying to feed him. It required a biohazard clean up." Rick paused to read her reception. "It was Matt's idea. He had terrible memories."

He fingered the supple leather of the horse's harness. "Matt is my brother, Anna, you know that. I'd do anything for him. He wanted the house remodeled, it was remodeled."

"What about Colombia?" she asked in a mortified whisper.

Rick produced two photographs from his breast pocket. "Do you recall seeing her on the security monitor?

"Sort of."

He held up a publicity shot of Vivi Morrison. "How about this one?"

"That's the woman from the beach who told me about the murder at the house."

"Congratulations, you've been duped by Veronique Moreau, both photos are the same woman. You survived, lots of vampires and mortals haven't."

"But I met her during the day, she was on the beach drinking coffee, walking a dog."

"She's using the drug; same drug Matt was on."

"What about my memories…. Who was pretty boy?"

"Sterling was taunting me, I was trying—"

"I remember Sterling was killed."

"Yes, you're right, Sterling was killed. I wasn't the one who killed him."

"Who else was there?" Her hand closed tightly around the plastic bottle. Rick shook his head slowly, his lips a thin, grim line. He said nothing, waiting. "But, I…"

"You were defending me," he explained gently. "Sterling suckered me, would have killed me if you hadn't swung five pounds of marble at him." Rick swept his hair off his forehead and sighed at the revelation. "You only wanted to disable him. His death was accidental."

Anna collapsed to the hay bale, her elbows on her thighs and her face in her hands.

"I had you thralled. I believed it would save your sanity. Why didn't you come to me?"

"If it were true, I thought you might have me killed."

"What have I ever done, or said, or demonstrated in any way, that I would harm you, ever?"

"But vampires are killers."

"We're *all* killers, if put between threats and the people we love. My kind once killed to feed. I've gone to considerable lengths to eradicate that."

Anna painfully looked up at him. "I feel like a jerk."

"After that stinging note, I'd say you kinda were." He listened to her inhale and exhale. "Were you coming back to California?

"No."

"What about your car?"

"The blue one is still in your garage. I haven't had time to think that far."

"I'm sorry Veronique got to you. If I had placed restrictions on you, we would have argued, you would have hated me. At least this time Veronique let you live. Frankly, you should stay the hell away from me, she may try again."

"I guess I'm safe here in the snow."

"At least you'll see her coming. As a mortal, you're vulnerable. If you were a vampire you would have defenses."

"You could always turn me."

"You just told me vampires are killers."

"You just told me *I'm* a killer. I'd be a double threat."

"It's true, you would be far less vulnerable."

"Then I should join your Family?"

"Oh, Cupcake, do you know what that means?"

"I do. Cat and I talked about it."

"Why didn't you talk to me?"

"I wanted an unbiased opinion. Did you think Matt would tell me the truth? I couldn't ask Lawrence. Adam is a shape-shifter. Cat was my only resource."

"I'm curious, what did she say?"

"Cat said not to jump into it. That I needed reasons other than you."

"You need better reasons than surviving Veronique too."

"The man I love is a vampire, we are all being threatened and the only strength we have is together."

"You're pretty smart for a kid. I won't deny I want to live a thousand lives with you. I would be the world's most deliriously happy vampire. I've had long enough without you. Together…we can never be too close."

"I love you too, Fitz."

"Then I will be the one you die to love?

"Evidently, seems its working out this way. What are you going to say to my parents?"

"First, we have to discuss the dowry. I like that horse, he's a nice gelding."

"He's twenty years old."

"He's a good boy. Got any other land? Cows? Chickens?"

"Just me. I do know how to thaw blood."

"Will you go to Ireland on business with me?"

"Business?"

"I can consult with your father about our personal merger at a later date. It might be better long distance."

"You know how hard-headed I am. Where do you think I learned it?"

* * * *

Jerry sat at the breakfast table, eating a piece of dessert left over from the party. Susan spied through the blinds at Anna and her dancing boss. "They're leaving the barn…"

Jerry's head didn't come up from the cobbler. "Is there a hoof pick in his eye?"

Susan shook her head.

Jerry's head snapped up at her silence. "Is he carrying his head under his arm?"

"They're smiling."

Jerry consulted his watch. "Does she look tumbled?" He drained the glass of milk and set it down, still holding his fork.

Susan laughed. "She's not crying anymore, and I don't see hay on her backside."

Jerry shook the fork at his wife. "I guess I can put this in the dishwasher, then. What are we bracing for? You didn't go into much detail last night. Lose her job?"

Susan shook her head.

"Engagement? Elopement?"

Susan shrugged and grimaced.

"Well, as long as we don't have to worry about their living in sin or a bun in the oven, I can be a reasonable man." Jerry carried his dirty dishes to the sink, he turned to Susan with a fisheye. "Don't let him charm you."

"Never."

* * * *

Rick scuffed off the snow on his boots, mindful of the highly polished floors. He removed his cap as he stepped through the door. Anna slipped her hand through Rick's elbow as they approached her parents.

"Mr. and Mrs. Curley, good evening. Thank you for welcoming me this weekend. I'm sure you've been wondering about the high drama I brought with me. I'm sorry about that. Is this a good place to talk?"

"Here around the kitchen table is fine," Jerry invited. "This is where we have most of our family discussions."

Susan moved to the sink. "I'll put some coffee on. Anna, why don't you get out some of those Buckeye candies you love?"

Anna shifted uncomfortably. "Mom, please don't go to any trouble."

"Nonsense, say what what's on your mind, Rick."

Rick pulled a chair out for Anna and sat next to her. He began with his hands folded on the table, as if in casual prayer. The glint of the overhead lights played on his watch face, and he self-consciously pulled his sleeve over his ornate, antique, hand crafted gold watch. It was his habit to straighten his family crest ring, proudly displaying the crest built over a slab of emerald.

Rick observed Jerry and Susan inspecting his hands and jewelry. Their eyes met, and they politely looked at him to begin the discussion. *They want their daughter well cared for.*

"I might have come in here last night and played the rich son of a bitch. I want you to know that's not who I am, well, most of the time. Before Anna left L.A., she was given some unflattering misinformation about me from a competitor. It was libelous. I regret she wasn't able to consult me before she left for the holidays. It would have saved everyone a great deal of pain." Rick reminded himself to take breaths between sentences.

Jerry levied a look over his eyeglasses. "That competitor wouldn't happen to be a former admirer, would it?"

*Yea, Jerry, being open-minded.* "No, as a matter of fact, she was my business partner's ex, but I won't deny she has an axe to grind. I came very close to putting her in prison. And if I put it kindly, I would have to call her unbalanced."

"Or psychopathic…" Anna muttered.

Rick shrugged. "You say potato…"

Susan poured coffees and placed them on the table. "Is our daughter in danger?"

The coffee smelled delicious and it would give Rick something to do with his hands. He picked up the cup and thought for a second. "I have extensive security and the threat has been distanced from us. Anna's safety is my primary concern."

Susan fastened him with an accusing look. "That sounds like a fancy way of saying she's in danger."

"I run an international business conglomerate. I travel the globe. Anna has accepted a position to supervise a project in Ireland. Just flying back and forth across the ocean can be considered a danger. If you're asking if she's in imminent danger by that woman's hand, I'd say no."

Susan gave a satisfied nod, and Anna let go a breath she probably didn't realize she'd been holding.

Rick stifled a laugh at Anna's over-enthusiastic tone of voice as she spoke: "Speaking of Ireland, Rick was headed there when his jet was grounded in Kentucky. It's been moved to Columbus and I need to be on that flight."

"So, Mr. Hiatt, you've got my curiosity piqued." Jerry scratched his beard. "You cut into the dance last night and had her rattled pretty good. She wouldn't walk you through the house to the barn an hour ago, but now life is good? Everyone is smiling and she's getting on a plane smaller than my barn to travel across an ocean…"

"Well, Mr. Curley, it's a very safe jet. You're welcome to inspect it before we leave." *Please don't open the aft door or the refrigerator.*

Anna hid behind her hands in mortification.

Susan shook her head. "Jerry, say what you're thinking. These kids probably have a schedule."

"Speaking plainly, I have one daughter. What are your intensions?"

Rick felt embarrassment roll off Anna. If truth be told, even a vampire could blush.

"Mr. Curley, I welcome your question. I understand your concern, and if Anna were my daughter, I'd ask the same." Rick took Anna's hand and placed it flat on the table. Gently, he rested his on top. "My intensions toward your daughter are entirely honorable—in the long-run. She initiated our meeting because of her concerns for my safety and the safety of my employees. We haven't personally known each other very long. We've seen quite a bit about how we react in different situations. Right now, she seems to like me, when she's not mad at me." He winked at Anna. "We enjoy working with each other and I respect her expertise. I'm not in it to break her heart." He opened his mouth to say more and shut it with a snap. *The next person who speaks, loses.* He read the satisfaction in the room. *If I had a contract, they would sign.*

Susan beamed. "Do you have to pack?"

Jerry pushed his chair away and came around the table to Rick who stood in response. "Does that jet have a telephone? I want to know when you've arrived safely."

"Yes, Sir, it does, and we'll be happy to check in."

"I'll just run upstairs and get my things." Anna turned on the stairs. "Daddy would it be okay if Player stayed here with you for a few weeks? If we take him to Ireland, he'll be quarantined."

"Of course." Jerry smiled. "We'll make him a good farm dog. He'll keep Bonkers on his toes."

Rick dug his hands into his pockets, he felt absolutely airborne. "Cupcake, if you don't see it upstairs, we can pick it up in New York."

Susan threw Jerry a pleased look and when Rick turned his back, he caught a hint of the word "Cupcake?"

* * * *

*Amazing what becomes commonplace*, Anna thought as she climbed aboard the jet and found her favorite seat next to the window. She watched Rick in conversation with the pilot and settled back. Fragmented half-thoughts chased themselves around what she considered her fractured mind. When her scattered thoughts about killing Sterling darkened and began to frighten her, she repeated *I do not know exactly what occurred, but it cannot hurt me and I'll confront it with help.* She realized dwelling on it threatened her sanity.

Rick buckled the now familiar briefcase into a seat. "We caught a break and we're in line for takeoff in fifteen minutes." He dropped into the seat next to her. "Need a pillow or a blanket or a drink or a kiss?"

Anna reclined parallel to him and reached for his hand. "I need to be un-thralled. If I got this way from thralling, certainly your people can undo it. Do you know how awful it is to have these terrible, vague memories?"

Rick pushed the armrests between their seats up and out of the way. He slid his arm around her and pulled her close. "I'm sorry, Cupcake, that must be unsettling. Time for Vampire 102. You see, it's something of a talent most of us employ. Personally, I don't need to thrall. I talk my way in and out of things, but the responders..."

Anna looked at him. "Whoa, whoa, whoa, whoa, whoa. What's a responder?"

"The Family, as you've heard me call it, has a hierarchy. You heard me speaking with the President in the limo. Do you remember that?"

Anna nodded.

"The President is head of the Vampire Council. We have elected area Representatives. I'm a Representative..."

"Is Matt a Representative?"

"No. Matt doesn't care for politics."

"Go on."

"We have a court system that interprets and enforces our laws. We have the responders who police our citizens, and there are other responders who are like Emergency Medical Technicians, like the woman who thralled you."

"A woman..." Anna gazed upward and then snapped back to Rick. "Was the woman named Raquel?"

"Could have been. I was, for lack of a better word, in a coma when the squad got to the room. I remember tossing you my phone and telling you who to call, and that's the last I remember. Once they stabilized me, thralling you was at my request. And I remember the responder who did it was a woman, but I honestly don't remember her name. If it's important to you, I can access that."

"Yes, please." She paused and considered the information. "You mentioned a biohazard cleanup at the house. Who does that?"

Rick nodded as he stretched in the reclining seat. "That's a responder branch that handles the morgue and hazardous materials. There you have Responder 101."

"If it took five minutes to thrall me, will it take five minutes to reverse it?"

Rick rolled on his side and stroked a strand of hair behind her ear. "Do you know what the thralling technique involves?"

"It's probably nothing like the dumb vampire movies."

Rick laughed. "Thank God, no. It's a form of hypnosis. For vampires, it's a survival mechanism. Our eyes, and attention on a mortal, if we chose to use them that way, induce a deep hypnotic trance, leaving them open to suggestion."

"You mean, you could moonlight opening weight loss clinics?"

"Now that's a revenue stream I've never considered." He shook his head at her. "But yeah, I'd be great at it. It took them about an hour to make you forget about Sterling…obviously not very well. The technician may need an in-service. However, I don't expect it would take longer than fifteen minutes or so to help you remember, since parts have come back to you so easily."

Anna turned on her side and snuggled into him. "Could you un-thrall me?"

Rick recognized her raw need. "If it will bring you peace, I will."

* * * *

In New York, after the jet was fueled and stocked, a uniformed Flight Attendant boarded, wheeling a Hartman tweed and leather suitcase behind her. She smiled. "I have a delivery for Ms. Curley?"

"Oh, how pretty! Thank you."

"My name is Charlotte, I'll be serving you this evening. The Captain informs me we'll be taking off in about thirty minutes. Is there anything I can get you before we're restricted to our seats?"

Rick reboarded the jet carrying a white cardboard pastry box tied with string. He stood like a proud twelve-year-old. "I've been told this is the finest New York Cheesecake in the city! I will have to defer to you dear, dear mortals to confirm it." Rick winked at Charlotte and whispered in her ear.

He returned to his seat with a split of Dom Pérignon and two flutes. He dropped a fresh strawberry into Anna's glass and poured the champagne.

"Oh, you're so romantic, and I love cheesecake."

Rick preened under her praise. "That's good, cuz I couldn't find a flan."

Anna beckoned him with one teasing finger. "Drop 'em Fitz."

"My trousers?" He played shocked. "Right here?"

"No. Your fangs."

He looked disappointed. "Oh. It's not like a light switch."

She licked her lips and a sliver of her pink tongue curled up at him. "Yes, it is."

"You know me too well." In mock resignation he dropped his head and his vampire came out to play.

She extended one graceful finger and pierced the tip. Squeezing a generous drop, she turned her finger over his glass. One, two, three drops tinted his champagne, and then he caught her finger between his lips. His brown eyes twinkled at the taste of her.

Rick let her nosh, as one of his chefs described, on a tray of sliced meats and cheeses with the champagne. She was giddy. He suspected that was the result of the relief his un-thralling gave her. His soft, even words describing the actual events surrounding Sterling's accidental death, freed her. He cemented his place in her life and then praised her level head when calling in the cavalry to save his undead life.

Rick kissed the back of Anna's fingers. "If you'll allow me to start again, I'll show you why no one will ever come between us." he whispered, only half kidding. He nodded his head toward the back of the jet.

Anna rolled into his embrace and he rose, carrying her cave-man style. Rick enjoyed her playfully paddling his ass as he walked toward the bedroom. "I really like this view." Anna giggled. "It's your best side."

Rick shook his shoulders to keep her giggling. "I'm gonna give you my best side!"

Inside the bedroom, he set her gently on her feet. *She is more than the curve of her hips, the shine on her lips.* He kissed her again; long drugging kisses that made her moan into his mouth and arch her hips up against him. *She's warm, like the summers of my youth.* Their hands explored the familiar peaks and valleys of each other's bodies and reignited the places where their play had united them.

"May I undress you?" Rick's whisper tickled over the shell of her ear. She nodded silently, raising both arms for him to start with her bulky angora sweater. He held it up to his nose and scented her excitement and her devotion. "Cupcake, you gave me a dream. It's been so long I thought I'd forgotten how to do that." Her blush was innocent but her expression hungry, and questing. Opening the pearl button of her soft wool skirt allowed it to drop to the carpet as he took her hand and she stepped over the flurry of colorful fabric. "Will you leave your panties on for now?" He pressed close and wrapped his arms around her to unclip her brassiere. "Let me free these, they want to come out and play." The beautiful buoyancy of her flesh bobbled with the jet's movement.

Relief flooded him with a kind of wicked determination. He growled softly when she pressed impossibly close to him, his eyes paled with need and his fangs descended. He ran his tongue lightly against his fangs and felt the cut. He tasted his own blood. The graze was light and healed instantly. If his information was correct, it would be dilute enough to give Anna the effect without causing that pesky amnesia. He kissed her again, their tongues tangling, and it didn't take her long to gasp as the unfamiliar sensations hit her. The high of vampire blood.

He quirked a grin watching her pupils dilate and hearing the tympani of her heart pound. Her body temperature rose incrementally with the rush of blood to her skin and nerves. *Delight of delights,* he thought, *we're both going to enjoy this!* He licked and sucked and nibbled his way down her neck and to the valley between her breasts.

* * * *

Anna felt his tongue was edged with fire as he licked a slow and erotic path down her body. Time suspended, her world expanded into the cosmos as he deliberately licked and nibbled and tasted every millimeter of her breast, finally making it to her nipple. Tracing her way through a constellation, she was near tears with need.

"Bite me, Rick! Please! Bite me!" she begged, her dilated eyes pleading with him, and his lips closed around the soft rosy peak. She could feel her blood pulsing there—he paused, accentuating her need. In his silence, his eyes questioned her as he grazed his own tongue. Then he bit swiftly and delicately into her nipple. That miniscule amount of his blood mingled with hers as he suckled her. Her pleasure was worth any blood he would bleed.

"Oh God!" The effect of the bite and the vampire blood brought a scream of ecstasy to her throat. She threw her fist into her mouth to muffle it.

* * * *

He chuckled at her inhibition. "You'll never have to be shy again, Cupcake." Rick sniffed at the invitingly heady scent of Anna's cum building within her. It sluiced inside her and pooled in her silky panties. He sealed the mark on her nipple and ventured down her abdomen to her hot center. His hands at her hips tore away the delicate fabric obstructing his prize.

He stroked her soft calves and caressed the backs of her knees, lifting them to see the beauty of her sex. She lay completely open to him. *Oh God!* He groaned. She flooded for him. He spread her lips and her thick cream spilled out. He dove to drink her essence off her glistening lips and thighs.

Anna bucked and keened beneath him. Her heady musk hung over them, he had given her the sensation, and she'd returned the gift of rich perfume. It spurred him to take her higher. His strong hands held her where he wanted her. He grasped her hips and drew her up to his mouth, and she was totally his.

"Bite me! Do it!" she beseeched through clenched teeth, writhing beneath him. "Please, let me come again! Bite me, Rick, please!"

Rick could not bear to inflict lasting damage or pain on Anna but knew the terrific sensitivity in the tender flesh on each side of her clitoris. He grazed her lightly, making sure the scratches were shallow and small. Again, he tapped his own tongue and let his blood mingle with hers as he lapped at her again and again. She exploded against him, screaming his name. She bucked so hard he had to draw back quickly to keep her from impaling herself on his fangs. And that was all the control he could muster.

As her body spasmed wildly beneath him, he flipped her on her knees and pressed her forward onto her hands. He entered her with one long, hard thrust. She threw her head back with a feral growl, hunkered down on her forearms, and drove her lovely, firm ass back into him. He spread his hands and caressed the curves where her cheeks became her thighs. He adored possessing her. Giving and taking, they exchanged passion with equal fervor. Rick lost his mind inside her, driving them both to ecstasy as he drilled into her over and over. The blood that stained his fingers scented the air as he worked her clit, driving them both into a frenzy. Anna, shining with sweat, shook when Rick's fangs sank into the delicate intersection of her neck and shoulder. Her sweet blood triggered his explosion. He emptied himself into her fisting flesh with a feral growl that echoed within the cabin and was drowned by the engine's drone. Pressed tightly against her back, he laved his bite marks, reigniting her climax as she moaned out the last of her energy.

*Is she ready for more? Can she take it?*

He wasn't done yet. He flipped her on her back again, drew her legs roughly apart and went for a spot he'd never touched before, her femoral artery, located in the juncture between her legs and pelvis. It was precarious, but Rick had the expertise. He was the master of this bite, and she was his world. As his long fangs broke the skin, Anna's world tilted and spun. He drew against her strongly, not out of control, but more passionately than ever before. She gasped, moaned, and he reveled in the sounds she made. A potent orgasm rocketed through her. She shook with the rapture of it, her heart pounding, her breath coming in deep gasps, and Rick still lapped at her.

He stroked his hardening cock with her cream and pressed into her slowly. As he scooped her up, her breasts to his chest, he sat back down on the bed and felt her legs encircle his hips. He would never release her, he would bargain with the Devil to hold her like this forever. He listened for the calming of her heart and breathing as she rode his length. His splayed hands held her sweet ass as he found his marks and he gently bit again. He shuddered inside her. She'd said she wanted him to feed from her. He'd actually taken very little, but the sensation of it all overwhelmed her. The look in her eyes told him Anna would remember this coupling.

He pulled the covers over them and reclined against the wall of pillows with her in his arms. Her eyes opened as he felt his cock relax and he beamed at her languid attempt to focus.

They exchanged "love yous" with their eyes as their bodies summed up the experience with sighs and moans. He murmured huskily. "I didn't mean to be so rough. Are you okay?"

Her smile peeked out at him, green eyes warm with love and consummation. She reached a soft palm out to cup his cheek. "I'm fine. That was…oh, Fitz… I don't want to lose this feeling. I love you too…"

He turned his face to kiss her palm and held her close against him. "See what happens when you make me crawl across the floor?"

Her smiling eyes narrowed playfully. "Was that you begging me to take you back?

*You're mine, Anna,* he thought possessively. *Mine.*

* * * *

She fell into that airy place between awareness and sleep, the place where every golden moment is saved and replayed at will, her words were breathy. "You were always mine, Fitz."

* * * *

*"Heya, Mom, Dad, and Wyatt!*

*The time difference is brutal, so I'm sending this video letter. This is Erne Castle, the original home of the Fitzjarrald Dukedom. We're turning it into a luxury resort. This Castle is hysterical. (No, I don't mean historical.) See this fireplace behind me? We have one houseboy who spends his entire day chopping wood and keeping the fires in every room roaring. I am still freezing, wrapped up in layers, and we just completed a million dollars-worth of HVAC work! I don't know how the Fitzjarrald's survived it. I'm seriously considering becoming a historical reenactor just, so I can wear their seven layers of wool clothing!"*

Anna walked the halls of the grey stone castle pointing her phone at tapestries and leaded glass windows, explaining the history behind them. She opened the study door that temporarily housed Rick's office, and waved at him, Matt and Adam. She could tell they'd heard her coming by the way they posed and waved, three angelic schoolboys, backs straight, hands folded neatly in front of them on the table.

*"Two weeks after we arrived, Rick's partner, Matt, arrived with his wife, Catherine. Adam is our resident bachelor. He says it's my job to find him a wife."* Anna closed the door and lowered her voice. *"With his looks it shouldn't be hard, right Mom?"*

Heading in the direction of the parlor, she stopped before a jumble of furniture. *"This will be the foyer—you have to imagine it without five rooms of furniture stacked in it. There's Cat, Matt's wife. Dad, isn't she pretty? The most perfect complexion I've ever seen."* Cat gave the camera an embarrassed, crinkled-nosed, smile and waved. *"Cat is working on some stories for international travel magazines, she's a writer."*

Anna made her way to the library. *"You are gonna choke when you see this. Have you ever seen a carved emerald? This is part of the collection I'm curating. It's the Fitzjarrald dirk (or dagger). It's been in the family since the 15th century and was the personal close-quarters weapon carried by the Duke, the head of the family. It was lost in the late 1700s and has only recently been returned."* Anna videoed the dirk from every possible angle. *"Mom, those are real diamonds and emeralds. Awesome, right?"* She tightened in on the carved emerald. *"This emerald alone is 82 karats. I still can't get over why anyone would carve an emerald, but it is beautiful, isn't it? You see the night bird on top? The carving is the Fitzjarrald family crest, and there's a great story about the night bird. In their early history, a night bird woke the Fitzjarrald's nursemaid and saved them from a fire, and that's how the night bird got to be part of the family crest."*

She climbed the remaining floors to the top of the crenellated castle and shot a panoramic image of the orange and purple sky at sunset. *"These crenellations..."* She pointed at the square indentations. *"...were the openings for guns and cannons, but we're having binoculars mounted on them, so people can get up close with the magnificent view."*

She finished by turning the lens on herself. For her good-bye, she showed them her best, fresh-washed face with her biggest smile.

*"Give Player a big hug from us, Okay? I love you all. Our grand opening date isn't firm, but Rick will send a jet to bring you over when it's ready. So make sure your passports are up to date. And Daddy—the jet is bigger than your barn!*

*Love,*

*Your Pumpkin."*

* * * *

Adam chuckled as the study door closed on Anna. "Isn't she cute when she's busy?"

Matt gave him an incredulous look. "She hasn't been busy by herself." His remark earned him raised eyebrows from Rick. "The old man here, stormed the castle, won the maiden, bedded her, blooded her, and mated with her." Matt stretched back in the club chair and extended his long legs. He readjusted himself and shot Rick a wry glance. "After all these years of being around us, Adam, this might be the first time you've seen a newly mated mortal. Cat was never like this. Anna's a walking testimony to the allure of fang on flesh. She makes every vamp around her want to pull up tough." Matt sat up suddenly, shifted forward in his chair, spread his knees and held an imaginary woman before him.

Rick watched Matt make his 'come face' and shook his head. "I *am* a lucky vampire."

Matt reclined and rubbed at the back of his neck as he drew his tongue over his lips. "I'd like a little romancing with Cat. Is there any corner of this castle that doesn't echo at the slightest moan? I don't want to assault your sensitive vamp ears."

Rick moved pens and paperclips around his desk top, his expression meek as a Sunday school teacher. "There's a lovely room on the fourth floor. It should be conducive to your 'well and good' intentions.

Matt smiled pleasantly. "And that should allow you time for your gymnastic workout with Anna."

Adam shook his head. "I definitely need a woman."

Rick nodded. "Right after this thing with Ronnie is settled, your sex life is our next priority."

Adam grimaced and looked between the two men.

Rick carried on. "Now, who do we know in the Hollywood community who's got access to Ronnie? They have to be a good sport."

Adam scrolled through the list of Gaoler members on his tablet. "Ah, Greg Reardon is a vamp, a great guy, and his sub is Jessie Gordon."

"Jessie, 'the crane,' Gordon?" Rick looked at the ceiling mural and imagined the young man floating naked in the clouds along with the angels.

"The one who looks like an underage choir boy but balls like a jackhammer?" Matt chuckled.

Adam nodded seriously. "One and the same."

Rick picked up his phone. "That'll work."

# 21

The television writer was coasting in this incarnation as Gregory Reardon. Greg had an endearing cleft in his chin to balance a full but receding hairline. His middle-aged everyman's face let him blend into the Hollywood film industry. Not so handsome that he was threatening, not so homely that he belonged in Washington, D.C. The gay lifestyle was well accepted these days in Hollywood, and Greg enjoyed being his unfettered, flamboyant self. When he realized he was the oldest staff writer, even by mortal standards, on his new gig with a cable network, he chalked it up to working in an industry that worshiped youth.

How hard would it be to write about the supernatural, when you were a three-hundred-year old vampire? He took hubris in writing a proper vampire, only to get shot down weekly by the network execs. After surviving February sweeps, Greg issued invitations to the cast and crew of Mystical Therapies for a weekend blow-out. Rick's call was therefore well-timed.

Greg watched with amusement as his 'guest of honor' struggled to park the mammoth Bentley in the politically correct, conservatively-sized L.A. parking space. The setting sun laid a blanket of pink and orange over the luau party decorations. Hopefully, all the party-goers who stayed the entire weekend would drink and screw enough to keep them in bed till dusk. If not, Greg would have to find a surrogate to host pool-time during the afternoons.

Bon vivant that he was, he stood in the doorway with a monster sized mai tai to greet Veronique. "Vivi, dear, you've had a whirlwind career. This time last year you were fighting to find a parking space at UCLA!" The paternal writer wrapped a platonic arm around the BoHo-chic actress and pressed the drink into her free hand. *I happen to know you were in Colombia living off fatted donors when you weren't peddling Humanité.*

"You know, I'm just counting my blessings," Veronique agreed. "Yeah, I'd like to blow off a little steam. What kind of man-candy have you got roaming these glass halls?" She brushed her hip against his board shorts. Greg knew she hadn't heard a thing he said since arriving, her gaze riveted from cock to cock to cock.

"We're not shy here, Vivi. If you feel the need for the setting sun on your buns, go ahead…" Greg sniffed her rutting hormones as she trotted in the direction of the pergola by the edge of the patio. She was as predictable as the tides.

His instincts had been right when he'd tapped his sub to play her love interest. Jesse Gordon was a preternaturally youthful vamp, and Greg had him spray-tanned and groomed like the stallion he was. Jesse would be the perfect target of her 'affections.' He had the lean, lithe musculature of a swimmer, except his speed was impeded by the colossal schlong he could barely tuck into the blue-green Speedo that matched his bedroom eyes. Greg observed the greedy spider moving in for her conquest. Her fingers flew immediately to Jesse's riot of dark chocolate waves. If she hadn't been tanked on Humanité, Jesse would have had fangs by midnight. *Sorry, sweet cheeks, he's been in the Family since 1859, and he's mine.*

* * * *

It was the withdrawal hunger again. Veronique was rousted from her rest by the bloody hunger for some fresh O positive. She sat up, her sensitive flesh sliding across silken sheets. She was nude in a strange bed with no accounting of the experience. Blackout drapes leaked sunlight around their perimeter. It was daytime, and the last thing she remembered was the party Friday night.

"Thank God you're awake!" Greg stood at her bedside holding a tumbler that smelled like bagged blood.

"Is that the best you've got?" she snapped. "And when did you become a member of the Family?"

Greg frowned. "My dear, I've been a vampire for three hundred years. You were on too much Humanité to notice. But now, as you can see, it's worn off."

Veronique developed a case of modesty and drew up the sheet. "What happened to me?"

"I'm sorry to say that beautiful boy you partied with Friday night drugged you, and that's not all…" His gaze shifted away nervously.

"You're scaring me, Greg. What's going on?"

"The little snot filmed the two of you having carnal knowledge and shopped it to TMI."

"What?"

"Afraid so, dearest. Of course, all the mortals think he's underage. We know better, but what can you do, out him as a vampire?"

"They think I had sex with a minor?"

"Yep. The studio's after your head. The police are a sniffing around your apartment. This is a clusterfuck."

Veronique buried her head in her knees. "Oh, fuck me!"

"That's what he did. I'm afraid you're persona non grata in Hollywood, maybe even in the United States."

Veronique submerged into self-pity as she drank the blood. "Everything was going so well!"

Greg nodded sadly. "Dicks can truly fuck you up!"

"Is there any hope of defending myself?"

"Not that I can see. You're more likely to wind up in jail, and sans Humanité, you'd have a rather unpleasant Polanski-esque time of it. If I were you, I'd get the hell out of Dodge."

"But where can I go?" Veronique could hear the whine in her own voice. "Back to Haiti?"

Greg considered for a moment. "No, you'd never make it past the security checks, plus, they have extradition." The two sat in silence and then he snapped his fingers. "I've got a friend with a yacht, but…"

"I could change my appearance."

"No, the anti-terrorism software is too sophisticated for that. They'd catch you on the screening… but they'd never look for you in a shipping crate."

"A shipping crate is so coarse! Why not a coffin?"

Greg considered. "Why not? We could send you to Mexico, you'd be safe there. You'd have a peaceful little rest. On his yacht it would take less than a day, and you'll rise refreshed and free."

Vivi Morrison was dead. Long live Veronique Moreau. She picked up her dying cell phone, confirming her fate and then arranged a bank wire. "Is it possible to go back to my apartment?" Greg shook his head. "I need something to wear, I have a few things squirreled away…"

"Give me a list. I'll find a way in…"

* * * *

Once out of Veronique's sight, Greg texted Rick. "She bought it! Departing via your transport at 2100 hours L.A. time. The pleasure was all mine. This stuff writes itself!"

He received a return text. "Greg, you've been a real sport. I.O.U."

The writer's fingers flew over the keyboard. "Let me write your biography. You could play yourself, you'd win an Oscar."

His heart sank at the reply. "Dear boy, biographies are for dead people. Do a fictionalized version and *you'll* win the Oscar."

* * * *

Rick slipped his phone back in his pocket and smiled at Anna. "We'll have a guest joining us soon."

She nodded. Rick walked from window to window, touching the new panes and recalling the ancient leaded glass. He approached the altar and ran a fond hand over the carved wood, smoothed by centuries of similar touches.

"You know, if the family hadn't fallen into disrepute, I would have been sent off to life in the Church, rather than becoming the Duke."

"So, you would have been a priest?"

"Most probably."

"Anglican or Catholic?"

Rick shrugged. "What does it matter?"

"That's true. If you'd become a priest, I wouldn't be here."

He stared up at the almost life-sized Christ crucified above the altar and then turned and looked at the empty seats. "Neither would I."

Anna laughed, and kissed him quickly. "I'm glad it worked out the way it did. This space will be so pretty for weddings and christenings."

"It's served that purpose for hundreds of years." Rick knelt under the altar and worked a stone out of the floor. It lifted cleanly to reveal a six-by-six inch open space. A leather pouch lay inside, awaiting the return of a little boy's hands. "I can't believe it's survived all these years." He stood holding his childhood treasures.

"What is that? How did you know it was there?"

"I put it there. I'll show you." He led her to a pew and opened the now brittle bag with great care. Ten knuckle bones and a disintegrating ball spilled out along with a crude wooden top and a marble knight from a long-forgotten chess set. He fished in the pouch with two long fingers and drew out an unmatched emerald earring. "These were the gaming systems of the 1500s. I played with them every day until I was sent to foster at nine years."

"So, these were your toys!"

"Yes, my most prized. Understanding I also had my horse and my dog and the family."

"Oh, these are so sweet! I'm trying to imagine you as a little boy…that's so long ago, do you still remember it?"

"Uh, yeah. Do you remember being a little girl?"

"Yes, but for me it wasn't five hundred years ago."

"I get it. Let me tell you about memory, Cupcake. Years are not remembered in time. They're remembered in experiences. So, I can't ask you to remember exactly what you were doing on any day, unless it was a remarkable day. But you could tell me exactly what happened on a special day."

"Like New Year's Eve?"

"You bet. I'll never forget it." He balanced the bones in his palm affectionately.

"I want lifetimes of memories with you."

Her words stopped him. "You know what that means…"

"Yes. I want you to turn me."

Rick went dizzy with joy, unfamiliar warmth spread from his heart, throughout his chest as elation grew within him. He worked to keep his voice modulated. "You've given this a lot of thought."

Anna straddled his lap, took his earnest face between her hands and smiled. "In this sacred place, I swear, I want to spend lifetimes with you."

Rick smiled back. "I guess we need to set a date."

* * * *

Rick and Matt delighted in hearing Veronique's impatient clawing at the coffin's lid for at least thirty minutes before they unsealed her. The shock on her face when they opened the lid was gratifying. The two vampires leaned over her.

"Well, our old friend, Veronique!" Rick said with false enthusiasm.

"You!" she spat back.

Matt drew her attention as he bent menacingly closer. "You've been a very naughty girl, again, Ronnie. Same old story, same old song and dance."

Veronique assessed her situation, seeking an escape route. Rick smiled broadly and shook his head. "Forget it. You wouldn't get to the door. And I'd be very happy to behead you myself."

"What do you want, Rick?" she growled through gritted teeth. "You've taken my money, my job, everything—"

"Poor, preyed upon psychopath."

"What do you want?" She crawled out of the coffin and stood defiantly before them.

"I was at your trial, Ms. Moreau. I distinctly heard the judge say any further use of Humanité would end in termination," Adam said pleasantly and turned to Rick "You voted on that new law, didn't you, Representative Hiatt?"

"Why, yes I did, Master Adam. It seems Ms. Moreau doesn't take Council authority seriously."

Matt tsked. "That's a sure way to be separated from your head."

Rick stepped forward, his face serious. "Last chance, Ronnie. You sign this confession admitting your illegal use of Humanité, and get out of our lives forever, or…"

"Or?" she sniped.

"Or, we'll take you to Geneva right now and present a stream of witnesses to your illegal use of the drug and then it's lights out."

Rick watched the wheels turn in her mind as she contemplated her choices. He saw the moment she concluded she had none.

"Fine. Give me the confession and a pen."

Rick handed both to her and waited as she signed. He held his insurance policy with satisfaction. "This is no game, Ronnie. You stay away from us, from our women, and our business. I see your fingerprints anywhere near us and I'll go medieval on your head."

"What am I supposed to do for money? You've left me nothing." She spun on her heel toward Matt. "How about you give me that 1.5 million dollars back that I was forced to pay you?"

Matt gave her a sardonic sneer. "I suggest you sell timeshares."

Rick stepped between them. "The jet is waiting to take you to Chad. They speak French there. I'm sure you'll find some nice despot to take you in. Whatever, stay the hell away from us or…"

"Yes, yes, I heard you. Where the hell is Chad?"

"Good. Adam will take you to the airport. Adieu!"

* * * *

Anna jumped up from her computer and ran to find Cat. "You have got to see this!" She danced from foot to foot waiting for Cat to confirm her find.

"Look at the second miniature down, the little boys. What does the catalogue label say?"

"Miniature portrait of brothers Richard and Niall Fitzjarrald, 1520." Cat read. She looked up at Anna and smiled.

"Does one of them look like Rick, do you think? Could it be Rick as a little boy?"

Cat studied the diminutive portrait. "They're so tiny it's hard to tell, but, could be. You're the expert. What do you think?"

"See those bones they're playing with?" Cat squinted and nodded. "Rick showed me knuckle bones he prized and played with as a little boy. And, he did have a brother named Niall, older by two years. Niall died shortly after this miniature was painted. Miniatures where like family photos, you know? Much more personal than the formal portraits. His family would have kept this miniature like we keep a phone photo…"

"It's for sale. Are you going to buy it for the history room? You should show it to Rick."

Anna dialed the contact number on the website. "I am going to buy it, but I'm not going to show it to Rick yet. I want it to be my mating gift to him." She held up an extended pinkie finger to Cat. "Pinkie swear with me you won't tell Rick or Matt. This is just perfect! I want something unique, something he wouldn't buy for himself…"

Cat laughed. "Okay, pinkie swear. See if you can get them to send it to Dublin. We can run into the city and pick it up."

* * * *

The remodel of the entire estate continued apace, everyone in their group having distinct responsibilities. In addition to Anna's curating historical elements, and Cat's developing marketing literature, the women found their greatest enjoyment in decorating four floors of the castle. Meanwhile, in addition to managing a multinational corporation, Rick, Matt and Adam supervised the renovation of the outlying buildings, stables, and golf course.

This particular night, the five of them found peace in gathering in the study over dinner. Rick was restless. The others watched him fret over a clipboard, drop it, and march to the bar to hastily pour a whiskey, add a few drops of A positive, and down it.

"This is grueling. You have to stay on these people to the letter." He turned and leaned against the makeshift bar. "How hard is it? Measure twice, cut once. I swear these flooring specialists are extortionists!"

Adam lowered his tablet and cocked his head. "You've built skyscrapers! What's the problem with a few board feet?"

Rick downed another drink and replaced the glass with a shove. "Not here. I think I've bought enough wood to cover the ceilings too."

Matt exchanged looks with the ladies and shook his head. "Oh, for the good old days when the only people you had to flog were your submissives."

Cat had a lap full of bridal magazines. "You know, the bridal industry will make us a small fortune. From what Anna has planned for your mating ceremony, I'm seeing a new revenue stream."

Rick pursed his lips. "Thank God this only happens once."

Anna circled him with the list of ceremony suppliers. She curled herself into his slack arms. "The ceremony only happens once but think of the anniversaries. If the sixtieth year is diamonds, what will we exchange at a century?"

Matt poked Cat with his elbow in an obvious stage whisper. "The high hard one."

Rick slanted him a dubious look. "I heard that!" He hooked Anna into a playful embrace. "What's the gift for fifty years?"

Anna consulted her list. "Gold."

"Then I'll give you twice as much gold." Rick kissed the top of her head.

* * * *

Veronique tapped an impatient toe in the filth of Chad's International Airport. *This country is completely unacceptable.* Rick Hiatt had a vengeful sense of humor and he could think again, if he expected her to stay in this God-forsaken hell-hole. She was eternally grateful that she'd had the presence of mind to keep her cell phone with her. She used the directory now and dialed.

"Mr. Nassar, please, Veronique Moreau calling." She waited an interminable amount of time for him to pick up.

"Veronique! I haven't heard from you since last year's unfortunate events. I'm sorry to hear about your Papa's death."

"Omar, it's good to hear your voice." She began tragically. "Yes, Papa is gone." She played Omar with a mournful beat of silence. "In the midst of my bereavement I've lost a bet."

"Oh, my dear, what can I do to help the fledgling of one of my oldest friends?"

Veronique sighed and winced at what she was about to do. "I'm stuck in Chad. Have you ever been to Chad?"

"Oh, dear child. Are you near the airport?"

"Yes. I am. I have found myself stranded without a passport." She sniffed dramatically. "Daylight is breaking, and I have nowhere to go to ground."

"Veronique, dear, you wait at the terminal, it's small but safe. The banking center is the most protected for you. I'm sending my plane. I'll arrange for your safe passage back to Haiti."

"I knew you could help me. I simply have no words! Thank you, thank you, thank you!"

"Please let me know you've arrived safely. Do you need help with the authorities there?"

"Thank you, but no, Omar, I still have many friends within the Haitian government."

* * * *

Settled in the leather luxury of Omar Nassar's private jet, Veronique plotted the ultimate revenge. Death was too immediate for Rick Hiatt and Matt Brenner. She intended for them to suffer long and cruelly. The most direct way to accomplish that was with the torturous deaths of their mates, the blame for which would be laid directly at their feet. If she were lucky, she'd come out of it a billion dollars ahead. *It's called doubling down.*

It was easy to rent a hotel room for a week in Chad. No one had reason to suspect it remained empty. It would take one day at most to have her passport replaced in Haiti, and another to get back to the United Kingdom.

* * * *

Anna and Cat hovered in the shadows of the staircase. Cat whispered, "What do you think they're up to?"

"Probably a little of what we're trying to pull off." Anna moved the curtain to hide from Matt and Rick who were getting into one of the property's Range Rovers.

"Well then, as soon as they're out of sight, we can boogie over to Dublin and pick up the miniature."

Anna gave the sky an assessing glance. "The weather is on your side, Cat, it's due to be overcast all day. If you ride in the back, will you be okay?"

Cat nodded. "Ready any time you are."

* * * *

Veronique watched the two women as they giggled their way down the sidewalk, paying no attention to their surroundings. *Typical.* Veronique clicked the cloned car key and made adjustments to the dome light. She loved the fact that Rick had an affinity for triple-black automobiles. She checked her pocket for the syringes. The one in her right pocket was a well-known human sedative. The one in her left pocket was a special cocktail of paralytics used to immobilize vampires. Relocking the doors, this spider just had to lay in wait.

Veronique reveled in her vampirism—no more puny human mimicry for her! Her vampire hearing easily detected familiar voices over the din of street sounds. Anticipation danced within her when she heard Anna's boots on the pavement. Her need burgeoned when the locks clicked. *Patience is a virtue.* Just as predicted, the ladies entered the front seat and clicked into safety belts. *Seat belts insure such a false sense of security.* Anna keyed the ignition and the radio drowned the sound of Veronique's movement. They sat chatting about their next stop. *What a rush!* Veronique palmed the two syringes, rose up from the back seat utilizing vampire speed, and simultaneously directed her aim into their necks. There was a small jolt of recognition in Anna's eyes as she slipped into oblivion. Cat's unresponsive gaze registered mute confusion.

Employing preternatural strength, she pulled Cat through the center console onto the back seat and then went to the driver's side to push Anna into a lump in the passenger's seat. Putting the car in gear, she floored the Range Rover into thin traffic earning a blare of horns. *Bite me.* She giggled, high on her conquest. Veronique followed the navigation system to a private dock.

The small boat she rented would be waiting for her. It invigorated her to buy the services of a strapping fisherman who was stupid enough to agree to transport a casket to Lamb Island after dark. She pulled into a private garage where her pre-rented pickup truck held one wide coffin.

It was nothing to load the women face to face into the casket and slide it into the covered truck bed. She hastily grabbed the duffle bag with clothes and some old school vampire restraints. Her undead heart nearly bounded out of her chest as she spied her fisherman smoking on the dock. *What a nasty habit.*

Veronique practiced her 'active grieving' skills while the coffin was maneuvered onto a landscape four-wheel vehicle. "Yes, I'm transporting my husband to the church's grave yard. He was a very private person." She lured the Irishman back to the chapel and when the burden was rolled into the aisle, she paused. "Are you hungry? I could go for a bite, couldn't you?" That gave her free rein of the use of a fairly manageable boat.

The old chapel was haunting at this hour. The full moon cast shadows of the monuments to earlier island residents. An ornate stone path led to an archaic well, it was mostly dry now and not exceptionally deep, but it would suit her purposes. Anna's body slumped in her arms. *Dead weight, what an apt description of Rick's little tart.* Cat's dead-eyed gaze shook even

Veronique's reserve. Before she lowered Matt's mate into the well she carefully tightened the titanium and silver manacles to her wrists, ankles and waist. It was tricky to get the two women chained together. It was a tight fit for three.

Veronique caught Cat's chin in her hand. "You are not mature enough to pull the bolt out of the ground, especially with your friend chained to you. Enjoy yourselves. I think it's marvelous to dine with friends, even more of an adventure when you dine *on* friends. By the way, enjoy the hallucinogens I've added to her blood." With that, Veronique accomplished what she knew Cat was unable to do, she climbed the walls like the spider she was. She wouldn't use her phone, she knew that was too easy to trace. Her brand-new tablet was just the thing. She used a virtual private network. She'd never get caught. A photo or two would lend credence to her claims. She checked her tablet and found just enough bars to send an email.

> *Dear Sirs,*
>
> *This is to inform you of the impending deaths of your mates. Attached is a photo that is proof of life, for however long it lasts. Be assured, once the paralytic wears off and the sun rises, Mrs. Brenner should find Ms. Curley's blood quite a tasty meal ready to eat. Rick, it was a challenge in close quarters to inflict suffering on a mortal. However, I believe the hallucinogens I've injected into your little Cupcake should keep her rattled all night, especially when Catherine begins to develop a hunger. Then, they can enjoy the trip together.*
>
> *Should you and Matt wish to prevent this horrific chain of events, please alter the articles of incorporation for the Consort Group International Board to install me as majority owner. If you move quickly enough, I may be able to get back to the damsels in distress before their trauma is too great. If your women are like you, the guilt of hurting one another would be devastating.*
>
> *Please have the necessary paperwork notarized and forwarded to my solicitor's office in care of this email. I'll expect hard copies to the address below within twelve hours. This should all make for an entertaining night.*
>
> *Don't fuck with me boys,*
> *Veronique Moreau*

She promptly received notification: *your message has been read.*

* * * *

"If we send this, they're dead. If we don't, they're dead." Rick paced, staring at a printed copy of the email.

Matt went into detective mode the minute Rick pressed the print button. "Adam has the chops to decode the IP address, they haven't been gone that long. The Rover was parked at a private garage at 5:45. This email was sent at 7:13.

"What good is an IP address when we have no location on the women?" Rick dropped the paper on the desk and threw up his hands.

All the tension of a kidnapping blew through Matt's cop mind. His training hadn't included him as the mark.

* * * *

Cat felt the damp soaking through her clothes and phantoms slithering across her skin. She knew she was restrained at her wrists, waist and ankles. She could only assume the restraint was tainted with silver. She could feel the burn. There was a sound of trickling water, she knew they were below ground level. She had seen the woman intermittently while she affixed the restraints. She felt Anna chained to face her, the mortal woman's body growing progressively colder. Cat felt the sensation of falling when the woman dropped them into the stony prison.

Matt brought her a treat of A negative for 'breakfast' today, and that had been how many hours ago? They rose early, each of them claiming 'things to do.' So, her last meal would have been around four in the afternoon. What time was it now? She searched every sense and found no time marker. At least she wasn't hungry now, she'd hang on to that. She prayed to the Creator for divine intervention. She had no other recourse.

* * * *

It was sub-marine heaven, that moment when your tummy is comfortably full, and the floating feeling transports your heart to your happiest place. Nessa glided with the current, at peace with herself and the universe, a time of perfect clarity.

* * * *

Anna struggled against the darkness. It came at her in mosaics of color, wicked, terrifying and frigid. She fought and found herself restrained. Did she dare try to open her eyes and see the cold body she was chained against? *What if it's Rick? What if he is truly dead?* The witch hadn't cackled, her voice was mellow and threatening. Images of being lowered into this hell flashed with stained glass fragmentation. Cat's rigid body was the cold, dead thing tied to her. Anna fought, testing the restraints. She was mired in chains and the stench of mold and moss. "Cat! Can't you move?" Anna shook her body vigorously to elicit a response. Cat's dead weight frightened her. In Anna's trance, Cat's blue eyes spun in musical movement and shattered. Anna screamed to the stars, "Dear God, help us!"

* * * *

Replete with her own dinner, Nessa scouted a swarm of eels and dove into their midst. If she carried a dozen or so back to her den, she would be greeted with smiles. And there it was again, that piercing wail reverberating within her, as if touched by a tuning fork. She was far too deep in the loch to hear sounds, which meant, this was a psychic scream. As she slipped gracefully toward the shore she felt an unnerving pluck to her spine. Agitated, she dropped the eels and turned her massive body in all four directions waiting for the cry to re-emerge. A golden eagle crested the tree tops and circled above her furiously, the screech causing Nessa to shake her head. This was no invitation to glide the air alongside her friend. This was a demand to be answered. "You heard it too? Where's it coming from?" The beauty of telepathy was the use of pictures in exchange for words. Nessa immediately saw an island in her mind's eye. But which island?

* * * *

Matt was grateful they hadn't yet put up walls separating the study from the great hall. It allowed him to monitor both Rick in mogul mode and the responders in search mode. Rick gestured him over to the desk. "I need you to sign where the arrows indicate."

"We agree that doing this will be our last-ditch effort? Statistically, paying the kidnapper just buys you a body. Do you expect more from Veronique?"

Rick fell into his chair, his head dropped back. "They are worth more than our fortune. Without Anna, I'll be nothing."

"I'm there with you." Matt washed a hand over his grim face. He picked up the pen and let Rick flip the pages as he signed.

"This covers all contingencies." Rick's voice broke.

Adam flagged Matt to the other side of the massive room. "The responders have established the possible radius of their location. Cameras all over Ireland are using facial recognition to search for her. So far, there's nothing, but search parties are out."

Matt was a caged man. "I'd feel like I was accomplishing something if I was out there. Adam, isn't there a way to take me up for an aerial view?"

Adam turned in frustration, walked toward the window and surveyed the darkness. "It's not like dropping your fangs. It's been ages since I shifted. The massacre was a visceral reaction to physical threats. I'm so out of touch with my dragon…"

"How much more threat do you want? You want me fangs out in your face?" Adam jumped back at Matt's instantaneous transformation.

"Matt, you know I'll do anything for you. I'll shift, but I won't take you up with me. If I can't hold it, you'll be jelly. Let me search the sea. It will take the responders some time to get to that area."

* * * *

Veronique scheduled a massage, manicure and pedicure once she docked the boat in Dundalk, Ireland. She relaxed on the massage table while she ruminated over all the hurdles Rick and Matt were jumping. *Somebody in this situation has to keep calm, might as well be me. It is tragic what cobblestones can do to a manicure.*

* * * *

Anna was not sure how long she napped. The music of the crickets and night sounds dragged her out of a multi-colored dream. Looking up, she saw the stars racing against the blue-black sky. She wasn't sure where her body ended, and Cat's began, they were that close. One moment she had perfect clarity, the next she railed against the chains. The shock of Cat touching her wrist broke her panic.

"Anna, she gave you a hallucinogen. What you're seeing isn't real."

"If this isn't real, where are we?"

"I think we're in a well."

Wide-eyed and open-mouthed, Anna swiveled her head around their prison and back to the sky. "Cat…" Her voice trailed out the name. "Your hair is brilliant as moonbeams. Your skin…" Anna leaned forward to brush her cheek against Cat's. "Your skin is like peaches. When is Rick coming to get us?"

Cat pulled back from Anna. "Honey, I don't know how they'll find us."

Anna shrugged back from Cat, pulling her closer. "Let me ask the eagle…"

* * * *

Cat sighed and found she could hang her head. Thank God, the paralytic was wearing off.

Anna's gaze darted around the dark hole and up to the sky. Cat couldn't imagine what she was seeing, but Anna described it well. "Can you see how we're all connected? Every creature has a silver cord…not you…I'm sorry…"

"That must be pretty." Cat swallowed hard, she tried to stare at the moss over Anna's shoulder. The contact between their cheeks stirred her awareness of the magnificent road map of veins under Anna's pale flesh. Cat's fangs began to burn. "What else do you see?" Cat would have Anna describe every cobble in the wall to keep her mind off impending hunger.

"Shh, shh, shh. The eagle's telling me…" Anna's voice was a whisper.

"What does he say?"

Anna shook her head insistently. "She…she says nature is in harmony with us. Her friend will be here soon. She says we shouldn't be afraid."

*Unless her friend packs O negative, she needs to be afraid.* "How long is 'soon'?" Cat bit her bottom lip.

Anna closed her eyes and absorbed the moonlight. "Before light."

* * * *

Adam felt the distress call immediately upon shifting. It was far less difficult than he'd anticipated, for it seemed the entire east coast of Ireland was alive with news of anguished female energy. The whales and eagles were especially disturbed. Adam reached out to them mentally and trembled at their replies. *At least they are alive.* He held on to that shred of hope.

His animal contacts were doing their best to triangulate the physical source of the tribulation. He hovered over the estuary and heard eagle song. *Find the singing eagle.*

His great form swerved away from the coast into the realm of the sea creatures. Great ombre wings beat to a high speed then folded tightly to his body. He dove deeply into the icy Irish Sea.

* * * *

Nessa caught the current and blessed the Creator for providing a strong tail wind to help propel her to the abandoned feminine souls. As her great golden wings powered her toward their lamentations, she felt the yin and yang of mortal and immortal souls trapped together. *What is the cataclysm that the green man speaks of?* "I beseech the Creator to guide our flight and deliver them to safety." Nessa quieted her mind and soared in anticipation.

"Where are you?" She heard the male energy strong and clear in her mind.

She peered down to gauge her location. Flying over Belfast, the desperate energy hit her like a tsunami, almost repelling her back over the water. She banked in flight and answered the call.

"Where are you?"

The tone of the answer was elated. "I'm in the Sea, not far from Skerries Island."

Nessa knew the voice, but it seemed a dim memory, one she could not readily place. The urgency of the situation overrode her curiosity. "I'm not far." She replied and sent him an aerial picture of Skerries Island. "I'll meet you on the beach."

"Do you know where they are?"

"Not yet, but we're getting closer."

* * * *

Cat's senses felt the pull of the moon. Her undead body was in sync with the tides and as the hungry waves ate up the shore, she needed to feed. She felt her flesh grow tight, and her nerves jumped at the night sounds that amplified with the moon's passing. Each of Anna's mortal systems cried out to be quieted. Cat's hunger was a tight string plucked by Anna's heartbeat and breaths. The roadmaps of blood were now teaming just inches from Cat. *Is it better to strike and feed, or warn her and scare her to death? Rick never put her in this situation. Hell, I'm not even prepared for this. Do I sip a bit each hour?*

"I don't want to scare you." Cat bowed her head, so Anna would not see the impatient vampire before her.

"I'm not scared. Are you scared?"

"Yes, I am, Anna. I need to feed, and I can't tell how the hallucinogen is going to affect my control."

"Ohhh. You're afraid you're going to turn me, and Rick will miss out." Anna swayed against Cat.

"Oh, honey, if it were only that simple. I'm afraid I won't be able to stop. I don't know how to turn anyone."

Anna's gaze left Cat's as it appeared she was hearing another conversation. Cat ground her jaw and prayed silently.

Anna tilted her head and shook her hair from her neck as best she could. "The Creator gives life; the Creator takes life. You don't have that power. Lean on her strength and trust."

Veronique knew exactly what horrors could be inflicted with these tight chains. It left Cat only a limited area from which to feed. If unchecked, Anna's death would be close up and psychedelic.

* * * *

Rick was head down over his driver. I was a clear night and the portable tee box was situated to aim golf balls off the west side of the castle. He cried an angry, "Fore!" The club head made contact with a mighty *thwack!* And the ball disappeared into the night. "Why don't they call?"

Matt shook his head, his hands deep in his jeans pockets as he paced well behind Rick's golf stance. "There's nothing to call about, I guess."

When the bucket of balls was empty, Rick pounded the club head into the roof floor. "When I find Veronique, I'll kill her." He gripped the club handle and the shaft near the head and bent the club in a pretzel.

"Get in line." Matt gazed dully into the distance.

Rick sighed and walked to his friend. "We have two and a half hours before we pull the trigger. I have a courier downstairs. We'll do it, Matt, because we won't have a choice if it comes to that, but I'm afraid it will seal their fates."

"Don't give up, buddy, I've seen cases turn on a dime."

"I wasn't at the Colosseum, but I'd swear, Veronique and Caligula were cut from the same cloth."

* * * *

Adam landed, his mind filled with the images the Orcas generated. The girls were on an island, or at least land near the sea. In the moonlight, Adam caught the sight of an infinitesimal golden shape undulating toward him. The shape formulated the closer it flew. Leathery golden wings moved gracefully in the icy air, closer and closer.

"Is that you, Adam?" The voice in his mind was unmistakably feminine and vaguely familiar.

"Who are you?" He paced the beach anxiously as the dragon drew closer. She was stunning. Ombre shades of shimmering white to yellow to rose gold graced her athletic form. He was certain he'd remember seeing her before. The scales and plates of her feminine form moved over agile withers and flanks. Her long neck moved in nimble observation and he heard a pleased sigh when their gazes met.

"Adam Lachlan, Prince of Flight's End." He heard affection in her voice.

"And you are?" He was enchanted but perturbed by her evasion.

"Nessa Clark, Princess of Fisherfield Forest." Her clawed feet caught the damp sand as she settled to earth silently.

"Cousin, you were a mere hatchling when last I saw you. What a beautiful lass you've become."

"And you are as handsome as the old women say. How did you tap into these feminine laments?"

"I didn't. These women are my dear friend's mates. I began an aerial search and heard the eagle and Orca songs."

"I believe I know where they are. A golden eagle confirmed the fears that distracted me from feeding. She's circled over Lamb Island and shown me the shapes restrained in a well."

"Can you show me?"

"Of course."

"My skills are rusty. This is only the second time I've shifted in two hundred years. If I can carry rescuers back, could you guard them until we arrive?"

"Hurry, Adam, I fear they have little time." Nessa nodded and launched herself over the Sea.

* * * *

Rick's head snapped up as Adam shot into the room. "What?"

"I've found them." He turned to Matt. "Send the responders to Lamb Island, there's a well behind the church." He turned to Rick. "You bring lengths of rope and bolt cutters, both of you meet me on the West Lawn. Hurry."

There was a whirlwind of activity around them, and in the few minutes it took them to do his bidding, the men were met by a gold and carmine fire dragon. Matt shot Rick a look of amazement. "A minute ago, he was naked in the study, and now he's going to carry us over water to an island?"

"You were the one who asked him to shift." Rick shrugged and scrambled up the great beast's proffered leg. They scarcely caught their grips when he lifted up, winging eastward, following the images in his mind's eye.

* * * *

*What do you do when the only person who can save your life will lose theirs doing it?* Cat could bite Anna now and regulate her draw, or she could put it off and lose all control. The night animals went to their nests and Cat's fangs dropped reflexively, scenting their blood. *It's been too long since feeding.* She dreaded the changing colors in the sky, signaling the approaching dawn. Although Anna insisted she could cover her and deflect the sun's rays, Cat feared they would not last the day. She shook her shoulders, waking Anna from another mind-expanding dream.

Anna's head lolled. "What?"

Cat hid her opalescent eyes and whispered, "Anna, I'm so sorry...I need to feed."

Anna was as gentle as a lamb to the slaughter. "I said it was okay."

Cat summoned her strength to bite cleanly and draw evenly. The sound of fang on flesh sickened her, but Anna simply fell toward her and sighed Rick's name. Cat's resilience reemerged, and she measured Anna's steady heartbeat.

*I need to stop.* She dug deep for the willpower and her fangs retracted seconds before the drug twisted and pulled her into a dark mire of regret. With all her heart, she wished she had asked more questions and prepared to be on her own. Cat twisted her face away from Anna as soon as she felt the colors of Anna's light course through her undead body.

She knew the sensation of flowing light was the result of the drug. But, how did she explain the huge golden dragon above them?

* * * *

Veronique grumbled in frustration when she realized her vamp body temperature hindered the use of her iPhone. "You!" She summoned the surprised receptionist. "Reach into my bag and grab my stylus. My nails are wet." The offended young woman did as requested with little enthusiasm. Veronique harrumphed again. There was no message waiting and no call from her solicitor. What did this mean? She couldn't believe those two Neanderthals would let their women die. *Where is chivalry?*

* * * *

Cat was plagued by hunger. The hallucinogen displayed Anna's life force flagrantly, at the same time removing Cat's restraint. Her need was mounting from fevered to frenzied. The compulsion to drop fangs won. The bite was ugly, Anna keened a mournful wail.

Nessa's wings shaded Cat from the rising sun's rays. She quivered at their torment, feeling Cat's remorse and Anna's fear. Her mind reached out to Adam. *"Where are you?"*

Adam's wings beat furiously as he gained the island's shoreline. *"Moments away."* His enormous shadow appeared at Nessa's side, and then she saw two men drop and roll to their feet.

* * * *

Rick ran to the well's edge. He used his Dom voice. "Cat! Stop!" Matt thrust the end of the rope into his hands and slipped down the well wall.

Cat startled at his arrival. "I can't stop," she pleaded, "help me."

Matt insinuated himself between the two women. "I'm here, baby, you'll be fine. Breathe with me."

Matt listened carefully to Anna's heartbeat, they'd arrived in the nick of time. He tried to make eye contact with her.

"She's hallucinating. The woman who brought us here gave her drugs. It's in me too…be careful…"

Matt nodded and bit his own wrist but held it above Anna's mouth. He caught her neck and whispered. "Anna, drink this." His blood flowed with the pressure exerted. Her thirsty tongue caught every drop. His arm rapidly healed and he re-bit to feed his mate. "Cat, baby, take what you need." His other arm encircled her lovingly.

Throughout the tense minutes Rick hovered over the well. "Matt? What's happening? Are they okay?"

Matt lifted his head from Cat's shoulder. "Working on it, buddy. They're chained together and attached to a bolt down here. If you'll carefully slide the bolt cutters down, we can ask Adam to lift us out."

"What about Anna, is she okay?" Rick insisted.

Matt reassessed Anna's appearance. "She's pretty shaken and disoriented. Nothing you can't help her with."

* * * *

Nessa's wings umbrellaed over them as Adam drew them steadily up to the ground. Rick belayed the rope, and then caught Anna into his arms. He brushed her snarled hair back and held her face between his hands. Relief swept over him. "Oh, Cupcake, I thought I'd lost you!" He rocked her against him, aware of her vaguely unfocused eyes.

"You're such a beautiful little boy. The girls are going to eat you up one day! You're so cute!"

Rick's smile froze, and he glanced up at Matt. "What's goin' on?"

"Veronique drugged her. And I've fed her some of my blood. Just don't take any of hers."

Rick studied her gaze and expression. "Well dear, this should be an interesting night." While he held her close, he watched Matt carry Cat to Nessa.

Cat peered up at the massive golden dragon. "I know you must have been the one who heard us. Words can't be enough, we're forever indebted to you. Thank you." Nessa bowed her regal head in response and one twinkling golden eye winked at them.

Matt begged back. "Excuse us, I have to get her inside. Thank you for keeping her safe."

Rick nodded and waved at Nessa as he followed the others into the chapel. Once he laid Anna on a pew he searched for abandoned clothes and ran out to Adam. "Thousands of years of being and you guys haven't developed a pouch to carry some clothes? We've got two uninitiated women who are gonna freak out when they see you shift back!" Adam nodded with a chuff as Rick strode back to the chapel.

Anna, Cat and Matt stood at the window watching Nessa and Adam say their goodbyes. Anna looked around with wide-eyed innocence. "They're dragons."

Cat nodded. "I know, sweetie, they're dragons."

The men shook their heads. "The chopper's here. We can head home."

Lieutenant Jan Kulczyk was the first of the responders to reach the chapel. "Good morning, Sirs." He saluted Rick and Matt. "I'm glad to see things ended well. I have good news. We have a bead on Veronique Moreau. We were able to hack into her tablet."

"How close is she?" Matt asked angrily.

"She's traveling a side road in the middle of a national park in Scotland."

Adam stepped forward. "I know that area. It's wilderness."

Rick nodded, his voice grim. "Perfect." He turned to Adam. "Will you see our ladies home and get them settled?"

"No worries." Adam patted Rick's shoulder.

Rick embraced Anna. "I have to take care of this, Cupcake. I'm sorry to leave you, but if I don't put and an end to this problem, it will come back to haunt us again. So, Adam will take good care of you, okay?" He watched as Matt gave Cat a similar goodbye embrace and they headed for Kulczyk's helicopter.

* * * *

It was a blessedly foggy and overcast morning in the Scottish Highlands. With any luck, this weather would hold until Veronique reached the airport at Inverness and was on her way to France. Bocelli's rendition of Nessun Dorma blasted through the speakers as she enjoyed her victory over Rick Hiatt. She'd received confirmation from her solicitor no more than two hours ago that the Articles of Incorporation had been received. She was instantaneously an incredibly wealthy woman, and she had bested that condescending son of a cur! Plans for the future would include…

"Damn! Why is this car coasting to a stop?" *Why can nothing ever be easy?* She steered to the shoulder of the road and riffled through the console for the rental papers.

Dialing her cell phone, she filed a formal request for roadside assistance.

"I regret it may be as long as forty-five minutes because of your remote location."

"Fine. I'll wait. I don't have much choice." She cut off the call and slammed the phone into the passenger's seat, and then billionaire dreams flew through her mind.

* * * *

"The electromagnetic pulse has disabled her car. We're about six-and-a-half kilometers from her," Kulczyk announced through their headphones.

Private McDonald handed Rick and Matt their Kevlar vests. "There's a TEC-9 with a fifty-round magazine. They're silver rounds, so, don't cross your streams." The Private winked.

Rick examined the gun and frowned. "I want something for closer quarters." McDonald passed Rick and Matt sheathed machetes. Rick nodded. "That should do the trick."

Kulczyk circled the copter to land in front of Veronique's sedan. Rick and Matt jumped from the sliding door, caps pulled low, and windbreakers covering their vests.

Veronique waved and called out. "I had no idea they'd send a helicopter. Can you take me all the way to Inverness?"

Rick held up a hand and nodded, keeping his face low until they were upon her.

As soon as she recognized her visitors, her eyes grew round and she poised to run. Rick's steely grasp held her in place. "Veronique Moreau, as a duly elected member of the Vampire Council, under their authority, I exercise the penalty for your confessed use of Humanité. The penalty is termination."

Matt stepped forward from behind her and with one swift slice her head lay on the ground. He glared at her collapsing body, devoid of regret. "That seems anticlimactic."

Rick gave him a sardonic look. "That's what it's like when you take out the trash."

They climbed into the chopper in time to hear Kulczyk on the radio. "We need a clean-up team to the following coordinates…"

# 22

Anna got back into the car at the private terminal. "I guess it will be a while before I see them. It was wonderful for Mom, Dad and Wyatt to have the run of the place. Player will be busy, don't you think?" Player, hearing his name, insinuated his giant head from the back seat.

"Don't slobber on the new car," Rick reprimanded.

"He's not slobbering, he's a good boy." Anna settled into her seat and turned back to Adam. "Are you ready for home and all it entails?"

Adam stretched crossways, battling the dog for backseat space. "When one of your people says the Queen is calling for you, you go. Especially when the Queen is your mother."

Anna shook her head in awe. "I had no idea I was surrounded by so much royalty. I'm sorry there's unrest within your clan."

Adam grew thoughtful. "It's not the unrest that disturbs me, it's that mother is refusing the normal right of succession and naming me king. I'm sure there's more to this summons than I know."

Anna's jaw dropped. "King?" The men smiled.

Rick glanced up to the rearview mirror and nodded. "You know you have our support, old man."

"I've always felt that in my heart, Rick. I'll message you when I arrive."

Rick pulled the car up to departing flights and the tall man unfolded from the back with his one suitcase.

As Rick pulled the car into traffic, the Bluetooth rang, incoming call. "Matt's calling."

*"Hey brother, I've got a big job on my hands. Sure, we can't call the King back to our payroll?*

"Nice try, Matt, we just dropped him off at the terminal. What's up? You don't need me, do you?"

Matt hesitated. *"I think you are going to have your own hands full for the next few weeks. You get to handle a fledgling."* Matt let out a maniacal laugh.

"Hey! I'm in the car," Anna protested.

Cat piped up. *"Everything will be fine, Annie. Don't listen to the men."*

Rick turned the car off the motorway as Matt continued. *"The Gaoler in Cannes is a hot mess."*

Cat cut in, *"But the ocean is beautiful."*

*"Whatever. I have about three weeks of work here, but we're headed back, so Anna will have company."*

Rick caught Anna's hand and gave it a quick kiss. "Okay, brother, we'll see you when we see you."

They rode in silence for a few miles. Rick scented Anna's jitters. "We've been through quite a bit in the last few months. I'm looking forward to tonight."

"It's certainly a bigger night than our wedding. It sort of puts the vows to the ultimate test, don't you think?"

Rick chuckled. "This is a first, I've never turned anyone who means so much to me."

Anna patted his thigh as he drove.

"You know, years from now, your family is going to wonder why we look the same as when they last saw us. Surely, if a group of your museum friends think you're pregnant after our romantic getaway, everyone is going to expect a visit from the stork soon."

Anna dismissed that with a wave of her hand. "I've already decided, I'm going to tell them you're sterile."

Rick laughed. "Great! Put it on me. I shoot blanks. Alrightie then, it sounds like you've covered all the contingencies. The only thing left is to do the deed."

Anna smiled. "I'm…" she took a deep breath and spun her emerald mating ring on her finger, "…nervous. But I think you have some techniques to calm me down."

"Only for you, Cupcake." He parked the car and took her hands. "This is not the first time a mortal has been turned. You're in good hands. I know you can do this."

* * * *

Anna didn't remember their steps to the bedroom. Their urgency was spent in deep embraces, feeling the contours of each other's bodies, their eyes wide and engaged. No kissing, no words. She cherished their gazes silently. Touching each other's faces with reverent hands, they were wide-eyed and panting. Anna arched her back, pressing her breasts into Rick's waiting hands.

He forced her against the wall, his arms framing her and their foreheads together. "Anna, these months together…we've consumed each other…shared pieces of our souls. I thought the world had grown too wide to find this peace again." His words stunned her, reducing her response to accepting silence. "Each occasion of our loving has stamped you as mine."

Anna's hands caressed his broad and muscled shoulders. She felt her heart open as it had in all of their frenzied and fevered couplings. "The further we entwine the more our lives change." He murmured.

"Fitz, you know you've ruined me for mortal men." Her eyes smiled dreamily at her own confession.

"And I've found myself speechless among women of my kind... but I've confessed this before. I want to give you everything."

Anna tightened her hold on his shoulders as he lifted her legs around his waist and pressed tighter to her clothed core. He bounded down the hall to the bedroom. Slow, long, open-mouthed kisses gave permission for more. They exhibited amazing control as they felt their way around each other.

Unilaterally, they surrendered. Flat hands peeled away clothing, each taking reverent time to regard the view of snug boxer briefs or a lacey bra. Growing urgency reduced them to throwing underclothes airborne as they rolled in the bed over the turned-down covers. Anna lay back and watched Rick crawl up the length of the bed to lie beside her, it was deliberate torrid romance in its truest sense. The sight of his paleness in the near darkness awestruck her. Her smile returned as she realized, *yes, my lover is a vampire, a very handsome and enticing vampire.* She braced herself to feel cold flesh and felt her own heat reflecting off him. Quickly, he absorbed her warmth and wrapped that back around her with his embrace.

Rick's mouth touched each measure of her. He laid out her arms and gently pressed his knee between hers. Anna's smile lit the bedroom as he cupped her breast and stroked her attentive nipples with his thumbs. She reached between them to catch his hard cock tapping at her belly. She wanted to feel him inside her *now* and knew it was way, way too soon. This was the prelude to a slow, comfortable screw. His extenuated ministrations piqued her curiosity, did she really know him before? It had been months since she first fancied his body over hers or wondered about the carnal skill he would bring to bed. She quivered, shaking and wet for him. He lingered, kissing her lips, seeking her tongue to dance with his. Wordlessly, they rolled to their sides and played at nibbling each other's hands and fingers. Anna traced the sculpture of his abs—this earned her his winning smile. It was part of the devilish leer he levied when he stole first blood. Now his eyes followed her busy fingers as they flowed over his body.

* * * *

"Cupcake, you know I can't stop now, I'm on the border..." his head dropped back at the sensation of her thumb working his cock, how she danced sensations over his velvet flesh, he gritted his teeth at the near flash of that darkness that could carry a mortal man to climax.

"Border? We need a passport where we're going?" She playfully bumped her hip into his.

"All we need is some give and some take. Be your beautiful self and let me, ahhh, let me." His lips silenced with the taste of her rosy nipple.

"What if I want to play with you?" Anna caught his face with her hands and kissed his forehead, nose and the dimple on his cheek.

"Oh, Cupcake, you know I believe my lady comes first. I don't want to rush. I may tie your hands to the bed posts...you are unspeakably delicious." Rick nuzzled Anna from her breasts to her navel. "Tell me, Anna, what do you want?" He was wrapped up so tightly in her allure...he was frozen in this moment. Rick raised up from her breasts to gaze at her face. She was softness and strength as he caught the sight of their body's profile in the half light of the bedroom. He watched her hands clutch at the sheets and she drew her knees up and captured him.

He would be held hostage in this bed, releasing her only when they had repeatedly blown every sensation through the roof, when their unrelenting caresses would strike that critical tipping point. She rolled in his arms, returning his caresses a bit stronger over each moment until her moan powered her roll over his chest in playful domination. Her cheek rested in the hollow of his collarbone, her hand caught his jaw and she kissed him. Her savory lips engaged his kiss, distracting, as she sinuously lay over him. Rick's mind blurred as she straddled him. His erection lurked under the fork of her legs; it stirred there in her wet heat as she pressed tighter, their fingers laced together as they fixed their gazes on each other. Rick waited for a response as he read the tilt of her head, the turn of her cheek.

What if he never wanted this heaven to end? It wouldn't, Rick's inner vamp lay in wait, hungry to prove the confirmation of their love. Anna didn't slide down from his hips. His light fingertips drew lazy paths up and down her thighs. With each trip up her thigh, his thumbs moved closer to finding a warm place to nestle within her delta. Her stiff back gave way to a fluid sway as his thumbs explored the folds of flesh, her back arching as his strokes circled over her clit. Anna purred as she curled forward, whipping Rick with her full mane of titian waves, her breasts brushing his chest as he gasped at her sensuously slow movements. His hands flew to catch her and kiss her silly, they locked lips as their tongues danced gently at first, then more deeply and slowly, Anna came up for air and turned her cheek to offer her neck.

Rick caught her hands in his and kissed the backs of both. "Not yet..."

Anna reared back again, looking blissful, as Rick's hands held her safe. She began to crawl back down alongside him, sharing more of her warmth with him. He rolled to catch her, press his knee between hers to gain his place between her thighs. His earnest brown eyes met hers and he watched tears gather. "Let me love you, Anna."

The sensations of his lips on hers were transcendent when he laid her back and took over their choreography. Rick spread her hands to her side, kissing back up her arm to nuzzle at her neck then trail down between her breasts to the divot of her navel. His cool lips gave her relief from the internal burn that had taken over her mortal flesh; he licked and kissed drawing a budding fang every now and then. For a moment Rick rested his chin on the delta of her thighs. Their eyes met, and Rick winked. Their eyes silently agreed, and Rick pressed on to taste her as he had so many nights before. His tongue fell on the folds of her flesh and her breath hitched. Light strokes danced in circles, whipping her into a euphoria of growing tension. Rick suckled her swelling flesh as low moans rose from her mouth.

Anna's knees widened and drew up as she slid into rapture, Rick buried his face within her, lapping, licking, kissing and nipping as she writhed. He grasped her hips and held her fast, keeping up his gentle pressure, taking her higher and higher.

Its origin was a light sigh that descended from the heavens, collecting the weight of all her fears and casting them away. When she came, she came hard. She shook in a personal darkness that exploded into a blue-white light.

And when she took flight, she found Rick there between her knees, covering himself with her dew as he begged for entry.

Outstretched hands reached for him and invited him within her. He paused and ran his hand through his hair, wet with her perspiration, her gaze locked on his smile and he pressed forward, inch by turgid inch. She felt his strength as they joined, each adoring the give and take of flesh within flesh. Her gasp was not fear, it was a gasp of feeling so deliriously at home with him between her thighs. He was a different man when he was with her.

"Tell me this is real…" he asked, balancing on his forearms while he found the pace to fill her completely. "This is real, really… phenomenal." Anna worked to return the favor. She caught him between her knees and rose to his thrusts, pressed on slowly, arduously and time stood still as their strength pulled them through sensual rapids.

Anna recognized the closed eyes, the flaring nostrils which led him on his own journey into bliss. He delivered tiny punctures, taking miniscule amounts of her blood. He looked rapturous and she shivered deliciously.

She felt it was their night, and this was their gift to each other, eternity. Anything boxed or gift-bagged or delivered would pale in comparison to their love, shared for centuries to come. Her heat swallowed him, triggering spasms between them.

She knew opalescent eyes laid in wait behind his eyelids. She could taste blood from his tongue's hurried rides over lengthened fangs. Within a slow kiss he snagged her tongue, and she hoped he tasted drops of her passionate blood. She felt him lengthen, harden, and quiver on the verge of climax. She sighed, urged him on with a whisper and tightened on him.

"Rick, take me with you." She offered her neck.

**The End**

**Blood Dragon, the third book of The Blood Trilogy**

Adam Lachlan, a tall drink of scrumptious masculinity, has been exiled from his dragon-shifter clan for the past two hundred years. His bad-boy charm has been harnessed to succeed as a Master Dom in the mortal world. He's spent decades isolating himself emotionally.

Willow Greer is beautiful, intelligent and charming. Men have pursued her, but she's flown from them all. Willow has a secret burden. Adopted in infancy and having no explanation for shifting into a Pegasus at puberty, she's cloistered herself romantically. Without knowing the full truth of her nature, how can she commit to love?

When Adam's fire meets Willow's short fuse, flirtation is on! At the onset, secrets are guarded, but once their true selves are revealed, the complications begin. Can they overcome the problems of romance between different shifter species? Will they drop their emotional baggage and risk love's bondage?

**Appetite for Blood, Prequel to the Blood Trilogy**

A revolution is roaring into the 1920s! Vampires, who previously killed to feed, now thrill to feed. The revolution is led by a four-hundred-year-old vampire, Rick Hiatt, and his newly turned ward, Matt Brenner. This is not the first time Rick has encountered the brutal treachery of the Moreau family of vampires, but he and Matt seek to make it the last.

Los Angelinos mortal and immortal are under attack by the entitled, remorseless Moreaus. Dragon-shifter Adam Lachlan and seductresses Venus and Luna, team up with Rick and Matt to put an end to the siege. Brute strength won't take these hellions down, but they might be hoodwinked into exposing themselves.

Read about the origins of the fast friendship between Matt, Rick, and Adam, and see how their BDSM empire grew from humble beginnings to an international conglomerate.

**Paperbacks and eBooks by Amber Anthony**

Appetite for Blood, Prequel to the Blood Trilogy
Blood Rising, Blood Trilogy Book 1
Blood Emerald, Blood Trilogy Book 2
Blood Dragon, Blood Trilogy Book 3

Blood Fugue, Tales from the Gaoler Book 1

Arise, My Darling
Becoming Gabriel

Roman's Revenge, Roman's Adventures Book 1
Roman's Rules, Roman's Adventures Book 2
Roman's Return, Roman's Adventures Book 3

**Follow Amber Anthony on**

All Author

BookBub

BookSprout

GoodReads

The Romance Reviews

https://AmberAnthonyWrites.com